Turning Point

Kimberly A. Mercy-Wagner

PAGE PUBLISHING
Conneaut Lake, PA

First originally published by Page Publishing 2018

ISBN 978-1-68409-395-3 (pbk)
ISBN 978-1-68409-396-0 (digital)

Printed in the United States of America

I dedicate this book, *Turning Point* to my loved ones who have passed: Robert Eric, Steven John, Richard George, Donna Joan, my dear father Richard John Mercy, and my loving husband Brendan Peter Wagner!!

I will always remember all of you with deep affection and lots of love. XOXOXO

CHAPTER

ONE

〰〰〰

*I*t's May 6, 2006. The assignment is to take out a fugitive named Carlos Garcia who is a 5'7" Hispanic male in his late twenties. Note: He has a rattlesnake tattoo that trails down his back. His recent address is 12 Lindsey Drive, apartment 12, South Central, Los Angeles, California. He has a past history of six convictions for drug trafficking and using and a warrant is out from the DEA (Drug Enforcement Administration) for his arrest. This time it's four counts of drug trafficking, dealing, and using cocaine, heroin, and crystal meth. Note: He is armed and dangerous. Go in with caution!

The next day six DEA agents are on duty. One agent is Keith Heiden, age 39, sandy blond hair, blue eyes, Irish Austrian, and 5'11 3/4". He is soft-spoken, sometimes quiet, keeps to himself, but he can be aggressive. He only has a few friends on the job. His past is fully confidential from almost everyone. He doesn't talk about his personal life to anyone other than his wife and Agent Peter Darling. This assignment is done every day, by training or the real scene. It is always strictly by the book, no heroes, just teamwork all the way. Agent Keith Heiden has done this assignment more than a thousand times.

It's May 7, 2006. Good evening California! The temperature is about fifty-six degrees with clear skies in Los Angeles. Here is the traffic update for the greater Los Angeles area. Agent Peter Darling turns off the truck engine; he is the head of the field team and Agent Keith Heiden's supervisor and best friend. They are ready to roll. At 7:00 pm, the six agents, including Agent Keith Heiden, are all wearing black government uniforms from head to foot with bullet-proof vests underneath jackets that state in white letters "DEA." This is posted in the front upper corner left side and on the back of the jackets. It is required to wear IDs when on duty.

Two agents, Liam Gallagher and Sean Tierney, are young, strong, and fresh out of DEA training in Quantico, Virginia. The agents are fully trained to step to the front; Agent Peter Darling and Agent Keith Heiden trained them. At the address 12 Lindsey Drive, Apartment 12, South Central Los Angeles, you can hear the sound of a knock at the front door. "Police, search warrant!!" Agent Liam Gallagher shouts out with a clear warning. No response from the criminal in the apartment. Suddenly, Agent Anderson Peters, comes in front holding a battering ram to give that one single forceful swing to open the door. The apartment key is not in the equation. The battering ram rips the door open!

All six agents walk in fast using caution. They're trained to be sharp and on their feet at all times. They all shout sporadically, "DEA! Get down now!" Agent Keith Heiden walks quickly as he holds his gun, a 9mm Glock. The adrenaline is pumping through his body; he is ready for anything.

"DEA!" shouts Agent Liam Gallagher, entering another room. Agent Heiden walks past Agent Brook without saying anything. In the corner of his eye, Agent Heiden gets a glimpse of the couple partying on the bed in their birthday suits. He forcefully turns the man around to see the large snake tattoo running down Carlos's back.

"Hey man! What are you doing?" Carlos's dark brown eyes are very wide with shock. Agent Heiden is moving slowly with his gun pointing at Carlos.

"Carlos Garcia, you're under arrest for four counts of drug trafficking. Please put your hands on your head!" Agent Heiden states, waiting for Carlos to put his hands on his head. He's feeling a strong, powerful aggression toward this man for no apparent reason. Agent Keith Heiden starts to push Carlos forcefully to the ground not even noticing that he didn't put on the handcuffs. He starts hitting him repeatedly with all his body weight. Carlos pleads in Spanish to the agent to spare his life. Keith blocks out all the surrounding sounds.

Three DEA agents quickly enter the room and pull Agent Heiden off Carlos. They desperately try to pin down Keith but it's a fight of muscles from all sides. One agent finally gets Keith's hand and suddenly without a second thought, he handcuffs him tightly behind his back. He's escorted into the living room and forced to sit on a dusty old chair. He sees Garcia's two girls, who have witnessed their daddy bleeding and crying from the pain that he just endured. Keith feels his heart drop as he sees what he's done. But for some strange reason, he can't remember what he did to Gracia. Keith sees the two girls accompanied out of the apartment by a social worker, not knowing if the children will ever see their parents again.

"Are you crazy, Keith? You almost killed Carlos, and he's now unconscious! What were you thinking?? I can't save you this time!" Special Agent Peter Darling yells.

Keith is feeling very low, as he is reprimanded by his supervisor and best friend. His job is on the line; his wife Justine is going to be so disappointed, and what will the kids think of their dad the head of the family? The future of Agent Keith Patrick Heiden is very shaky. He puts his head down with shame and starts to cry.

It is now Monday, May 7, 2007, one year after the Carlos Garcia case and Agent Keith Patrick Heiden's breakdown. Keith almost lost everything he had worked for. His job and his family were on the line. Agent Peter Darling has been watching every move he makes while supervising him. Keith is grounded from fieldwork and doing desk duty until the director and other high authority officials make a final decision on his future with the DEA Internal Affairs Department. Carlos Garcia and Keith Heiden settled out of court and went through arbitration. The settlement is closed to the public. Keith and Carlos have a restraining order not to talk about the agreement to anyone except their wives. Keith is not arrested for his actions, and both parties agreed to the settlement. The restraining order also keeps both parties a hundred feet away from each other.

CHAPTER
TWO

〰〰〰

A government letter was given to Agent Keith Patrick Heiden. He must obey it, or an arrest warrant will be issued to him by the DEA's Internal Affairs and the State of California's District Attorney's, office. Agent Heiden needs to see a professional psychologist. Please note: sessions are going to start at 11:00 a.m. on May 7, 2007, at Agent Keith Heiden' s home in Pacific Palisades, California. He is only allowed two missed appointments with the doctor.

It is now May 7, 2007, and time is tight for Keith. He cares for a three-year-old who will be four on June 30th. His son's name is Colin. He takes a lot of energy out of Keith. Colin loves to talk now, and he gets cranky very easily if he doesn't get his way. He runs, jumps, throws things, and his new thing is spitting at you. Keith is always at the breaking point when dealing with his son. Colin finally sleeps for his nap at 11:00 a.m. until 12:00 or 1:00 p.m., but not later than that. It is a good time to start therapy.

Dr. Elise Sheppard walks toward the front door. The house is very new, and the front door has red oak wood carved with different designs of leaves and branches. Dr. Sheppard can see a shadow image of a man walking toward her from the design glass imbedded in the door. The door opens in front of Dr. Sheppard. Keith standing there wearing a dark blue long-sleeved shirt, blue jeans, and comfortable sneakers. His steady blue eyes look tired and stressed as he stands in front of Dr. Sheppard.

"Hello, Mr. Heiden. My name is Dr. Elise Sheppard. I'm your psychologist. We spoke over the phone about today's appointment being mandatory by the DEA of Los Angeles and the USA government," says Dr. Sheppard, as she puts her hand out as a friendly and professional gesture.

Keith shakes the doctor's hand. "Hello, Dr. Sheppard, thank you for coming. Come in. Did you find the house okay?"

Dr. Sheppard walks into the Heiden's lovely home. The living room is huge with soft color tones that look like the theme design all around the house. It is a very soft and friendly home atmosphere.

"Please sit down and make yourself comfortable," Keith states, as he closes the front door behind him. He automatically locks the bottom and top locks for safety reasons.

In the living room on the left side are two large tan couches facing parallel to each other. There is a lovely table in between, and two lounge chairs are on opposite sides. Dr. Sheppard sits on the end of one of the tan couches. She can face Mr. Heiden if he is sitting on the lounge chair closer to the front.

"Yes, I did, but your front gate guard didn't have my name," Dr. Sheppard replies, as she takes out her notepad, her business card, and Mr. Heiden's case story on what happened last year to the day. Dr. Sheppard places everything on the table trying not to scratch it.

"I don't understand. I gave them your name two days ago… I don't understand… Coffee is brewing if you want some. We can take a break in between our session," Keith states, trying to make the situation more comfortable. Telling one's personal life history to a total stranger, who's getting good money to see him, is very difficult. Keith found out from his job that they are paying Dr. Sheppard for therapy sessions, that are well overdue for Mr. Heiden.

"A break for coffee sounds good to me. Let's start, shall we?" remarks Dr. Sheppard, as she opens Mr. Keith Heiden's case file # 279425 and tries to think of ways to talk about the situation with her new client.

"On May 6, 2006, in East Los Angeles, you had a warrant for the arrest of a Mr. Carlos Garcia. You were in the master bedroom and apprehended a Mr. Carlos Garcia for a warrant out for his arrest on four counts of dealing and using drugs. You were about to put handcuffs on Mr. Carlos Garcia when you just snapped, pushing

Garcia forcefully down to the floor for no legal reasons. You started to beat on Garcia, with full force, punching, and kicking him. You gave him two broken legs and arms, a broken nose, four cracked ribs, and a concussion. Well, what brought on this violent assault toward Mr. Garcia? Mr. Heiden, can you please tell me what brought on this angry, aggressive act of abuse?" asks Dr. Sheppard, as she sits back on the comfortable couch. Elise is wearing an expensive suit in light gray bought in Beverly Hills. She doesn't wear any rings on her thin graceful fingers. Her light brown hair is straight, long, and very healthy looking. It is about shoulder length. She has dark skin from her father's side, and she tans very easily from the California sun. Dr. Sheppard's hazel eyes show a lot of emotion.

Keith sits quietly waiting for Dr. Sheppard to finish. "I'm sorry, Dr. Sheppard, I don't remember. I blacked out. The only thing I remember is that I was handcuffed, and I was sitting on a chair looking at two little kids crying. Believe me, that is all I remember!" Keith states, with a straight, serious face and those blue eyes shining intensely.

"So you blacked out?" asks Dr. Sheppard. She is not sure she heard Mr. Heiden right.

"Yes," Keith states to Dr. Sheppard, not showing any emotion.

Dr. Sheppard understands what a blackout means. It could be caused by anything, like a car accident, some kind of abuse, the loss of a job, etc. It is a situation that causes the mind to shut down when it can't deal with the problem at hand.

"Is this the first time that you blacked out?" Dr. Sheppard asks. Mr. Heiden's case file is opened on her lap, and she tries to figure out what her next question will be.

"Yes," Keith answers, as he sits back on the chair and tries to focus on what Dr. Sheppard is asking.

"Are you sure you don't remember? Mr. Heiden, I'm trying to help you deal with why you would hurt this man. So I'm going to ask you again. Do you remember, or don't you want to remember?" asks Dr. Sheppard. She senses that Mr. Heiden will not be able to give her the information very easily.

"I blacked out… I don't remember… Why are you asking me the same question? I know you have a lot more to ask," replies Keith, feeling uncomfortable and getting a little annoyed.

"Mr. Heiden, I can tell from your body position that you are very uncomfortable. You know I have just begun asking you questions. Will you please work with me? You are making my job very difficult. By the look of that big scar on your left ear and the red marks on your hands, it seems like you were abused. If I may ask, how did you get your scars?" questions Dr. Sheppard.

Keith looks at his hands, which were his only protection from his father who used a wide leather belt on him. He's thinking about plastic surgery, but it's too expensive since he is trying to save for the kids' college funds. Right now, his wife, Justine, his daughter, Erin, his sons, Patrick, Mitchell, and Colin, along with Reese, the chocolate male lab, are his primary concern.

"This was my thirteenth birthday present from my dad. Anything else?" Keith replies sarcastically.

"You don't like anyone asking you about your scars?" questions Dr. Sheppard, uncrossing her legs, as they are getting cramped.

"I don't like talking about me or my personal life," Keith answers with a clear, stern voice, which gives Dr. Sheppard a clue to back off a little.

"Okay, let's go in another direction with our questions… What do you do for fun?" asks Dr. Sheppard, trying to relax Keith.

"Fun? Is that a question?" Keith asks with a very confused look on his face.

"Yes, fun," replies Dr. Sheppard.

"Fun? I thought your question about my left ear was difficult to answer!" Keith replies with a confused but relaxed look on his face.

"You have a young son named Colin, right?"

Keith smiles thinking that Colin really brings joy into his life. "Yes, Colin is going to be four this June. Hopefully, he will go to a good prekindergarten this September. My summer fun is trying to find a good school for him. Well, I play with him and his toys, and I'm teaching him his alphabet and counting up to ten. We watch cartoons for only half an hour. I don't want my kids to watch too much television, and I make sure that the rule is enforced. He is a very smart kid for a three-year-old. I try not to say anything bad in front of him. His little brain can hold lots of information," Keith announces. He turns the volume up on the baby monitor so he can hear Colin, if necessary.

He hears the sound of a small child sleeping as Dr. Sheppard smiles. Dr. Elise Sheppard is thirty-five years old, never been married, and has no wish to in the near future. She has dated a lot of different men over the years, but Elise is married to her career. She graduated fourth in her class from Yale University. Her dad, Dr. Charlie Forester Sheppard, a heart surgeon at Yale University Hospital, is very proud of his little girl. Elise gets a call from dad every day. They are very close, especially since Elise's mother died in a car accident seven years ago. She still shakes from the thought of the unfortunate event but keeps these terrible feelings to herself.

"Mr. Heiden, what do you want out of these therapy sessions?" Dr. Sheppard asks, while looking at Keith to see his reaction. Keith is very relaxed now as he looks back at Dr. Sheppard.

"I just want to go back to work and be fully active. Doing paperwork and filing is not my cup of tea. I know that I'm grounded from fieldwork right now, but I also know your evaluation will make a difference for my career. Dr. Sheppard, I don't want to pressure you, but I'm itching to get back out there!" Keith announces strongly.

"Well, you know that you're not ready for fieldwork right now. This is our first day. I don't know what the future holds, and you have a lot of baggage from your past and present to work through. Let's just take one step at a time," Dr. Sheppard states, as she watches Keith's response.

"Fair enough… Dr. Sheppard, do you want some coffee?" Keith asks, as he gets up with the baby monitor still in his hands.

"That sounds great," Elise says, as she gets up from the couch and walks behind Keith to the kitchen.

Dr. Sheppard can't help but notice the mess Colin made from his morning breakfast. He is an untamed monkey. "Dr. Sheppard, what do you take in your coffee?" Keith asks, placing two cups on the corner counter and pouring a fresh cup of coffee for Dr. Sheppard.

As Keith begins to pour coffee into the second cup, he accidentally misses and the coffee lands on his left hand.

"Damn!" Keith exclaims, sitting the Krups white coffee pot back on its base and trying to hold his hand. The pain starts to make it tremble. He quickly puts his hand in cold water to relieve the burning.

"What happened? Mr. Heiden, what's wrong?" Elise says, leaning over to aid Keith.

"I'm fine," he states, with an intense sharp voice. "Please leave me alone!"

At that moment the baby monitor begins to vibrate and Keith hears Colin crying. "Damn it!" This is all he needs. Colin is awake now, and his hand is burning at the same time. He takes a towel and wraps it quickly around his hand, trying to hide his injury from Dr. Sheppard.

This is all too much for him to handle in one morning.

"Please, Dr. Sheppard, I'm fine. I think it is better if you leave now. We will pick up on Wednesday at the same time. Please understand?" he pleads with a sharp, but sad voice. His intense blue eyes show that he needs help but not right now.

"Please let yourself out. Thanks," Keith requests. Dr. Sheppard looks at him as she walks away. He covers his hand showing that he is ashamed of what happened to him and walks up the stairs to Colin. As Dr. Sheppard starts to clean the mess that was made, she hears Keith over the baby monitor.

"What's wrong, Colin? It's okay. If Daddy scared you, I'm sorry. I didn't mean to," Keith says in a very soft voice. "Daddy!" Colin cries out.

"It's okay. Go back to sleep. I'm right here."

Keith knows that Dr. Sheppard is going to hear everything that is said through the baby monitor. He's making it sound like he's okay. The situation is handled, even though his face is flushed with anger and despair. Hiding his true feelings is not easy, but it is part of his life.

Dr. Sheppard leaves the Heidens' house feeling very confused and troubled. Taking on Keith Heiden as a client is not an easy task.

"I need coffee," she says out loud in front of the Heidens' home, as she puts her sunglasses on and walks away.

Keith looks outside through the guest bedroom window and sees Dr. Sheppard walking away. He knows now that the doctor will not go away easily. Even though it is the first session of the therapy, it is going to be very stressful talking about his childhood, especially to a total stranger.

As Keith watches Dr. Sheppard get into her red 2006 Volvo S41 and drive away, many questions race through his mind. Why does he need a therapist now after all these years? Is someone really after his position? Why has this drama hit him so suddenly now? Dealing with his past and present is his personal business. He must take responsibility for controlling his anger and blackouts before they happen again.

"Keith, what are you doing?" asks Justine, his wife. She is a slight woman, 5'7" and 112 lbs with very curly blond hair and light blue but sharp eyes. As Justine walks toward Keith, she can tell by his mannerisms that he is hurt. They have been together for four and then married of eighteen years. So she knows him well. Both hold each other as Keith moves Justine's hair. He remembers when he had a Quartz watch on and for some reason it got caught in Justine's tight curly hair. The watch was never to be found again!

"Keith, you are going through with this doctor!" Justine shouts as she pushes away from Keith. They have a lot of baggage since the Jose Medina case ten years ago.

"I don't want to see a doctor, especially a therapist! They are crazier than their patients!" exclaims Keith, holding his hand for extra comfort.

"You're incredible! After what happened to all of us last year! You have jeopardized your job and our family. I can't take the drama anymore!" shouts Justine, slamming the door before the real fighting begins.

Keith looks at his wife and thinks to himself, *Here we go again! She's putting another needle into the voodoo doll that has my name on it. This doll has been in the picture since the first day they met. I bet that her whole family helped her make it. I can imagine how many needles are already in the voodoo doll a.k.a. Keith or maybe I don't want to know.*

"You never understood what I'm going through! I console you every minute, but you never can meet me halfway on my needs!" shouts Keith.

"I'm telling you right now, I supported you since your family disowned you! My family and I took you in when you were at your worst!" Justine viciously shouts at Keith. She's instantly in his face and extremely angry. As Justine slaps Keith across his face it echoes through the house. Keith puts his head down in shame like a child. "I'm sorry!"

"Why don't you stand up for yourself? Take control of what you are doing! If you lose your job, everything that we have will be gone in a second. Your income supports us. You make me sick to my stomach! You're a self-centered person! Grow up!" As Justine leaves the room Keith becomes teary-eyed, feeling confused and unworthy.

Justine stomps to the master bedroom and locks the door, leaving Keith feeling helpless and abused. Who will save him from Justine, and who will save Justine from Keith?

CHAPTER
THREE

〰〰〰〰〰〰〰〰〰〰〰〰〰〰〰〰〰〰〰〰〰〰〰〰〰〰〰〰〰〰〰〰〰〰〰〰

*D*r. Sheppard's schedule this Tuesday morning is light. It's a great time to catch up on her paperwork with a fresh cup of coffee. The sound of the phone ringing breaks her concentration. "Good morning. Dr. Elise Sheppard, how can I help you today?" she asks, using her business voice.

"Hello, my name is Agent Peter Darling from the DEA Department in Los Angeles."

The voice sounds friendly. "I'm Agent Keith Heiden's supervisor. How is he doing in his sessions? I know you can't give me all the details because of the patient's confidentially oath, but if you can give me anything at all that would be great!" asks Agent Peter Darling.

"It is going to be hard work for both parties, even though I just started. I'm hopeful that we'll make some progress," announces Elise, as she takes a sip of her hot coffee.

"That's good! I know it's going to be a slow process. Agent Heiden starts work at 8:00 p.m. tonight. Do you have time this evening to come down to the department to evaluate him? Believe me, it will be worth the trip," says Agent Darling.

"Sure." Elise answers, thinking about this little field trip with some concern and interest at the same time.

"That's great! I'll put your name at the security gate. There you will meet Terrance Jackson; who will take good care of you until I come down to see you. The address is 1435 Federal Drive, in downtown Los Angeles. We will keep Agent Heiden in the dark about tonight. Before I forget, I also have some cases for you to review. I know that you have a lot on your plate, so let me know if you want the additional work. I'll understand either way. I can find another psychologist to take on the cases, but I'd like to give you the first pick. What is the saying, killing two birds with one stone?" he laughingly says.

"Thank you, I will accept your invitation as well as the cases," Elise answers, as she looks at the pile of work in front of her.

It's taken her at least a month to catch up without coffee breaks in between. Dr. Jonathan Daniels dropped off all the resumes for the receptionist position this morning. When that position is filled, Elise will finally see her whole desk; right now she can't remember what kind of wood her desk is made out of.

"Thank you, Dr. Sheppard. See you tonight. It was great talking to you. Good-bye," says Agent Peter Darling.

"Good-bye," Elise hangs up the phone, gets up from her desk, and opens her briefcase, a graduation gift from Dad. She takes out her PDA and types in the 8:30 p.m. appointment for tonight at the DEA.

Elise sees Dr. Jonathan Daniels through her office window. He's another therapist and a very good friend. He helps her with business and her personal life. Jonathan is a fifty-four-year-old man with green eyes and salt and pepper colored hair. Due to his laid-back and slow-moving manner, he looks shorter than his 5'10" frame. Elise pushes him to date, because there is someone for everyone.

She walks out of her office to get his attention, "Jonathan, do you have a minute?" she asks. He hands Elise a donut from Dunkin Donuts and an extra large fresh coffee with milk but no sugar.

"Thanks, how did you know?" She closes her hand around the cup for extra comfort to wake herself up.

Jonathan loves his coffee at Circle K. It's a large coffee, very light with three packages of Sweet and Low.

"I saw your coffee emergency light flashing. I always have a minute for you," he states, with a smile on his face.

Jonathan is wearing a suit that should have been brought back to the Salvation Army clothing bin a long time ago. One day Elise went to the Santa Monica Mall with Jonathan to update his wardrobe. He cried like a baby throughout the whole process.

"Agent Peter Darling from the DEA Department in Los Angeles just called me two minutes ago. I have an appointment at 8:30 p.m. with him, and he also has more cases for me. The real reason he called, however, is to evaluate Agent Heiden while I'm there. What do you think?" she asks, while drinking a little bit of her coffee.

"Go for it! If you can get new cases and evaluate Agent Heiden at the same time, you couldn't ask for anything better than that! Just tell me the details tomorrow!" Jonathan replies, as he smiles at Elise, and she responds back by giving him a wink.

"No problem, I think it's going to be very interesting," Elise announces, drinking her coffee very slowly.

Elise walks back to her office looking at all the paperwork that needs to be addressed. As she types the information into her data program, she hopes that help will come soon. She begins to think to herself; what if she falls down and hits her head against her desk? Papers will cover her. No one will ever find her, because the cleaning lady doesn't even dare to clean her office. Jonathan is not fast in response time so he won't know. Her body will start to smell. Maybe her patients will call to make additional appointments, except Mr. Heiden, who she doesn't think will call at all.

CHAPTER

FOUR

*A*s she enters the federal building, Dr. Elise Sheppard feels somewhat overwhelmed. In the main lobby she walks over the crest seal of the United State Drug Enforcement Administration. She sees many people with business suits throughout the building. As she heads toward the security gate, Elise spots a guard with a name tag that says, "Terrance (Jackson)."

He smiles at her and says, "Can you please show me your ID and put your briefcase and pocketbook on the moving belt?" Another officer looks through Dr. Sheppard's things; on the other side of the scanner she picks up her items. As she walks to the gate, Elise is stopped by a scanner stick that searches her body for any concealed weapons. The guard gives Dr. Sheppard her California drivers license and calls Agent Darling.

"Dr. Sheppard, please stand to the side so I can do my job," states Mr. Jackson, as he guides her to a safe place. Elise continues to observe the people as they walk through the gate. She can't help but think that they are always being looked at under a microscope through the government's eye. The time is now 8:40 p.m. Elise sees a gentleman walking towards her.

"Hi, Dr. Elise Sheppard?" asks the man. His cream-colored tie is slightly darker than his shirt and looks quite nice with his distinguished-looking black suit. The DEA ID clip is very noticeable in his outside pocket.

"Yes, you must be Agent Peter Darling?" Elise replies, as she shakes the agent's hand. His thin, well-fit body looks taller than it's

6'2" height and complements his brown hair and interesting light brown eyes.

"Hello, I'm sorry for the delay. I was making sure that Agent Heiden is in tonight," Peter states with a friendly smile.

As they begin their walk toward the first of many doors they will encounter in their travels, Agent Darling looks straight at Elise to get her full attention.

"Dr. Sheppard, I need to inform you about some strict ground rules before we enter. Please listen to me at all times, try not to walk away from me, and look straight ahead. There is a lot of highly confidential information here that is sealed to the public. That's why there are very few outside visitors. If you were not assigned to come to visit today, you wouldn't be able to get into this section of the DEA Department. There is a visiting area on the first floor for outside people who can come to see their family members who work here. Oh, I almost forgot. Try not to talk to any agents. If they start a conversation that is different… I hope I covered everything… Short version, just stay close to me and there won't be any problems," Peter announces to Elise.

"Okay, just stay close to you at all times and keep my nose clean… Got it!" Elise answers. She feels very important with the DEA visitor's pass around her neck.

"You're my responsibility now," he says with a smile, trying to get Elise to relax.

"Yes, Agent Darling," she answers with a smile on her face.

"Good! I didn't want to really sound like my father," says Peter, smiling right back at her.

Elise starts to laugh at what Agent Darling has just said. They start walking toward the door using swipe card keys to access their way. It's like walking through a maze. They finally see the main secret entrance to the DEA Department. Peter uses his backhand, and the monitor shows Agent Peter Darling's government picture and signature. The touchpad states, "Information accepted."

The doors open into the main section of the United States Drug Enforcement Administration. Elise never saw such a secretive department. She works for the government but never went into a building like this before. They contact her by e-mail or voice mail, giving her assignments for the week ahead. This is the first time that Elise is welcomed on a tour. They walk toward Agent Darling's office. As she sits down in a comfortable chair, she sees children's toys around the room. If she didn't know better she could be in Toys "R" Us rather than a government agency.

"If I may ask, are you selling these toys on E-Bay?" she questions, waiting for Agent Darling to answer her.

"I wish! These are my toys, which give me a happy, light feeling during stressful hours at work," answers Peter with a friendly smile. He opens his desk to find something making a lot of noise. "Where is it?" he says to himself, feeling around a messy drawer full of toys. "Come on!"

As Elise gets up from her chair, pictures of men, women, teenagers, toddlers, and infants of all ages catch her eye. These pictures are on the wall with the saying "All Walks of Life."

"Who are these people on the wall? What is their importance?" she asks, with total interest.

"Those pictures are a reminder for me and others in the department. They are the people we couldn't save this year. It tells us that drugs kill every minute and at any age. Here are five new cases of different agents that need your help. Please review these cases as soon as you can. Here is my business card in case you need my help in any way," Peter comments and hands over the files and business card to Elise.

She puts the new information into the briefcase and closes it automatically. As she looks up at Agent Darling, he tries to get candy out of a Pez container with Daffy Duck's head. "Do you want one?" he says with a wink.

"No, thank you," she replies with a smile, as Agent Darling continues to act like a teenager.

As Elise looks around the room, she sees some personal pictures of Peter. One with four children immediately catches her eye. The three boys are wearing white polo shirts with tan pants, and the teenage girl has a white summer dress on. Is Agent Darling married, she wonders even though there is no wedding band in sight? Or perhaps he is the favorite uncle in the family? Her thoughts are interrupted by a loud knock at the door.

"Come in," says Agent Darling, as he continues to eat a pez.

Agent Keith Heiden walks into the office. He feels like he is trapped inside the famous ride at Walt Disney, "It's a Small World." He focuses on a tiny clown with big eyes in the hot air balloon. This little character is holding a picket sign that says, "Help me!" He is always a little fearful when entering Peter's office.

"Hey Keith," Peter says with a smile on his face. He tries to get some reaction from Keith other than just business.

"Hello. Here are the reports and the compact disk that you wanted from yesterday," Keith states, as he passes the completed work to Agent Darling. Peter starts to take a quick look at the reports. Keith feels very closed in and extremely uncomfortable. The cartoons appear ready to attack him at any moment.

"I still have to go over it, but it looks good so far. By any chance, do you have the four reports that I had requested four days ago?" Peter asks, as he looks at Keith intently.

"Peter, I finished those reports at the first deadline you gave me. As always, I have to wait for other people to respond to my reports. I'm dealing with snails for DEA staff!" Keith states loudly, as he turns his head and sees Dr. Elise Sheppard sitting quietly observing the two agents talking about work. "I'm sorry. Hello, Dr. Sheppard. I didn't see you there."

"That's okay." Elise smiles at Keith. He's a little surprised to see the doctor. He doesn't like surprises at all. Keith has to know at all times what he is up against. His father loved to play games with Keith's mental and physical state.

"Peter, why didn't you tell me that Dr. Sheppard was here?" Keith says with an annoyed tone in his voice.

"You didn't ask. So if you can get me those reports before work is over, that will be great," Peter states in a tone Keith knows means business. "You have to interrogate a criminal in twenty minutes. He is in room # 24, and here is all the information on the gentleman." Peter states, as he hands over the file to Keith. "We have to talk one on one about a matter that needs to be addressed."

Keith looks at his boss in frustration. Sometimes he asks too much of his staff. "Peter, it's not as easy as it sounds. It's going to take a lot more time to find the files. Can you give me till Friday?" he pleads.

"Sorry, Keith, I can't accommodate you. You must give me those reports by the end of the work day. The bosses upstairs are breathing down my neck! I will have to reprimand you, and I don't want to do that! You're pushing me up against the wall. Just do it!" Peter shouts back at Keith to give him a strong clue that this is business, not personal.

"Sorry, I didn't know you were tied up in knots!" Keith says with a give-me-a-break look at Peter. "Okay I'll see you in twenty minutes, and I'll try to get the reports in by the end of the work day. Bye, Dr. Sheppard," Keith says offhandedly, as Elise looks up at him.

"Good-bye."

Minutes later Elise and Agent Peter Darling walk toward the interrogation room. There are many monitors that see inside the room at different angles. They show a young man in his early twenties sitting behind a table with a bottle of water beside him. Three different agents are sitting down at their stations waiting for the interrogation to begin. Elise sees Keith walk toward the agents.

Keith is dressed all in black with his gun besides his hip with his ID and badge showing. He looks very professional, moving like a soldier with little or no expression on his face. His strong outside personality hides a very different Keith on the inside. He signs a couple of forms and then looks directly at Dr. Sheppard without saying a word. Elise knows now that she is falling for him big time. She feels like a teenager. She dated her boyfriend in college for many years. They were about to be married, but she realized she couldn't go through with it. She knew that she wasn't ready to get married then, but the passage of time changes things.

As Keith enters the room he sees a young adult sitting and waiting quietly. "Place your bets, agents," remarks Agent Darling, waving a $20 bill above his head. The agents are taking out their money to bet about $20 or $30 dollars or more. There is a lot of excitement as they hand their bills over to Agent Darling.

Elise looks very confused as she asks, "You guys place bets?"

"Yes, this is betting time, Dr. Sheppard. The bet is that our boy Heiden can stare at anyone in the room without saying a word. The person will get nervous until he or she pleads their hearts out, pouring out a full confession in about twenty minutes or less. It will be great to see," says Peter with a smile, as he winks at Elise. "So, Dr. Sheppard, are you going to place your bet on our golden child?" He looks at her with excitement as her eyes light up.

"Why not?" she replies with a big smile. She is really beginning to like Peter. Every class needs a clown, so why not the DEA Department of LA?

Dr. Sheppard walks up to the window to see Agent Heiden, but he is unable to see her. Keith is standing against the wall without any expression, while the suspect is moving around the room like an untamed alley cat trying to get out of his cage. He is about 5'5", wearing loose-fitting jeans and a black T-shirt with the words "Party Hardy!" The dirty-looking young man is very jumpy, as if he's still on a high kick.

As he runs to the window to get anyone's attention you can hear him cry out, "Hey, is this guy from special ed?"

Elise asks, "How long can Agent Heiden remain silent?" One of the agents answers the question. "He can hold his position a very long time. The longest was about four hours until the criminal needed a bathroom break. Then Agent Heiden took his bathroom break. How sweet was that?"

"Thanks for the information. This helps Dr. Sheppard understand what's going on, because she is looking at me strangely," Peter says, starting to laugh out loud.

The other agents are laughing with him. They like to joke around a lot to release some tension that is felt every minute in the DEA department. Half the time Agent Darling starts the jokes without even realizing it.

"Man, what happened to your ear? You look deformed or something!" yells the suspect. Keith gives him a bizarre look that means, "back off or else!!" He steps away from Agent Heiden. "Okay, man, I will stand back. Just don't bite." The suspect slowly sits down in the chair with his back to the wall. It bothers him that he can't read this agent. On the streets of LA, he knows his homeboys well, but you have to know your opponents even better. He can't figure out this man in black. Keith starts to walk around the room, trying to keep himself focused. The twenty minutes that have gone by seem like an eternity.

The only break in silence is the sound of Keith coughing. Then suddenly the tension increases when Agent Heiden leans over the table and directly stares into the suspect's doped up eyes.

"Okay! I'll talk!" wails the suspect. At that moment Keith turns his head and looks directly at Dr. Sheppard, the intensity of his eyes penetrate the window between them. She feels an unexpected cold chill run through her body.

An agent on the other side of the window lowers the volume in the interrogation room as the suspect continues to give his statement. The agents file out, some happy about their winnings and others sadly empty-handed. A few minutes later Elise and Peter walk out to the main lobby to say their goodbyes. Elise doesn't see Keith again, which saddens her, but perhaps it's a good thing.

CHAPTER

FIVE

〜〜〜〜〜〜〜〜〜〜〜〜〜〜〜〜〜〜〜〜〜〜〜〜〜〜〜〜〜〜〜〜〜〜〜〜〜〜〜

*I*t is 9:00 a.m. on a Wednesday as Dr. Elise Sheppard walks to her office, unlocks the door, and enters. She sees all the files of patients that need her attention and lots of resumes the secretarial job. Elise has to double her orders for coffee because her job needs her. The question is, does she want the job? She sits down at her desk, turns on the computer, and looks at all the mail in front of her. The phone rings. "Dr. Elise Sheppard," she answers in a personal voice.

"Hello, Dr. Sheppard. This is Peter Darling, remember me?" asks the gentleman with a friendly voice. Elise is opening her mail from yesterday and trying to keep a conversation going at the same time. "Hello, Agent Darling. How can I help you today?" she asks. She begins to think of Peter as a grown man trapped in a teenage mind, or better yet a bad boy with a government badge. How sweet is that?

"I'm calling because I'm single and you're single. So do you want to go out with me?" asks Peter, as he walks around his very messy apartment looking for his car keys. "I will tell you that it's going to be fun!"

"Agent Darling…do you mean a date? It's a conflict of interest because Keith is your partner and my patient. I really don't think it is in the best interest of Mr. Heiden. We can jeopardize his future in the DEA Department," Elise states to Agent Darling.

"Come on, Elise, take a chance in life and go out with me! I know that we'll have lots of fun! Don't worry. I'll be watching our boy closely when he works underneath me. Other than being late

26

more than once, he is doing well. I must find out about the schedule time. I don't have to be his supervisor either. He can be assigned to a different section of the department," he states, still looking for his car keys. He really wants to get to the gym, since he's been eating a lot of his mother's cooking on the weekends. Peter is trying to keep fit, especially since he plans to travel a lot before the big forty in two years. If he doesn't find his keys, he won't be going anywhere.

"I have to think about this, Peter, and I'll let you know. I have your number," Elise states. "Listen, I don't want you to change departments because of me." She thinks this could be fun, and at the same time, she wonders how she would handle Mr. Heiden if she goes out with his supervisor and best friend.

"Does that mean that you'll consider going out with me?" he asks. "Believe me we won't talk about our golden boy!"

"It seems fair. Okay, I'll go out with you," Elise says, with a big smile on her face. She feels like a teenager again. It reminds her of the last day of school when Tommy Landers asked her out. She'll never forget that summer. It was great until Tommy moved to a different state. She will always have the memories along with the love letters, pictures, and some flowers that are now dried in her personal album.

"That's great! I have to go now, but I'll call you by the end of the day. We can set up a date for the weekend. Take care of yourself, and I'll call you soon," Peter remarks, as he spots his keys near the coffee pot. Now he can finish a cup of fresh coffee and the omelet that has been waiting for him.

CHAPTER

SIX

///

*I*t is 11:00 a.m. on a Wednesday, and Dr. Elise Sheppard should be at the front door any minute now. Colin is too wired up to take a nap. It is a hit or miss with him. Keith closes the gates to the kitchen and upstairs, so Colin can't go in there. The goal is to keep Colin in the living room, so Keith doesn't have to look too far for him. Keith hopes he won't get into too much trouble this way. Colin's toys, snacks, and a sippy cup with fresh water are set up on the table as the doorbell rings.

"Mommy!" Colin runs to the door waiting to give her a big hug.

"Colin, it's not mommy. It's a doctor," Keith answers, as he walks toward the front door.

"I want Mommy!" Colin whimpers, as he pulls on Keith's clothes. "I want Mommy!"

"Colin, please be a good boy for Daddy!" Keith pleads anxiously to his little son, as he holds Colin firmly and opens the door at the same time. How does Keith use his DEA skills in this situation?

"Hello, Colin, Mr. Heiden." Dr. Sheppard smiles, as she watches Keith struggle with a little child who is an identical image of her patient.

"Hello, Dr. Sheppard. Please come in. Can you please close the front door behind us? Thanks," Keith says, as he holds Colin's hand and walks towards the living room.

"Sure," replies Dr. Sheppard, as she watches Keith and Colin.

It is nice to see a father and son bond together especially these days. Elise is getting that strange feeling of love for Mr. Heiden again. She did make herself promise to shut this feeling out when working with Keith, but it's not going to be easy.

"Colin, remember what I said early this morning? You have to be a good boy for me. You're going to be good, right?" Keith says with an amiable and soft voice.

"Okay, Daddy. Daddy, I want Mommy! Mommy!" Colin's tears are running down his face. Keith takes a few tissues out of the box and wipes his runny nose.

"I'm sorry, Dr. Sheppard. Please sit down," Keith urges. "When Colin doesn't take a nap, this is what happens," Keith says, as he watches his little one walk around the living room.

"I see," says Dr. Sheppard, as she makes herself comfortable on the couch. She smoothes her suit and easily crosses her legs, unaware of Keith watching her. He turns quickly to look in Colin's direction.

"Colin, don't run too fast or you will get hurt," Keith says, as he stands in the middle of the living room. Keith looks at Dr. Sheppard. "I hope you don't mind if I sit down on the floor and play with Colin?"

"I don't mind at all. This is going to be interesting," Dr. Sheppard replies with a smile. She is feeling flushed, strange inside and begins to nervously laugh out loud. Keith doesn't understand what Elise is laughing about.

She thinks it is good to have a client interact with someone or something they enjoy. It helps them to relax and answer questions more easily.

"I don't know about that!" Keith says, as he sits down next to Colin and all his toys.

"How does it feel being a father?" Dr. Sheppard asks.

"Shocking!" replies Keith sarcastically, as he watches Colin bring him all his toys. "Colin, I don't need all the toys on my lap, but thank you." As Colin sits on his daddy's lap, he begins to squirm.

"Colin, you're hurting me. If you want to sit on me, you can't move so much," Keith reminds his son, as he tries to look at Dr. Sheppard. "Colin, you are moving too much. Please get off my lap,"

Keith says, as he removes Colin and sees Elise laughing at the whole episode.

"No! Lap!" Colin cries out, with a shriek that pierces right through Keith's left ear.

"Colin, please don't yell in my ear. That hurts Daddy. Try to be a good boy." Keith looks really tired. He worked last night from 8:00 p.m. till 9:00 a.m., and now Colin won't even nap. Colin gets up from his dad's lap. "Okay, Daddy." He starts to walk around the living room making funny noises, as Keith watches his every move.

"Please, Dr. Sheppard, don't mind me. Continue with the questions," Keith says, as he sits there with the toys lying on his lap and around him.

"Are you the disciplinarian in your family?" Dr. Sheppard asks, as they continue to hear Colin making crazy sounds in different parts of the living room.

"Believe it or not, yes. Colin, what are you doing?" Keith doesn't get an answer from Colin.

"Colin! Answer Daddy! I hope you are not underneath the couch? Colin William Heiden!" Keith shouts. As he gets up the toys, fall off his lap, and he starts to search for his son.

"Justine didn't want the job. She told me that she would give in by looking into her children's somber, sorry eyes." Keith is still walking around the living room trying to find the identical half pint of himself.

As Elise crosses her legs to give Colin an easy exit from underneath the couch, she asks, "How do you feel?"

"I'm trying to shape up four kids, and it is not at all easy. Colin Heiden, answer me now! One, two, three… Now you're in big trouble, mister!"

"Help me!" cries a little voice underneath the couch opposite Dr. Sheppard. Elise starts to laugh as she sees a little boy that can get into trouble so quickly. Keith is behind the couch pulling Colin's body out of the cramped space. The little child's laughter echoes throughout the first floor of the home.

"Get out of there! Hold on!" Keith calls to his three-year-old. He carefully tries to pull his little son out from underneath the couch. Dr. Sheppard hears the drama behind the couch, and she starts to giggle.

"Thank you, Daddy." As the laughter stops, Colin has tears in his blue eyes once again.

Keith walks Colin to the time-out chair in the corner of the living room. "Colin Heiden, you didn't listen to Daddy. Now, I want you to sit down on the time-out stool and face the wall. You know what to do." Keith gives a direct order to his three-year-old son. "You have to sit for five minutes. If you get off the chair before the time is up, you will have to start all over. Do you understand, Colin? Now sit down."

"No!" Colin wails. You can hear the shriek as it echoes throughout the house.

"Listen!" Keith begins to whisper into his son's little ear. His body and facial expressions are becoming very tense. Colin finally stops crying and sits in the little chair with no demands. Whatever Keith said to his son worked instantly. Keith sits down on a chair near Dr. Sheppard and tries to catch his breath from the little drama. "What about kids?"

Dr. Sheppard starts to laugh again. "I'm sorry," she is feeling very silly and very hot inside, and she doesn't know why she is acting this way. "Is it hot in here, or it is just me?"

"Are you okay, Dr. Sheppard?" Keith looks concerned and confused by Elise's actions.

"I'm fine," she replies, as she tries to hide her embarrassment. She begins to talk to herself. "Elise, try to relax. You must hold back these feelings you have for Keith Heiden."

Keith looks at Colin, as he waits for him to move off the stool. As Dr. Sheppard thinks about Keith's past, she finds it very interesting to see how he is handling his son.

"How do you deal so well with your kids since you had a terrible childhood?" Dr. Sheppard asks, as she looks at Keith who is still watching Colin.

"I made a promise to myself not to be like my father, and I take it one day at a time," answers Keith.

"If you were your father, what would have happened to Colin today?" questions Dr. Sheppard, as she looks at Mr. Heiden for his reaction.

"Colin would have to do a lot of praying if he planned on taking his next breath," states Keith with a cold, stern voice as he looks directly at Dr. Sheppard. Those intense blue eyes send chills down her spine.

Then he turns his attention back to his son. "Colin, you have four minutes," Keith announces, looking at his imported European watch.

"Okay," says a sad little voice filled with sniffles.

"Doesn't it break your heart?" asks Dr. Sheppard, feeling sorry for little Colin crying on the time-out stool in the corner of the room.

"You sound like my wife Justine. If you give into the kids, you just make it worse. I'm trying to teach them discipline and respect," he responds back.

"What about you? What did your father teach you?" Dr. Sheppard asks, waiting to see what Keith's answer will be.

Keith has a confused look on his face. He is either thinking about the question, or he doesn't understand what Dr. Sheppard is trying to say. "Mr. Heiden, do you understand the question I'm asking you?" Dr. Sheppard asks, as she waits for Keith's reaction.

"Daddy, I want to get up!" Colin wails.

"Colin, sit down. I'm not saying it again! Please sit down! It is going to be a very long day for you and for me! If you want to play you have to sit first," Keith states, with a clear but firm voice. Colin sits down on the stool and begins to cry loudly.

Keith looks at Dr. Sheppard, "My dad didn't have any true feelings about raising me correctly. He was a very cold man with no heart. If he had one, he wouldn't have done what he did to me."

"You truly think that?" asks Dr. Sheppard, putting Keith's case file on her left side.

"Yes, I do. Abuse was all I ever knew from him," Keith answers. He gets up and walks over the Colin's snack, and his sippy cup. As he gives the little bag of carrots and the sippy cup to his hungry lit-

tle master. Colin looks up and smiles weakly. "Thank you, Daddy."
Keith lovingly pats Colin's head.

"Dr. Sheppard, I don't know what you want from me. I'm
trapped in my abuse. I don't know how I should feel. Maybe I should
feel like a lost puppy in a shelter?" he asks. "How do I wake up from
the nightmare I have to deal with every day?"

"It's not going to be easy," she replies sympathetically.

"I know… Colin, you can get up now. What do you want to
eat for lunch? You can have peanut butter and jelly or grilled cheese?"
Keith asks as he gets up from the chair. Colin moves quickly from the
time-out stool and puts his carrots and sippy cup down on the floor.

"Daddy, Daddy, potty!" he exclaims, as he tries to hold himself
and wipe his tears at the same time.

"Okay, Colin, let's go to the bathroom." Keith puts his hand
out to Colin. "Dr. Sheppard, I know we still have a half hour of our
session to finish today. We can sit outside on the patio since it is a
nice day. Help yourself to a drink, and I'll be right out," he states, as
he walks with Colin to the hallway bathroom.

"That's fine, thank you," replies Dr. Sheppard.

Elise Sheppard suddenly feels very thirsty from the morning
drama. She opens the stainless steel refrigerator to find everything
labeled and packed very neatly. There is no junk food in sight.

"Hello, Keith!" Dr. Sheppard doesn't recognize the voice of the
woman who has just entered the house. As Elise takes out a bottle
of water and closes the refrigerator door, she sees a woman in her
late thirties from the corner of her eye. She is about 5'7" with a
thin frame and wearing a very light off-white business suit. Her long
blond curly hair is held back with a clip, which emphasizes her high
forehead and very sharp, clear blue eyes. She is wearing a 4-karat
diamond engagement ring and a wedding band set with 2-karat dia-
monds. Both rings are in a platinum setting.

"Oh hello, I'm Dr. Elise Sheppard, Mr. Heiden's psychologist,"
she states, putting her hand out as a friendly gesture.

"Do all doctors open their client's refrigerators?" replies the
woman, without acknowledging Elise's outstretched hand.

"Only the hungry ones," Dr. Sheppard replies with a smile.

"I'm Mrs. Heiden. Where is my husband?" she states with a cool tone. Mrs. Heiden is feeling some concern with the situation. A stranger just opens the refrigerator and helps herself to a bottle of water while husband and child are nowhere to be found.

"Mommy!" Colin is wearing a Teenage Mutant Ninja Turtles' shirt, blue jeans, and little white sneakers that have red lights, which flash when he moves. He runs into Justine's open arms, hugging her legs.

"Hello, Colin. Were you a good boy?" Justine smiles when she sees her baby boy. She knows that Colin is growing up. In September he is going into pre-K. "He was on the time-out stool just once. For the most part, he is a good boy. Right, Colin?" Keith announces with a smile on his face. It warms his heart to see Colin hugging Justine with such love and affection.

"Yes, Daddy." Colin smiles, as he's moving his little body to release his pump energy. He is little, but he is really fast on his feet when he wants to be. Colin begins to yell, "Teenage Mutant Ninja Tur…tles!" He loves to have an audience, and he begins to race from one room to another without a care in the world.

"Colin, please don't run!" Keith commands with a smile on his face. It makes him happy to see his son enjoying himself.

"I can see you ladies have already met," Keith says, as he looks at the two women and smiles at them. He seems relaxed and very friendly now. I guess family will do that. It certainly makes him smile from ear to ear.

"Justine, I hope you don't mind that Dr. Sheppard and I are going outside to finish our session," he says, as he sees Justine walking toward him. He kisses her on the cheek and gently strokes her arm.

"That's fine. I have the Johnson's house on Plum Avenue!" Justine announces, as she tries to get Keith's attention.

"That's great, Justine!" He smiles at her, as he picks up the peanut butter jar to make Colin's lunch. "I can do that, Keith. You go finish with the doctor." Justine takes the jar out of Keith's hand slowly and gracefully. Their hands touch, and she smiles at Keith, showing Dr. Sheppard that there is no room for another woman in his life.

"Thanks." A little surprised that Justine is so touchy, but it feels nice to be wanted. Suddenly he has a strange feeling as he thinks to himself, *What are you trying to ask me? What do you really want from me? What are you going to say or do to me after the doctor leaves?* Dr. Sheppard has a strong feeling that Justine abuses Keith emotionally and physically. Elise feels sick inside, seeing these two lives eaten away little by little by abuse. She wants to address this matter but doesn't know how to approach it with either party.

The last ten yrs of their eighteen-year marriage has been rocky, because they are both headstrong and stubborn. Keith and Justine need to work on their relationship, but where do they start?

CHAPTER
SEVEN

A few minutes later Keith and Elise walk outside to the patio. Dr. Sheppard places her bottle of water on the light tan table and sits down in one of the four comfortable chairs. Keith holds his glass of ice tea as they settle themselves and get ready to finish their therapy session. The weather is sunny, and the breeze is a cool one. It is a perfect day to sit in the backyard, which is filled with many different palm trees, colorful flowers, a huge swimming pool, and a play area for Colin. Keith smiles, as he thinks of all the quality time he's spent out here with his family. He has certainly put the barbeque to good use.

"I hope we won't be distracted out here. I know we've already wasted a lot of time. Sorry about that," Keith says.

"You don't have to be sorry. Things happen," Elise claims, opening her notepad.

"You are from a family of nine?" Dr. Sheppard asks, as she takes a thirst-quenching drink from her water bottle.

"Yes, my mother had four sets of twins. She was in the newspaper many years ago. I'm the only one that is not a twin, the fifth child out of a group of eight siblings. I have not spoken to any of them in twenty-two years," he states, taking a drink from his cold ice tea.

"That is amazing, four sets of twins! I know for a fact it was a full house!" Elise remarks, with a huge smile on her face. "If you had a chance to meet them, would you?" she asks, looking at her patient for a reaction but seeing only sadness inside his blue eyes.

"Yes, it was a full house. I don't know, maybe not," he replies, trying to relax in his chair. It is not easy for Keith to get comfortable with so many difficult questions being thrown at him.

"Why?" Elise asks, as she takes a drink of water.

"Because it was twenty-two years ago, and I have nothing to say to them. They are total strangers to me," he states coldly while he looks at the floor to avoid Dr. Sheppard's eyes.

"How about your parents? What about your mother? Did you have any relationship with her?" Elise opens Keith's case file and is ready to write.

"They were drunks who didn't seem to have a care in the world. I don't think they cared if I was dead or alive. I was disowned by my family three days before my high school graduation." Keith replies sorrowfully. The only people who knew about his childhood were Justine and Peter. It makes him very uncomfortable to speak about this to Dr. Sheppard.

Keith remembers all too well the day that he was disowned by his family. He went out with a couple of friends three days before his graduation from St. Michael's Roman Catholic High School. After drinking ten beers or more he drove his father's 1985 Cadillac Eldorado home. As he parked the car on the front lawn mowing down all his mother's flowers, he had no idea what destruction he might have caused on the drive to his house. He rushed into his home and interrupted his father's meeting with two Japanese businessmen. He began laughing and cursing and suddenly vomited all over one client's brand-new shoes. Everyone began yelling at Keith as the two men left the house. Keith's father lost the account and the company. His pension, stocks, and bonds were also in jeopardy. All that he had worked for over the past fifteen or more years could be lost because of his spoiled, rotten son. Keith received a painful beating with his father's belt and was then kicked out of the house. He never saw his family again.

Keith shakes his head to get his mind back on track dreading what is ahead of him. He glances at Dr. Sheppard's cleavage quickly before putting his head down, and as he tries to be discreet from his adolescent behavior before, she takes note. But it's too late. Elise gives a smile that she's flattered by the extra attention from her new patient. Keith finds her to be smart and attractive, so how could you not look? He feels that he must avoid any more distractions.

"Why are you putting your head down?" asks Dr. Sheppard. She knows that an abused person can readily show signs of despair and have difficulty looking at someone directly.

"I don't know. Maybe I just do it automatically," he says very softly. But Keith knows exactly why he is doing it.

"Are you shamed of what happened to you in the past?" questions Dr. Sheppard cautiously.

"Yes, I'm ashamed that I couldn't fight back," Keith answers moving in his chair uncomfortably. He gets up from his seat and walks around the yard, glancing at the doctor then at his dog Reese who is lying on the grass rolling around on his back. As he watches his dog, "just being a dog," Keith smiles weakly.

Elise doesn't see that moment because she is writing on her notepad. She must be careful of the questions that she asks Keith. "I have a question that has been on my mind since I got here. Why didn't you run away or tell a policeman or a teacher at school about your troubled life?" Dr. Sheppard asks, using a calm voice as she looks at Keith.

At that instant, Keith looks directly at Dr. Sheppard and sits straight up in his chair. "I never thought of running away. Where would I go? The system would put me back into another abusive home. Besides, I didn't want my father to know that I would tell anyone about my life. It was a very dark secret, and my dad was a very scary man. He was terribly controlling and had a strong hold on everyone in the family, especially me," Keith answers emphatically. He could feel the chills down his back as he recalled his childhood.

Once again Keith puts his head down and grits his teeth to hold back any tears that might start uncontrollably. "I would try to hide from my father every time he came home, because I knew I was going to get the strap. I would run quickly to the kitchen to grab some food and then run back to my room. One day my father said to me, 'The game is to get the prey,' and I was the prey! My childhood was a game to him. Once or twice I would win, but he would win most of the time. I hate games!" Keith states strongly, as if he was yelling directly at his father. His body is completely tense, and Elise can see every vein in his neck. She knows he wants to be left alone.

"If you did win, what would happen?" Dr. Sheppard asks. Keith gives her a strange look almost like Reese, the family chocolate lab, who tilts his head to one side when trying to understand what is being said.

"You mean to lose a game?" he asks, as he picks up his head and looks directly at the doctor without blinking.

As she looks at her patient she thinks about how his emotions change in a split second. One minute he is filled with anger and aggression, and a second later he is overwhelmed with sadness. Although Elise has dealt with many similar patients, Keith's case is very extreme. She has to be very careful with her questions.

"No, I mean to win a game."

Keith smiles a little bit. "If I didn't get a beating for that day, I considered it a win and a good day for me. I only wanted to be left alone. That was all I asked for my miserable life." The smile is gone and Keith's voice is suddenly weak.

As Elise tries to hold back her own tears, she can only imagine what her patient went through. How awful it must have been for Keith to feel so unwanted and used at the same time. "You know it is not your fault. The blame is on your parents, and you need to understand and accept that so your healing can begin," replies Dr. Sheppard in a very soothing, calm voice. "I'm sorry that you felt so unwanted. Did you feel like an outcast?"

"All the time," Keith replies, holding his head in his hands.

"Did you try to kill yourself? Please try to be honest with your answer," she replies calmly, as she looks for some sign that will indicate Keith is ready to pick up his head and move on.

"I tried a couple of times. As you can see it didn't work out," Keith answers sarcastically. He continues to squirm in his chair trying to find some comfort in this difficult situation.

"Did you seriously hurt yourself in your efforts to do away with your life?" questions Dr. Sheppard.

"No, because I received enough punishment from the monster who slept in the room next door to me. I could never trust or believe in myself. I always doubted my abilities. Even though my father cheated during our games, I never thought I could beat him," he answers sadly.

"Did you ever hurt another individual or an animal?" she asks. Elise will not be surprised if his answer is yes to this question.

"No!" He yells sharply. *How could she ask such a question? Does she believe I could do this?* He thinks to himself.

"If your father had a heart attack would you help him get emergency care?" Elise asks cautiously.

"I would call 911 for help, but I wouldn't do anything else," answers Keith.

Elise does not react to any of Keith's answers, as she continues to write on her notepad. "If you ran away and had one item to bring, what would it be and why?"

"Does it have to be just one item? I would take all my books. When I read it took me to a different, kinder place. It would help my childhood pain go away," Keith replies sadly.

"How were holidays and birthdays for you? Do you remember any good times?" asks Dr. Sheppard as she begins to see Keith getting upset again.

"Holidays were never a happy time for me," he replies dejectedly, without even lifting up his head. "I never had a Christmas dinner with all the trimmings. I ate the leftovers that people didn't eat on their plates. When I saw Christmas presents with my name on the boxes, my father quickly gave them to my brothers. Even my brothers would laugh at me while they opened the gifts that were meant for me. My birthdays passed without a word. There was never a celebration, because they didn't care if I was born into this world or not."

Elise gets up from the patio chair as she waits for Keith's next response. "Mr. Heiden, were you continually afraid for your life as a child?"

"That's a stupid question, Dr. Sheppard. If you were in my shoes wouldn't you be?" he responds in exasperation as he lifts his head just enough to see a little bit of Elise's cleavage. Chills go quickly down her spine as she catches Keith's look.

He moves his head just enough to get a full view of her breast. Elise smiles, and without saying a word, she leans forward to give Keith a better look.

She has a strong feeling that there is very little intimacy between Keith and Justine in the bedroom. "Yes, I would be," Elise says softly. "If you had a chance to go back to the past, how would you change it?"

"I'd kill the asshole!" he cries with an angry voice, as he picks up his head for the last time. The intensity in his blue eyes causes Elise to sit down. She backs away with some fear because of the complexity of Keith's emotions.

Elise saw a sign of this aggression when they first met. Now she's sure that she wants to continue with this line of questioning. Elise wonders how far she can go without being attacked by her patient, but she is willing to take the chance in order to help Keith. In her mind she thinks, *Let's go for it!*

She clears her throat to get her question out, "Can you tell me how you would kill your dad if you had the opportunity?"

"It's a secret," replies Keith in a very calm, but stern voice. Without a minute to spare Elise says, "I want to help you. Can I please help you?"

"Why do you want to help me?" Keith inquiries without blinking. "You don't even know me?"

"You're in pain, and I want to help you," Elise replies with concern in her voice. She knows how important it is for Keith to trust her completely. In order for patients to open up, they must have full trust in their therapists. It is a very slow process, and only time will tell how long it will be for Keith.

"I still don't understand why you want to help me. I'm a little confused about what you really want," pleads Keith. He sits back on the chair and focuses on Dr. Sheppard's eyes. His body position tells the doctor that he can relax and still have full control.

"I'm your friend, and I can feel your pain. Whatever you want I'll help you, just say the word," replies Elise in a soft, soothing voice.

"I don't have any friends. No one likes me! They would call me the elephant man like the one in the old movie. Why do I need friends if they only want to call me names? You're not my friend! You will call me names like the others do! Go away! Why are you in my face? Leave me alone!" Keith shouts as his face reddens.

Elise sees Justine near the sliding doors, as the drama unfolds in the backyard. She knows that she must concentrate on her patient to try to get his full trust. If Justine interferes, it will only bring more tension into the session. Suddenly, Justine walks outside with her arms crossed.

"Dr. Sheppard, it's time to finish with my husband's therapy session," she demands, indifferent to Keith's state of mind. Justine walks back into the house without giving Elise a chance to respond. Dr. Sheppard shakes her head in amazement at Justine's uncaring attitude and thinks, *She is truly the universal bitch of Southern California!* This is going to be a very long summer at the Heiden house.

"I have to go now, but I will be back. We can continue this conversation the next time, all right?" she asks, trying not to push the button too far. She has no choice but to end the session; since Justine is on her back trying to be the center of attention. As Elise gets up from her chair, she sees no immediate reaction from Keith.

Keith zones out for a minute and doesn't hear what Dr. Sheppard has just said. "Oh, I'm sorry," he replies instinctively, as he gets up slowly, and walks toward the kitchen trying to collect his thoughts. Elise picks up her briefcase and pocketbook and follows Keith to the front door. As he opens the door; he just looks at her without saying a single word.

"I think we made progress, and I hope you feel the same way. Thank you and have a good day." Dr. Sheppard walks out of the house.

"I'm not sure, you too," replies Keith, with a look of concern on his face, as he closes the door and locks it. Keith suddenly feels very stressed and exhausted at the same time. As he takes a deep breath and rubs his tired eyes, he wonders what will occur next with Justine. The session took longer than he had hoped.

CHAPTER

EIGHT

//

*K*eith walks into the kitchen and sees Justine in a light off white outfit. She is holding a laundry basket full of colored wash from the first load of millions to come. Justine puts the basket down on the kitchen table and starts to fold the clothes. There is a look of disappointment on Justine's face, and she seems ready to attack her husband for no reason at all.

"Are you angry with me?" he asks, with a very concerned and confused look on this face. "What did I do?"

"You let Dr. Sheppard help herself to a bottle of water from our refrigerator!" Justine yells, as she stops folding the clean clothes. "How could you do such a thing?"

"I told her to help herself to a drink! What's wrong with that?" he demands. It is not even 12:30 p.m. and the fighting has begun.

"Where were you?" yells Justine.

"Colin had to go to the bathroom, and I had to attend to his needs!" Keith shouts at Justine, giving her a clue to back off.

"You let her open the refrigerator!" Justine proclaims dramatically, with her hands waving in the air.

"Is that it?! She opened the refrigerator? I really think that your blond hair is curled too tight, because you're nuts!" Keith shouts. "Justine, what is the big issue? I know you have one!"

"I don't want Dr. Sheppard roaming around our house! We have too much at stake!" Justine protests, as she watches her husband pace back and forth across the kitchen.

"The only access that Dr. Sheppard had to our house is the living room, kitchen, and the backyard! Give me a break!" Keith exclaims in frustration. As he looks at Justine trying to read into her eyes, he hopes to give her a clue to back down from this fight. Most of the time they argue with such vengeance and never seem to come up with any answers, or even a compromise.

"This is all we need right now! The doctor already knows what happened last year, and if she investigates our house, she may find out what occurred ten years ago! We lost a lot of money from the Garcia case. You put this family in danger financially and emotionally. Did you ever think about our family before you went off the deep end?" The echoes from Justine's shouts travel throughout the house. It's very apparent that she is continually embarrassed by Keith's actions.

"I know, Justine. You have constantly repeated this to me throughout my life! What do you want from me? Believe me, I pay the price every day!" Keith shouts.

"You're not paying enough in my eyes! You tell the kids all the time to take responsibility for their actions! What about you, do you take responsibility? Well, Keith, congratulations on a job well done! Sometimes you make me sick to my stomach! I can't even look at you, and for being a true jackass today you can do all the laundry! I mean all of it! You can also bring your things down to the couch and sleep there until I see fit to call you back," shouts Justine, as she suddenly walks toward Keith and slaps him across the face. Her slap catches Keith by his left eye, and it begins to throb immediately. "You're lucky Colin is taking his nap," she cries out. "I'm so sick and tired of your shit!"

Justine walks away calmly not looking back, and Keith slowly walks to the hallway bathroom. He looks into the mirror and sees a brand-new injury. Her engagement ring and wedding band must have cut him near his eye, and he can't open it. Cleaning his wounds have become routine, especially since Justine is continually vexed with him. He realizes that she is getting more aggressive every day and very callous, just like him and his father.

Keith takes extra care to clean up his injuries. He always hid his unhealthy home life because he must protect himself and his family. As a child Keith would feel so much pain from the abusive attacks that he always wanted to call in sick to school. His parents would never let him stay home and told him to go to school or else. Sometimes he would cry for hours, but there wasn't anybody to save his lost soul. No one knows that Justine is very abusive toward him, and he wouldn't hit back because she is a lady. He wonders what will become of him and Justine, and how will they keep the family together?

CHAPTER
NINE

〰〰〰〰〰〰〰〰〰〰〰〰〰〰〰〰〰〰〰〰〰〰〰〰〰〰〰〰〰〰〰

*J*ustine Catherine Anderson remembers the first day that she met her husband. It was graduation day for Keith Patrick Heiden. He had just gotten his diploma from St. Michael's Roman Catholic High School, and he was still wearing his light blue cap and gown on this sunny day in 1985. As she looked more closely at Keith, she could see his body shake as he cried quietly. He was sitting against a true date palm tree with his new high school diploma grasped tightly in his bruised hands. Justine summoned up her courage and walked over to the young man who desperately needed to talk to someone. She had occasionally seen Keith at school as he waited for the bus to arrive. He also was the same age as her brother Jack. Justine sat down next to him and began speaking to Keith gently. Her manner was soft and calm. You would think that they had been friends for years. It took him a half hour to finally open up to Justine, but then the occurrences of the last three days came tumbling out. He told her he had nowhere to live. He just had $5 in his pocket and the clothes on his back. Keith had stayed at his friend's house for the past three days, but he felt unwelcomed and decided it was time to leave. Within two hours Justine managed to convince her parents, and Keith moved in with them under a strict guideline of rules.

While he stayed with the Andersons, he worked extra jobs to help the family. Soon after that he applied for a job at the DEA Department in LA. He worked very hard at the DEA. Keith became a special agent five years into the job. During that time he studied at the University of California and received a masters in Criminal

Justice and Police Science. Keith achieved high grades in school and success at his job.

He moved out of Justine's home after three years and found an apartment nearby. When he was twenty-two he married Justine in Hawaii on April 22, 1989, and that same year their beautiful twins were born. Erin Kaitlyn and Patrick Keith were the first additions to the Heiden family on July 4. They struggled at first, but it was easier once Keith became a special agent. Finally, all was going well, and he hoped his past wouldn't catch up with him.

Justine slowly walks upstairs to the master bedroom. She feels exhausted and exasperated from the drama of the day. She also real-Izes that she slapped Keith across the face once again. Justine can get so crazy when Keith doesn't take a stand for himself. He just shies away like a little turtle putting his head back into his shell and not dealing with the issue at hand. She just can't deal with any more drama.

The real estate market is very slow, and she doesn't think she'll see a very big commission any time soon. Although the Johnson house on Plum Avenue is a great deal, she wants more. Justine goes to the office every day to get the hot spots on the big deals. She also goes door to door to get her name out there in the public eye. She keeps herself in top notch shape at all times. It's important that Justine gets a manicure, pedicure, and a facial every other week. She works out every morning before Colin wakes up. Her clothes are always in tip-top shape and the newest on the fashion scene. She especially has an expensive taste for shoes, particularly three-inch high heels.

One day Reese went upstairs and destroyed Justine's designer shoes. They were highly expensive, and she didn't have the courage to tell Keith about the price. That's why there is now a doggie run in the backyard. She doesn't like dogs anyway. Justine thinks they smell, and she hates picking up after them. Keith always wanted a big dog to call his own. He told Justine how he once had a dog that was supposedly a birthday present. The dog was never given a name, however, and Keith was never allowed to play with it or interact with it in any way. His job was to clean up the dog's mess every day. Keith remembers that he also was given dog food to eat for punishment at times. Now Keith has a chance to show affection and be attentive to his animals. His first family dog was a yellow lab named Travis, who was a devoted friend for thirteen years, and now he has Reese, the chocolate lab. Keith enjoys being around animals; he also watches the DEA Narcotics Canine Unit while they are in training.

Justine's cell phone suddenly rings. "Hello, Justine Heiden," she answers. Her voice suddenly changes to a real estate mode.

"Hello, Justine, do you have a minute?" asks the man on the other end of the line.

"Yes, I do." Justine slowly closes the master bedroom door and retreats to her lounge chair. It's the perfect spot to relax and read a good novel while covered in a soft, cozy blanket. The stone and marble fireplace across from the lounge chair caught their eyes when they first saw the house two years ago. Keith usually sits in the lounge across from hers but half the time he ends up falling asleep there in business suit.

Keith was nowhere in sight so it was a perfect time to talk to Treat. After all, she hadn't heard from him in a week. "Treat, I really don't have a lot of time to talk to you. What do you want?" she asks, trying to speak softly. It wouldn't be wise for Keith to hear her, and she didn't want to wake Colin up.

"Justine, do you miss me? Why do you stay with that loser? I treat you better than that so-called husband of yours! I know he has money, but he doesn't give you the love that you truly need!" Treat Miller cries out over the phone line. "Please, Justine, can I please see you? I really miss you! It's not fair! I thought we had something? Do you feel anything for me?"

"I don't know what I want. It's not that easy. I have responsibilities to take care of. I know that my life is not a Danielle Steel novel. Please try to understand. I don't want to give you mixed messages, but I need some space for now!" Justine pleads, as she wraps the long cashmere blanket around her for warmth.

"I need you, Justine. I truly love you. Let's run away from this so-called life and go to Mexico! We can buy a house on the beach and make tropical drinks at the tiki bar. I can give you a better life! I don't have money like your husband, but we can work it out. Will you run off into the sunset with me? I love you, Justine, always remember that," pleads Treat.

She covers herself with the blanket in the hope that her pain will go away. Justine cries out, "I don't know what you want! I have my children here. I just can't leave them because of a new love that blossomed last year. It's not fair to them and will cause more pain in my heart! I hope you understand; I need more time!"

"Justine, you're a great woman, and I hope you make a decision soon. Because I really miss you."

She smiles and laughs a little over what her lover has said. "Listen, Treat, I will call you soon, but I can't think right now. Just please understand that I need more time."

"Be honest, Justine, do you still love your husband after what happened last year? Your life will be destroyed by him. He's callous, recalcitrant, and abominable! The list is endless," Treat exclaims.

"Listen to me, I know what I'm up against. I lived with the man for eighteen years, so don't tell me about his special qualities. I know first-hand! I need time. Can you give me space?"

"Okay, Justine, if that's what you want. I'll call you in a couple of weeks." He says in a soft voice.

"Thanks, Treat. You know that I love you?" Justine cries, as she wipes the tears from her cheek.

"Yes, I know… Good-bye, Justine, I love you." Then the phone line goes dead.

The conversation ends but the questions have just started. She begins to cry even more from all the drama in her life. As she stares at her diamond engagement ring and wedding band, Justine wonders if she loves Keith. Is it possible that she just feels sorry for him because of his abused past, or is there a true foundation of love?

Justine wipes away her tears as she hears a knock at the bedroom door. Keith walks into the room and focuses on Justine with a look of consternation on his face.

"I'm so sorry!" he says.

"I forgive you. I'm sorry that I hit you. Does it hurt?" she says as she sits up straight in her comfortable lounge chair and looks at Keith.

Keith stops in his tracks as he heads toward the bathroom. In a split second, he has been brought back to his past. The words of his drunken father ring in his ears. "I'm sorry that I hit you. Does it hurt?" These words continue to echo through his head. It appears to Keith that Justine has become a cut-throat individual like his father!

As the afternoon wears on Justine becomes friendlier towards Keith. Their conversation is pleasant, and she is being extremely nice. It always seems to be the same soap opera drama; the one who abuses his or her victim will later console that person. It was the same shit with Keith's father over and over again, just a different day. The worst part of it is that Keith notices the kids are paying the price. He feels that he can't share his secret with any outsiders, so the vicious evil cycle continues.

CHAPTER

TEN

〰〰〰〰〰〰〰〰〰〰〰〰〰〰〰〰〰〰〰〰〰〰〰〰〰〰〰〰〰〰〰〰

*T*he work day is over for Keith at nine on Thursday morning. Generally, it is a twelve or thirteen hour day at work for a lot of the DEA special agents. In Keith's world, the word "sleep" means only four or five hours a day, if he's lucky. He really likes the weekend hours, because Justine is a great help in the morning before she leaves. Then Erin takes over by caring for Colin, and she also watches over Patrick and Mitch. When the family pitches in, it saves a lot of money on daycare.

Keith doesn't want a stranger raising the kids. The time schedules that Justine and Keith have worked out are for the best. The weekends are great because Keith has the opportunity to catch up on the sleep he missed during the week. Everyone is quiet in the master bedroom, and it shows him how well the family can work together. He never felt any family support in his childhood.

As Keith makes his way toward his SUV, his cell phone rings. It's 9:15 a.m. and the caller ID shows no number. He puts the cell phone on the base device as he turns on his truck.

As Keith presses the speaker button on his cell phone he hears, "Mr. Heiden!"

"Mr. Keith Heiden, I need to see you. How about tonight?" asks a man with an English accent. Keith tries to recognize the voice, but he draws a complete blank.

"I'm sorry I didn't catch your name?" Keith asks, trying to get additional information.

"My name is Preston Williamson, and I work for Interpol in Great Britain. What would be a good day and time for me to meet with you?"

"Interpol sounds very serious. Why do you need to see me? Can you fill me in on what you want from the DEA Dept and me? I'm leaving work now. Maybe we can meet at 9:00 p.m. tonight?" Keith states, trying to turn on the SUV engine.

"That would be fine. See you at 9:00 p.m.," answers Preston Williamson.

"Do you need the address to the DEA from Los Angeles?" asks Keith as he puts on his dark sunglasses.

"Thanks, but I already have the address. The only thing that I'm missing is talking to you one on one," Preston says with a very soft English accent.

"Okay, I'll put your name down with a security guard at the gate, and I'll see you then," Keith states as he turns on the engine. He is ready to go home and hopes that he will get two or three hours of sleep, that is if Colin lets him.

"Thank you, I'll see you at 9:00 p.m. Have a good day," states Preston.

"Thank you. See you later," replies Keith.

A knock on the passenger side window of the SUV makes Keith jump out of his skin. The door opens and Agent Peter Richard Darling slides automatically into the passenger seat. Peter has dark brown hair and light brown eyes and stands about 6'1". He tries to work out as much as he can in his free time. You know how county desk jobs are! You have to keep in shape especially if you're a field agent catching those bad guys!

"You should have that reaction all the time when you see me! It's so funny to see your body jump ten feet into the air!" Peter smiles as he starts to laugh. "I have to tell Agent Gallagher and Tierney. They will get a big kick out of it. Can you drive me home? My car is in the shop until tomorrow," Peter remarks as he continues to laugh.

They both just completed thirteen hours on the job, and Peter doesn't seem at all tired. Keith is amazed by this, and he is getting exhausted by just looking at him. Driving through the morning rush hour traffic in the LA area is always fun to do after working very long hours.

Keith takes off his sunglasses for a minute and Peter notices his eye.

"What happened to your left eye? You have a nice red mark with a deep cut. Did Justine hit you again?" Peter asks with a concerned look on his face.

Keith puts his sunglasses on quickly and tries not to make a major deal of it. This could be a whole conversation as they drive to Peter's apartment. "It's not a big deal. I deserved it, and it doesn't hurt that much," he solemnly states.

"You're a troubled liar! You're crazy! How can you let her do that to you! I'm going to talk to her and try to stop this madness! She is out of control!" Peter shouts. He wants Keith to open his eyes and see what he sees.

"That will be the day. As I told you before it's fine! Please don't worry about it. I'll take care of it. Please don't talk to Justine," Keith pleads to Peter, who is shaking his head in disbelief.

"Then you need to address this situation to Dr. Sheppard! If you don't put your foot down Justine is going to abuse you over and over again! You need to speak to the doctor and let her know what you are going through!" Peter shouts.

As Keith looks straight ahead, he takes out some tissues from the armrest compartment to wipe his nose.

"I know that you're trying to help, and I greatly appreciate all that you've done for me and my family. But, Peter, this is my problem, so please respect my wishes and let it go."

At thirty-eight, Agent Peter Darling still looks good. He tries to keep up with the young girls, but he knows that he's getting older. Sometimes he acts like an uncontrollable teenager who will never grow up. There are times when he doesn't understand why he and Keith are best of friends. Peter feels sorry for Keith because of his horrible past. He was best man at Keith and Justine's wedding in Hawaii. He's also the godfather of all their kids as well as their legal guardian. Peter is now a blood brother, his best friend, boss, and supervisor to Keith.

Peter's relationship with Julia Ulrich went downhill very quickly ten years ago. He feels his best friend was partly to blame along with Jose Medina.

"I don't want you to be beaten up by a blond!" Peter laughs at his absurd statement, as Keith just stares at him. "Seriously, Keith, you'll have to do a double shift tonight for not giving me the four files I needed on Tuesday, and then you'll have Monday night off," Peter states.

A double shift is when an agent works overtime and the agents usually get to pick the workday, but now Keith is being watched. If he's being reprimanded, under the close supervision of Agent Peter Darling, this will not help his defense. Sometimes Keith really thinks that he was born to fail.

"Have you been sniffing black markers again? You're really making me do a double shift because of four files?" asks Keith incredulously as he turns to Peter for a split second.

Peter starts to laugh continuously for over a minute, and then he becomes serious. "I'm guilty as charged. I do sniff black markers. How did you know? Yes, I needed them on my desk by Tuesday when your work was done. You didn't give them to me so this happened! You're so lucky that you will be working a double shift with pay, and you're able to keep your ego intact at the same time. You should count your blessings that you have me as your supervisor and not Agent Jack Forrester! Listen, Keith, if you get in trouble you have to pay for your mistakes."

"I still can't believe you're my supervisor!" Keith sees Peter as more of a friend and a clown than a supervisor. "I'm sorry I couldn't locate those four files. I searched high and low and even asked the people that I gave the files to. For some strange reason they stated that they didn't have my work, and my signature is not on record showing that they were signed over to them. Peter, I don't know what's going on! I think someone is playing with me!" he shouts.

"This is just great!" Keith sighs, as he thinks to himself, *We're stuck in rush-hour traffic moving negative zero on Route 5 of the Santa Ana Freeway. With Peter in the car it's going to be a very long ride!*

"Are you sure that cut doesn't hurt? Because looking at you, my eye hurts. Listen, those files were going to the district attorney's office that Wednesday morning. They're ready to build cases and start the arraignment processes. That didn't happen! So you're grounded under my watch until I can investigate what happened and why. This is not going to be easy!" Peter says with a wide yawn. "Do you know you're in deep shit? I just don't know what is happening to you! The DA is out for your blood, and you may be arrested for tampering with the files. I feel that something big is going to happen, and I won't be able to save you. My hands will be tied at this point, Keith, so you better put your attorney on speed dial. It is going to be a very bumpy ride from this day forward!"

"It doesn't hurt," Keith puts his dark sunglasses on again. "I can't believe what you just said to me," he says, with a strong feeling of rejection from his wife and now his job. He looks straight ahead at the traffic while he tries to comprehend what Peter has just said to him. If he is arrested by the request of the DA, Justine will take the kids and leave him without looking back.

As Keith starts to shake, he desperately tries to hide any signs of breaking down on Route 5. Peter sees his partner breaking apart in front of him.

"Keith, I should never have told you! I'm so stupid! Look at you shaking like a leaf!" he bursts out sympathetically. "Why don't you pull over and let me take the wheel?"

"Thanks for your concern but I'm fine," Keith responds, as he tries to recover his control.

"You're crying without making any sound! Shit, what did your father do to you? Keith, come on. I know that you're hurt!" Peter shouts, as he really wants to take the wheel before they have an accident.

"I'm fine, don't worry about me. Please just try to keep me out of jail!" Keith replies hoarsely. "We had a big fight yesterday, and this will put her over the top."

"Are you crazy? Justine will have your head on a silver platter! You can't tell her about this! She's already out of her mind!" Peter exclaims with exasperation in his voice.

"I have to tell her before she finds out from someone else," Keith replies sadly, still looking at the traffic. The tears have stopped, but he is filled with emotion.

"Seriously, do you want another cut on your other eye? She is a highly aggressive lady with her own issues. Listen, Keith just hold off. There is no need to say anything about what might or might not happen," pleads Peter.

"Okay," Keith says with a soft voice.

"Good, now you're thinking with your brain instead of your Irish-Austrian butt!" giggles Peter, as he looks at Keith for a minute to see if he's listening and not just "yessing him."

"You have a point there," Keith answers. He takes a deep breath and continues. "I have another problem. Peter, I really think that Justine is jealous of Dr. Elise Sheppard."

"To see two women at each other! Boy, I don't need HBO for this!" Peter laughs, smiling from ear to ear. "A catfight between two grown intelligent women! How sweet is that? Listen, I'll talk to Justine on your behalf about the double shift. She loves me and she will give in to me. I wouldn't stop looking for the files, though." He leans back in the passenger seat and tries to get comfortable. It's a good time to take that nap.

"That would be great, thanks. Justine thinks that you are annoying, but she puts up with you for my benefit." Keith smiles as he takes a quick glimpse at his partner.

"I'll talk to her and don't worry, because Uncle Peter has your back. I won't say anything about her abusive behavior toward you, but I can't make any promises." He yawns as he lowers the seat back. He closes his eyes to try and dream of the blond California hottie at the beach.

Keith sometimes wonders what makes Peter tick. Is there an on and off switch somewhere? The kids love him to death, and he brings a lot of laughter into the house. He's like a stray cat that comes up to the front door and scratches diligently waiting for food to arrive.

"I know that you will confront Justine about her abusiveness. If that happens, you have to promise me that you'll give me enough time to get out of the country. Peter, by any chance, did you pick Dr.

Sheppard as my therapist?" Keith asks with a yawn. "Stop looking at me funny! My eye doesn't hurt," he snaps.

Peter starts to laugh and answers, "Sure, when I win the lottery then I will believe that your eye doesn't hurt! I have to speak to our private investigator, Paul Lauren, (a retiree from the LAPD) to see if your relationship with Justine is at all normal. I really hope that Dr. Sheppard can help you! I didn't pick the doctor. The heads of the DEA Department did." He combs his hair back with his hands and looks at himself through the internal mirror. "Do you like Dr. Sheppard?"

Keith looks at him for a minute and then puts his focus back toward the very slow-moving traffic. "I guess she's okay. I know we have a lot more therapy to go. Did you get more information on Treat Miller?"

"I have to speak to our private investigator, Paul Lauren. "I know that he has something for us. He's very good at what he does. He's worked in the business for two years now, and he gets the job done quickly and smoothly. I'll call him tonight and get an update on Treat, and then I'll let you know what will happen next," Peter replies with a yawn.

"Thanks," Keith responds, as he continues to wait for the traffic to move. Maybe it would've been smarter to take another route home.

"Do you know that our Justine is having an affair with Treat?" Peter asks.

"Yes, I know," Keith answers sharply. "I might be a husband and father but being a DEA agent flows strongly through my veins at all times!"

"As long as we have enough evidence to pick up the jackass and to put the low-life that he is in a jail cell at Pelican Bay State Prison or California State Prison, it doesn't matter to me where he ends up. I'll be satisfied as long as he's locked up for the rest of his life! Then he won't be able to console Justine anymore!" Keith states sharply, as he quickly looks at his best friend.

Peter loudly insists, "Don't worry, we'll get the low-life! I hope you can save your marriage, because I really don't want you guys to get a divorce."

"Believe me it's not going to come to that. I received a very unusual phone call from a man named Preston Williamson from England. He works for Interpol and wants to meet me. I said yes for nine tonight," Keith states as he looks at Peter to see his reaction. The traffic is finally moving at a faster pace, and they can comfortably drive sixty-five miles per hour.

Peter has a surprised look and says, "Interpol? What does he want from you? Do you know the reason why he needs to meet you? This sounds very fishy if you ask me."

"Don't worry. I'm going to use all my DEA training skills for this operation. He didn't tell me any details over the phone, but I will keep you informed every step of the way. I know that's what you want as a concerned boss, best friend, and very annoying 'brother.'" Now Keith is finally up to the correct speed on the highway.

"Aw, how thoughtful of you to think of me in your plans! What a Hallmark moment! Yes, I need to know. Babysitting you has not been easy these days. I want to know everything from the conversations you have with this man, to what your plans are without involving the DEA department. You already have a red mark under your name. If I find out that you're taking DEA information, I'm going to give you a wedgie and put your white underwear over your head!" Peter states as he looks at Keith for his reaction.

"We were so close to having a normal adult conversation," Keith replies. He shakes his head in disappointment and asks himself, "why can't I find a normal friend?" Keith continues, "I will keep you informed of any more information that comes my way. I need your support on this! I can't do this alone!"

Peter answers, "Fine, I'll get the information that you need in order to get something good from this guy, Mr. Williamson." Then he starts to laugh. "I crack myself up!" he thinks to himself. "The more that I know the better chance you'll have to keep your job until retirement." He looks at his buddy and smiles. "Keith you're so cute and gullible!"

Keith shakes his head. "Listen, Peter, I have a bad feeling that something is going to surface from the ten-year-old Medina case. Just get ready to make a 180-degree turn!"

Both agents become quiet as they go into their own individual thoughts. What's next? Do they have a plan, if any?

CHAPTER
ELEVEN

*T*hursday afternoon arrives quickly, and Elise walks down the office hallway to get herself some fresh coffee. She notices that no one in the office replenished the caffeine supplies over the work week, so she decides to go get some coffee outside the office. It's a great day for a drive. Within half an hour she is in Orange County where Justine Heiden works. Elise finds a nice parking space for her new red 2007 Volvo. As she walks through town a sign catches her eye. The California Realtors is where Justine works, and Elise looks around the office for her as she enters.

"Hello, welcome to California Realty. How can I help you today?" asks the receptionist as she proudly wears her "Jennifer G." nametag. She's in her mid-twenties, a jumpy young thing with healthy brown hair and blond highlights. Her skin is very smooth, and she doesn't need any makeup. It really makes Elise sick to her stomach to see someone that young and beautiful in front of her. She looks at Elise with a smile that says happy to meet you. Elise is envious as she sees her perfect white teeth.

"Hello, Jennifer, can I please speak to Mrs. Justine Heiden?" asks Elise, who sees a lot of different colored notes all around her work station.

"She is behind you towards your left side," Jennifer replies, as she uses a ballpoint pen to direct Elise.

Dr. Sheppard turns around and sees Justine Heiden, which gives Elise a cold chill down her spine. Justine laughs at something the realtor agent has said. She opens the front door to let herself out.

"I have to go, guys! Please call me on my cell if you need me!" Justine announces to anyone who will listen. She walks outside the building and feels the warm breeze, still unaware that Dr. Sheppard is walking behind her.

Elise takes a deep breath. "Mrs. Heiden," she says to get her attention. Justine stops in her tracks and turns around as she responds to the woman's voice. "Yes," she answers, using her real estate voice.

"Hello, Mrs. Heiden. It's Dr. Sheppard, remember me?" Elise declares as she offers her hand to Justine in a friendly gesture. How odd it is that Justine doesn't return the expression! She is a real estate agent who needs to interact with people to help make a commission for the month.

"Yes, I know who you are! What do you want, Dr. Sheppard? I'm very busy," she states with an annoyed tone in her voice.

"Mrs. Heiden, I'm sorry that I scared you the other day, and I'd like to explain what happened. Keith told me to help myself to a drink, so I took a bottle of water. That's why you saw me opening your refrigerator," Elise explains, as she sees the unhappy and confused look on Justine's face.

"Dr. Sheppard, who do you think you are? My husband is your patient, and I've just heard you call him by his first name! He is to you and always will be Mr. Heiden!" Justine snaps back. "So you just happened to be in the neighborhood, and just happened to find me at my place of work? Give me a break, Dr. Sheppard. What do you really want?" Justine asks as she takes a glimpse at the time on her watch. She has to eat something before heading back to work.

"I know there is a lot of heavy tension between you and your husband. You guys can talk to me about your marriage. I'm a very good listener. I can try to help you fix your problems. Just say the word, and I'm there for you. Your husband's sessions are going well, but we have a lot work to do, and it's going to be a long journey," Elise states, using a calm professional voice.

"My marriage is none of your business! Is this the real core of my husband's problem? You have no right! I know that my husband wouldn't even think about talking to you on a personal matter that is between us and no one else! Even if we went to a therapist about our marriage, it wouldn't be with you!" Justine shouts loud enough for anyone to hear. "Don't even look in my direction!" she screams, as she walks away from Dr. Sheppard. Elise feels tightness in her chest, and she is totally embarrassed. Elise is also very angry at the way she has been spoken to. Her job is her passion.

Still using her calm voice, she says, "You know, Mrs. Heiden, you're a total bitch. You abuse your husband verbally and maybe physically too. I bet that he has to ask for permission to do things around the house, especially going to the bathroom." Her feeling is that Mrs. Heiden is unstable, very controlling, aggressive, and has a very cold heart. She always wants to be the center of attention in her small life, even though Mr. Heiden needs extra attention because of the instability in his life.

"Dr. Sheppard! How dare you? Who do you think you are, calling me a bitch? Leave me alone, or I will call the police! Your job is to get my husband, Mr. Heiden to you, his job back so that he is fully active! That's what you get paid for, so do it!" Justine shouts. She walks quickly away and doesn't even look over her shoulder to see what Dr. Sheppard is doing.

Elise shakes her head. She can't believe what just happened. *I'm hungry*, she thinks, as she looks around to see where she can eat in this town. Everything is very clean and that includes the public garbage cans. American flags, attached to the streetlights on South Willshire Boulevard, wave in the air. Lots of different stores line the streets, but the one that catches her eye is the dog grooming place, "Paws with Style." Everything, however, seems way over Dr. Sheppard's budget.

One hour passes since Elise has lunch at her favorite place, Panera Bread. It is time to go back to work. She puts her large diet Coke on her desk, then walks a little and falls on the floor between her desk and office chair. Elise feels no pain and begins to laugh out loud. The phone rings and she gets up slowly from the floor and brushes herself off. "Hello, Dr. Sheppard," she says with a clear voice that is ready to turn into a fit of laughter.

"Hello, Dr. Sheppard, this is Keith Heiden," he says with a tone of annoyance.

Elise place herself in her comfortable office chair. "Hello, how can I help you, Mr. Heiden?"

"Dr. Sheppard, why did you call my wife a bitch?" Keith asks sharply.

Elise suddenly begins to laugh, and for a split second she has forgotten that she is on the phone with Mr. Heiden.

"Dr. Sheppard, you're laughing! Do you think my wife is a prostitute on Hollywood Boulevard?" he snaps.

"No, no, of course not," she replies, trying to contain herself from bursting into laughter again.

Elise pulls the phone away from her ear, because Mr. Heiden is yelling so loud. As she begins to drink her large diet Coke, she presses the speaker button and hears the sound of Mr. Heiden breathing heavily.

"Dr. Sheppard, you didn't answer my question! Why would you call my wife a degrading name?" he asks with a sharper tone in his voice that he uses on his own kids.

"I was angry at the time. I don't remember if I called her that," she states. Elise feels at this point that she just wants to get him off the phone. Mr. Heiden is not a pleasant person to talk to, but Agent Peter Darling is a very different story. She burst out laughing again.

"I expect this kind of behavior from my teenage kids, Dr. Sheppard, but you're a professional and should act like one! How dare you talk to my wife that way about our marriage! It's amazing that you really think my wife abuses me! Why don't you stick to what you're paid to do!" yells Keith furiously.

"You both have a problem with your marriage, and I have a very strong feeling that Justine abuses you verbally and sometimes physically. How do you know what questions I'm paid to ask you? I know I never told you, or did I?" Elise asks between her giggles.

"Because I have a copy of your questions," he says, as he walks through the huge kitchen.

As Elise continues her phone conversation she can hear the sounds of the show *Blue Clues* coming from the TV. The sound of Colin making crazy noises can also be heard.

Then she asks, "That information is confidential! How did you get it?" As she leans back in her office chair.

"Maybe I will tell you one day. Please don't go near my wife again, if you value your license!" he shouts, as he tries to give doctor giggles a clue that he's very serious.

"Mr. Heiden, I don't take to threats!" Elise snaps back.

"Listen, Dr. Sheppard. You cornered my wife to answer your questions, and that was none of your business! It's not a threat. I'm telling you if it happens again, I will take your license away!" shouts Keith. His voice shakes Elise's inner ears, and suddenly she feels a cold chill down her spine.

Elise responds, "Mr. Heiden, it is not my intention to make your wife afraid of me! I'm sorry for all of it. I take my work seriously!"

"This is great! Practice your freedom of speech. That's the American way, but it causes a lot of problems for me and what I want. Stay away from my wife! I just got an earful from her, and I don't like to be yelled at!" he shouts, as he hangs up the phone.

The sound of the dial tone echoes through the office while Elise starts to laugh again. Why try to reason with a patient that's totally unstable? She always puts herself in this position; you would think she would learn by now.

CHAPTER
TWELVE

*I*t's 2:15 a.m. Wednesday, May 16, when the phone rings on the nightstand besides Elise's bed. "Hello," she says sleepily, as she lies on her comfortable queen-sized bed. Her blankets are a safe haven for her very tired body. She always feels that she sleeps on a cloud in the sky close to her mother. Elise knows that her mother is watching and protecting her at all times.

"Elise, it's Jonathan!" His voice sounds very serious.

"What's up?" asks Elise.

"You have to go to Mr. Heiden's house now!" Jonathan exclaims.

"Jonathan, it's two thirty in the morning and my next session with Mr. Heiden is at 11:00 a.m. today," she states, as she rubs her tired brown eyes to wake up.

"According to his son, Mitch, Mr. Heiden is having a panic attack," continues Jonathan. "Can you go over there as soon as possible?"

"Jonathan, I'm so tired!" cries Elise, as she puts her head on the pillow.

"I will buy all the Dunkin Donuts coffee for a month if you do this! Please? I will love you forever!" replies Jonathan.

"Okay," Elise answers as she turns on a nightstand light.

"You're the best! Good night. I want to know everything on Monday. Please remember that I have to go to Washington D.C., and I'm leaving at 10:00 a.m. for my flight. You can go to work late. Just come in around noon. I will leave a voice message to the staff on your behalf," he announces.

"Okay, Jonathan, you owe me big time for this. I think a two month's supply of Dunkin Donuts coffee should do the trick!" she hints to her boss.

"Fine, Elise, don't push it," he answers with a laugh.

While driving, Elise tries to focus on the road. The radio is playing the top 10 music hits, and she has a small cup of coffee in the holder. She grabbed whatever she could find on the bedroom floor and threw it on. It's too early in the morning for Elise to think about looking pretty. The time is 3:00 am, as Elise arrives at the Heidens' house. The front door light is on and solar lights are glowing around the yard giving an extra dramatic effect. The neighborhood is very quiet, however, and Elise wonders what is happening on the other side of the front door.

She walks up to the front door, and it opens quickly. "You have to come in and see this!" exclaims a young boy about the age of 12 or 13. Mitch is the adopted son of the Heidens. He has black hair and dark brown eyes and became a part of the family eight years ago. "I'm sorry, Dr. Sheppard, my name is Mitch. I'm just very worried about my dad. Can you please help him?"

"Mitchell! Dr. Sheppard, it's not that bad. It happens a couple of times a night," Justine cries, as she walks down the large staircase. "I'm sorry, Dr. Sheppard, that you had to come down here for nothing. Mitch, please show the doctor to the front door. Have a good night, and I'm sorry for your time."

"No, Mom, I want the doctor to see what is going on with Dad!" Mitch shouts, as he appears to be very upset over the whole situation.

"Mitchell Paul Heiden! Remember what your father told you about listening to me! You're disobeying me, and I won't have it!" Justine yells, as she tightly holds Mitch's arm. She gives her son a stern look as if to say, "Don't you even dare to scream for Dr. Sheppard."

"Do you want me to tell your father that you're not respecting me?"

"No, Mom, please I'll be good... Okay, we won't go upstairs," Mitch replies dejectedly and gives his mother a sign to let go of his arm.

Keith screams at the top of his lungs through the master bedroom doors. "Please, Dad, no more spankings! I'm sorry, I won't do it again! No! It hurts, please, Dad. It really hurts, and I'll be a good boy! No, no, please no! I don't know what I did! I'm sorry, Dad!" The sound of his cries travels down from the second floor. "Please, Dad, no more. I'm sorry for whatever I did!"

It suddenly becomes clear to Elise that this family has a lot of serious problems. Especially Justine Heiden, who controls everything and uses her alpha skills on everyone in the house. It doesn't seem like Keith's problems are a major concern. He's going through a troubled ordeal every night, but no one is coming to his aid, except Mitch. He really wants to save his father from despair, but his mom is blocking the way. It's a very sad situation all around. Where do you start the healing?

"I'm sorry that my son called you so early in the morning. Thank you for coming," Mrs. Heiden says while she opens the front door. Dr. Sheppard rushes out of the house and she begins to cry softly. Once she gets into her car the tears begin to flow like a river. "What kind of monster was his father? Why would he single out Keith to abuse? Why did he choose one child out of his nine children?"

Justine locks the front door and turns on the alarm system. She turns off all first floor lights and takes a quick glimpse at Reese sleeping on the kitchen floor. She walks upstairs where she finds her comfortable white robe and fuzzy slippers. On the second floor, she sees Mitch with a very concerned look on his face.

"Mom, are you going to tell Dad what I did?" Mitch asks with tears in his eyes, as he rubs his arm where it stills hurts.

"I don't know yet. It depends on how I feel when I wake up in the morning. Good night, Mitch." Justine replies, as she walks into the master bedroom. Mitch sees a little glimpse of his dad sleeping, as Justine quickly closes the door in front of him.

It is around 8:30 a.m. and Mitch didn't sleep at all. He knows that his mom might tell his dad about last night. Mitch doesn't like to get into trouble, and he rarely disobeys his parents. But he knows that his dad is very strict, especially when it comes to breaking the rules. Mitch loves his dad, but sometimes the punishments to him and his siblings are just too harsh. He misses the school bus as he tries to listen to his parents' conversation through the bedroom door. The voices are muffled as he puts his ear against the door.

"Mommy! Mommy!" Colin screams, as he stands up on his bed and holds onto the railing. "Mommy!"

Mitch jumps quickly away from the door, startled by Colin's screams. He loses his balance as the master bedroom door opens. He falls directly in front of his father.

Keith smiles sleepily at Mitch. "Good morning, son." He's wearing his cotton light blue pajamas and tan slippers that he received for Christmas last year from one of his kids. "Can you please get up?" he says as he walks over Mitch.

"Daddy! Daddy potty!" Colin shouts cheerfully. He is ready and waiting to be swooped up, so he can start another adventurous day as a three-year-old. Keith picks up Colin from his bedroom and walks to the hallway bathroom without skipping a beat.

Mitch walks back to his bedroom, crawls into his twin bed, and wraps himself in his soft blankets, as he tries to fall back to sleep. Twenty minutes later he hears a knock at his door. "Mitch, can you please open the door? We need to talk," his dad says quietly.

"Dad, can we talk later? I really don't feel well, and I need some extra sleep," he replies dejectedly, as he covers his head with his blankets.

"Sorry, Mitch. You missed the school bus, and I need to know why. Please open the door now," he states firmly.

Mitch gets up slowly wrapping his blanket around him. "Okay." He unlocks the door and Keith walks quietly into the room. "What's wrong, Mitchell?"

Mitch crawls back into his comfortable twin bed. "I just don't want to go to school today, and I didn't sleep at all last night. Can I get some more sleep?" he pleads.

"Mitchell, please, can you sit up? I really need your full attention!" Keith commands, as he sits on his son's desk chair. Mitch leans his back against the wall to keep his sleepy body from falling over like dead weight

"I guess Mom told you about me early this morning?" he asks without opening his eyes.

"Yes, she did. She's not very happy with your behavior and I'm not either. You didn't listen to her and disobeyed an order. You called Dr. Sheppard at 2:00 a.m. when your mother told you not to! Can you explain to me why?" he asks, as he rubs his tired blue eyes and yawns at the same time. Keith still feels exhausted. His schedule is way off because of the extra job hours they are asking him to do.

Keith's work schedule is not a normal nine-to-five job, Monday through Friday. In the DEA world agents really are on call 24/7. He has crazy nights at work, and he needs to catch up on his sleep. Once in a while, Peter will ask him to work on weekend nights. In this situation he gets off one or two nights during the week. He's getting older now, and he feels it when he moves. Both his home life and work are getting to him. He knows that he needs a vacation, but his 24/7 existence wants him to go and go. Maybe in his next life he will take that vacation. Don't forget that extra sleep!

"Dad, I was worried about you! You keep screaming in your sleep, like you're reliving bad moments all over again. I guess in this family the others are used to your screams in the middle of the night, but I'm not. I can't go to sleep because I feel your pain. I know that you saved me from my troubled past. All I remember is my biological father shooting needles filled with heroin up his arm. Dad, I'm not trying to get out of punishment, but I just worry about you!" Mitch states, as he opens his eyes a little bit to see his dad's reaction.

"Mitchell, don't worry about me. I guess I had a nightmare. I don't remember. Maybe that's a good thing. That's why I have a therapist to chew my ear off with her questions. Just be a good kid, get good grades, and stay out of trouble. Hopefully you will be a well-rounded adult. I'm not angry with you. I'm just very surprised that you would call Dr. Sheppard at 2:00 a.m. It's not like you to do this kind of thing. Your mom told me that you disobeyed her, and I'm not happy about that. For your punishment there will be no TV or video games for two weeks. Also, I would be extremely angry with you if Dr. Sheppard had seen me in that kind of state. So, Mitch, I'm giving you warning about that. Please don't call the doctor in the middle of the night, or there will be hell to pay! Do you understand?" Keith commands.

"Dad, you didn't have a nightmare. You were experiencing the horrible ordeals of your past!" Mitch states strongly. He feels that there is something terribly wrong and that his father needs help right away.

"Please, Mitch. It's not your concern. Yes, it's my past, and I have to deal with it every day for the rest of my life. So please let me deal with it in my own way." Keith stands tall, showing that he is strong and not to be reckoned with.

"Okay, I will let it go. Yes, sir. I'm sorry about calling Dr. Sheppard. It won't happen again, I promise. I will listen to Mom from now on, but two weeks?" Mitch asks quickly.

"Yes, two weeks! I'll let you sleep for another hour, and then you have to get up. I will make you a hearty breakfast so you can eat, and then you have to catch up on your schoolwork that you missed today. Also you can help me take care of Colin. I will call the school to tell them you'll be back tomorrow. Please do not make this a habit," Keith states, as he continues to rub his tired eyes.

"Okay, thanks, Dad," Mitch says, as he sinks his head back into the pillow.

Keith closes the door softly and walks down the stairs. He quickly catches a glimpse of Justine at the bottom to the stairs with her arms folded. The expression on her face says it all. "It's too early to start in with you!" Keith exclaims, as he intentionally bumps into her as he passes. He sees Colin and smiles. He is eating a banana from his Teenage Mutant Ninja Turtles bowl while he sits in his booster seat. "Hi, Daddy!"

With a soft voice Keith remarks, "Hello, Colin, please don't talk with your mouth full. Finish the banana in your mouth and then you can talk. Okay?"

Colin swallows than smiles at his dad. "It's kicking good!" he shouts, as he starts to make crazy sounds.

Justine briskly walks toward the kitchen, and she looks at Keith with tension in her crystal blue eyes. "You didn't punish him for what happened last night? How will he ever learn if he gets away with things?" asks Justine. She is wearing a cream-colored business suit and she shakes her curly head of hair, which is held down with a designer clip, as she speaks. Keith walks away from Colin calmly not to scare his little boy.

"I punished Mitch for disobeying you, but not for calling Dr. Sheppard! I gave him a stern warning. Dr. Sheppard didn't see me in my shocked state, but if she had, it would be a different story!" he screams. He starts to get some food out of the refrigerator to make breakfast.

"Oh please! He called Dr. Sheppard at 2:00 a.m.! I want you to punish him because he did that!" Justine shouts back, as she looks directly into his tired blue eyes.

"Justine, if you feel that strongly about it, you punish him!" he shouts right back at her.

"That's your job, Keith, not mine! So do your job! If you do, it won't happen again! When your father almost beat the life out of you, did you do it again? I think not!" Justine shouts into Keith's face while Mitch walks into the kitchen. Suddenly Justine slaps Keith extremely hard across the face. Mitch and Colin jump out of their skins as the drama unfolds before their eyes.

"Mom, what are you doing?" Mitch yells while Colin starts to cry from his chair and then screams, "Daddy!"

Justine just ignores what Mitch asked as well as Colin's cries. She zones her crystal sharp blue eyes on her husband. Suddenly Justine reacts with a smile on her face and laughs out loud which echoes throughout the first floor. Keith automatically puts his head down in front of the queen lion while the tears roll down his cheek. His body starts to shake a little as Justine looks at her watch, a Fossil Polly Brown. "I have to go now. Love you all! See you guys later, have a good day!" Justine walks quickly toward the front door, and she picks up her purse and her English dark brown soft leather briefcase on her path.

"Bye, Mommy!" Colin screams and wipes his tiny tears from his face.

"Bye Colin. Be a good boy for Daddy!" She says as they hear the sound of the front door closing.

Keith feels totally embarrassed in front of the kids as his head is still down. Mitch is in total shock by what he just had seen, and he thinks to himself about what happened just two seconds ago. *Why did his mom slap his dad in the face? Does this happen every day when he's in school? What can he do for his dad right now?"*

Mitch tries to ease the tension that has already begun before the early morning news comes on T.V. "Dad, I didn't hear much," he states. To make him feel better is not going to be easy an task. He can help take the pain away, but how can he help the healing? Keith starts to shut down into a safe zone. It's a routine for a person who is abused to shut down after an aggressive ordeal.

"You're not a good liar but thanks anyway. Please promise me, Mitch, you won't tell anyone?" he cries out. His head is still down.

"Does this happen a lot? I don't think it's a good idea. Maybe we should tell Dr. Sheppard. She is coming today, right?" Mitch asks his father softly. His dad just stands still like a tree without any movement.

"Sometimes I know it's my fault." Keith picks up his head to give his son a clue to keep the secret. His blue eyes are watery and bloodshot. "Please promise me!" he pleads to his son. He walks slowly to get some tissues to wipe his runny nose. Mitch sees his father breaking apart in front of his dark brown eyes. His abused body and mind has taken over his father. "It's not your fault. I saw it all!" Mitch states.

He pleads with a cracked voice, "Please respect my wish and don't tell anyone about this."

"Okay, Dad, I will keep the promise because you want me to. I still think it's not a good idea," he says softly to put his two cents in. Mitch decides to take a little advantage for his own needs. "Listen, Dad, I'll keep this promise if you sponge my two weeks punishment?" asks Mitch, as he stands tall and waits for his dad's answer.

"Thank you… What did you ask me?" Keith walks closely to his son to overpower his son's sorry request. He smiles the way his abusive father did before the strapping started. As his body begins to tense up again, he says, "Mitch, I'm not going to answer your question! Who do you think you're talking to? I punished you for a totally different situation! Don't you dare blackmail me!"

"Okay, I'll back off but come on, Dad, to promise something like this is not a good thing. It will only make matters worse!" Mitch states.

"Please, Mitchell! Just do it with no back talk! I will handle this situation between your mother and me. If I need your help I will ask you! Don't even try to feel your oats because you're almost at the teenager stage! Please understand what I'm up against. Listen, Mitchell, please don't fight me when I need your help. I'm not a well man as you know," Keith exclaims and tries to hold himself back without breaking apart. A sharp pain crawls through his body.

Mitch sees his dad's face in pain. "Okay, Dad, I'm sorry. I will do as you wish."

Keith takes a very deep breath to collect his thoughts and to calm himself down. His demeanor changes and minutes later he says in his soft voice, "Thank you, Mitch. Please watch Colin. I'm sorry that I can't make you guys breakfast at this time. You can get some cereal if you want. I'll be back. I'm going to take a shower and get ready before Dr. Sheppard comes. I won't be long." Keith states.

"Teenage Mutual Ninja Tu…tules!" the little three-year-old monster shouts loudly with all his might.

"Thanks, no problem," Mitch quickly answers without a fight.

He replies, "Thanks, Mitch." Then he walks away and stops himself. A strange uneasy feeling sets up. How does he deal with Mitch now? The questions remain, "What can he say to his son? "Mitchell, this is normal between your mother and me. Please don't be alarmed we're used to it." Keith smiles but he really wants to say the three very important words "I love you" to his brave son. During Keith's childhood those words were not said and had no meaning.

"I know what you're about to say! I can see it in your eyes. Right back at you," Mitch states while he opens up a box of Cheerios and pours a bowl for him and Colin.

Keith was upset and sad throughout Dr. Sheppard's therapy session. Elise knows that there is something strange going on with Mr. Heiden, but she doesn't bring up the subject. She decides to let it go.

He answers her questions quietly. Elise tries to make small talk with Keith, but he will never really take part in such conversation especially today of all days.

After the therapy session, Keith was quiet and sad throughout the day. To spend time with Mitch and Colin is very nice. Colin dances like a maniac to the song by Avril Lavigne, "Runway." Keith laughs and smiles to see his three-year-old being crazy, jumping like a caveman and making a lot of noise. Keith gets the extra sleep he needed before the other family members come home. To get ready for work that night he wants to be alone, but life has other plans for him.

An 8 by 11 inch unmarked brown envelope addressed to Keith Heiden arrived by mail that afternoon.

CHAPTER
THIRTEEN

~~~~~~

*S*t. Francis Roman Catholic is a pre-kindergarten, elementary, middle and high school in Pacific Palisades that the Heiden's children go to for education. Mitchell Paul is twelve years old and goes to the middle school. Erin Kaitlyn and Patrick Keith Heiden both go to the high school. The private school tuition to support the children's education is very expensive, and that is why Keith works thirteen hours five days a week.

"Hello," Patrick says, as he stands at 5'11 1/2" tall with light blond hair and his mother's crystal light blue eyes but is the spitting image of his dad. Patrick picks his activities well with both sports and girls. He's not into the school thing as his grades will show. His grade point average is meager, and he cuts a lot of classes. He therefore gets grounded a lot by his strict dad, who doesn't understand the life of American teenagers. He tries to put a short leash on Patrick's bad behavior, but he doesn't give untoward his father's demands or threats. They both are fighters like two gladiators and battle for hours. Both are total opposites.

"Good afternoon, Mr. Heiden, are you ready for a job again?" the man states on the other side of the cell phone line.

"I'll get your stuff today." Patrick says as he looks around the outside campus grounds with lots of flowers and Phoenix Canariensis Canary Island Data Palm trees. His body feels the sun on his face. He wears the designer shades that he brought with his allowance money. His mom gives him his allowance once a week to clean the first floor with Erin, the sister that he never wanted.

A couple of months ago his dad found out that Patrick didn't do his share of chores, and he was grounded for a month with no allowance until he could show full responsibility for his actions. He never received any allowance money until this day. The young Luke Skywalker, Patrick, borrows from the daughter of Gabb the Hutt's sister, Erin. Let's just say it is a very long IOU. So Patrick has to be very nice and not step on Erin's toes, or she will go directly to Dad and punishment will be forced right then and there. His social life will be no more under Mr. Keith Heiden's rules.

"Patrick, the goods are in the same place. So you can pick it up, and I'll call you back for the delivery date and time for your next job," the man states with the British accent on the other side of the cell phone line. "I wish you luck, on the job, Mr. Heiden. If it goes well you will be rewarded, and if not, well, I hope it doesn't come to that. I'll call you soon. So, do the job!!"

"Wait!" Patrick shouts.

"What, Mr. Heiden? Do you have a question? Please tell me?" the British gentleman asks with a very calm voice.

"I'm not really sure that I want to do this. Please can I sit this mission out? I really have a bad feeling about this job!" he asks with a very nervous tone in his voice.

The British gentleman dismisses Patrick's pleas. "Don't worry, Mr. Heiden, I'll call you for additional instructions. Try not to get into too much trouble at school. Good-bye."

As Patrick takes a look at the St. Francis Roman Catholic School Letter, he makes a face that says, "He's so dead." It states that he's suspended for one week from school for cutting classes and not giving assignments on time. Also, Principal Eileen Cross wants to meet with Patrick's parents on this matter. Patrick just wants to dig a deep hole and bury himself in it. He walks toward his physics class, late as usual. Another late slip to top his day that already went south.

Patrick walks slowly into Mr. Guy Fisher's physics class. "Well, Mr. Heiden, we are so happy you finally came into class," the teacher claims, as he writes a pink detention slip.

Patrick says to himself, *Another pink detention slip to add to my collection. I'm so dead! The emperor of the dark side of the force will kill me.* He hits his head on the desk. "I'm totally screwed."

Hours later the St. Francis Roman Catholic School bus stops on the block where the Heiden kids live. The other kids that live in the gated community walk off the bus, and Erin walks with her friends. She doesn't notice that Patrick is behind her walking at a very slow pace. He tries to think how to get out of this punishment. Ten minutes later Patrick looks at the driveway and sees his parents' vehicles. His knees become weak and a getting into trouble headache comes into play. There's a lot of tension put on him with this job he's been asked to do and now dealing with his very damaged father. Something is not right in the universe.

Patrick's cell phone rings, "Hello." he takes it out of his school uniform pocket.

"Hello, Patrick, you were going to call me today…so what happened?" asks a teenage girl with a sweet voice.

"Hey, Melissa. I've been busy this week. I didn't see you in school today." Patrick stops walking in the direction of his home. Melissa Master is Patrick's girlfriend for a month now. He didn't tell his dad that he's dating but his mom knows. One of the family rules is to meet the person that you're thinking of dating before going out, Like going to the movies.

"I didn't feel good today, but I'll see you tomorrow. You're in trouble again?" Melissa asks in a soft voice.

Patrick starts to walk down the long block that he lives on. He declares, "Yes, I'm suspended for one week from school. My dad is going to kill me when he finds out!"

"Patrick, how can we spend any time together if you're always punished? This is totally not fair to me! Please don't call me until you're free! You know I have a life, and I can't wait for you. I'll see you at school. I wish you the best but it's over between us! "I'm sorry but it has to be," Melissa states then suddenly the phone line goes dead.

"Melissa! Melissa!" Patrick shouts, as he presses the redial button on his cellphone to get back his almost ex-girlfriend on the line.

His heart drops ten stories without a safety net in sight. Losing her was not an option.

"Hello," her voice comes back on the line. "What do you want, Patrick?" She knows it's him because she has caller identification on her cell phone.

Patrick pleads his case as he stops in his tracks. "Melissa, please give me a chance. You have to listen to me! I love you! Please don't leave me, because I'm grounded. I won't be the same without you." His voice starts to crack. "Please, Melissa, give me another chance?"

"Patrick, your dad is too strict! You have to be a man! Call me if you become that man, not a mouse! You can see me if you have free time on your hands, not locked up in your bedroom! Good-bye, I'll see you around," Melissa cries as she hangs up the phone.

"Great! Just great!" Patrick shouts, as he takes a deep breath and wipes the tears off his face. He walks toward his home but is not ready to deal with his father. He's always on the edge for no reason at all, and Patrick can push him off the cliff at anytime. He can handle a good solid fight with his dad, but to get the sentences, that's a totally different story.

He opens the front door of his home and hears everyone making some sort of noise talking to one another. It gets crazy after 3:00pm during the work week. Colin runs into the living room wearing a party hat with a rubber band tight around his head. Babbling noises come out of his pre-k mouth. Justine walks into the living room. "Colin, my love, I have to take your party hat off your head." She gently takes the hat off Colin's head. "Thank you, my little handsome man."

"Okay, Mommy. Hi, Patrick!" Colin screams with all his little lungs. He looks up at his big brother with his blue eyes and smiles. "Hi Patrick!"

"Hi, Colin," Patrick says with a smile. As he's thinking in his teenage mind, how many different spots there are to hide the heroin and cocaine without being noticed, by anyone especially his dad and Uncle Peter. Colin walks around the house without a care in the world. He has the time of his life by making crazy noises without speaking many words. He likes to repeat what people say in front of him. Favorite words are "daddy," "mommy," "Patrick," "Erin," "Mitch." He has trouble saying "Reese" and of course "Uncle Peter." Colin loves his Uncle Peter.

Justine looks at Patrick with a big smile on her face. "Hi honey, did you have a good day at school?" she asks while she gives him a kiss and a hug.

He makes a strange face while his mother is kissing him for the millionth time. "I think, I've gotten too old for kisses from my mom. I guess school was okay, Melissa broke up with me just a minute ago," Patrick states with those sad light blues eyes.

Justine and Keith have a different way of giving affection toward their children. She gives her love with lots of hugs and kisses. She also spoils them without Keith noticing. He's unable to provide that type of affection. He tries to give them protection from the outside world, as well as discipline and his time for any support they might need.

Justine cries, "You're never too old to get your mother's kisses and hugs. I'm sorry about you and Melissa. Is there something that I can do for you?" She gives her oldest son a supportive hug.

Patrick slowly pulls away from his mother's hug, "Can you talk to her mom on my behalf?" I know that you're good friends he asks sadly.

"Patrick, your dad wants to talk to you in the kitchen," Justine states, as she tries to console him from his broken heart. She can't believe that her oldest son is having girl problems; it's touching and sad at the same time. "I'll try to talk to Melissa's mother about the situation but there is no guarantee it's going to work… Go ahead your dad is waiting for you."

Patrick walks slowly into the kitchen and watches his dad cooking dinner. "Hi, Dad. You wanted to talk me?" He smells of private school all over his tired body which makes him sick to his stomach. He's very hungry, and he just wants to play some games on his x-box before dinner starts. But first it's important to get his uniform off his aching body.

His dad presses the interior light to see the inside of the oven and the ham. He looks at Patrick and sees his son trying to get some of his uniform clothes off his body.

"Patrick, please make sure your clothes go into your room if they are clean. Also, don't wrap your clean clothes into a ball. It's extra work to iron them out. If they are dirty clothes, put them into the hamper. Once again, it is located upstairs or in the laundry room, not underneath your bed! How was school today?" Keith asks his teenage son.

Patrick replies, "Right bedroom or hamper, got it. I guess it was okay. Two minutes ago, my girlfriend, Melissa, broke up with me." He looks at his dad, as if he was an evil emperor from the dark side of the force, waiting to take away Patrick a.k.a. Luke Skywalker power from the force.

Keith has a concerned look on his face, and he feels a little sad for what his son is going through. He says, "I'm sorry to hear that, son."

"I bet you are." Patrick replies in a very smart aleck remark tone of voice. He tries to give his dad a clue that he is very upset about what happened with Melissa and him.

"Excuse me!" Keith snaps back. He quickly walks over to his son without blinking his tense blue eyes really to attack his teenage son. "Rethink what you're about to say next. It will be your first and last remark you'll ever make! Do you understand?" Keith roars as a king lion does when he gets upset with one of his young clubs. He looks straight into his son's crystal blue eyes for a very fast response to back down.

"Sorry, Dad it won't happen again," Patrick cries as he puts his head down to the king lion of the Heiden clan. "I'm just upset that Melissa broke up with me!"

Keith feels his son has a broken heart, and then he asks as he becomes more relaxed. "I think she broke up with you because you are not spending enough time with her." He moves around the kitchen area and tries to get dinner ready. "As I said before I'm truly sorry for what happened to you. Hopefully in time it will blow over and you guys will get back together."

Patrick reacts suddenly. He picks up his head to what his dad just said and looks straight into his father's controlling blue eyes. "I'm not spending anytime with her, because I'm punished all my teenage life!" he exclaims and throws his hands up in the air and accidentally hits his dad in the head.

"Ouch," Keith cries out at he rubs his head from the fast blow. "Please watch where your hands go!" He says to himself, *I hope I don't get a headache from this. He has a good swing.*

"Sorry," Patrick replies with a sound of laughter. As he realizes what he just did, hit his dad in the head with his hand. *How funny is that, and should I do it again?*

"That's not my problem, Patrick." Still rubbing his head from his teenage son's below. "You get into trouble, and I have to correct you. Listen, to see you on the weekends is not my plan for fun... I think sometimes I'm the one who's punished, not you. Son, your mother tells me that you haven't done your chores. Is this true or not?" he asks without any expression on his face.

"I don't know," he answers while he pulls out his white shirt underneath his pants.

"That's an insufficient answer, yes or no! Patrick, I'm not happy when you don't listen to your mother when I'm not around! Just this morning I grounded Mitch for the same thing! Patrick, just because your allowance is frozen you can't take advantage of not doing your responsibly in this family! We all have to work together not go against each other," Keith states to his son and tries to finish making dinner at the same time. "Please don't borrow any money from your sister. If you borrow money you must pay it back. That's only fair. Do you understand what I'm saying to you?"

Patrick answers, "Sure." He slightly looks and sees a light tan envelope that caught his crystal blue eyes. He notices that the envelope came from the school about his suspension for one week. His parents put the mail near the kitchen phone. They didn't rush to open it because half were bills.

"This is your only warning! If you don't comply you know what happens next?" Keith announces as he looks at his watch.

"Okay," Patrick replies while he yawns in front of his dad. Can I go now? Patrick walks nearby his dad and tries to get closer to the envelope without him noticing.

"Patrick, can you please watch the dinner for one second? I have to talk to your mother for a minute," he asks while washing his hands under the steel kitchen sink.

"No problem," he answers, as he looks at his dad ready for him to leave the room.

Any minute now the school letter is mine.

As Keith wipes his hands on a paper towel, he says, "Thanks, I'll be back in a minute." He puts his foot on the lever to open the lid to a tall steel garbage can to throw the towel out. He looks at Patrick directly and smiles at him, then he walks away toward the front of the house. Patrick quickly sees the sender address from his school and puts the envelope into the inside pocket of his uniform jacket.

"I got you," responds his older sister Erin. Only by five minutes apart at birth and that voice can break a person's face automatically. Patrick turns his body around to the sound and he snaps, "Why don't you go to Death Valley and decay yourself!" He smiles at what he just said to his ugly sister.

"What a comeback. I caught your hands in the cookie jar once again. Patrick, why don't you just surrender? You know the longer you keep secrets the deeper the sentences will be?" Erin states, as she sees her brother being annoying as ever.

It's not easy to be a twin; Erin tries to stay away from Patrick. She wishes that she wasn't related to him. Since Patrick gets into trouble her social life is never the same. The news is now posted all over the Greater Los Angeles area. Erin has to cover her face in public because she's so ashamed of her brother's actions.

"Listen, mother hen! You think you can get brownie points."

"Maybe but I haven't been punished for a long time." Erin smiles proudly with no worries being under her dad's radar.

"Okay, you want a war? Bring it on, girlfriend! I can get you in trouble with no problem. It's like walking on water," Patrick states. *Erin is so ugly especially when the sun hits her. I think my eyes are starting to burn by looking at her.*

"Patrick Keith Heiden!" Keith vigorously shouts while he walks into the kitchen. He sees a pot of boiling water overflowing because the burner was too high. Unexpectedly Patrick's body jumps out of his skin when his dad shouts his name with surprise. He turns around to see what his dad is yelling at. It's never a good sign when your full name is announced to the world.

"I just told you to watch the food for a minute! What's wrong with you? Do you have a brain in that head of yours?" Keith exclaims while he quickly walks to the stove. He lowers down the flame and takes the lid off the pot. Meanwhile, Erin sticks her tongue out and gives a message to her twin brother, "You got in trouble."

"Dad, did she have to be born?" Patrick pleads to his dad to send her back to wherever she came from. Keith has a confused look on his face. "What? Just set the table!"

Twenty minutes later dinner is ready at the Heiden house. Keith always makes luscious meals, and it takes about two hours to prepare. Tonight it's a honey-baked ham with sides of sweet potatoes, cream of spinach, and carrots. Some of the kids don't like the same vegetables so there are steamed vegetables, corn, and string beans as well. We can't forget the homemade biscuits. Patrick and Erin start to talk like ordinary human beings. Then it ends up to a be a full-fledged argument most all the time. Justine always tries to break up the fight, but it never works out the way she hopes. Keith is always in his own little world. He puts his head down and eats his food fast and rarely looks up to see the drama unfold at the dinner table. He just keeps to himself and helps Colin eat his meal. No facial expression from Keith; he looks directly at the other end of the dining room table. Justine screams at the kids to stop their yelling. She tries so hard to control the situation, but lots of times she doesn't get any responses from her abused damaged husband. Maybe this time it will be different or not? It's a hit or miss.

"Keith, you can try to help me!!" Justine commands. Whatever she says it snaps Keith out of the frozen state. Suddenly his body becomes tense with an angry look on his face with what he sees in front of him.

He shouts, "Patrick and Erin, stop this instant or else!" He gives a final command that makes everyone jump up from his or her seats. He doesn't even notice the similarity in his voice, that makes him sound like his father. "I don't want to hear or see you guys disrespect your mother! If you do, the repercussion will be strong! Is this how you treat your mother when I'm not around? Answer me!" Keith demands sternly, as he hits his hand on the dining room table. He gives a very cold abusive look to his kids as they stop in their tracks.

Without haste, Patrick puts his head down and tries to avoid his father's state of mind. "I don't know," he says quickly.

"Is that your answer?" he shouts with full force. Mitch slowly eats his food without even looking up and not a sound Colin cries loudly and tries to get more food at the same time from his dad. Keith gives some food to his little son and continues with the problem at hand.

"Erin, what's you answer to all of this?" Keith asks his little girl.

Erin is now a young seventeen-year-old woman soon to be eighteen in July. She's the spitting image of Justine but with Keith's blue eyes. Erin stands at 5'7" and she is very intelligent. Keith is in total shock that his little girl is so beautiful, and the boys in town know it too. He will do anything to have the boys not look in Erin's direction. In her early teens, Keith use to scare them away, but he can't do that now. He already knows about Erin's new boyfriend, Christopher Masterson. They have been dating for five or six months. Keith is not very happy that he didn't see this young man first before the love drama started. One of the Heidens' house rules is to meet the date before Erin thinks about going out with that person. He's not too worried how Erin will handle herself, but it's the boys that are his concern. He taught her and Justine self-defense, and he said one day. "If it's necessary to kick butt with no regard."

"I know that we have disrespected Mom, but I don't know why we did it. It just happened." Erin cries to answer her very strict dad, and she still has her head down. She has read every book on abuse and how the mind works. They both love a challenge to the will of the mind and body. Keith has met his match to bring him down from extreme aggression.

"Interesting Erin, have been you reading abuse books lately?" he asks with a calm voice but not surprised at all that one of his children would read to be ahead of the game.

Erin picks up her head up and answers, "Yes, Dad, I've been reading abuse books. That is the only answer I can give you right now." She tries to be careful in her approach and thinks of her next move. Keith shakes his head and tries to get this push of aggression out of his system. But for some reason, it's not working out at this time.

Suddenly Keith's body shakes uncontrollably; it's the reaction that he gets when being abusive. "Fine your answer is not acceptable in my book! I will not take this kind of behavior! You have disrespected your mother and me! I don't take this situation lightly! You guys have a very serious problem that needs to be addressed right now! You are both grounded for one month each! This will not happen again! Do you understand? I didn't hear you, once again, do you understand?" Keith roars out to his cubs to obey now. His face turns beet red with a heavy breathe, and with his tense blue eyes he can bring down anyone that tries to confront him.

"You can't do this! Patrick started it!" Erin screams, as she stands up from her chair and points her index finger directly at her loser twin brother who is sitting across from her.

Patrick suddenly picks up his head and gives a look to his sister to shut up or else. "Hey!" he replies.

"Please sit down, Erin. I'm not done here!" Keith shouts as the volume of his voice shakes throughout the first floor of the house. Erin sits down quietly and begins to cry. She could barely keep her head up to answer her controlling father.

"You and your brother are going to write an apology letter to your mother. In this letter you will tell us your reason why you feel that disrespecting your mother is a good thing or not! What you think being grounded for one month will teach you! Please leave the letters on the kitchen table by Saturday morning when I come home after a double shift at work. Do I make myself clear?" Keith commands of the twins. "We didn't raise you this way, did we?"

"No, Dad." The both kids answer at once to avoid more conflict with their dad.

Keith shouts, "Once again, do you understand what I said to you?"

They have their heads down to show respect to the king lion of the leader of the pack of the Heiden family. They feel a shame. "Yes, Dad, sorry about our behavior. It wouldn't happen again," Erin answers as the tears fall down her cheek.

Patrick cries out, "Hey, what she just said."

Justine smiles at her husband and she says, "Thank you Keith." She's very proud of him taking control of the kids. "Thank you."

Keith looks at Justine without any expression on his face. He puts his attention directly towards Colin and starts to feed his little master. His mood slowly becomes relaxed and the aggression goes away inch by inch. The kids begin to eat quickly and quietly throughout the dinnertime to avoid their father's wrath.

Two hours later everything seems to be almost normal at the Heiden's house. Keith walks out of the home at 6:30 p.m. to head for work. As he walks to his SUV, he sees on the window blades a large manila envelope. He takes if off the truck but doesn't open it, because it might be crucial evidence. He drives away with the evidence laying on the passenger seat; he wants to open it right away, but then his cell phone rings in his business suit pants pocket. He puts his phone on the holder, fastens it and presses the speaker button. "Heiden," he shouts.

"Hello, Keith, my best buddy," the sound of Peter's friendly voice comes through the cell phone line. "I know you're coming into work tonight but I'm sorry to say. I would like you to know that time will go a little faster if you can get your government butt in here at 7:00 p.m, not the time you're thinking which is 8:00 p.m."

"What are you talking about? I'm scheduled for 8:00 p.m. and I don't remember you telling me about the time change! I really think you should check the records," Keith snaps while he drives out the community gate and waves "hi or goodbye" to the man who works at the security gate house. He thinks to himself, "What if he's wrong on the time?" Sometimes he does think he's right but lately, he's not on top of his game. Especially when it comes down to his family and Justine always yelling at him out of the blue.

"Listen, Keith, it's really 7:00 p.m. This is not good with DEA Internal Affairs. They already know that you missed work twice. You can't put me in this position explaining to the people ahead of us that Agent Keith Heiden doesn't do the things he should do. This is not fair to me! Just get in here as fast as you can!" Peter shouts at Keith. He doesn't like to yell but it becomes a habit with Keith.

"Fine," Keith answers with a sound of a whimper in his voice. He feels uneasy when he gets yelled at from anyone. During his abused life getting yelled at was part of an everyday routine. Now he feels that the pressure from Justine makes him scold the kids. He's not happy at all. She makes him go over the limit when it comes down to disciplining the children.

He knows that Justine can destroy anything that comes near her. Keith thinks that she's very aggressive towards people and lots of time it's towards him. He remembers a very nasty fight three weeks after Carlos Garcia's case was over. It brought Justine over the edge because they lost a lot of money from an arbitration case, and Keith's job was on the line. She screamed and yelled at him in the famiy room, and then suddenly she took a wooden bat from the kids' toys. She beat him repeatedly with the bat, and he didn't plead for his life. Keith thought maybe he deserved the beating from her or he's very sick in the head that this is a normal thing at home. That week he called in sick from work because he received lots of black and blues and his right arm was broken in two places. He told everyone that he fell off the ladder that day, and that it didn't hurt as much as it looked. Till this day Keith still cries about what happened that sent Justine over the edge. He's very scared of her but always keeps a close watch on her at all times. He never told Peter the real story, but he has a strong feeling something went south.

CHAPTER
FOURTEEN

*I*t's around 8:00 p.m. and Keith tries to get his body and his mind ready for the long hours ahead of him. He checks into the DEA of Los Angeles right on time in his mind but something happened he can't explain. His office is always clean and his papers are where he leaves them the night before. He deals with a lot of paperwork and post it notes that say call people back. The DEA work is very detail oriented and everything is noted and signed in every part of the department. Jennifer Chan, a petite Asian lady in her mid-forties, makes Keith's work a little easier to handle. She schedules different meetings, training agents on canines and has many other responsibilities. Jennifer entertains by giving fortune cookie wisdom of the day from her grandparents. She always has a smile on her face when you see her.

Keith puts his personal items down and starts to yawn and stretch his extremely tried body.

He really hates double shifts, especially when he is just doing office duties. Being grounded for little over a year is not pretty and puts him in a stressful mode all the time.

Keith sits behind his desk looking at different pictures of his family around him which life to boring office and some taste of joy into his county job. A German stein that sits in front on his desk with little chocolate candies inside, was given to him by his mother-in-law for no reason accept to show him that he is loved. She always refills the chocolate for Heiden. He is very moved that his mother in-law cares so much for the lost soul of her son in-law. She gives Keith only one rule. Just take one chocolate a day. The joy of the chocolate will bring a smile to your face and she is correct. Keith opens the German beer stein, take one piece of needed chocolate and eats it very slowly as a smile of happiness appears on his face. They both talk once a day in German. Keith understands German from his father, who was born in Austria and came to America at the age of five. Austria has different dialects in the German language. Keith taught all the kids German. Now it's Colin's turn. He believes that knowing a different language will challenge their minds. Keith gets to work, opens the mail, and looks at his meetings, social events, additional training, and etc., every day.

He makes sure he answers all his mail and voice mails by the end of his workday.

There is one letter that catches his eye. He opens the envelope that states to the parents of Mr. Patrick Keith Heiden. Keith calls home and reads the letter while the phone rings on the other line. "Hello," Justine answers.

"Hello, Justine, how are you doing?" he asks while he puts the letter down on the desk. He pushes the speaker button and starts to type one of the reports of thousands more to do while burning the midnight oil at work. "I'm fine, how about you and work?" she asks in a friendly voice. He hears through the phone line the background of the kids talking very loudly and the sound of echoes of laughter while Reese is barking at something.

"I'm okay. It's just business as usual here. Justine, I'm calling you because I found out why Patrick is suspended from school again. He has one week for skipping classes and not giving the assignments in on time. So now we have to find out what he's into during school hours, and why he's failing all of his classes. Can I please speak to our golden child?" Keith requests, as he starts to type away in the computer system.

"I can't believe this! Sure, he's right here in the kitchen... Patrick, your dad wants to speak to you now!" Keith hears a conversation between Justine and Patrick, and he can tell by her tone that she's not very happy.

"Mom, I don't know what you're talking about!" exclaims Patrick.

"Patrick, your father wants to talk to you now, not later!" she commands. "Patrick Keith Heiden, your father is waiting!"

Patrick picks up the receiver and presses the speakerphone bottom. "Hi, Dad! This speakerphone is so cool! I don't know why Mom's curls are in knots," Patrick says in a friendly voice.

"Patrick, please take me off speakerphone. I really have to talk to you." Patrick presses the button and the sound of the other family members in the background are no more. "Patrick, what did you do with the letter from your school?" Keith continues to focus on his typing and talk on the phone at the same time. It's a gift that he has perfected since the early days.

"I took it and ripped it up... Oh man!" he shouts, screaming words out loud that make him sound like a truck driver. "How do you know?"

"Patrick, maybe one day I'll tell you when you're older. You're grounded for two months for taking the envelope and not telling us what happened today at school. The sentence for your chores is still up in the air. Son, you and I are going to have a very serious talk about your problems at school. So find a comfortable seat because you will be in it for a long time explaining to me why you are suspended, and why you are failing all your classes!" Keith states, as he sees a tall British gentleman standing on the other side of his office door talking to Jennifer.

"Dad, can you hear my side of the story? So... I am grounded for the total of three months?! Dad, I won't have a summer!" Patrick cries while he looks at his mother at the same time. Justine is pacing back and forth throughout the kitchen. She shakes her head in disbelief with a disappointed look on her face. She's ready and waiting to give her two cents about her son's behavior. Patrick starts to cry a little. He knows that he'll never have a chance with Melissa now.

"Yes...the total of three months, and that includes what happened at dinner time. I'm very sorry that you won't have a summer, but you brought this on yourself. You know I would love to hear your explanation, but I have to go now. What you did was wrong, and that is why you're punished for your choices. Please tell your mom I'll call her tomorrow, and I love you guys. Behave, okay? I'll see you soon, bye, Patrick," Keith announces with a soft but firm voice. The adventure of parenthood, oh, how sweet it is! What will come up next?

"Dad! Hello, Dad!" Patrick shouts into the phone but only hears the dial tone. Erin walks by Patrick and starts to laugh, "Don't you get it! He's not on the other line, moron!"

"Why don't you just throw yourself into the Pacific Ocean, so that sharks can eat you!" Patrick snaps back, while he tries to wipe the tears off his face quickly before his older sister notices.

"I don't know what to do with that one!" Erin says as she laughs. "Boy, Patrick, you really messed yourself up this time! Being punished for the whole summer is rough. I'm happy I'm not you!"

CHAPTER

FIFTEEN

~~~~~~

*K*eith puts on the latex gloves and peels off the tape that says "Evidence" from the large envelope. He walks over to a lamp and turns it on to see it clearly, as he slowly takes out the items. There are about twenty pictures taken of him and Dr. Sheppard. They showed different shots of everyday activities, going to the store, going to coffee houses, and so on. Peter walks into Keith's office and sees the pictures on the glass table. There is a post-it not attached to a picture. It says, "you're going to get another package like this one on Monday. Look out for it. Have a good day."

"Someone has a thing for you guys." He laughs, trying to release the tension.

"Can you take these pictures and get fingerprints out of them? Also, try to find out their origin. I need a name!" Keith exclaims. "I'm sorry about the mix up on the time. Was it 7:00 p.m. or 8:00 p.m.?"

"It was 7:00 p.m.," Peter states, as he suddenly sees his best buddy put his head down in shame. He feels badly as he witnesses Keith's strange behavior. "Keith, it's okay. Please don't worry. Uncle Peter will fix the problem." Then Peter gives a supporting punch to Keith's right arm. "There, does that feel better? You know sometimes we forget the important things in life like being somewhere on time. You're dealing with a lot of stress right now. Between the Garcia case and now, your drop-dead gorgeous, hot, young therapist asking a million questions, it's not easy," teases Peter.

"Did Chucky E. Cheese give you some of your intelligence?" Keith asks with a surprised look on his face.

"Sometimes you surprise me!" replies Peter and laughs. As always Keith doesn't respond.

"Don't worry, I'm on it!" Peter states, as he carefully puts the pictures and envelope into a large plastic evidence bag. He takes off the latex gloves and gives Keith a friendly smile. Peter quietly walks out of the office and sees Jenny, Keith's secretary, sitting behind her desk. She immediately passes Peter and knocks on the boss's door slowly opening it.

"You like Mr. Williamson now?" Jenny asks with a smile on her face.

"Thanks, Jenny. Send him in." Keith is ready to introduce himself although it's still scary at times. He finds it difficult to show any friendly emotions towards other people when he first meets them. All this stems from the abuse he received as a child.

"Mr. Williamson, thanks for coming over so late." Keith has been ready for this meeting for a while. Preston works for the International Criminal Police Organization, otherwise known as Interpol. Both men shake hands. Keith appears small at 5'11" next to Mr. Williamson's 6'4" frame.

"Mr. Heiden, it's nice to meet you. You have a comfortable office," Preston states while he looks at different personal pictures around the room. An interesting mug of some sort sits on the desk that catches Preston's attention. A modern office is not like your average government style interior, and that's good for the staff of the DEA dept. It makes you feel special.

"I try very hard to be as comfortable as I can," Keith replies, as he looks at Mr. Williamson standing tall in his European-made business suit. "Please sit down and make yourself comfortable." Keith walks toward his desk as he thinks of all the work he has to do. There is typing, filing, debriefing of other agents and witnesses to question. There is also the interrogation of suspects or criminals. Nowadays Keith has to raise his hand to get permission for a bathroom break. As he sits behind his desk, he tries to remember all the things he has to do before the double shift is over.

"Thank you," Preston Williamson replies, as he fits his long body into a lightweight chair.

"I hope you don't mind that I have to type reports into the computer system while we talk," Keith says apologetically, as he looks at Preston for his reaction.

Preston gives a friendly smile, "It's not a problem. It's your office, and you made the rules. Before we talk, however, I'd like to ask you about that interesting mug on your desk."

"Oh, this thing? It's called a beer stein, and it's from Germany. My mother-in-law was born and raised in the country, and one day she gave me this thoughtful present." Keith smiles as he remembers the day he received the gift. He's very touched that someone would give him a present from their heart for no reason at all.

His mother-in-law, Gertrude Adalicia Bauer Anderson, is a very interesting woman. She is headstrong on what she wants in life and has no regrets. She and Keith are close, like a mother and son relationship. He's very touched by Gertrude and doesn't understand why she would go out of her way to make him comfortable. Justine and her mother don't have a good relationship. She's daddy's little girl all the way. They're so close; they almost have the same personality, and it's very scary at times from where Keith is standing.

"A beer stein? I'm sorry, I still don't understand. What it is?" Preston asks with a very confused look on his face.

"It's a large mug that has very unique art carved into it. This one has my last name engraved on the bottom. It holds a lot of beer!" Keith holds the tall, heavy mug up to show Mr. Williamson from a different view. He's like a child showing his special item at show and tell in school. Keith glows and feels very relaxed. He slowly and carefully puts the mug down in it's place. He remembers how his brother and sister, Christopher and Jennifer, had given him a very touching gift. It was a black Cross Pen that he lost when his family disowned him.

Preston laughs. "I can understand in this day and age that work can be hard, and you need that beer," he states. He understands that fully coming from England. He loves to spend quality time with his chums and have some drinks of Cask Ale beer at a local pub near his town. Preston opens his briefcase made out of Italian leather and takes out a tan-colored case file to show the agent.

"That would be a good idea, but I don't think so. There are little chocolates imported from Germany inside. I know it brings a smile to my face when I have one. It works every time. Please take one." Keith opens the beer stein with a friendly smile on his face. They are like two little boys going into the cookie jar without anyone noticing. Preston takes a piece of heavenly creamy milk chocolate and puts it in his mouth. "Hmm, this is really good! Thank you."

Keith types away on the computer and looks at Mr. Williamson from time to time. He tries not to be rude to the person who's present in his office.

"How can the DEA Department help Interpol?" Keith asks, as he stops typing and looks at Preston.

"I'm happy that you asked that question," Preston says, as he puts down a case file with the Interpol seal on it. Keith gets his attention and opens the file. There is a red stamp that says "copy" on each paper. He attentively reads every word and comprehends all the facts that are in front of him. During Keith's childhood reading a lot of books helped him deal with his abuse. It was a great escape from what he was going through; now it helps in his job when he deals with reading a lot of paperwork.

As he turns each page, he sees information that contains some Interpol codes and abbreviations that he doesn't understand. Minutes later he closes the file and starts to rub his tired blue eyes. "This case file is just full of facts about where he goes and stays in different parts of England, Europe, and United States. I don't recognize a lot of the Interpol codes and abbreviations. From the information that we have in the DEA database, we don't have a case against him. Mr. Williamson, I still don't know what you want from me and the DEA Department"

"Agent Heiden, do you know what Interpol does?" asks Mr. Williamson, as he looks at Keith for a response to his questions.

"I guess, but I know you will give me a history lesson," Keith remarks sharply. He starts to type again.

Preston is suddenly taken back by the sudden change of tone in Agent Heiden's voice. He's willing to let it go and not ask any questions. Preston thinks to himself, maybe Agent Heiden is moody because of the amount of his workload and long hours. Or, perhaps the pressure is getting to him.

Preston states, "Think of us as the CIA of the planet's police force. We track down the suspects and collect all the information that is needed. Then we give this information to the local authorities around the world. We do the legwork to make your job easier."

"Okay, you still didn't give me an answer to my question?'" Keith asks with a friendly but firm tone in his voice, as he takes the mouse and clicks the printer icon on the top left hand corner of his computer screen. Seconds later the laser printer starts to print away.

As Keith turns his head to look to his right, Preston notices that Agent Heiden's left eye has a cut above it. Keith tries to focus by blinking, but he is exhausted and is continuously yawning. He doesn't know why he is so tired. Maybe it's all the stress, but his double shift has just begun, and he must conserve his energy for the work ahead.

"Agent Heiden, you can help Interpol get additional information on Mr. Jude Henderson while he's in the states. Last week he was seen in California. Not to change the subject, but I could really use a glass of water. It has been a long flight from London," He sighs, as he rubs his neck and leans back in the office chair.

As Keith focuses in on Preston, he says automatically, "How rude of me! I'm sorry." He gets up and quickly walks over to the refrigerator pulling out two cold water bottles. "Sorry about that," he says as he automatically puts his head down because of his behavior.

Mr. Williamson looks confused over Keith's strange reaction. "Thank you. Are you okay, Agent Heiden?" Preston asks in a soft voice. Keith doesn't answer as he continues to sit there with his head down and his body shaking.

Preston notices a rapid behavior change from Agent Heiden, but he is unable to locate the main source. As an Interpol investigator, you have to see all sides. It's the same with DEA agents who are always on guard, even when they are sleeping! Preston Williamson looks at Keith's left ear as well as his hands. He sees it all the time on the streets of Los Angeles, and he hears a lot of stories. His mum used to tell him to explore the real world when he was young. "I'm sorry for your pain. I can see it in your ear, hands, and eye."

As Keith picks up his head, he answers Preston and says, "Thank you." He seems shy and a little upset about what Mr. Williamson might ask next. Will it be a question, about the scars on his left ear and hands? Or could it be the cut on his eye? Keith tries to take out paper from the printer.

Preston coughs, so Keith knows he's still in the room. "I need your help for additional information. If we work together, we can get Jude Henderson. He's very dangerous but you deal with that every day," adds Mr. Williamson, as he takes a long drink of water and sits back in the comfortable chair. Preston can sleep for days anywhere after long hours on an airplane. Now that England's time zone is an eight hour difference, it's getting harder for Preston to move his body and put it in relax mode; hopefully he'll get lucky and grab a few hours of sleep.

"I'm sorry, what's Mr. Henderson doing here? You never filled me in on the details, and I can't help you without a good reason! You're wasting my time, and I have a lot on my plate right now!" Keith announces as his voice cracks. The department knows that they work extremely hard and have a great deal of stress.

"Mr. Henderson has been working for Jose Medina and the crew for many months now, and he's going international. He already has New York, Florida, and other states that are listed on the memo in the file. I know that the DEA gets updated information every half hour to be one step ahead of crime. Henderson already started to spread the Medina drug fest all around the world. Now he's in Los Angeles and he's making his move on the streets. He lures young children from the age of fourteen and up. Jose Medina's drug operation works by buying and selling drugs to children or adults in all towns. Mr. Henderson is building an empire with lots of contacts from Jose Medina. I have a very strong feeling that something big is going to happen within a couple of months. It's going to be a very interesting summer in Los Angeles!" Mr. Williamson exclaims and takes another drink of his water. Preston still can't get used to the hot, dry weather of California. It's so different from England.

"This is all very interesting. If I can help you, I only have a limited amount of access to information. I think you have the wrong guy for the job! I have not been fully active for over a year now. You can try to get a different agent. I can give you several names," Keith announces while he gets the second batch of printouts.

"That's very funny." Mr. Williamson laughs. Preston feels deeply honored that Keith is opening up to him, or maybe he's just venting. He thinks that Agent Heiden is a very entertaining American.

Keith shakes his head with confusion. "My record is not the cleanest. I can help you find an agent for this assignment!"

"I don't need to see your record. What you did or didn't do doesn't interest me. Your goal is to get Jose Medina and his men. My mission is to apprehend Mr. Jude Henderson. I'm not giving you any pressure right now, but I really need an answer by the end of next week," Mr. Williamson announces, as he gets up from his chair and throws away the finished bottle of water. He looks at Keith for a response, while the agent looks at his report that's coming out of the printer.

"Agent Heiden, did you hear me?" Mr. Williamson snaps, as he tries to get the agent's full attention.

"I'm sorry. So you're not interested in my record? If I were you, I'd rethink that!" Keith walks to his desk and sits in his comfortable office chair. "What additional information do you want from DEA?"

"Agent Heiden, I need you to help get Jude Henderson, and I know you have a lot at stake. But by the expression on your face, you are not giving in to my request," he states and tries to adjust his tired, aching, body.

"Mr. Williamson, any information that I can give you is the same that you give to me. We share information to get the bad guys. It's called open communication between agencies!" Keith answers sarcastically. "Do you think that I have more information then you have? I'm sorry Mr. Williamson, but you're wasting my time and yours! I really have a lot of work to do, and I hope you don't mind letting yourself out!" Keith responds without the blink of an eye to the British gentleman standing in front of him.

"Please consider my offer. Believe me, it will be worthwhile in the end. You can keep the file. I have another one in my hotel. We can talk about the details later." Mr. Williamson shakes Agent Heiden's hand and gives him a friendly smile.

"Thank you for the water and that delicious chocolate!" He smiles just thinking about the chocolate.

Keith goes right back to his office chair and smiles. "I'm happy that you enjoyed the snacks."

"Please think about my offer. I'll call you later in the week. Have a good night," Mr. Williamson says. Preston walks out of Keith's office and gives Jenny a friendly wave.

Jenny cheerfully smiles. "Good-bye Mr. Williamson."

"Good-bye, Jenny," Mr. Williamson says in his charming British way.

CHAPTER
SIXTEEN

lise rushes toward Star Bucks near her home in San Marino. She just put on comfortable clothes because it's Saturday morning, May 19, and she has agreed to meet Keith Heiden at 11:00 a.m. She looks at her watch as she enters Star Bucks. It is now nine thirty. Elise is especially jumpy this morning before her morning coffee. She fidgets impatiently on the busy line.

"Miguel! I need a venti double latté Costa Rican coffee, and fast!" Elise looks tired after a girl's night out with her old college friends. They're in town for a couple of weeks. She drank a lot of shots as well as chocolate and lemon martinis. Then she wonders why she has a throbbing headache and hangover.

"What's wrong, girlfriend?" Miguel Sanchez asks. He's the manager at Star Bucks for more than three years now. He always watches over Elise because she helped him find an apartment in her complex. Now they are best friends who watch out for each other.

"I think I had too much to drink last night, but who's counting, right?" Elise says with a very weak smile.

She tries so hard to wake up, but she's not a morning person. That's why she start her workday at 10:00 or 11:00 a.m., depending on how she feels. Elise tries to work just three hours on Saturday so she can catch up on paperwork. She doesn't usually see patients, and just thinking about seeing Mr. Heiden makes her want a stronger drink than coffee. He's very hard to handle and although she can't put her finger on it, she feels like a child who's dealing with a strict father.

Miguel gives Elise a long overdue coffee. "Here you go, sweetie. It's hot! Let's get together this Friday. I'll call you. That coffee was $2.75." Elise hands him the money and without missing a beat, she says, "Thanks Miguel." She gives him a sleepy smile and adds, "I would love to get together with you on Friday. I miss talking to you."

"Me too, girlfriend! You hang in there!" yells Miguel through the Saturday crowd noise.

Elise walks out of Star Bucks and sees that her sneaker is untied. "Great!" She says out in the open public.

As she squats down to fix it, she is suddenly pushed forward and lands face first on the sidewalk. Her coffee pours out of the plastic cup and her body goes into shock for a quick minute. There goes $2.75! No-oo-o!

"I'm sorry. Are you okay?" asks the man with an English accent, while he helps Elise get up from the sidewalk. She feels very cold from the liquid that has trailed down her back and overpowered by the smell of coffee!

"Are you crazy?!" she shouts for anyone to hear.

"I'm sorry. I will pay for any damages," the Englishman says, as he looks at Elise with concern in his clear blue eyes.

"What about my $2.75 coffee? That's what I need right now!" Elise cries indignantly.

"Of course, Whatever you want. Again, I am so sorry!" says the gentleman. He takes a very expensive wallet out of his Italian suit pocket and pulls out a one hundred dollar bill.

"Please take it! It's the least that I can do. Hopefully, this will make your day!" he exclaims with a friendly smile.

Elise knows very well not to take anything from strangers, especially a hundred dollars. In this case, however, she'll take her chances. "Thank you. It's only $20 for damages not one hundred," she replies as she tries hard to shake off the uncomfortable feeling of ice coffee dripping down her body. Elise just wants to go home. Her headache is worse than ever and her ego and pride are hurt. She takes the $100 out of the Englishman's hand. "Thank you," Elise states, as she picks up her pocketbook and walks away from the handsome gentleman.

A few minutes later, Elise gets herself a fresh cup of hot coffee. As she starts to walk to her Volvo, she looks down to avoid any eye contact because of her appearance. While driving away, Elise pushes her very wet body forward, so her back will dry up faster from the high AC coming out of the vents. She lost a lot of time, so she can't go home and change. She'll have to drink the coffee and smell like one too.

An hour passes by as Elise finally arrives at Mr. Heiden's house. She looks at her watch and the time is now 11:20 a.m. Although she is almost dry now, her clothes are sticking to her skin like crazy glue. She begins to think to herself, *Why did I ever wake up today?* It's a little late now, as she presses on the doorbell of the Heiden's house. Elise quickly tries to fix herself and whatever can be saved of her hair.

The sounds of the doorbell echo throughout the huge house. Keith yells something that is barely audible, as his head is burrowed beneath the pillows, and the blankets are covering his body. He knows for a fact that the person is not leaving any time soon. Patrick is no help, because he's a very heavy sleeper. Colin has just gone down for his routine nap, and Erin and Mitch have gone to their grandparents' house. Justine went to work. The doorbell rings again and the echoes pierce Keith's brain, make him get up from his very comfortable California king size bed. He tries to hold back his anger and decides in his sleepy state of mind not to say hi when he opens the front door.

While Elise is waiting for someone to come to the front door, she looks around the neighborhood. Its lovely weather and the people are taking the time to do outside activities. Some are walking their dogs, riding their bikes, playing basketball, or skateboarding down the street. It's nice to experience life, especially when Elise has to get ready to deal with her patient.

The front door slowly opens and Keith stands on the other side. He looks very tired since he just got home four hours ago. Working a double shift is taking a toll on him physically and mentally these days. He is wearing lightweight navy blue pajamas covered with the same color expensive robe and tan slippers on his feet. His sandy blond hair is messed up from sleeping. Keith rubs his blue eyes, but the person is still at the front door.

"Dr. Sheppard, what are you doing here?" Keith asks with a sleepy voice and confused look on his face. He blinks rapidly and tries to avoid the sun shining in his eyes.

"Hi," says Dr. Sheppard, as she tries to balance herself by holding her briefcase and pocketbook on her shoulder at the same time. "I'm sorry that I'm late. I know that we had an appointment as 11:00 a.m."

Elise looks at her watch. "Okay it's now 11:30am. Once again, I'm sorry that I'm late." Suddenly, Elise looks at her patient, and her heart starts to beat rapidly. Her hands become sweaty. Elise realizes that she has a major teenage crush on him. Even though he looks extremely exhausted and not very attractive at this moment, that doesn't matter to Elise. She starts to giggle, and Keith becomes aggravated because his doctor is acting very weird.

"Sorry, inside joke," she answers quickly as she continues to giggle.

"Dr. Sheppard, why do you smell like coffee? I called you Thursday afternoon and left messages on your cell and office phones. I just got home at 8 a.m. after working long hours. I'm really exhausted and not in the mood to talk to anyone right now. Is it possible for us to have a double session on Monday at 11:00 a.m.?" Keith asks, as he leans his sleepy body against the front door to support himself.

"Wait a minute. Hold on!" Elise listens to her voice messages from her cell phone. A few minutes later her face becomes as red as her car, and suddenly she feels embarrassed in front of Mr. Heiden. She starts to laugh. "Oh, I'm so sorry!"

Keith thinks to himself, *Does she know what she's doing?* Should he be very concerned at this point? Maybe he should look for another therapist like right away. His face immediately turns beet red, and he shouts with anger, "Next time listen to your voicemail!" Suddenly the door slams in front of Dr. Sheppard. She hears the locks turn and the sound of the alarm system click on. Elise sees Keith's shadow walk away from the front door, and then he's gone.

"Hello, hello. That's just great!" Dr. Sheppard feels upset and embarrassed that Mr. Heiden talked down to her like she's one of his naughty children.

She starts to laugh. Her day is not going as planned!

CHAPTER

SEVENTEEN

~s Elise begins to leave, a light tan cat startles her as it walks over her feet and meows. She wonders if it's a feral cat or part of the Heiden household.

"Hello cat," Elise says as she smiles.

The cat quickly runs away from Dr. Sheppard and heads in the direction of the Heiden's backyard.

"Cat! Wait! Don't go in there!" Elise walks fast and looks as she stands on tippy toes to see where the cat went.

As she is about to open the gate, she suddenly hears the sound of a man clearing his throat. "Miss, can you please put your hands up in the air so I can see them! Please turn around slowly and face me! I mean slowly!" a man states with a calm voice. His mind is clear, and he shows no emotion as he speaks.

Elise puts her hands above her head and turns around slowly. As she looks at the man holding the gun all she can think of is how Irish looking he is.

"My name is Agent Liam Gallagher from DEA. Please state your name and the reason why you're trespassing!" he says in a firm voice. "Search her." Agent Gallagher gives a direct order to one of the agents behind him. The agent slowly searches Dr. Elise Sheppard, as he carefully pats her from head to toe.

"There are no weapons, sir. It's all clear. I'll check her briefcase and purse," announces the DEA agent as he looks directly at Agent Gallagher.

"Please answer my questions. What is your name, and why are you trespassing on this property?" asks Agent Gallagher as he continues to point his gun at Elise. As an afterthought he asks, "Why do you smell of coffee?"

"My name is Dr. Elise Sheppard. I'm Mr. Heiden's therapist." Then she asks, "Shouldn't you know my name? The reason why I smell like coffee… Well, that's a long story."

"The briefcase and purse are clear, sir," the DEA agent states, as he steps back to give the doctor some room to breathe.

"Please put your hands down very slowly and show me your ID," commands Agent Gallagher as he puts his gun back into his holster.

He's feeling very tired, as his double shift is almost over. Liam can't wait to drink some beers with his friends. Maybe he'll watch some Stephen King movies and play lots of Xbox games.

Dr. Sheppard slowly opens her Gucci wallet and takes out her California license. Elise gives it to Agent Liam Gallagher without saying a word. He holds her ID in his hand and sees that Dr. Sheppard is an exact match.

A second later the agent gives Elise back her license and states, "Dr. Elise Sheppard, it still doesn't explain the why you were peeking into the backyard."

"I had an appointment today with Mr. Heiden. Unfortunately, the plans were changed at the last minute," Elise answers, as she looks at Agent Liam Gallagher.

He stands 6'2" tall with red hair, deep brown eyes, and a fair-skinned complexion. His face is very red and covered with freckles. Elise had never met a man with red hair before. She thought it looked fake.

"Dr. Sheppard, Agent Heiden just finished a double shift, and I bet he's sleeping now. So why were you near the backyard fence peeking in?" Gallagher asks again, as he puts his gun back into his holster.

Suddenly a dog starts to bark. Agent Gallagher and Dr. Sheppard immediately turn to look in the direction of all the commotion.

Liam asks with a stern voice, "Agent Tierney, what's wrong with Trooper?"

A well-trained drug-sniffing search dog, Trooper is a very handsome three-year-old German Sheppard. Trooper's attention is on the car in front of him. As Agent Tierney, tries to hold him back Trooper is determined to crawl underneath the car. Agent Sean Tierney looks a bit like Colin Farrell, the movie actor. He's 5'9" with dark brown hair and eyes. Liam and Sean have been best friends since they started together on the job.

Agent Sean Tierney shouts loudly, "Trooper is barking at this red Volvo in front of the Heiden's house!" Trooper's body show signs that he is ready to go. He seems to be saying, "Don't try to stop me, I'm going in!"

"That's my car! Get that dog away from my vehicle!" Elise shouts, with her hands waving in every direction. Liam and Elise both walk towards the car to get a better look the drama that is unfolding.

"Dr. Sheppard, can you please open your car door. It's called search and seize noted in the Fourth Amendment of the Constitution. In this case, we have probable cause that a crime may have been committed." Agent Gallagher commands, as he dials from his cell phone while he looks closely at the doctor and Agent Tierney.

"Agent Gallagher…right? I don't really care what amendment you're trying to preach to me! I think you still need a warrant!" Elise states, as she feels a little uncomfortable in her sticky coffee smelling sneakers. She knows a tiny bit of the law, but her family is into the medical field.

Liam is not at all surprised with the doctor's reaction. A lot of people including shrinks don't like cops, especially living in Los Angeles after the Rodney King case against the LAPD. Who can blame them for not liking the men and women in blue? Everyone was shocked after that terrible event, but it happened and now we have to move on. Liam doesn't need the doctor telling him what to do. He is about to call a judge. *Get out of my head, woman!* He says to himself.

Liam commands, "Dr. Sheppard, please stay here. I'll be right back," he continues, as he walks away to get some privacy and talk to Judge Larry Davis on his cell phone.

Liam knows all too well that a woman like Dr. Sheppard can get very dramatic in less than a second. He has five sisters, not including his mom in his equation. The girls in the house were loud and headstrong individuals, so it made life very interesting for Liam, his three brothers, and dad. He's surprised that he still has his hearing from all the women family fights. Elise is getting very upset that DEA agents are treating her like a criminal. She walks back and forth like an untamed lion ready to attack.

She thinks to herself, *What to do next if anything? Do I need a lawyer? What are my rights?*

Elise is very scared about what's unfolding in front of her. She's not having a very good day!

A navy Nissan Maxima 2006 pulls up and parks a few inches behind Elise's Volvo. Peter gets out of the car and walks toward Elise. "Hello, Dr. Elise Sheppard," he says with a friendly voice.

"Hello, Agent Peter Darling," Elise responds, as she remembers the conversation they had the other day.

A big date with Peter the great. This will be very interesting, she thinking in the mind. He gives a new meaning to the word "character."

"I know that we didn't really talk about our first date plans. Do you have any ideas?" he asks with a friendly smile on his face as he looks at the pretty doctor in front of him. Peter then turns his attention on Trooper who is barking at the hot red car. He puts two and two together and asks, "What's going on with Dr. Sheppard's car?"

"Trooper might have found something underneath the doctor's car," the agent answers, as he tries to stop Trooper from lunging.

Then Peter looks at the doctor directly and says, "I'm sorry about the mess. I guess Agent Gallagher is calling for a warrant to search your car. We have to do everything by the book. You know how it is." He says apologetically.

"It's just not my day!" Elise exclaims while she rubs her tried stressful eyes.

"I fully understand. We just have to rule out any suspicion of any kind. Then we can move on." he states with a concerned look on his face. "Dr. Sheppard, if I may ask what happened to you?" Peter can't help but notice Elise's total disarray. Maybe it's a new look, but why does she smell like burnt coffee? he begins to pounder.

"It's a very long story," Elise answers, as she uses her hands once again to fix her hair. She really is not in the mood to tell her tale of woe again.

"Well, I'm here to take you for a drive somewhere. Where do you want to go? I'm not going to kidnap you. I just want to make you comfortable in this situation until the search warrant comes in," Peter asks, as he looks at Elise for a reaction to his request.

"Sure, I want to go home, take a nice hot shower, and put on some comfortable clothes," she says, as she picks up her belongings. Elise is relieved that she won't have to smell like the latest coffee that just came out of Star Bucks anymore. She loves to drink the coffee, not wear it! That's a little extreme. She does have some concern about the situation taking place, however. She also feels uneasy about taking a ride with gentleman from the DEA department that she only met once, even though she has had an occasional phone conversation with him. She does think Peter is a nice guy, nonetheless, and wouldn't allow any harm to come her way.

"Then let's go!" Peter replies, as he opens the door for the doctor to get in.

Peter's mother is from Kirovohrad, Ukraine. She came to America after meeting Peter's dad. They bumped into each other on a dirt road, where his mom fell with her family's clean laundry and everything landed directly in the mud. They started to laugh out loud and that was the beginning of their relationship.

Peter's mom is a great cook. He especially has great memories of her cooking when he was a child. His mother came from a very poor but loving family in the Ukraine. Her family values stand tall in the Darling family. Peter had a great childhood with his close-knit family. They call every day, and they all get together two weekends a month. Peter feels heartily sorry for Keith since his childhood was so sad. If he could give a little joy back to Keith, he would. Peter knows Keith has a long journey ahead of him.

A half hour later, there is still no update on the request for a warrant. Peter will be posted updates every half hour by Agent

Gallagher. Dr. Sheppard gets out of Peter's car and walks to her apartment, as Peter decides to wait outside and get some Starbucks coffee for both of them. Someone takes a lot of pictures from afar of Peter and Elise as they are drinking coffee, talking, and laughing together. They are just having a good old time with each other, but someone wants more.

The time is 1 p.m. when Peter and Dr. Sheppard arrive at the Heiden's house. Peter walks into the home to see what's up with the family. Elise stands on the sidewalk as Agent Gallagher walks over to her and shows her the warrant to search the car.

As Liam gives her the warrant he says, "I'm sorry if it went down this way but I have to do my job. Please understand my situation." As Elise opens the warrant, she thinks, how this really tops my day! It takes all her strength not to start cursing in French and English!

"Dr. Sheppard, can you please open your car now?" commands Agent Gallagher. A few minutes pass by, "Please open the car door, or I will have to use force!" Elise takes her car keys out of her purse and presses the button to unlock the car. The doors open to the Volvo. Agent Sean Tierney enters with Agent Trooper from the Narcotics Canine Unit. The furry DEA agent wants to jump into the interior of Dr. Elise Sheppard's car. Trooper starts to bark forcefully. It's part of the dog's job to get excited.

A minute later Agent Sean Tierney states forcefully, "Dr. Sheppard, I need you to open the trunk!" At the same time he tries to hold Trooper back with his collar and leash.

"Dr. Sheppard, please open the trunk," commands Agent Liam Gallagher for a second time.

"Fine! I'm calling my lawyer! This is not right!" exclaims Elise, as she feels very annoyed at the whole situation. Then she gives a stern look to Agent Liam Gallagher and says, "You're going to pay for this little drama! Believe me!"

Liam answers with a smile, "I wouldn't be surprised, Dr. Sheppard!"

"You think you're all man with a bag of chips holding a gun in your hand!" Elise shouts.

"Dr. Sheppard, you can save your drama for your lawyer, because I'm just doing my job. If that's a crime, sue me!" Liam states with a calm voice.

The trunk opens and Trooper begins his job. This is what he's been trained to do since he was a puppy. He's a very smart canine, one of the best breeds of intelligence. The DEA Department is very proud of their furry agents in the Narcotic Canine Unit. If the canine is injured or suddenly dies while on duty, it is a federal crime. The narcotic canine will get a federal funeral with an American flag covering it's coffin and pictures of remembrance from the Drug Enforcement Administration placed in the main lobby.

"What are you doing? That dog is getting hair all over and scratching the interior!" Dr. Sheppard shouts, as she paces back and forth on the sidewalk. "Get that beast out of my car now!"

Minutes later Peter walks out of the Heiden's house. He sees a lot of drama unfolding in the front yard. As he stands next to Agent Gallagher, he says, "Did you find anything in the car?"

Exhaustion has just hit Liam with full force. He rubs his brown eyes and yawns at the same time trying to keep himself awake. Only a couple of hours left to work, then home. The serious factor is sleep. He knows he needs it desperately. He still has to go back to the office of the DEA Department to take off his uniform and fill out paper work. By the time he finishes it will be about 6:00 p.m. and sweet extra money for the Irishman, but still no sleep comes into play anytime soon.

Liam was born and raised in Boston. He's a well-rounded person surrounded by a very big Irish family with lots of love and support. The family was very sad that Liam moved so far away to pursue his career. He joined the Drug Enforcement Administration, which was one of many choices that he looked into. Liam had seen many crimes in his past in the dangerous sections of Boston. It's sad that one of America's historical cities needs a lot of help. His parents are so cool and down to earth. They stated to Liam one day, "When ever you want to come back home to visit, we have a ticket with your name on it!" Liam doesn't understand Keith's childhood. He feels very sorry that he didn't have a family like his. Every time Liam sees

Keith he wants to do something extra to make him comfortable in his work. Other agents think that Liam is kissing butt to his second boss, but he really cares for Keith

Agent Sean Tierney and Trooper search every corner of the car. Suddenly Trooper stops and begins to focus his attention under the car. Peter and Elise look in Sean's direction. Agent Tierney tries to figure out why Trooper is going Co Jo underneath the car.

"Agent Darling and Gallagher, I think there is something underneath the car! May I proceed with caution, Agent Darling?"

"Yes, proceed with caution, and Agent Gallagher will assist you. I will observe the situation from here," Peter commands. He stands next to Elise and gives support if anything goes down.

Agent Sean Tierney puts Trooper in the DEA company navy color SUV vehicle and locks him in the back seat. There is lots of water for Trooper in a plastic container, and he can rest with two automatic fans cooling him at the same time. Agent Tierney walks back to his equipment, which consists of two mirrors and a very long pole. Tierney has a steady hand with nerves of steel as he holds the mirrors.

Sean Tierney is from the deep south of Loganville, Georgia. It's a very small town with Baptist church values. Sean's dad is a military soldier, who served as a marine for thirty-two years. Now that he's retired he likes to fish with old school friends. Sean's mom goes to church every day for twelve o'clock mass. She raised four boys while her husband was on duty. Sean had a great childhood with lots of love and laughter in the household. His parents are proud of their boys. Two of them had joined the military. Sean entered the world of the DEA in California, and the other son went to work on Wall Street in New York. Sean doesn't know Keith very well, but he knows that Agent Heiden has his back if something happens.

Sean sees through the mirror wand that reflects what seems to be clear plastic bags and a note attached to them. It looks like cocaine and heroin, but Sean is not really sure from where he's standing. Agent Gallagher is typing instructions from a wireless laptop computer to a gripping hook robot. It's built on four wheels and made of titanium. It also has a digital camera on it and drives up to seventy-five miles with a speed of one to twenty miles per hour. The gripping hook slowly maneuvers its way to Dr. Sheppard's car and goes underneath taking out the two packages.

Minutes later the agents are collecting all the evidence to build an arrest or case on Dr. Sheppard. "We have something!" Agent Tierney shouts, as he holds an evidence bag that says, DEA property and inside the plastic is two bags of drugs.

"Liam and Sean, please analyze all the evidence and fingerprints on the car!" Agent Peter Darling commands the young agents.

"I can't believe you! You have no rights to do this!" Dr. Sheppard yells directly into Peter's face.

"Dr. Sheppard, please step away from my space! We have a lot to talk about. We will go inside Agent Heiden's house and I will debrief you," Peter states, as he really doesn't mind having the hot therapist close to him, but she smells of old coffee for some strange reason.

"Agent Gallagher and Tierney, clean shop and bring Dr. Sheppard's car to the DEA evidence parking lot to look over," Peter shouts the order.

"Yes, sir!" Both agents answer at the same time. Agent Gallagher and Tierney are extremely tired. Now it is time and a half as the job continues.

"Agent Darling, you have no right to do this to me! I need my car. What am I going to do without my transportation?" Who's going to pay for my car when your pig paws are all over it?!" shouts Elise with arms flaring up in the sky, like she's ready to take off!

"Dr. Sheppard, I'll take care of you until everything pans out. Now, I have to debrief you about what happened this morning. So let's begin," Peter states and walks with the very hot doctor. She's very fit, maybe a vegetarian like all Californians. Peter can pick a good mate and he loves to party hard. Maybe a little too hard at his age; within two years he will be forty. He's not looking forward to that mid-age drama, not by a long shot.

Charlie Winsborrow is Peter's good friend from college days. He didn't become adventurous until turning forty in March. He's that kind of guy that would sign up for the x-games on TV. Now he does everything; ski diving, bungee jumping, pinning down an alligator, on any kind of adventure which he will do in a heartbeat. I guess he feels like a twenty year old in his forties. Whatever suits his fancy.

CHAPTER

EIGHTEEN

*P*eter unlocks the Heiden's front door, "Hello, Hello," he yells into the house. Colin hears him and runs quickly from the back of the house to the front door. "Uncle Peter!" he yells as he gives Peter a very big hug on his leg, and Dr. Sheppard smiles from ear to ear at the scene in front of her. Colin loves Peter like he was his daddy.

Peter cheerfully states, "Hey buddy!" He picks his little friend up and holds him tightly. "Did you miss me?" Colin tries to get out of Peter's arms. "Do you want to get down?"

"Down!" Peter puts Keith's little clone down, and immediately he starts to run and make crazy noises that travel throughout the house.

"That boy has talent!" Peter laughs.

Elise joins in and laughs too. I guess Peter has a way to make people smile and be happy. She feels comfortable around Agent Darling. There are no waves of stress coming from him. He's the total opposite of Keith, generally a happy-go-lucky guy who gets a kick out of having an audience to entertain. Peter thinks that Dr. Sheppard is cute and has a smoking body even though there is still a hint of smell of coffee on her.

"Hey, Uncle Peter!" Patrick exclaims, as he comes down the wide staircase, dressed in the latest teenage fashion. "Hello, Patrick." Peter gives him a hug to show his love. Keith rarely shows affection to his kids, so Peter is there to fill in the void.

"Dr. Sheppard, this is Patrick, the second oldest in the Heiden clan," Peter announces proudly. He really loves the kids. They all hold a special place in his heart.

"Hello, Patrick. You certainly have your mother's eyes!" Elise states, as she exchanges a handshake with the teenager. He looks like Keith except for his eye color.

"Hello, Dr. Sheppard, I'm glad to meet you. Yes, I have my mother's eyes, and that's why I get out of trouble with the girls. How's my dad's therapy going?" asks Patrick with a charming smile that can drop ladies' hearts in a split second.

"He's doing fine, although we still have a lot of work ahead of us," Elise answers, as she gives Patrick a smile. Peter puts his arm around Patrick, like a father will do to a son. You can see that Peter is more of a father than Keith is to his own kids. It's sad, but true. Hopefully that will change in time.

"Where's your dad?" Peter asks, as he looks at the teenager.

"He's outside in the backyard reading the *Los Angeles Times*," Patrick replies, while he scratches his head. He realizes that he doesn't see his little monster brother around. "Great, where did you go…you little…," he says under his breath.

"What did you say?" Peter asks in a friendly but concerned voice.

"Nothing, Uncle Peter," he responds, as he scans the living room trying to find a hint of blond hair sticking out from behind the couch.

"What kind of mood is he in?" Peter asks with major concern. Keith's mood will determine whether Elise's debriefing will go smoothly or not.

"If you're asking if he's in a happy mood, that never happens. But he's tolerable today. Can I go now?" Patrick asks, as he looks around for Colin, and tries to keep up with the little person wearing red flashing light sneakers.

Patrick has to care for his little brother with fast legs for two weeks. This order was given by the King Lion of the Heiden clan. It's not what you call fun in a teenager's world, and Patrick tries to hold Colin down in one place. This is not easy because he's always ready to go somewhere and touch everything in his pre-k path. He's like "Animal," a puppet character on the Muppets. Patrick doesn't know how his parents raised him and Erin at that age. They must have been on heavy drugs from his daddy's job, or lots of babysitters through the years.

"So you're suspended for one week from school? What did you do to get that? So, you're grounded. How many months this time?" Peter ask. "You're worse than me when I was your age!" He laughs as his whole body shakes like jello. Peter really misses the teenage life with all his experiences. Oh, the good old days!

"Damn, Uncle Peter! What's with all these questions?! You sound like dad! I'm a teenager not a criminal!" Patrick roars with an annoyed look on his face as if to say, *You're embarrassing me right in front of Dr. Sheppard. Can you stop! She's not that bad looking for a doctor. Even though she talks to crazy people, and that includes my dad. He should've been put in a straight jacket a long time ago and locked in a rubber room for the rest of his life.*

"Patrick, watch your language! There's a lady in the house!" Peter states, as he gives his famous friendly smile to Elise, like he gives to all the ladies out there.

"Sorry… Dad has grounded me for three months. Can I go now? I have to take care of Colin for the one week that I'm out of school," Patrick states, as he tries to concentrate on finding Colin. "It's not a walk in the park…you know what I'm saying?"

"That's the whole summer, buddy!" shocked look of disbelief on his face, because Keith can go overboard when he disciplines his children. He's a total drill sergeant, and he doesn't have to be because they are really good kids. Peter has seen bad kids in his day, and the Heiden kids are angels compared to others out there. "Boy, Patrick, you really got your dad angry this time! Weren't you just grounded recently before this incident?"

"Yes, two months ago, and I know it's the whole summer. You don't have to remind me! Dad is not very happy with me right now. I'm positive that he's off medication when he punishes me," Patrick solemnly says. Then suddenly he has an idea and quickly says it before he forgets to ask. With a burst of energy Patrick pleads to his favorite uncle. "Uncle Peter, can you talk to Dad on my behalf? He really likes you and maybe he will reduce my sentence!" He gives Peter a friendly but sad smile which says, please help me!

Peter laughs, "Patrick, to be honest, it really depends if the full moon is out tonight not if your dad likes me or not. Anyway he sentenced you already! I can't help you once the punishment is handed out. It would be a totally different story if I was around before he pulled the lever of the electric chair, but I wasn't. I'm so sorry! It's very difficult to override his decision once it's set in stone. Sorry, buddy, I can't help this time…but have a great summer anyway!"

"Thanks for nothing, Uncle Peter!" Patrick replies with an annoyed tone in his voice. He thinks that sometimes Uncle Peter is not right in the noodle or maybe that's all the time.

Peter walks toward Patrick and smacks him on the back of his head to respond to the teenager's smart remark. "Hey, don't be that way!"

"Ouch, Uncle Peter, that hurt!" Patrick rubs his head. "Why did you hit me?"

"Because I can!" Peter laughs. "You're so lucky that I didn't kick you on your English, German, Irish, and Austrian, butt for acting like a spoiled brat!" Peter proclaims with a smile on his face. "Go ahead take care of your little brother before I decide to give you that kick on your seat where your brains are!" Peter then rubs his hand on the teenager's blond hair affectionately.

"I guess…" Patrick mumbles softly. "See you… It's very nice to meet you, Dr. Sheppard." He shoots a friendly smile at Elise.

"It's nice to meet you too. Take care of yourself and stay out of trouble," Elise claims, as she gives him a friendly smile. She tries not to stare into Patrick's sharp blue eyes, but can't resist.

"Thanks for caring. I really think trouble comes my way," Patrick announces, as he looks directly at Dr. Sheppard, engaging her with that smile that can melt ladies' hearts. "See you later."

Elise is thinking to herself, Patrick must be a handful when it comes down to dealing with the girls. His parents really have their work cut out for them keeping him in line.

Peter sees young Heiden walking around the house and calling Colin's name. He smiles as he looks at Patrick all grown up and becoming a young adult. It seems like only yesterday that he became an uncle for the newborn twins, Erin and Patrick.

"He's cute!" Elise states, as she tries to remember her nephews back in Connecticut. Lately she misses her family and doesn't really know when she'll be back to see them. Hopefully soon because they keep asking her to come home to visit, especially when the holidays roll around. Peter just gives his famous friendly smile as he responds.

"Yes, he's very adorable and deadly at the same time!" Peter laughs and shakes his head. "Dr. Sheppard, let's go in the kitchen and you can tell me all about it," he responds.

They walk towards the huge kitchen, and Elise makes sure she has a clear view of Keith, as she sits down. She watches Keith from afar as he reads today's newspaper while wearing his dark sunglasses.

"I need a drink," Elise exclaims, as she feels stressed out from the day.

Peter walks over to the refrigerator and slowly opens the door to see the food stacked neatly and labeled accordingly. "Man, my boy needs some friends! He has too much time on his hands! Who in their right mind writes labels on cheese? It's only cheese, not Queen Elizabeth's fine food?!" he states loudly as he shakes his head in disbelief. "He's one sick individual!"

Elise laughs releasing some of the tension of today's drama, and Peter amuses her too. He likes Elise's laugh. It has a very girlish sound. To hear laughter in this house is very rare. Only once in a blue moon. Justine will laugh at Peter when he tells a joke. Keith is a serious person and only laughs if the kids do something that catches his eye. You have a better chance of hitting the lottery than hearing laughter coming from Keith.

"Peter, I really need that drink!" Elise persistently exclaims, as she is ready to jump out of her skin.

"Oh, that drink! Okay, where do they store the sauce?" he asks loudly, as he opens different cabinets in the kitchen. "I'm not finding it… Let me ask Keith if he knows…be right back." Peter walks out to the backyard, as Elise continues to watch him read the newspaper. Keith has no idea Peter is standing right next to him.

"Hello, Peter, what do you want?" Keith asks, without blinking an eye or losing his spot. He's focused on reading about the rise in food costs.

"I didn't think that you saw me or heard me coming," Peter states, while he has a song in his head. He starts dancing in place.

"I'm a father and DEA agent! I see more than you think. What are you doing?" Keith asks without looking up at Peter. He can feel him making moves.

"I'm dancing to the song in my head. Where is your alcohol?" he asks as he dances on the side where Keith sits.

Elise's laughter echoes throughout the kitchen. At that moment Colin walks toward the sliding door. He begins to bang on it with his little hands, making crazy sounds at the same time. He tries to get anyone's attention to play with him while both men continue their conversation. Colin gets louder. "Uncle Peter! Play with me!" His little voice echoes thought out the kitchen through the other side of the sliding doors. Peter walks to the kitchen, and Keith starts on the crossword puzzle. He's not concerned with what his kids are doing. Does Keith know that Dr. Sheppard is in the kitchen or not? He tries to relax with Reese sleeping underneath the patio table to get some shade. Peter walks back into the kitchen and Colin suddenly runs away.

"You are too funny!" Elise states as she giggle. Peter flashes one of his famous friendly smiles to the doctor.

"I know, I try to keep my audience entertained," Peter replies. Colin runs around the house and stops in front of Peter, as Patrick continues to try and catch up with Speedy Gonzales in his flashing light sneakers.

"Uncle Peter, gummy bear?" Colin yells, as he puts his little hand above his head.

"Thank you, Colin, "Peter says with a friendly voice and takes about three gummy bears gently from his little buddy's hands. "Kicking good!" He smiles at the half-pint image of his best friend.

"You're welcome, Uncle Peter!" he shouts, then he runs away leaving Peter, Dr. Sheppard, and Patrick to their own devices.

"Patrick, can you and Colin go into another room? I need to speak with Dr. Sheppard alone." Peter requests, as he looks at Patrick, to get a quick response.

"Okay, Uncle Peter, whatever you say. Colin, where are you?" Patrick looks around for his little over-energetic brother. Seconds later Patrick finds Colin and says with a soft voice, "Let's go into the family room and play!" He takes his little brother's hand, and they walk together without any problems.

The family room is large enough for a full-size pool table, two couches, and a fifty-five-inch flat screen T.V. So there are a lot of things for the pre-k youngster to keep busy with for a couple of hours, hopefully until lunchtime.

Colin runs back to see his favorite uncle again and gives him a huge smile. "Bye, Uncle Peter! Play?" he screams and Patrick comes out of the family room to get the half pint so he can watch him closely in one spot.

"Yes, Colin. I'll play with you right after I finish talking to Dr. Sheppard. Okay, little buddy?" Peter asks with a huge smile. Peter has two nephews Steven and Shane, who are about Colin's age. He does seem closer to Colin than his real nephews, but he loves them the same way.

"Okay!" Less than a second later, Colin runs into the family room leaving Patrick in the dust.

"Thanks, Patrick." Peter walks in the direction of the liquor cabinet. A bottle of red wine is what the doctor ordered. He walks toward Elise with one hand holding a Waterford crystal wine glass and the other the bottle of fine wine.

"Okay, Elise, let's get started. Can you please tell me everything you did early this morning before we met?" he says, as he pours the red wine into the Irish crystal glass. She thinks to herself; *It's about time!*

"Well, I went to Star Bucks to get some coffee, and then I walked outside and I noticed that my sneaker was untied. I bent down to tie it, and suddenly I felt cold liquid in my hair and down my back. It was cold coffee! That made my morning!" she announced. Elise takes a drink of fine red wine. She really doesn't care where it came from, and all she knows is that she needs a real drink to calm her nerves.

"Please continue," Peter says while he takes a sip of his cold water.

"This guy was so fine! He had a British accent, and he looked like James Bond. He said sorry to me for bumping into me. He gave me a hundred dollar bill for my troubles. He was a good guy! Too bad I didn't get his number," Elise feels a little tipsy very quickly. *Oh no! I'm running out of wine in my glass! I really need some and fast! Peter looks cute right about now.* "Can I please have another?" she asks, as she holds up her empty glass like she's the Statue of Liberty.

"Okay, this is it, no more. Keith will have my head!" he states as he looks at Elise and takes a glimpse outside at Keith. He's still zoned out and not aware of the drama that's about to brew in the kitchen or he knows but doesn't want to look. Elise feels funny inside while she stares at the red wine being poured into the Irish crystal glass. Her head moves to follow the twirling liquor coming down like a funnel.

"Peter, I love you!" Elise smiles from ear to ear, not realizing that she's acting like a total fool without any one's help.

Peter has a look of concern on his face and asks, "Elise, did you eat today?" He sees that she's going down very fast, and that means she didn't eat anything yet. Peter shakes his head and thinks to himself, *She's one very messed up shrink! It's also kind of sexy in a way, laughs a little cute too.*

"No! Should I have eaten something?" Elise replies with a smile still on her face, and she starts to giggle like a schoolgirl.

"Great!" Peter quickly opens the refrigerator to see if there is any food available to settle her stomach. Elise starts to drink the red wine like it's a bottle of cold water. Peter looks at Elise and starts to laugh, "You're one crazy doctor!"

"That's why they give me the big bucks!" she states as she wraps her hands around the wine glass like it's hot cocoa in a mug. "I'm just having a bad morning! I need to just chill out," Elise sighs as she takes another sip of the beautiful red wine.

"Peter, I thought you were kidding about a drink!" Keith shouts, as he sees his therapist acting like a drunken sailor. He thinks to himself: *This person is the one helping me with my emotional and bad behavior issues? Please shoot me now!* Keith knows that Dr. Sheppard is almost at the bottom of her drink and he must disengage the situation quickly. He takes the Irish crystal wine glass away and pours the wine down the sink.

"Hey, that's mine! You...you...yo...u have no right to do that!" Elise stutters and burps without a second to spare.

"Oh...yeah!" Peter laughs. "Please, Elise, have another drink!" Keith gives an unpleasant look to the two morons in his kitchen.

"I can't believe she can't hold one drink in her system! This is how she acts?" Keith roars. He is both angry and annoyed, as he puts the bottle back on the high shelf.

"It was a second glass. She drank them down in less than five minutes," Peter whispers with a scared and very concerned look on his face. The only witness is Elise who's now very drunk and silly. So she doesn't help to save Peter's life from his best friend's wrath.

"What?" Keith shouts, as the sound echoes and pierce Elise's ears. "You're incredible! I can't leave you alone for a second in my house! It's like I'm dealing with Patrick all over again!"

"Ouch, that hurts! You're not nice!" she screams, as she tries to stop that person from yelling.

"Sorry, the doctor is having a very bad day, and she didn't eat yet," Peter says quickly before Keith explodes.

Keith yells directly at Peter, "What the hell are you doing? Do you know that you have an adolescent brain? You've gotten my therapist drunk, and she didn't eat yet! What were you thinking? Just great! You're making your Uncle Peter move to ask her out on a date at Chucky E. Cheese! Listen, Don Juan, I don't need my therapist in this condition!" He quickly walks over to make some food for Elise. A plain sandwich will help her stomach settle, especially if it's full of alcohol.

"Dr. Sheppard, I'm making you a fresh pot of coffee," Keith states, as he sees her in the state of being silly. He never understood why people would drink and laugh at nothing. His parents used to do the same thing. They drunk all they could and then laughed for hours over nothing. "I'm going to make you that coffee."

"No!" Elise shouts like Colin.

Keith becomes extremely angry and upset. He feels the tension building up throughout his body. Three minutes later a sandwich is made for Elise. She acts like a drunken fool from the streets of Hollywood Blvd. He walks over to Elise and he says, "Dr. Sheppard, please eat this sandwich. It will help your stomach. Try to eat slowly... I'm going to make you some coffee." Keith puts the sandwich close to Elise, as she continues to laugh. He is getting extremely annoyed. Suddenly Keith's hands start to shake rapidly, and he tries to hide his aggression. He takes three deep breaths and tries to calm himself down. Peter notices that his best friend is not doing well. He tries to block the situation and walks toward the doctor quickly.

"Elise, please eat your food. It will help you a lot, and you won't get sick," Pete requests, as he sits near her for comfort. He tries to put his body in front of Elise so Keith doesn't see more than he has.

She says with a smile and giggles, "You're very funny, Peter."

"You made her this way! It's your responsibility to sober her up! All I need is to see Justine walking into this! I'll be in Reese's dog-house and my tail in between my legs!" Keith yells, while his voice vibrates throughout the house. "You're on your own! I don't want any part of this! Where are my kids?"

"Relax, Keith, it will be fine! You don't have to worry. Uncle Peter is here to save the day," Peter announces, as he tries very hard not to get his partner more upset then he already is.

"That's what I'm worried about! My kids?" Keith states, a painful headache is crawling up to the surface.

"I'm sorry, your boys are playing in the family room," Peter replies, as he rubs his head to alleviate some tension.

Keith commands, "Peter, try not to forget to make coffee for the doctor!" He walks directly to the family room without looking back at the two clowns left in the kitchen.

Half an hour passes and Keith and his two boys are out to get some lunch. He needs to breathe some of that fresh air and spend alone time with his boys. Elise retraces her steps from that morning, and Agents Gallagher and Tierney come up empty handed! There were no drugs in Elise Sheppard's car, and she is free to go. The so-called drugs were really flour and herbs sprayed with "Seal Drug Spray" or "SDS." It's a spray with a very strong drug scent which drives the drug-sniffing dogs crazy.

"Agent Darling, when is Agent Heiden coming back?" Liam asks, as he looks at Peter flicking around a paper football. "Dr. Sheppard, we are sorry for any inconvenience that the DEA has put you through. You're in the clear, and you're not charged with anything. You can go home."

"Thank you, Agent Gallagher, right?" Elise asks, as she tries to remember the young agent's name, as the liquor in her system continues to wear off.

"He's coming back later tonight, and he wants everyone gone before Justine comes home," Peter answers.

That evening, Justine walks into the house later than usual. Everyone is sleeping including Reese who's laying on the kitchen floor underneath the kitchen table. As always the house is totally spotless. She feels overwhelmed for some reason or another; maybe it's the stress at work. It seems that she's not making her quota this month, and it's showing in her appearance. She just wants a big break so she can become a partner in the firm. She has been there since they opened up in the early nineties and she has made her mark in the business.

She takes the full "bottle of poison" from the top shelf. For some strange reason her hands start to shake rapidly. She tries to take a drink and without warning the bottle drops. It shatters all over the kitchen floor scaring Reese. Russian vodka travels quickly. What a mess! Justine walks slowly to the table and cries out loud for anyone to help her, but no one answers her call.

CHAPTER

NINETEEN

*I*t's May 20, Sunday morning at 5:00 a.m. Everyone is asleep at the Heiden house. A large package addressed to Mr. Keith Heiden leans against the front door. Erin wakes up at 8:26 a.m. and puts the box on her father's desk when she spots it outside.

Later that day, Keith and Justine finish up their food shopping; they begin to walk back towards their black SUV. Justine is pushing the cart as Colin sits in the front and babbles away. Keith's cell phone rings in the jean's left pocket. "Hello, Heiden." He looks directly at his family as they walk toward their black SUV. "Mr. Heiden, do you like games? I like games. Let's play one," said a British man with a very deep accent on the other side of the phone line. "Tic tock tic tock." He suddenly runs toward Justine and rushes to pick Colin up from the shopping cart seat without even thinking twice.

He runs toward his wife and takes a tight grip on her right arm. "Get away from the SUV!" he commands with a firm tone as if to say "now, not later!" Most of the time Justine doesn't take Keith seriously.

She suddenly tries to pull away from him. Justine wears the pants in the family and everyone knows it, especially Keith. "Stop, Keith. What the hell are you doing?" she demands an answer.

"Something terrible is going to happen, and I don't want to be here when it does! Come on, woman!" he shouts, as he tries desperately for her to go his way. She's a freakin' unstable pain in my ass mule! Justine acts more like a child than all of their kids put together.

"I'm not moving an inch until you tell me what's going on! Answer me, Keith! Stop being an ass," she screams.

He tries with all his might to pull Justine and Colin to safety. Suddenly a great explosion from the truck shoots fire into the sky. Metal, glass, and other parts of the vehicle rip away and others are thrown about twenty feet. It's a domino effect from the SUV's explosion which cause other vehicles to be destroyed too. People are screaming all around the parking lot. Some are dead and others are injured. The sounds of sirens start coming closer to the scene.

Keith snaps back to reality by a piercing scream from Colin. A very sharp pain shoots through his body as he continues to move toward his family to help them. Justine is crying, as she holds onto her right leg that has a piece of metal embedded in the back of it.

"Justine, look at me! I'm going to take the metal slowly out of your leg! You need to listen carefully! Try not to move your leg!" Keith commands. He slowly gets up to balance his body and leans against the Honda Accord that is behind him. His first thought is to see if the car has any first aid supplies. As his mind races he picks the lock of the car and breaks the car window.

As Justine continues to cry, Keith is vaguely aware of other people running aimlessly trying to get medical help. There are dead bodies strewn around on the pavement, and the visibility is very murky as smoke, flames, and potent gas rise into the air.

Minutes later Keith gets into the car and opens the trunk, searching for anything he can find. He's trained to shut down his feelings to save others. As a child, he also had to shut down his feelings. All his abusive injuries were cared for by a personal physician who was paid very well not to ask questions.

Justine lays helplessly holding her leg and crying from the extreme pain. Colin screams from the top of his little lungs. Keith holds a white sheet and uses all his might to rip up pieces and throw the others over his shoulder. Colin is crying aimlessly not knowing what just happened to him. Blood is coming out of his little ears. His eardrums burst from the loud noise of the explosion. Colin stands next to his mother, and Keith gives him a soft kiss to comfort him. "Don't worry. Daddy will take care of everything. You're so brave and I love you!" Keith says, even though Colin is unable to hear a thing.

"Justine, I have to administer to your injury! I'm not going to lie. It's going to hurt!" Keith shouts to her and tries to get his wife's full attention. Hopefully she won't pass out from the shock and loss of blood.

"Justine, you need to lean towards your left side so I can see what I'm up against!" Keith commands and helps guide her to the position. Try not to put any pressure on the injury. Keith leans toward her to get the body strength he needs and takes a deep breath, "Justine, please stay still. I'm going to take the metal out of your leg! Try to be strong! Are you ready?" The ripped white sheet around her leg should slow the blood flow.

With a look of distress on her face, Justine screams loudly, "Keith no more! No more, it hurts! Please stop!"

"Justine! Look at me!" he shouts loudly. "I just started. I have to do this! If I don't you will lose your leg!"

He takes a deep breath and looks at Justine. "I'm going to count to three. Ready!" he states and sees Colin still standing by his mother. His tiny face shows a lot of pain.

He looks directly into his wife's crystal blue eyes. "One…two…three," he says in a firm but soft voice. Keith pulls the metal out slowly not to damage the muscles or major arteries. His hands start to shake slightly but he just needs to control what he sees and complete the job. It's a very difficult situation. Justine screams from the top of her lungs and makes Keith's job even more stressful. He knows how to block out noises, but it's painful to see his family scared and hurt.

"Justine! You have to relax. Relax, please don't move! Please don't move, Justine! Don't move. I almost have it!" His hands have a steady lock on the sheet metal as the blood continues to come out. Keith is unable to see anything. Any sudden movement Justine makes can kill her.

"Try not to move your leg. Don't move! Do you understand?" he shouts louder to let Justine know it is very serious. He feels the metal slowly coming out and begins to feel the pain from his injuries. He looks at what's left of his truck and tries to take control of the situation. It's not easy for him. He has a lot of questions about what went down today.

CHAPTER
TWENTY

The fire trucks from different cities of the Los Angeles area came very quickly along with the LAPD. Seven ambulances arrived at the scene within ten minutes of each other. The Heiden family was taken to the Cedars-Sinai Medical Center. Four hours later, Justine is release from the hospital with pain medication prescriptions and twenty stitches on her back right leg. She's tough and walks with crutches as she gets into her parent's car. Keith and Colin will have to stay overnight for observation. Keith has three broken ribs, bruises throughout his body, and his scars need attention, but father and son are doing all right.

Three hours later, Peter has been making calls to smooth everything over. KCALA news stated that a car bomb could have been a terrorist plot. As Dr. Sheppard walks into the hospital she sees Agent Pete Darling standing in the waiting room. "Agent Darling, you're not allowed to use a cell phone in the hospital," Elise orders with a smile.

Elise wears an expensive business suit that is imported from Italy. "Hey, beautiful." Peter's eyes are glowing as he sees the doctor.

"Did you hear anything new?" Elise asks.

"Keith wants to be alone in the room until they release him from the hospital. He might be going home by tomorrow. Colin's hearing is back to normal, and he was discharged early his morning," Peter answers, as he continues to hold onto Elise. "Do you want to go to Chucky E. Cheese?"

"Sure, why not! I have a couple of hours to kill before I see my client at 4:00 p.m.," she states with a big smile on her face. They both walk out the hospital holding hands.

Wednesday afternoon is crazy for Justine while she tries to get everything ready for Keith to come home. She hops by with crutches on one side of her to balance herself. At the same time she spots a pile of paper on the table. "Whose papers are these on the kitchen table? I want them cleared up and off my table today and not tomorrow!" Justine shouts.

"Justine, Colin seems okay," exclaims William Cooper Anderson with a deep British accent. Justine's father was born and raised in London England. "He's saying Teenage Mutant Ninja Turtles and is running everywhere in the house." He smiles, as he remembers his kids being crazy like that, and he's very happy. William loves to capture that moment with his grandkids.

"Yes, he runs around like nothing happened. Keith is coming home tomorrow if the doctor gives him a clean bill of health." She smiles and feels the love that was lost for over a year. Hopefully the feeling will stand for a while.

"I think I can wait for him to come home," he says with the same tone he always has when talking about his loser son-in-law.

William Cooper Anderson never really liked Keith since the first day they met. Justine had pleaded with her father that she would do anything if Keith Heiden could live with them just until he got on his feet. She stated that he didn't have a place to live after being disowned by his family just three days before his graduation. Till this day, William doesn't really know what happened to Keith. Why did he get kicked out of his home? How did he receive scars on his hands and left ear? William made a promise to his wife Gertrude not to ask questions on this very touchy subject. She said, "If Keith wants to tell us about what happened then he will on his own terms. We're doing this for our Justine. She's a great daughter and we can give this wish to her to help this poor lad in his time of need." Deep down inside William's gut, he wished he had never made that promise. Of all the luck Justine is now married to Keith, and she'll never tell her father the real story about Keith's life. William doesn't really care about Keith; he just wants him out of his daughter's life. There is something about Keith that William doesn't like, but he can't put his finger on it. He wishes that Justine had married one of the champs that came from England or Scotland that he knew from business or friendship William still hopes that Justine will divorce Keith but it's highly unlikely. Hopefully some wishes can come true.

"I know that you don't like him, Dad! You tell me every minute when you see me. Be nice for the kids' sake. They don't want to hear that their grandfather says bad things about their father," Justine replies, as she tries to collect all the papers from the kitchen table.

"Well dear, he's the elephant man! I don't like how he treats the kids. He's too strict and verbally abusive towards them. You should really think about how Keith raises the children when you're not at home. He's a scary man. He should be in a straight jacket for the rest of his life!" William shouts, and he doesn't care who hears the conversation. He loves his little girl so much. "I love you, Justine, and I don't want you hurt in any shape or form. Whenever you finally decide to leave him, your mother and I will help you make your transaction complete. You can live with us, or I can get you a home anywhere in Europe. Just say the word. I'll take care of all the loose ends," William announces, as he tries so hard to give his sweet Justine anything she wants. William walks closer to Justine, "Look, my darling, I'm just looking out for your best interest. I love you, and I don't want you to get hurt. You have to believe it when I say this. I don't want you around Keith because he's dangerous!"

Justine stops collecting the papers on the kitchen table and looks directly into her father's crystal blue eyes. "Justine, you should have taken the check the first time and left him before you married him."

Justine remembered the conversation that she had with her father. He tried to convince her to leave her soon-to-be husband. It was two hours before she was going to walk down to the alter from the top of the hill in Hawaii overlooking the ocean. She stated that day, "Dad, I'm having his children, and I can't leave him! Where would I go? How would I live with twins on the way?" she claimed with tears forming in her eyes. Justine shakes her head to get back to the present time.

"I made the check out to you! You're set for life without that abused loser of a husband of yours. Your mother and I will help you raise the children. Now the offer still stands and I'll make it worth-while. I'll give you everything so you can leave the bloody bastard!" William announces.

"Grandpa, what are you talking about?" Patrick shouts, as he stands in the kitchen. He has a confused look on his face. "I can't believe what I'm hearing!" *My mother and grandfather are planning to destroy her marriage! They don't even care what we feel about this situation. I know that my mother is deadly when her path is crossed, but this is the extreme. It's not a secret that my grandfather doesn't like my dad. When they're in the same room, they exchange dirty looks to take each other down without touching. It's pretty funny but scary at the same time. Grandfather loves to talk to anyone. That's his own business to spread his charm to make the big bucks. He's loaded and he always had a few hundred in his very expensive wallet. I always love it when I get gifts from him. He outdoes my dad any day.*

"Patrick, it's nothing. Please let it go," Justine orders her oldest son.

"It must be something! Grandfather, you're giving Mom a bribe to leave my dad?" Patrick snaps back.

"It's not how it sounds," Justine snaps back to stop her son from knowing any more than he knows.

"Please, Mom, don't patronize me! I know what I heard and what I see! I know that I'm not book smart like Erin, but I have my intuition. This smells like bad cheese. Grandfather, I love you and always will, but if you're badmouthing my father, then you're doing the same to me. It hurts my heart. So try to think about that the next time you say something bad about my dad," demands Patrick as he looks adamantly at his mother and grandfather.

"I'm sorry, Patrick, I didn't know that you had such strong feelings about your dad. I'll think twice about what I'm going to say, but it's not going to be easy," William states with a smile on his face. "You see, son, your father doesn't like me and I don't like him."

Justine walks over to her son and grabs onto his arm tightly, "Please don't tell your father!"

"I don't think it's your call! Let me go!" Patrick exclaims, as he pulls his arm away from his mom. He knows that his mother can be very controlling to get what she wants, and it doesn't really matter who she steps on to the top. Patrick looks at his mother as if to say "try me!" Justine and her father know he means business!

"Hello, Justine... Your honey is home!" Peter shouts. His voice echoes through the first floor of the huge house. "Keith, do you want the team to be here for security? Your SUV is going to be a bitch to fix, but I can get a great deal on tires." He smiles and laughs at the same time, as he tries to lighten up the stress for his injured friend.

Keith just looks at Peter in a strange way to his goofy partner in crime. "Yes, I also need to see the evidence on those pictures, and later we have to talk, right?" Keith asks, making a face from the pain that shoots throughout his aching body. "I'll tell Justine about the pictures and extra security."

Peter looks surprised as he replies, "The pictures? I didn't get an update as of yet, but I'll get the answer soon... I hope. There are other situations that need to be addressed. There were twelve deaths and six cars were damaged during the car bombing. Please don't worry; I'm taking care of everything. The press wants to know about you being at the scene of the car bomb. They want to know if this is a terrorist attack toward Americans. The FBI and Home Land Security is going to investigate this matter. You're an agent that is always on call 24/7 so you get a new SUV with all the trimmings."

"To be honest I need a painkiller right now," Keith states. Then he walks slowly toward the kitchen. "Just get everything fixed with no roadblocks. Just get it done." He looks straight into Peter's eyes. "Can you stay here for a couple of days until Justine and I can put a handle on things at home?" Keith takes a long deep breath and then he says, "Can I get reimbursed for the groceries. It was about $349. I have the receipt in my wallet. Do you want it to confirm my loss?"

Peter answers with a surprised look on his face that Keith would ask a question like that. "I'm sure you can get reimbursed, but I'll find out about that. Just give me your receipt." He starts to laugh from out of the blue. "Sure, I will stay here as long as you want."

Keith shakes his head in frustration as he gives the receipt to Peter. "Peter, why do I have to pull teeth just have a normal adult conversation with you? Thanks if you can get me the money for food."

Keith is extremely stressed. It's getting way too personal. He has to think ten times faster in order for him and his family to live another day. He's afraid that Justine will talk him into taking an early retirement from the DEA. Keith knows that's not an option; he loves his job too much and it's part of him. He lives and breathes, "DEA", even though he had a heavy set back ten years ago. He's not willing to throw in the towel yet. However, with the safety of his family in danger, he might have to give up being a government special agent and be a full time stay-at-home dad. He stands his ground and puts up a good fight to make his point to his wife. He needs to be in the job that he loves, but it's not going to be easy. It's going to be a very, long, hot, dry summer at the Heiden's house because of the arguments that will occur between Keith and Justine and not just because of the weather.

Peter laughs at Keith's reaction. "Don't worry, Keith, I'll stay here until you guys are settled back into your daily routine."

Both agents walk into the kitchen and see Justine making a salad for the company that is here already. There will be more to come as well. "Hi, Justine, you're making a big salad. Are you planning for a lot of company?" Keith gives her a kiss on her soft cheek. He feels very blessed that she is alive.

"No, just a few people, my parents, sisters, brothers, nephews, nieces, and their spouses just a few people coming. You know the normal crowd. We need all the family in this house because you're home and we are all alive," Justine states with a smile on her face. She's very happy that her husband is alive and saved her and Colin. She walks very carefully because of her injury, as she gets dinner ready. Justine is not used to the kitchen area as she tries to find things. It's really Keith's territory, not hers.

"Just a few people." He smiles. You can always count on Justine to get family members over. It's a good thing they live in a huge house that can hold many guests. Justine gets into Keith's heart and this is one of those moments.

"Do you need help? What are we having for dinner?" Keith asks, as she struggles to find things in the kitchen. She's not a very good cook, but she's great at cleaning, especially when she has to pick up after their three lazy boys.

"I'm ordering seven different pizzas from Roma's Pizza Restaurant in town. Also, Keith, you have a message on the phone. We didn't erase it. I think you should answer it since it could be important," suggests Justine, as she mixes the ingredients into the salad.

Keith picks up the phone to listen to the messages. "Hello, this message is for Mr. Keith Heiden. My name is Summer Morgan. I'm one of the funeral directors from Longwood Funeral Home. I'm sorry to say, but your father, Mr. Conrad Van Heiden, died yesterday of a heart attack. Your mother wanted me to call you with this important information. There are two wakes. One being held on Thursday from 7:00 p.m. to 9:00 p.m. and one tomorrow at 12:00 p.m. to 3:00 p.m. The funeral mass will be from 12:00 p.m. to 1:00 p.m. as well as the burial at 3:00 p.m. on Friday. It will be held at St. Gabrielle Roman Catholic Church and the cemetery in San Bernardino. I hope you can make it. We send condolences from the Longwood Funeral Home. If you have any questions please call 305-555-7297 for additional information. Thank you."

Keith writes down all the information that he needs on some note paper that is next to the phone. He vaguely sees all of Justine's family members come through the kitchen and others parts of the house. William (Justine's father) carries seven pizzas into the dinner room. The table is set in sections, different sodas, plastic dinner plates, utensils, and napkins. He sees his kids coming into the kitchen and greeting the other family members. There are hugs and kisses and smiles all around. Everyone is talking away or moving to different parts of the house, but no sounds are coming into Keith's ears. He only hears his broken heart fall to a deep dark place. His blue eyes try to focus on what's in front of him. "Justine!" He shouts to override everyone's conversations. She turns her head and sees her husband go into shock.

"Keith, what's wrong. Are you hurt? Please tell me! You're scaring me! Keith!" Justine yells in dismay. Suddenly he falls to the kitchen floor. "Someone call Dr. Clark! He's in the phonebook! Everyone is around Keith, and Justine tries to help in any way. She starts crying for help, and then she sits with him on the kitchen floor just holding him tightly. "Keith, please! Don't go into shock now. We need you! Can someone call Dr. Richard Clark now!" she screams with all her might.

CHAPTER
TWENTY-ONE

*T*wenty minutes later the other family members helped Keith into the bedroom. Justine changes Keith into comfortable clothes and lays him on the bed. As he stares into space not saying a word, there is a knock on the bedroom door.

"Come in," whispers Justine, as she puts a soft blue blanket over Keith. She is blinking very hard to keep her tears from overflowing down her cheeks.

"Hi, Justine, Dr. Clark is on his way to check up on Keith. The phone message was about his father. I called the funeral director back. She said he died yesterday of a sudden heart attack," Peter claims, as he sees his best friend not responding to anything around him. He seems to be in a state of shock and in his safe zone. Often an abused person will go through this to avoid any pain. Keith is resting now Justine briskly walks outside, and she closes the master bedroom door very slowly without causing any more noise.

"Thanks for the information. Dr. Clark will look after Keith's needs. I remember one time long ago when he went into this state of shock. I think it was the Jose Medina case. It was not easy to bring him out of it. I don't know what to do at this point," Justine cries, as Peter gives her a hug to console her.

As Peter pulls slowly away from Justine he notices that all her crying didn't help her makeup. It's not a pretty sight from where he's standing. She looks like Rocky Raccoon! But in a soothing voice he says, "Justine, you have to be strong for the family. If not then I have to take over, and that wouldn't be pretty. I'll help the family because

Keith picked me as legal guardian. I don't know why! Maybe he was on heavy medication at the time!" Peter states then laughs while he looks at Justine. She laughs a little and starts to cry again. "Let's go downstairs, and we all can take turns looking after him from time to time." Peter says calmly. He wants Justine to know that everything will be all right.

"Okay," she cries, as she walks downstairs and sees the look of concern from all her family members.

"Justine, everyone is starting to eat. Do you think you can eat something?" William states, as he guides his daughter to the kitchen.

Everyone gets a chance to console Justine. It was Keith's dad who had just passed on, but no one seems to care at this point. Some of her family members are afraid of Keith because his behavior is not normal. They don't understand Keith's situation, or maybe they don't want to hear it. Her side of the family just plays along with Keith's needs and tries to be a part of things for Justine's sake. In the family eyes, it doesn't mean anything to them. They always felt that Justine could do much better.

Justine walks to the bedroom door and opens it to see Dr. Clark taking Keith's pulse. He's still in a state of shock, just staring and blinking rapidly. "Hello, Dr. Clark, how is he?" she asks with two slices of plain pizza on a plastic plate for Keith. Justine tries to help her husband eat his dinner. Keith slowly chews the pizza without saying a word.

Dr. Richard is forty-seven. He stands at 6'2" with light brown hair sprinkled with gray, which brings out his dark gray eyes. He now lives in Beverly Hills with his second wife Sarah who is in her mid-twenties. He has two great boys, Taylor 13, and Travis 15, from his first marriage, and he works in the family business. Now he has his own practice in Brentwood. He knows the Heiden family very well since Erin and Patrick were born. Dr. Clark made a promise many years back that he would be Keith's personal physician. He only comes to Mr. Heiden's aid and he's aware of Keith's abused childhood. It did set Richard back when he first saw Keith's abused body lots of scars and old bruised that never healed. At first, he was afraid to examine his patient for fear it would hurt him, but it's now a routine. He does feel sad to see Keith that way, but he's a doctor first and friend second.

Justine thinks to herself *it's too bad that Richard is taken.* Then she gives him a weak smile showing her concern without anything else clouding her mind.

"Hello, Justine, he's fine. His blood pressure is normal, but it's his state of mind I'm worried about. I think you should call Dr. Sheppard. Maybe she can snap him out of this," suggests Dr. Clark.

"Dr. Clark, I'm not going to call Dr. Sheppard! I can handle this problem by myself! This is not the first time that Keith was in shock. It's going to take some time for him to come around, but we'll be patient and wait," Justine snaps back.

"Justine, please forgive me... I'm just a little concerned that's all. I've know you guys before the twins were born, and I really hope that we're friends. Don't get me wrong; I like being your personal physician... Well, you know... I care," he sighs, as he collects his thoughts. "Please accept my apology, and I hope that you didn't think something else. That's not my intentions," Dr. Clark pleads his case, as he knows very well not to cross Mrs. Heiden if you want to live.

"That's okay, Dr. Clark. I know that you're worried, and I don't mean to snap at you. I can handle the situation, and I don't need Dr. Sheppard to make matters worse. I hope you'll understand."

Peter talks to Agent Gallagher and Tierney about what's going on with Agent Heiden and his situation. Peter wants everything to run smoothly. He gives a direct order to the agents to guard the Heiden family. Peter and Keith are total opposites. One loves to watch TV and is not a big reader, and other one doesn't watch TV and loves to read every book that is published. What a very strange world we live in! Who can understand why they are best of friends?

CHAPTER
TWENTY-TWO

The time is now 7:00 a.m. Friday, May 25, and a large envelope with Keith's name and home address was put on his nightstand. Keith gets up slowly still feeling the pain in his ribs. The key is to the take it very slowly when moving in any different direction. He takes his pajamas off carefully without making a sound. He doesn't know what to do or how to feel with the news that his father has died.

Keith turns on the warm water in his luxury shower. He starts to clean himself with soap throughout his body and shampooing his hair. He tried to relax his body. As the warm shower covers him the pains of his past come to the surface about his childhood and father. Suddenly Keith starts to cry in the shower; he finally realizes that his father is dead Even though he never had a normal father-and-son relationship it's very hard to explain the overwhelming feeling of grief. The tears pour down his face and his blue eyes become red and unable to see what's in front of him. He can deal with a lot in his life but lost of something that he can't get back; it's difficult. He never lost a family member before. The thoughts run through his mind. How can he feel this way about a man that gave him heartaches throughout his life? Why is he crying? Somehow he feel as if Justine is now the image of his father; it's very scary to deal with her behavior and save the kids in the long run. Keith realizes that he's trap in his nightmare, and he feels that the air he breathes is closing.

A few minutes later Keith collects himself. He slowly dries his body and tries not to put any pressure on his ribs. He thinks that he bruised them because of the explosion. He gets dressed in a short sleeve light blue shirt that Justine had bought him and tan shorts. We can't forget his comfortable sandals and other items that she bought as well. He never really buys his own clothes. He thinks it's too much of a headache. He decides to change into his dark suit after breakfast, if he can eat anything at all. Keith walks toward his nightstand, and he puts his wedding band on his left index finger. Then without a minute to spare he puts on the latex gloves that were in his drawer. Keith opens the envelope and sees different pictures of Justine and Treat having sex in a hotel. His blue eyes become wide open. Keith flips each picture and it becomes hard for him to chew to continue looking. Suddenly Keith drops the pictures on the floor and runs into the master bathroom throwing up into the toilet. Five minutes go by, and Keith is besides himself as he tries to clean himself off. It's an emotional roller coaster for him. He must compose himself as it is the morning they are burying his monster father. Keith doesn't understand why Justine went to the extreme. Is it because of what he did ten years ago? He knows that she is a stranger in the bed such as between the fight and other drama that comes to play; it's not a moment to play Kenny G. songs.

He puts all the pictures back in the envelope, seals it, and replaces it on his nightstand. The pictures make his stomach turn. He doesn't have time to burn them. He runs into the bathroom and throws up again. Twenty minutes later Keith collects himself even though he wants to find Treat and bust his head into a clement wall. He just wants to give him a little headache, that's all. When Justine finds out, the drama will start with lots of fireworks and it's not even the Fourth of July.

CHAPTER
TWENTY-THREE

A half hour later, Keith takes a peek at his kids sleeping peacefully. He walks slowly not realizing that Agent Gallagher holds a blood pressure machine and another piece of equipment this hand at the bottom of the stairs. Keith is now aware of the fact that Justine didn't sleep next to him last night, and he begins to wonder to himself where she is.

Agent Liam Gallagher gives an aghast look at Keith. He didn't know that anyone is up so early from last night catastrophic. "Oh, good morning, sir, from all the agents we are so very sorry for your loss. Agent Darling has something to tell you. He's in the kitchen," he states out, trying to hold the equipment in his hands and getting very intense from his boss. He gets a very cold chill down his back. "Yes, if there's anything else that I can do for you? Please just ask."

"Thank you but no," Keith answers with a very soft voice and his blues eyes overflowing with tears. As he looks at Agent Liam Gallagher, a strong, young man, he remembers that he was that way in his prime.

"I'll be outside if you need me for anything. There are five other agents beside me that have secured the area," states Agent Gallagher.

"Thank you, Agent Gallagher. I'll keep you posted if I need anything," Keith says, closing the front door behind him. This agent is doing well in the department; he has a bright future ahead of him. Keith takes a deep breath to focus in store for him today.

"Keith, are the kids asleep?" Peter asks, looking at his confused buddy, as he walks around with an apron on decorated with apples and pears.

"Yes, I like them that way until 9:00 a.m., but with my luck Colin will scream to be picked up to go to the bathroom. Then the others will start to get up one by one," Keith announces feeling very helpless today. Seeing that the coffee pot is not done brewing, he waits for it to finish before asking about Justine.

"So how long did I sleep last night, and what's going on?" Keith asks in a weak voice, as he looks at Peter.

"You slept for a long time. I guess Dr. Clark had given you good drugs. I think you want to sit down for what I'm about to tell you," says Peter. "Can you please sit down. This is a very serious matter."

Keith dismisses Peter's request, as he walks by him. He opens to the refrigerator to get items to make breakfast and he says, "I really can't sit. Peter, the kids are getting up soon, and I have to make breakfast. You going to eat with us?" he asks, as he juggles a box of pancake mix and fruit containers.

Peter looks at his zoned out partner in crime, and he thinks to himself that Keith's father must have really messed up his life. "Thanks for including me in the family breakfast."

"What?" Keith asks with a sharp quick response. Peter realizes that Colin always says that word, and he got that from his dad.

Peter takes a deep breath and begins to speak. "Seriously, Keith, you really need to sit down, because what I'm about to say is not good."

"Peter, I'm not into playing games so just tell me," Keith says without looking at his damaged partner.

"I found Justine passed out on the couch in the family room. Does she lay on the couch often?" he asks, as he takes off the out-dated apron before it kills his sexy image that he's proud of and perfected over his adult years.

"Good, you found her! Sometimes Justine will go to the family room to distress herself after a busy workday, and when she's not ready to deal with the family right away. But for the most part it will

143

be me stressing her out!" Keith answers with a sigh of relief in his voice.

"At times she lies down on the couch and has a glass of white wine. She covers herself with a cashmere blanket and watches TV. Once in awhile she'll fall asleep till the morning leaving the T.V. on all night."

"Why are you asking? Is she still sleeping in the family room? I really need to talk to her," Keith states, without skipping a beat on making the breakfast. He is cutting up assorted fruit and washing the strawberries, trying to save them at the same time before entering Peter's mouth. He can't forget the golden delicious apples from California, the blueberries, and the bananas as well.

"Here's the thing, Justine passed out on the couch with an empty bottle of Russian vodka besides her. Agent Gallagher, Tierney, brought her to the hospital to get her stomach pumped. Then she was brought to hospital then to Western Rehab Center for the additional care that she really needs. I have the number if you want to speak to her." Peter announces, as he sees Keith's facial expression become very confused and concerned. Peter has a thought. Maybe it wasn't the greatest idea to tell him at this moment in time.

Suddenly, Keith stops preparing breakfast as he tries to keep his mixed feelings about Justine to himself. Not to lose it in front of Peter, Keith asks in a clear voice, "You're telling me that Justine drank the whole bottle of Russian vodka? Where were you in all of this?" At this moment an extremely sharp pain comes down Keith's whole body. He just can't take any more drama!

"Yes, Justine drank Russian vodka last night. I was at home, but the three agents beside Liam and Sean were taking good care of her, and they made sure that everything is fully secure. Believe me everything is fine now," Peter answers and picks up a small bowl of strawberries that was just washed. "Mmm good."

Keith is shocked and full of disbelief at Peter's answers. "Peter, why didn't you stay here overnight? I have two extra guest bedrooms for you anytime! You are always welcome, especially if you need to crash from your many girlfriends that kick you out of their apartments. I thought we a family?" he says. "I really need you especially today. Now Justine is sick and I have to explain to the kids why mommy is not home…and finding more pictures, that is a different story. I'll tell you later… and it's not going to be a good day."

"Keith, we are family! Sometimes I like to go back to my place and hang! Do you want me to explain to the kids about their mom?" Peter states, as he licks his fingers that are covered in strawberries. "Sometimes you act like a spoiled child! Everyone has to listen and care to your every need!"

"Thanks for the offer, but I think I need to talk to the kids alone… I'm a spoiled child always get what I want? That's really funny!" Keith announces with a smirk on his face. "After what's gone on today and what I've gone through in my childhood, I'm spoiled rotten! Well, I'm trying very hard to protect my past, my family, and what I hear and see on the job." Keith looks up at Peter as if to say, "Peter, what the hell are you doing?" He looks in the refrigerator and tries to find more fruit to replace what has just been devoured. "Peter, please don't eat any more food until the kids come down to have their breakfast!!"

"I shouldn't have eaten all the strawberries, and I'm sorry for what I just said, but sometimes you do act obnoxious! Then every-body has to bow down to your behavior," Peter says, as he washes the white dish under the sink.

"No, that's how you think of me! I get it…my family, and I are a burden to you! Your single life has been interrupted; so you're blam-ing us, I'm so sorry that we are a burden! I don't want you to miss out on your social life!" he shouts as his body becomes weak in the knees. Keith starts to whimper. He puts his head down says to himself; this kitchen floor needs a good cleaning!

In a concerned voice Peter asks, "Are you okay?" He suddenly sees Keith about to break down. Within a split second his friend can turn his emotions from nice guy to dismal, temperamental, and aggressive. It was very scary for Peter to witness. He remembered back to when they first met, and Keith acted this way because of his abusive past.

"I'm fine," he responds, as he picks up his head. "I just got recent pictures of Justine and her new lover, Treat Miller. Let me tell you that they weren't pretty... I feel sick to my stomach! Why aren't these pancakes cooking?" Keith states with a confused look on his face.

Peter walks over to the stove and says, "You didn't have the flame on under the pan. I'm very sorry to hear the news about Justine but I'm not surprised." Keith shakes his head in disbelief and replies in a soft voice, "I know it was going to come to this. Thanks."

"Maybe it's a good thing that I'm staying over for a while... If you're unable to cook, there's something very wrong with you!" Peter announces as he tries very hard not to laugh. "I almost forgot to give you the number to the rehabilitation center so you can talk to Justine... When you are ready, of course. You need some sugar! Out of nowhere, Peter gives Keith a bear hug. "Peter!"

"Thanks," Keith answers, as he pulls away quickly before he is attacked again with his so-called male bonding. Peter gives a friendly smile for extra support as if to say that I'm here for you if you need me. I'll put all my personal events on hold just for you and only you, because I love you!

CHAPTER
TWENTY-FOUR

wenty minutes later all the kids come down to join Peter and Keith for breakfast. Keith keeps to himself and Peter tries to relax. Erin helps Colin with his food, and they exchange smiles from time to time. There are a few words spoken between Patrick and Mitch.

The time is now 12:00 p.m. and both Keith and Colin go upstairs to take their naps, while Patrick and Mitch play pool in the family room before heading to the funeral. Peter goes for a swim in the pool and tries to unwine as he prepares for the events ahead.

A woman in her mid-thirties enters the Heiden house without anyone noticing. She softly closes the front door behind her and quickly walks to the living room area. She hears the sound of dishes being washed in the kitchen as her hazel eyes look around and see a lot of children's toys scattered all over. Two ipads and a laptop computer are on the table with the internet still on. There is school work all around the floor as well as a plate of some leftover food. The young lady walks over to the fireplace mantle and looks at the pictures of the Heiden family. There is one picture that especially catches her eye. It's is a wedding picture of Keith and Justine standing close to each other. She was holding a Hawaiian boutonniere and wearing a White Orchid lei around her neck. Keith was wearing a Maile-style Ti Leaf and Orchid lei around his neck. They looked very young and happy. In one picture Patrick is hugging Erin. It looks like they were about seven or eight. There's another photo with all the family members and their dog. Mitch looks like he is nine or ten and he is posted in his hockey uniform. Last but not least, Colin smiles at the camera. Family pictures bring a lot of character to a home and show how with much love. Suddenly a smile forms on her face because what she sees is touching to the heart… It's called family.

As she walks into the kitchen, she recognizes the young woman by the sink. A teenager wearing a purple jumpsuit jacket and designer jean shorts with white sneakers is washing the dishes. The young lady looks up, and her behavior immediately changes as she looks with surprise at the woman in front of her.

"What are you doing here, Dr. Sheppard? How did you get into the house? I didn't hear a knock or the doorbell ring?" Erin asks with a look of disbelief on her face. She says to herself: *This lady has some nerve inviting herself into my home. It's like she's part of the family or something! Who the hell does think she is! She's really a piece of work by far! I don't think that dad would have a therapy session today with his estranged father being buried. If he's having a therapy session, I didn't hear about it. Sometimes I'm the last one to know anything in this family. Reese knows more than I do.*

Suddenly, Erin's cell phone rings. She quickly takes out the phone to see who's calling and realizes it's Christopher. Erin and Christopher have been together for over six months now. His name is Christopher Masterson and he comes from a very wealthy family. His grandfather and father have a family business together. They own many exclusive golf clubs all over California and Florida. Erin's mom had met him and thinks that he's a very charming and good-looking young man. Christopher said to Erin that he's totally afraid to meet her father. One day he overheard Mr. Heiden yelling at Patrick. His angry voice traveled through the phone line and almost pierced Christopher's right eardrum. Someday he'll meet Mr. Heiden when he's tough enough to take on a death challenge.

Erin decides to put the call to voicemail, and she'll call him back later when she gets some privacy. "Hello, you must be Erin? The front door was unlocked and I walked in," Dr. Sheppard answers with a calm voice. She tries to show that she's not a dangerous therapist. Elise has a strong feeling that she came here for a personal matter. It's very scary that this young lady looks just like Mrs. Bitchy

Heiden. She does see that Erin, Patrick, and Colin have family similarities since they're related, but not Mitch because he was adopted.

Erin decides to stop cleaning the dishes and wants to say what's on her mind without interruptions or distractions. "You should have knocked, Dr. Sheppard. This is not a good time to see my father! As you know we had a death in the family." *It's sad that I didn't know my grandfather or my dad's family. I heard stories from Mom but not from the horse's mouth. I guess he's totally ashamed of the whole situation. Dad looks sad when my mom's family comes by for a visit, especially on holidays or events.* "Sorry, but he's not able to talk...especially to you! So why don't you go away and never come back ever again!"

"I'm sorry about your loss, Erin. I'm here to help your father. I'm not the enemy. I just want to help in any way I can," Elise pleads, but she's not surprised at Erin's behavior and feels very strongly in her feeling to protect the family. This is the same kind of behavior that Mrs. Heiden (the over control freak) would do if they had met again. I guess the apples don't far fall from the tree!

"You don't help. You only make matters worse, not better!" Erin screams, as she stops to dry a dinner plate. "Just admit it, Dr. Sheppard, that you have a major thing for my father!" *It's truly sick that this so-called doctor is fixated with my dad.*

"Erin, I'm sorry, but I don't know what you're talking about!" Elise says, as she tries to cover her traces quickly. "Please, Erin, in this situation it's very important for me to speak to your dad. In his state of mind, he really needs my help. I have had experience with many people in the same circumstances like your dad. He can go either way. He may go into total shock or become highly aggressive," Dr. Sheppard pleads, as she tries to make a very serious matter run smoothly. "So please, Erin, let me help!"

"Whatever! I really don't want to hear this therapy shit from you! Dr. Sheppard, you're the reason why my family is in disarray!" Erin cries, as she tries to give the doctor a clue to go away.

"Erin, please explain to me why you have negative feelings toward me? This is our first time meeting and you don't like me?" Elise asks with a soft professional voice. She won't admit that she has a thing for Mr. Heiden. Although he's a very confused individual, there is something that's pulling her toward him. "What did I do to upset you?"

"I don't know, Dr. Sheppard. Maybe your evilness travels with a broom and goes to different families. Then you destroy their lives! You're a piece of work!" Erin shouts, as she's ready to explode. She wipes her hands on a paper towel and suddenly out of the blue and without a second thought, Erin picks up a clean expensive dinner plate and throws it directly at Dr. Sheppard.

Elise quickly moves out of the way. The plate misses her and shatters against the kitchen wall behind her leaving a nice dent. Keith quickly walks into the kitchen and sees what has just happened.

"Erin Kaitlyn Heiden!" he shouts in such a way that both Dr. Sheppard, and Erin jump out of their skins. Then suddenly Erin automatically puts are head down because the lion king has just roared. Keith walks into the kitchen with a shocked look on his face. He wears a short shelved light blue shirt, light grey color khaki shorts and black sandals. His arms and legs show a few scars.

Keith looks very concerned as he sees his beautiful daughter and the doctor in conflict. He asks in a strong but calm voice, "Dr. Sheppard, are you okay? Please tell me if you're hurt. I have a first aid kit in the bathroom," he says. Keith knows what to do in any emergency situation. He turns his head a little and focuses his blue eyes on the broken plate that shattered into pieces. He'll be blamed for this, not his daughter. *Justine is going to have my head on a silver platter when she sees this dent in the wall.* "Dr. Sheppard, please tell me if you need anything!"

"Mr. Heiden, thank you for your help but it's not a big deal. The plate missed me by an inch or more. So you really don't have to worry. I'm fine. Thanks again," Dr. Sheppard answers quickly and calmly. She tries to avoid having the teenage girl get into more trouble than she's already in. He sees what's in front of him and has a very strong bad taste in his mouth. Keith is ready to attack any minute now. *Deep down I know that all women are crazy in their pretty heads. I have witnessed cat fights between my sisters, Justine, and Erin and now my therapist is in the mix of insanity, to put it lightly.*

"Dr. Sheppard, you're kidding me, right? It's not a big deal? My daughter just threw a dinner plate at you, and you're taking this lightly?" Keith snaps furiously. "Are you out of your mind? I'm sorry, you're a therapist. Of course you're out of your mind. What was I thinking?"

"I'm not upset because the plate didn't hit me. I'm fine. Thank you for being concerned for my well-being. Please don't punish your daughter, because nothing serious happened. Let's move on!" Elise pleads, as she tries to get a point across to her abused patient. The look on his face, however, tells her it's going to take a lot more convincing, or even a miracle.

"Listen, I don't take this lightly. My daughter should know better!" he roars, as he looks directly at Erin. Her head is still down and her body starts to quiver. The sound of Erin's cries echo throughout the kitchen. "Erin, look at me when I'm talking to you!" Keith shouts. He walks closer to Erin to get her full attention and to get straight answers to his questions. Erin slowly lifts her head up and looks at her controlling father. *What if I have an itch that needs to be scratched will he get angrier than he is? I'm so scared right now!*

"Erin, please give me an intelligent answer as to why you would throw a plate at Dr. Sheppard. Were you planning to really hurt her?"

It breaks his heart to see his lovely daughter who he adores so much do an insane thing. He knows for a fact that Justine would pull this kind of stunt, but Erin? Keith doesn't like to make his little girl cry, but he's not here to collect any brownie points for the best father of the year award. Deep down inside it's his duty as a parent to discipline the children. Justine said it more than once that it is his duty, not hers. But the truth of the matter is they both had agreed before the twins were born that he'd take on the responsibility. He doesn't like it, but he'll do it.

"We were just talking, and I just got angry for some reason. I don't know why I suddenly threw the plate. I'm sorry, Dad! Please forgive me!" Erin pleads. "I'm sorry!" Her tears come down like a spring morning rain. "Dad, can we please discuss this matter in private?" She moans, as she looks at her father as if to say, this is embarrassing! Suddenly Erin looks at Dr. Sheppard for help.

"No, we may not! I'm not finished talking to you, young lady! Don't look at Dr. Sheppard. Look at me, Erin!" She obeys without a fight and looks at him with those sad puppy blue eyes. To see her father angry makes Erin extremely concerned. What's going to happen next? It's been a very long time since Erin had seen her father in this state. She wonders, does the dinnertime drama the other night count? Erin feels very ashamed and scared. She promised herself that she would never experience this again after getting in trouble with her loser twin brother. *I guess all bets are off at this point. I'm not having any luck this month.* "At least you admit that you threw the plate at the doctor. Maybe that will help you get a lesser sentence! Why are you sorry? Because you got caught in the act or the plate missed Dr. Sheppard? Did you really want the plate to hit her?" Keith asks, as he looks directly at Erin to wait for her to answer quickly. "How would you feel if she got seriously hurt and had to go to the hospital for emergency surgery?"

Elise interrupts and puts her two second into the conversation that's going south. "I think you're taking this situation way out of the ballpark! There are no injuries… So please, Mr. Heiden, let it go." Keith gives deaf ears to her plead.

Seconds go by and Erin doesn't answer. It's not a smart thing to do right now but for some reason she's unable to get any words out of her mouth. She tries to give a correct answer and dig herself out of the six foot hole. This time Erin doesn't receive any help from Patrick; it's all her. Her face shows that she's extremely upset while the tears are coming down like heavy rain, but it doesn't change her father's mode. "When I ask a question I want you to answer right now, not later. So, Erin, explain to me in simple terms, why would you do such an insane thing?" A second goes by and silence fill the room. "I'm not going to ask again!"

"I'm sorry, Dad, I don't know why I threw the plate at Dr. Sheppard but I did. I promise it won't happen again," Erin pleads. By the look of his body, he's ready to disengage the problem with an attack which is if necessary. You can hear the sound of him breathing heavily, not a good sign.

"Yes, you'll never do it again! I should really get my answers out of your backside!" Keith shouts directly at his daughter. Erin suddenly gives a surprise look as if to say, "You can't do that. I'm almost eighteen years old!"

Dr. Sheppard interrupts, "Mr. Heiden!" She tries to stop her patient from doing a ludicrous thing. She's set back, but not at all surprise a because of his state of mind. That's why she's hired to be his therapist; she knows that it's going to be a long summer.

"I'm so sorry!" she cries, as her tears quickly roll down her smooth face. Keith just dismissed his daughter's Oscar performance. "I'm truly sorry! Please, Dad, accept my apology!" Erin pleads, as she tries to save herself from the additional embarrassment that has already brewed up. *Dad never hit us. I guess because of his childhood. I Remember, I had fallen on my butt hard on ice a local skating rink a local staking ring. I received a huge bruise from the embarrassing fall; it hurt like hell for days after. To make matters worse and till this day, my friends wouldn't give up on telling other people. I can't imagine a spanking!* Even though he was a that point especially with Patrick many times, he never laid a finger on him. I really think he wanted too. When he yells it really feels like you're getting hit.

"Mr. Heiden that's a little extreme! It's not necessary for this kind of behavior!" Elise pleads, as she tries to stop the madness. She's not taking any chances, especially coming from her illogical patient.

Suddenly, Keith interrupts the doctor and snaps back, "Dr. Sheppard, please don't interrupt me when I'm disciplining my daughter!!.....It's called a threat and only a threat!!I just wanted to scare her out of her skin!....That's what I do best....Believe me, I wasn't planning on spanking her, even though she deserves it from pulling this stunt!"

Keith looks directly at his daughter with no emotion while Erin cries and feels degraded. This feeling that overcomes him stems from the pain of his childhood suffering. This sense of happiness and pleasure truly comes from the abuse received from his father oh, that unconditional love!!

"Agent Heiden, as I said before, she didn't hurt me! There's no harm done. So please let it go!" Elise pleads with a tone that she now means business. This situation is more difficult than writing her thesis on psychology. This patient is a very headstrong and extremely stubborn individual. *I'm putting this mildly. I really need a vacation!*

"Give me a break! Do you have a brain in that head of yours?" My dad used to say that to me and as always his answer would be no. For some strange reason, it always worked in my favor to get myself out of deeper trouble. "You're making light of this situation. You could've been seriously hurt, and with my luck these days, I would have to pay for all your medical bills! You also could have be sued my ass for millions! But hey, I'm only giving my two cents on how it would go down!" Keith sarcastically roars, as he sees his daughter slowly wiping her nose and tears away from her soft young skin. Erin tries not to be noticed but it's too late.

Elise snaps back with what needs to be said, "I think you're behavior is totally ludicrous!"

"I really don't give a rat's ass! You can take your professional Yale holier-than-thou attitude and you know what you can do with it! Dr. Sheppard, this is not a therapy session! I really think you're out of line if you want to go down the path of ludicrous behavior," Keith retorts with a tone that tells Elise she is really pissing him off.

Elise is about to say something to defend her actions once again and then… "Please, Dad, don't yell at Dr. Sheppard!" Erin pleads, as she tries to avoid an embarrassing situation. "I caused this drama, not Dr. Sheppard."

Keith tries desperately to ignore his lovely daughter's please and not to look at his therapist because he's embarrassed.

A minute later he says, "Dr. Sheppard, I just wanted to find out why she threw a plate at you. Also, it's my parenting duties to correct my children and make them become good citizens. To be honest, Dr. Sheppard, I'm really having a bad day and it doesn't seem to be getting any better!" Keith takes a deep breath. "By any chance did you receive my phone voice messages that I left you?"

"Sorry, but I didn't have a chance to check my messages. I think I left my cell phone at my friend's house last night or in my office… Thanks for reminding me to check them before the work week starts up again," Elise answers with a tone that shows she is not taking her problem seriously.

"You have to be shitting me! Dr. Sheppard, I really don't need extra drama! Please you must go now. It's going to be a trying day for me," Keith says. "I'll walk you out," he says very deliberately.

"I understand," Elise softly answers.

The doctor remembers all too well the loss of a family member. A drunk driver had taken her mother, Elizabeth Monique Sheppard, away from this world. The boy was only seventeen. He drove on the wrong side of traffic and head on into Elise's mom. She died instantly. The police found out that he was under the influence of alcohol over ten times the legal limit. This terrible and forgotten accident occurred three hours before Elise's college graduation. It had taken all of her body strength to walk up to that podium to receive her doctorate. It should've been a day of joy, not pain. The young man who caused the accident only got fifteen years behind bars, and he'll be out soon. Elise doesn't know why this happened. He'll be starting his adult life free as a bird, as she continues to mourn the loss of her mother. Where is the justice in that?

"Please, sweetheart, apologize to Dr. Sheppard," Keith asks in a soft but firm voice. He feels his heart has fallen into many tiny pieces and he knows all too well that he's going to get an ear full from his wife. For some strange reason, in Justine's eyes he can never do right. He tries very hard to please her, but there is never any light at the end of the tunnel. Keith knows that they have a lot of tension between them. In any relationship, it takes two or tango, but they're not even stepping on the dance floor.

Erin walks slowly toward Dr. Sheppard and looks directly into her eyes. The young teenager is 5'7" and the therapist is 5'5", but that doesn't factor in because Erin feels very small right now. "Please forgive me, Dr. Sheppard. I'm truly sorry for what I've done," she cries with her voice cracking.

"You're forgiven, Erin," Elise answers with a soft voice and a smile. She tries to make her understand it's only and no harm is done, and I had forgotten it already. Elise really wants to say something funny, but she doesn't think that Mr. Heiden would approve.

"Please, Erin, finish the dishes and clean up the broken plate. Also please get dressed, because we have to go soon," Keith softly says. "You're going to pay for the plate and the dent in the wall from your allowance. I'm not happy with your behavior, but I know that you have learned your lesson. However, you are grounded for another month Erin. I really hope you understand. That I made disapprove of what you do at times but I will always I love you."

"Yes, Dad, I'm sorry," Erin says, as she thinks to herself, *Maybe, if I use my little girl charm, my sentence will be shortened?*. "I know I have myself to blame, and I'm very sorry for that!" she solemnly answers, as she looks at her dad with puppy dog's eyes. Finally, it's going her way. *It's about time. I thought I would have to travel down the river without any paddles or life jacket. Sometimes you just have to get Dad tired of fighting, and then he'll give up.* Ten minutes go by and Keith doesn't answer her. Not a good sign. "I know that you're doing your job as a parent and again I'm sorry. Please understand that!" she answers.

"I know that you're sorry, but also I've put on some additional punishment. You'll have to write an apology letter to Dr. Sheppard," he orders with a soft tone in his voice. He now knows that Justine will be extremely infuriated when she finds out what he did to their precious daughter. Keith sometimes doesn't care what Justine has to say or think in this kind of situation. He won't back down when he know he is right.

"Yes, sir," Erin answers quickly with no back talk, unlike Patrick, who always tries to push Dad over the edge. Even if his punishment is harsh, Patrick doesn't really care, especially when he gets his point across. It gives him a chuckle when he gets his father into a frenzy. He loves it! Patrick thinks it's a hobby that he's perfected over the years. He has given Erin a few hints. He especially told her never let Dad see you break down under pressure.

"Mr. Heiden, that's not necessary, Erin already apologized to me!" Elise interrupts, as she tries to reason with her patient. She finds his behavior abnormal and it needs to stop right now! Elise has the strength to take him. Maybe she had a second wind or her fifth cup of coffee. Caffeine will do it every time!

Keith looks annoyed as he snaps back, "Dr. Sheppard, this is how I discipline my children! I've written a lot of letters throughout my childhood and it works! It states they're very sorry for what they're done! They need to discuss why their punishment is necessary. My children all know the routine!"

Elise interrupts, "Like spanking? Is that one of their other punishments."

"What the hell are you talking about?" he roars back. "I never hit my kids, especially with my history. You already know that!" He releases a long sigh. "You'll get Erin's apology letter next time we're at our lovely therapy session. Please, Dr. Sheppard, you have to leave now! I have a very long day ahead of me," Keith announces, and he quickly walks away leaving the women alone in the kitchen.

Erin slowly goes back to cleaning the dishes. Hopefully, for the final time, the tears roll down her young face. She wipes them gently off her nose with a napkin and looks at the therapist with a sorrowful demeanor.

Elise feels troubled that Erin was yelled at by her abused patient. "I'm so very sorry, Erin. I didn't mean for you to be get grounded, especially for a month," she says in a soft friendly voice. "I'm truly sorry." Elise remembered getting yelled at in front of friends by her father because she was late coming home one evening. To Elise it was totally unfair for her father to behave in such an unjust manner. Elise was grounded for a week for not calling home. It's embarrassing and it can scare a child for a long time. She understands at the time he was scared and concerned for the welfare of his precious daughter.

"Does your father always give you guys harsh punishments, or is this a rare situation?" she asks. Elise knows the answer but wants to hear it from the one that has experienced it.

"I wish this were a rare situation, but it's not. Thanks, Dr. Sheppard, you're sweet for caring," Erin answers. "I'll be fine and I'm sorry for what I did. It wasn't the brightest moment in my life. Once again please forgive me. I really hope it doesn't hurt my father's record with you."

"Please don't think about things like that. I do forgive you, and I know that you're under a lot of stress right now. Well, good-bye, please take care of yourself and keep your head up," Elise softly says to ease the young teenager's pain.

"Thank you and good-bye," Erin says with a weak smile on her face. She sees Dr. Sheppard walk away from the kitchen. Erin does think that the doctor has a lot of work ahead of her dealing with her father. She wishes her all the best because she really needs it and that's no joke.

The feeling of sadness travels throughout the house. As Dr. Sheppard meets her destination, she wants to say something that would make her patient feel a little better. Keith slowly opens the front door, and Elise walks out and turns quickly looking for the right "Hallmark words."

Keith interrupts and says, "I'm so sorry for my daughter's actions. I promise that you'll get an apology letter the next time we have a therapy session. I'll call you next week to begin my therapy sessions again. Please, Dr. Sheppard, don't call me until then. I need to spend time with my family, especially after what happened recently. Good-bye, have a good day," he exclaims, as he shuts the door.

"I need a cup of very strong coffee," Elise shouts, as the warm sun shines on her face. Then she quickly puts on her designer sunglasses that she bought on Rodeo Drive. It was a birthday present to herself. Elise believe that she should treat yourself with a gift for your birthday, something that no one would ever get for you. It really works because five years ago, she bought herself one-way ticket to California and never looked back. She's very happy that she made that decision.

Elise feels very concerned about Keith, Justine and his family. Now that she is thinking about it, where is the queen of the family anyway?

CHAPTER
TWENTY-FIVE

An hour later everyone is getting dressed for the funeral that starts at 3pm. The kids are running in different directions making a lot of sounds on the second floor. "Dad, I can't find my tie!" Mitch shouts through the hallway.

Keith saved Mitch's life, and now he is part of the Heiden family after being adopted nine years later. The DEA department arrested John and Faith Pollack with warrants of charges of four counts of drug trafficking, cocaine possession, child abuse and neglect. It's not a very good town for a white child in a minority community. Four DEA agents had to bring the Pollocks out in handcuffs and four-year-old Mitch saw everything. He was underneath the kitchen table crying. Such a sad little boy that was very dirty and smelled of urine.

"Hi, Mitch," said a DEA agent very softly, as he popped his head under the kitchen table.

"Mitch, my name is Keith."

"I want to help you. Can you please take my hand?" he asked with a calm voice that a little child would understand and not be afraid of. Keith tried to convince him that it was okay and he would be safe now.

"No, I want my mommy!" Mitch cried with little tears streaming down his face. "I want my mommy!"

"I know, son. Please give me your hand and we will go," Keith said with a soft voice to a very scared child.

Mitch took Keith's hand slowly. Minutes later they walked outside and found a social worker waiting.

"Thank you," said the lady from the state of California. She was a heavy-set woman with a few facial hairs that needed to be taken care of.

The social worker put Mitch into a child safety car set in the back of the car and headed towards a local hospital. "What is going to happen to him?" Keith asked, as he looks at the child through the window.

"You know how the government works. He'll be in the system like every other child in the Los Angeles area," she answered.

"How do I go about adopting him?" he asked with a concerned and serious look on his face.

The started social worker replied, "You're kidding, right?"

"No, I'm not!" Keith answered without a blink of any eye.

"Well, you have to file paperwork and apply for forester care It depends on how long the case takes and whether or not another family member wants him," the social worker answered.

"Thanks," he replied, as he looked at Mitch again. They both waves goodbyes to each other.

"I wish you all the luck because you need it big time," she said laughing at the same time.

After a long year of paper work and court dates, Mitchell Paul Pollack was finally adopted by the Heiden family. It was great to have a new family member, especially for Erin and Patrick, but for Justine it took a long time for her to adjust to being someone else's mom. Maybe because she didn't have him naturally and the subject of adoption never came up. Having twins was already a handful, but another kid was a shock. Justine knew that he really needed a mother and she'd tried but it wasn't going to be easy for both parties. Keith was just touched that he save a little boy's life.

CHAPTER
TWENTY-SIX

Peter walks toward the master bedroom and sees the kids passing by down the hallway. You can hear the exchange of conversations between them. Patrick gives a loving punch in the arm to Mitch as they pass each other. Colin plays alone in his bedroom while making crazy noises. Peter knocks on the door not knowing what kind of state his partner will be in.

"Come in!" Keith answers, as his voice travels through the door. Peter opens it slowly. The master bedroom is larger than Peter's apartment all together. The amazing marble fireplace takes your breath away, and his and hers walk-in closets are the size of a two car garage. The master bathroom has a whirlpool shower and large tub fit for a king. The two matching sinks complete the picture. Peter would love to hang in the room for just a couple of hours!

"Keith, where are you?" he solemnly asks, as he looks around for his crazy agent and best friend.

"I'm here!" Keith answers.

"Are you playing hide and seek?" he laughs, as he scratches his dark brown thick mane.

"What? No! I'm underneath the bed!" the voice cries out.

Sticking out like a sore thumb are Keith's legs underneath the California King size bed. "If you're desperate for money I can give you some. You don't have to crawl underneath the bed to get spare change!" Peter laughs.

"No, I'm trying to find my wedding band!" Keith answers with frustration, as he holds a small LCD black flashlight. "This morning

Colin was playing with it without me knowing it until it was too late. Now I have to find it before Justine has my head! She notices everything that's out of place," he replies.

"Justine is the last person to keep things straight!" Peter snaps.

"Peter… I know. You don't have to rub it in," Keith answers. "I know that you have my back, but please give me space so I can fix this."

"You can try but because I love you, and I consider you a brother I want to help you!" Peter snaps. "What are you afraid of?"

"I really can't have this heart-to-heart conversation right now, because I'm underneath this bed, and I'm afraid that I'll be stuck here for the rest of my life!" Keith answers. "Where the hell is it?"

Peter laughs and uses his DEA skills to look around the room to find this one small but lethal piece of jewelry. Peter thinks that this ring is a dangerous weapon that people are forced to wear. You can get locked down into an endless marriage with it and this is not Peter's plan.

"Bingo!" he states, as he sees the item on a dresser.

Keith picks up his head like a groundhog coming out of his hole. "Thanks," he answers, as he walks to the dresser and without a second thought puts the ring on his left ring finger. Then Keith wipes himself off.

Keith remembers the day he was about to marry Justine. He was so nervous; he felt that he was having an out-of-body experience. Also what made matters worse was he completely forgot to buy wedding bands before the special event started. They were married in Hawaii overlooking the ocean from afar, and it was the most beautiful moment in their young lives. When they got to the honeymoon suite Justine was very upset with Keith because of the rings; she made him sleep on the couch. That was not a good sign to start out as husband and wife.

"Listen, Keith, I'm trying to protect you from yourself," Peter says.

"Yes, I understand. Please give me space to take care of it!" Keith answers.

"She's out of control! This is her second affair, and now she's a heavy drinker! How are you going to handle her without calling in the SWAT team? You would kill yourself before you kill her, and I know that for a fact! This is a road that you don't want to be on or get directions for. I love you both but you don't love each other, and shit happens. Please be careful, and I'll be watching!" Peter announces, as he thinks that this tough love is the way to go for both of them. Justine and Keith are poison together, and there is no happy medium.

"I know that I owe you some money for getting the PI, and you have a right to say your piece because you care. Just please respect my wishes and give me the space that I really need," Keith pleads. "Believe me, Peter, I'm very tired of fighting with you or anyone else who loves me."

"Okay...okay... I'll back off for now, but trust me I'll be back." Peter sighs. "Everyone is getting ready, and we're just waiting for you. Is there anything that I can do for you? Do you want me to tell the kids what happened to Justine?" he asks.

"Thanks for the warning! I'll have a talk with the kids myself. I'm not ready to tell them that their mom is extremely sick, and she won't be with us for a of couple days, but it's one of my many duties as a father. I'll tell them before we head out to the funeral. Peter, can you please keep a close eye on my kids? Can you stay over for a couple of days until Justine is settled back home? I just need some breathing room especially today," he quietly asks.

"No problem...whatever you need! Keith, I'll stay over for as long as you want me to, and I'll help watch over the kids. I truly understand that you need some breathing room....Whatever you need, I'm there for you," Peter answers. "I wish I had the words for you to help deal with the pain that you're going through. I don't know what I will do when my dad passes away," he says honestly.

"Peter, you don't have to say anything. I know that you're heartfelt on my lost. Thank you. You're helping me by being at my side," Keith replies. "I'll be down in a minute." His eyes feel like they're going to pop out of his head from all the crying that he has already done. He realizes that it's not going to be easy by any means, and he knows for sure that the waterworks will start up again. The question is will the tears stop before he really embarrasses himself in public?

"Before I go to check up on the kids, can you explain to me what happened in the kitchen? I heard you read the riot act to Erin. You shouted through the sliding glass doors, because I heard you while swimming in your pool. You never yelled at her like that before," Peter asks with some concern.

"Hey, not my finest moment of practicing my parenting skills. I caught Erin throwing a dinner plate at Dr. Sheppard," Keith answers, as he rubs his eyes to release some tension.

"Why didn't you invite me to the Greek wedding? You know that I love a good party!" Peter asks with a laugh. Just seeing women fight is so dam sexy.

Keith gives Peter a confused look. "No, Peter! Are you stupid? Erin intentionally tried to hit Dr. Sheppard with an expensive dinner plate. Thank God, she didn't get hurt, but if she did I would be responsible for the medical bills, and I can't see myself making pizzas at Chucky E. Cheese!" Keith announces.

It would be very comical to see Keith wearing a Chucky E Cheese polyester, non-breathable uniform while making pizza in the back room. "I think they have a good medical plan!" Peter laughs, as he tries to make a light situation. Peter loves to bust his chops when he can. He thinks Keith is too serious about life and should let his hair down and enjoy what's around him.

"We'll never be on the same page," Keith says, as he shakes his head in disbelief. "I'm in deep shit, and you don't care that I'm going down to the wolves!"

Keith's Broadway performance is so good that it makes Peter laugh harder and he thinks that he peed in his pants. "Everybody thinks that I'm the joker in this relationship! Please, Keith, you're not going down to the wolves, whatever that means! I'll talk to Dr. Sheppard and see what I can do," Peter replies, as he rubs his head. I really need that heavy drink right now!

"Please, I don't need you to talk on my behalf to Dr. Sheppard. I'll never forgive myself if you do. Just give me a few minutes then

I'll talk to the kids. Also can you please take time to clean the living room from top to bottom it's horrendous," Keith requests, as he looks in the mirror to make sure his black tie is on straight.

Peter pats Keith's shoulder for extra support. "Okay I'll tell the kids to clean up downstairs, but when you said that huge word you really lost me." He laughs again. Peter's emotions can't be avoided.

Keith tilts his head like Reese (his dog) and asks, "What?"

"Never mind! I'll check on the kids," Peter answers, as he walks toward the door and turns around. "I'm sorry, Keith, for your loss. How do you feel?"

"Thanks for caring, Peter. You know that I wasn't surprised to get the call about my father's death. His terrible habits finally caught up with him…like smoking, drinking, and womanizing," sighs Keith. "Justine is in rehab, and that really doesn't help matters. It's not good at all. What did I get myself into by marrying her?"

Peter walks toward Keith and gives a supportive hug that he desperately needed. A second goes by and Keith breaks away and Peter says, "My father and I have a solid relationship. I can't imagine what you're going through. Now that your father passed on, you'll never have that relationship with him."

"I'm trying to understand what you're really getting at." Keith says, with a confused look

"Sorry, I'm a little confused," he answers.

"Now, you know how I feel," Keith solemnly replies, as he walks over to the door and opens it. "Peter, can you please give me a few minutes to collect myself, and I'll be right down shortly to talk to the kids."

"Sure no problem," Peter quickly answers, as he walks out of the master bedroom. Suddenly he turns around to say something to Keith. "I love you!" Keith is not in the mood what so ever especially for Peter. He gives him a strange look, and without a single clue, he shuts the door in Peter's face. "Okay, I'll call you or you call me!"

Twenty minutes go by and Peter is outside near the front garage doors. He walks in and out of his SUV. He places the garbage in a plastic bag. Keith holds Colin in his arms, as Peter sees and hears the Heiden family walk away from the house and toward his SUV.

Everyone is wearing black for the funeral to honor a grandfather that the kids never knew but just heard about.

No one says anything; they all just place themselves in the SUV to get to the destination quicker. You can feel the air very thick with solitude, and you know that someone passed on recently. Also, Justine is not here so it's hard for everyone because of what happened to her. It's a lovely California day to spend on the beach or doing some outdoor activity because the sun is shining in full force and the temperature is about seventy-five degrees. It's just a nice day to celebrate life instead of death.

CHAPTER
TWENTY-SEVEN

After driving one hour, the SUV enters St. Gabrielle Cemetery in San Bernardino. It's a peaceful resting place to say goodbye to loved ones. The lawn is Irish green and of course freshly groomed. There are lots of extraordinary flowers and palm trees that cover the grounds. In the center of the cemetery is a huge statue of St. Gabrielle the Archangel (patron of communication workers). It stands twelve feet high and overlooks the cemetery grounds.

Keith looks at his children and says, "Okay, kids, your Uncle Peter is in charge. Please listen to him as you do for me, especially you, Patrick."

"Hey, why is it always me? Look at Erin! She's the ugliest of the bunch!" Patrick shouts, then he realizes where he is. "Sorry, Dad."

"That's okay, Patrick," says Keith, as he gives a weak smile. He takes a deep breath while he tries to hold back the tears that might be creeping up to the surface. "I almost forgot, your Uncle Peter will stay with us for a few days until your mother and I settle back into our daily routine. Please just behave and we won't have problems," he orders in a soft voice.

Everyone gets out of the SUV and Keith catches a glimpse of people walking toward the burial site. His blue eyes spot a woman, and he shows some recognition. That could be his mother, but he's not sure from afar. He stands quietly while analyzing his estranged family members walking toward a cement staircase heading up a hill. Everyone looks so much older. Has it been twenty-three years? He starts walking toward the crowd; the kids and Peter follow him.

Peter's dad (Daniel Richard Darling) never hurt him like Keith's dad, but Peter did have a bad experience with him. It was only once. Peter was around thirteen or fourteen years of age when he was caught peeing on a grape tree on their family's wine property. The grape tree was young, but now it was dying and had to be replaced because of Peter's stupid stunt. He was grounded for two months and had to work every day after school, including weekends at the family business to pay for the new tree. It taught Peter an important lesson. He realized that he really hurt his dad emotionally and financially. Peter made a promise to himself to straighten his life out, although he knew it wouldn't be easy. "Trouble," was his middle name, and he always liked a good joke, especially if it was played on someone else.

Although Peter still wants to play jokes on people, he doesn't want to hurt anyone. He loves his dad and he promised himself never to hurt him again. Daniel is grateful that his son has such a good friend in Keith. He knows that Keith will watch over him and try to keep Peter in line. Daniel has also been a father figure to Keith over the years. It's certainly filled a void in Keith's life, and it's a way for him to say, "Thank you for taking good care of our son."

A lady dressed in a professional black business suit introduces herself to Keith by shaking hands, and they exchange conversation while they walk to the burial site.

An American flag lays on top of the coffin. The people start to gather around to show their loving support for one another. You can hear crying that seems to override the birds singing. The lady says her goodbyes to Keith and then walks away from the mourners. He turns to face his estranged family members and the coffin which is less than five feet away.

A Roman Catholic priest stands near the coffin to give the last blessing to the deceased. "Please let's begin! Let's stand solemnly to say our farewell. This is the final destination for Conrad Van Heiden, a son, brother, brother-in-law, uncle, friend, husband, father, and grandfather. We'll miss him deeply and love him forever. He leaves his beloved wife, his nine children, and twenty-six grandchildren. He had faithfully served his country in the United States Marine Corp."

The priest starts out with the sign of the cross to begin the prayer service. "Let us pray! Lord, open your arms to Conrad Van Heiden. Make him comfortable to meet with his parents and grandparents. As his body finally rests in the soul of mother earth please don't forget his loved ones left behind. Protect them Lord." The Father walks around the coffin and sprinkles holy water. "Ashes to ashes dust to dust. We say our last good-byes until me meet again! In the name of the Father the Son and the Holy Spirit, Amen! Thank you for coming and God bless you!" he says.

Minutes later the twenty-one gun salute begins. Seven young marines stand very straight in a vertical line, waiting for their orders from the head officer.

"Fire!!" shouts a Marine officer, and the shots hit the air twenty-one times to honor their fallen ex-Marine, Conrad Van Heiden. They paid their respects to their fallen comrade who served this great country for freedom.

Colin starts to cry and scream because the shots are too loud for his tiny ears. Erin tries to comfort her little brother by holding his hand.

Ten minutes later the two young Marines stand across on each side folding the American flag in a triangle shape. The American flag is given to the high officer and he slowly walks to Keith's mother and says, "Mrs. Heiden this flag is from the United States Marines and this great country, and we're truly sorry for your loss." He carefully hands over the American flag to her, and she starts to cry. It echoes in Keith's ears. He never liked to hear his mother cry, especially when he was a little boy. Even to this day, it breaks his heart to hear it. The Marine gives a statue to Mrs. Heiden out of highest respect for her loss and for Mr. Heiden too.

The people start to form a single line and slowly walk to say their last good-byes to Conrad. One by one they place their red roses down on the coffin. They all hug and share their tears with one another for comfort. Keith silently waits to be the last one at the coffin. Then it's his turn and he sighs to release any stress. He can hear his heart beat faster as he gets closer to the final meeting with his dad. He didn't go to the wake to see his dad lying peacefully in the casket. Keith knows that his dad is inside the box. Also with Keith's luck these days Conrad will jump out of the coffin and pull him inside! Keith's emotions are coming up to the surface; it all depends on which emotion comes out first: anger, sadness, happiness, frustration, or that feeling of being comfortable in his boxers. Keith thinks it's not a good idea to take off his dark sunglasses because he knows that his eyes are already bloodshot from crying this morning. He tries to focus on what's in front of him. His hand starts to shake as he tries to put the single rose on the coffin. It's done. Finally he's dead and Keith can live his life in peace. "Ouch…you bastard!" Keith shouts, as he notices that one of the thorns from the rose pokes his finger. I guess his dad was getting the last word and laughing too! Keith starts to suck the blood from the cut to make the bleeding stop. Shit that hurts!

A minute later, Keith feels overwhelmed with remorse, but for some strange reason, he was very satisfied at the same time. He secretly wipes his nose with a tissue. Then suddenly his head starts to throb. He can feel his brain trying to get out of his skull. Peter walks toward his best friend and says, "I'm really sorry, Keith, but I need to speak to you."

"Sorry…what?" Keith asks solemnly, as he turns his head around and looks at Peter. His partner looks concerned for some reason or another, but he knows that he will find out soon enough.

"I know you need some more time to be alone, but Colin is getting cranky again. I think the kids want to leave soon. Your monsters are getting hungry eyes, and they're staring strangely at me. I might be their main course if I don't get the real food fast," Peter announces, as he smiles at Keith.

Peter knows that if his father passed on, he'd never be the same. He and his dad are very close; he's more of a big brother than dad at times. They can talk and laugh for hours over just about nothing at all. They really enjoy each other's company. Peter is well aware that Keith gets very jealous and sad when he sees them together. He gets extremely quiet and quickly leaves the room without anyone noticing that he's gone.

Keith looks at his watch and says, "I didn't notice the time." He's a little surprised how fast the time goes, especially when you're lost in thoughts.

"Listen Keith, I'll take them to get something to eat. I'll come back for you in about half an hour or forty-five minutes at best," Peter softly answers.

"Okay," he says with a crackle in his voice. Keith takes out his wallet from his front suit pocket. As he opens it he finds two twenties and a paper receipt from Exxon, which was the last time he had pumped gas before his SUV exploded. Shit! My life really sucks right now!

"I've got it, Keith!" Peter cries, as he tries to stop his inconsolable partner from taking money out of his wallet.

"Peter, they're my kids and my responsibility," Keith announces with a look of concern.

"I know, and I'm very happy for that," he laughs. "I'm just taking them out for dinner, not to Vegas! Please don't worry about it!" Peter announces. "Uncle Peter has it and I'll be back. I'm not going to kidnap them. You'll get your kids back in one piece."

"Thank you, but you don't have to do that!" Keith cries, as he takes a glimpse of his great kids. They're waiting patiently for Uncle Peter to come back.

"It's the least that I can do for you, especially at this time of need," Peter says. "I'll pick up some food for you."

"Thanks, Peter, you're a great friend. I don't know what I would do without you," Keith replies.

"I know you can't do anything without me!" he replies, as he smiles back at his best friend. "I'll be back for you," Peter answers, and he walks away toward the Heiden kids. "I'll call you when we're close by so we can pick you up."

"Thanks, Peter," Keith answers.

Minutes later Keith walks around the grounds, and he decides to sit on a bench under a huge palm tree. He tries to relax as he waits for Peter. He closes his eyes and just listens to birds singing until…

"Keith," an old woman says with an Irish accent.

Shit! He sees a petite lady with a very Irish complexion and deep blue eyes looking at him. She wears her gray hair short and her face shows the strain of many years of hardship. Keith slowly stands up without saying a single word.

"Do you remember me? I'm your mother!" the gentle old lady asks. She doesn't realize that her voice is cracking under pressure. She knows why she's so nervous, because she's standing less than an inch from her long-lost son. She really missed him so much and always prayed for his safety. She says to herself, why didn't he get plastic surgery on his left ear and hands? It was the worst day for the whole family especially for Keith.

"Yes, but I want to forget," he snaps. Keith wants her to leave before something worse happens.

"I had a feeling that you would come…and I'm so happy to see you," she says, as she focuses on her son's platinum wedding band. She's relieved that he has someone that loves him the way he is. "I can see that you're married. I guess those were your kids. They look a lot like you. They're beautiful," she announces, as she tries to break down the invisible wall that was planted a long time ago.

"What do you want, Megan?" Keith snaps with a sharp tone of anger. *Don't test me, woman!*

"I guess I lost the title of mom?" she cries, as her windpipe begins to close.

"You never had it! So what do you want?" he asks again, as his hands begin to shake.

"Listen to me before you get angry!" she pleads. "Now that your father is dead the family and I really want you back, especially me. I know that it was his wish and his alone to disown you from the family. But things have changed and he's gone and his wishes died with him. Do you have the heart to let us in?" Megan exclaims, as she tries to hold back her tears.

"You want me to come back after the family disowned me for twenty-three years of my life? You have some nerve! What do you think? Are you going to try to control my life again where you left off? I had begged and pleaded for Dad's forgiveness over the years, but he never responded back to me! Now you and the family want me back? You're a piece of shit!" Keith shouts, as he feels veins popping out of his throat.

Even though it's a very dangerous move on her part, Megan suddenly puts her hand on his arm. She doesn't want him to walk away because she's afraid if she lets go it would be the last time she'll ever see her son. Keith doesn't fight back because he knows Megan needs to get everything off her chest before she leaves.

"Keith, your father wrote this letter three days before his death. I guess he knew the end was near. Anyway, he called me out of the blue and asked me to come over and pick it up. His special instructions were to give it to you. I had to do this in person, not by mail, and make sure you take it with no questions asked," Megan says, as she slowly opens her black purse and takes out a business envelope. It looks pretty heavy inside. "I guess it's all the answers you're looking for," she says solemnly.

As Keith takes the letter from her, Megan accidentally touches his scars. He flinches a little but doesn't say anything about the situation. Yes, the envelope does feel heavy, and he can only imagine what might be inside. Then Keith places the letter in his inside suit pocket without saying a word to the old lady that's staring at him.

"I don't know if you know but we saw you graduate from St. Michaels Roman Catholic High School and also from the University of Southern California. We were so proud of you and your accomplishments!" Megan states, as she looks at her son. She's amazed how he has aged, but she can still recognize him from across the street. Keith looks like Conrad, but he has her Irish complexion. Her husband was attractive but had a dark side to him and she wonders if Keith is the same way. What kind of life does Keith have now? Is he truly happy? Megan really wants to know if Keith is getting professional help, like seeing a therapist. Does he abuse his children as he was abused?

He looks at his mom straight in the eye. "You both came to my graduation? You never came to me after the ceremony to tell me," Keith says, as his voice cracks. He suddenly feels overwhelmed with the shocking news. He never thought that they had an ounce of compassion or love in their cold hearts.

"It's hard to explain but at the time your father didn't want to come to you. I tried very hard to convince him to apologize before it was too late. Well, I was trapped in a loveless marriage, and I didn't have anywhere to go to escape from him," she sighs and continues, "The truth of the matter is, he really didn't want to disown you, but at the time he was still extremely angry. I'm really sorry about the whole situation. I know that your father was ashamed of himself for the whole thing. I was afraid that I would never see you again, but here you are. You look great!"

"Get on with it, lady!" Keith roars.

"Your father changed physically and emotionally because of his overwhelming guilt. He was heartbroken and depressed after you. A lot of things changed. We both stopped drinking, and he wasn't abusive to anyone anymore. You know that he was very proud of you and always loved you! I love you too!" she cries, as she tries to get her son to understand their side of the story.

"You both had a very strange way of showing it!! I didn't have a childhood because you ripped it out from under me! You have some nerve," he shouts as he walks away. Keith tries desperately not to look back to see his mother's reaction.

"Keith…please wait!" she shouts, as she tries not to let her fifth child walk away from her forever. "Please don't leave!"

He stops in his tracks but still no sight of Peter's SUV. Keith hears the sound of footsteps behind him. He takes a deep breath and turns around. *How do I get this lady to leave me alone?*

Megan says in a soft voice, "Please take Jennifer's and Christopher's business cards. You remember your older sister and brother? They really want to speak to you and maybe you can get together. I know that you guys were very close. Please take them!" Keith sees her fair-skinned petite hands holding two business cards in front of him. He also notices that they are shaking like a leaf. I guess he's making her react this way, because Keith looks like Conrad.

Megan accidentally touches his hand while giving the business cards to him. Keith automatically flinches a little, not because it hurts anymore but because someone touched his hand without warning. Keith puts the cards in to his business suit jacket, not realizing that the letter is close to his heart as well. He walks past his mother without saying good-bye. As Peter's SUV pulls up, Keith sighs in relief and continues to walk away not looking back at the lady who didn't save him from hell. He enters the passenger side and sits down automatically without saying a single word.

"Are you okay? I have some dinner for you. It's your favorite tuna fish with a sprinkle of lemon and lettuce on rye and some ice tea to wash it down," Peter announces, as he passes the food to his best friend. Keith zones out for a minute as the paper bag is waving in front of his face.

He quietly takes the bag of food. "Thank you," he answers with a soft voice.

Peter asks again, "Are you okay?" He has a strong feeling that Keith is going to take his loss very hard for the next couple of days. It's one to those love-hate relationships that is unexplained to a person who has a normal family life with great parents.

Mitch sits right next to his father and says with excitement in his voice, "Dad, I had a triple hamburger with extra garlic pickles!" He loves his food; it's his safe-haven for all the problems in his little world, but he wouldn't go overboard to get heavy.

"That's great, Mitch!" Keith answers.

"Mitch, don't be a drama queen. You didn't have that triple, you had the double!"

Mitch turns around to see his big brother in the backseat. "Patrick, I know what I had! It was a triple burger, and that's why I have to unbutton my pants to get breathing room!" he claims and laughs without a second to spare.

Peter, Erin and Colin laugh too, as Keith quietly eats his sandwich.

"Give me a break! You're a drama queen!" Patrick says, as he looks outside and sees his grandma Heiden just standing alone on the edge of the grass. She looks helpless just waiting for her son to come back.

CHAPTER
TWENTY-EIGHT

he DEA Department is always busy, especially where Liam is standing. He walks to his workstation and looks at a file of the Jose Medina's case to see if anything out of the ordinary catches his eye. Liam sits down behind his desk and takes a look at the pictures of his huge (five brothers and four sisters) Irish family from Boston, Massachusetts. He thinks his family takes up the greater population of the city of Boston because of its size! He sees other pictures of his neighborhood, childhood, college and new friends too. There is one photo that was taken three years ago with Peter, Keith, Sean, and him at Palm Springs. They were at a company golf weekend, and they all had a great time. Keith looks especially happy in the picture, and Liam is honored to call him his friend and respect him for being his boss as well.

"Excuse me, Agent Gallagher," says a young man by the name of Todd Steinblum. A smart but disheveled young man of twenty-seven, Todd graduated from Georgetown University in Virginia with a masters degree in computer science. He got hired by the DEA department two months ago; he's very good at what he does. Todd loves to tell stories about the DEA world to his new sexy wife, Anastasia Slovickski. She stands at 5'11", skinny with light brown hair and piercing green eyes which is a sharp contrast to Todd 5'4" frame. Anastasia comes from Russia. She was a Mail Order Bride from a foreign affair international dating services and now lives in America.

"Hello, Todd, how can I help you?" Liam asks, as he takes a glimpse above and sees Todd looking as unkempt as ever.

"I need to look at your computer for a minute. You have to get out from behind your desk so I can do my magic," Todd orders, as he looks at Liam. Todd, as you can see, is not afraid of anyone, even if they have a gun attached to their hip.

"Todd, don't you guys have a workstation like a networking mainframe or something for that matter? I'm really busy right now! Can you come back in two or three hours? Just give me some time to finish what I'm doing, then the computer is all yours, I promise!" Liam announces, as he tries to tell the little tech fly to go away.

"We do have a networking mainframe and workstation, but I have to get everyone's computer up to speed first. So move!" he shouts, as he holds a compact disk and notepad.

"How long will this take? I really have to do my work! Agent Forrester is on my back!" Liam replies, as he gets up from his office chair.

"It will take at least an hour or two as long as I'm not interrupted. I thought Agent Heiden's dad's funeral was today?" he asks.

"Yes, the funeral is today, and Agent Heiden asked me to check on some things while he's gone. So, try to make it fast, okay Todd!" Liam announces, as he looks directly at the little computer nerd. He puts the Jose Medina file down on his desk and steps away not noticing Todd's deceptive eyes focused on the file. "Listen, Todd, don't touch anything that you're not assigned for...just the computer and that's it!"

"Hey, whatever. I'll try to make it as fast as possible. Please give me some room so I can do the work without smelling your bad breath behind me!" Todd orders, as he pushes all of his tiny body weight so Liam gets a clue to move away. He takes out the compact disk from the plastic case that's labeled x27 files. Todd puts in the disk and watches the computer load up the software as he looks at his watch to see the times. Todd lets Liam know that he is a very busy man who doesn't have time for small talk, especially with people like Liam who he feels is below him.

"Todd, I'll be back within half an hour to see how far you are, and then you can get out of my chair. I'll be back," he states then walks away so the nerd can play his computer games. "Don't get too comfortable and make a dent in my chair. Trust me, I'll be back very soon!" Liam exclaims, as he walks away leaving Todd alone in his disheveled mess.

"Let's see," Todd says out loud, as he sees the little hourglass icon. As he waits for the program to kick into the hard drive, he slowly moves his tech fingers. He tries to make sure not to move any papers that have post-it notes on them. There is a lot of information on the Jose Medina drug family business; fifteen years of work and still the case is open. Todd learned how to read fast; it's like brushing his teeth in the morning. It's something that needs to be learned because he has to read a lot of books in the computer world. He already knows a lot of information on the Jose Medina family something really caught his eye, and he can't wait to tell his supermodel wife the bit of good news. He knows that she loves her Polish-Jewish little nerd.

"Todd, my mouse is not working again! I don't remember what you told me the last time!" says Agent Sean Tierney, as he walks toward Liam's desk. "Hey, little man, what are you doing?!"

"Nothing!" Todd answers, as he tries to hide the reading material from Liam's desk. "What do you want, Sean?"

"My mouse is not working again. I need to get some files done! So can you fix it?" he pleads, with a very deep southern accent.

Todd has a funny feeling about this whole situation, and he says sarcastically, "For someone that's saying his last good-byes to his old man, Agent Heiden is really putting a lot of pressure on you to get things done."

"Listen, little weasel I never told you that Agent Heiden or any other agent gave us an order! Don't you dare give me any back talk!" Sean shouts.

"I didn't know that you and Heiden were lovers," Todd snaps back. He just loves to cause trouble.

Sean walks closer to Todd and asks, "What did you say, little man?"

"Do you want to start something? Bring it on!" Todd shouts, as he steps on Sean's shoes. "Listen, Georgia boy, back off if you want your mouse again! So you better stand down!" he commands. Sean is a little taller than Todd, and he is sure that he can take him down just by blowing on him.

"Get off my feet, geek boy! What are you going to do, give me a computer virus? Bring it on, tech boy!" Sean exclaims with a smile.

"Sean, stop it before you take his highlighter away from his pocket protector!" Liam laughs, as he looks at Todd while holding his partner back before he does something that he'll regret. "Are you finished yet?" Liam snaps.

"I didn't start yet; I'm being hassled by your number 2 guy! Besides, it's going to take longer than I thought. The program has to be recognized by the hard drive. You'll have to give me at least an hour or more to get my work done. I'll call you when it's done... and it won't be early!" Todd states with an annoyed tone in his voice. Liam stands and hovers over him as if it will make his job faster. He never gets the respect that he deserves, especially concerning management of the computer system for the DEA Department. Todd thinks everyone should kiss his pocket protector for what he does.

"Just get it done, Todd! I'll give you another half hour but that's it. I need to do my work!" Liam orders with a stern look. It's no joke that he needs word to work at his desk. Liam thinks that Todd is an annoying computer tech bug that wouldn't go away easily. He's very smart for what he does but that's it.

"Liam, he was bad mouthing Agent Heiden!" Sean yells at Liam and anyone else to hear.

"Listen, Sean, we have to mind our own business because our government ass is hanging by Agent Jack Forrester! He's after blood, and I hear that Agent Heiden is getting a new supervisor, and it might be him and us too," Liam says.

"That's not good at all, does he know?" Sean asks with a look of concern. He just wants to do his job without any tension, but everyday it is a different story, especially in the government world.

"Not yet. We'll have to watch his back from now on," Liam says, as he feels there are going to be major changes in the department, and it won't be a pretty sight!

"That's no problem! I have to go now. I'll have to find another computer boy that will help me in my situation. Liam, are we having lunch in forty-five minutes?" Sean says.

"Yes, let's meet out front," Liam states

"Good, I'll see you then," Sean answers, as he walks away from his partner and the nerd.

"Now we're talking!" Todd yells, but no one is really listening.

An hour later, Todd walks out of the DEA building as a smile shows on his face because he sees his lovely 5'11" supermodel wife. She has long light brown hair and wears a lightweight summer dress showing off her sexy legs. Todd reaches his destination and kisses the woman that's waiting to have lunch with him.

Todd was a single man from southern California who needed someone to rub his "pocket protector." His friends from the computer clubs said, "If you're hungry for love you should go on Mail Brides from the internet. These women come from all different parts of the world, Europe, Russia, Asia, Africa, and more, looking to come to America to meet eligible men for marriage and then citizenship. It's costly and it takes about a year or more to get everything finalized, but it can be done and it's legal in the States. Two years later Anastasia is now married to Todd and lives in a little apartment near the highway. She knows that she won't live there for long, and that her comrades from Russia will come for her and save her from this boring American lifestyle with Todd. It's only a matter of time before the Russian mob who she had worked for before she came to the United States come to get her.

"That is hot!" Liam announces, as he strains his eyes to look at a very tall attractive woman standing right next to the computer geek Todd. "Sean, I think there's something wrong with the universe, because I can't believe what I'm seeing!" Liam exclaims.

"Holy cow batman! Do you see what I see?" Sean asks, as he laughs while Liam's mouth is just wide open and ready for the bugs to enter.

Liam walks over to Todd and his hot girlfriend. "Excuse me, Todd, can I take a picture with my camera phone? You guys are so damn cute together!"

"Sure that would be great…right, honey?" Todd asks, as he smiles proudly ready to show off his "hot to trot" wife. He especially gets a kick out of the men's dumbfounded expressions!

Liam shouts, "Smile," as he takes the picture. He sees a very odd couple in front of him. You have a six-foot woman standing next to her man of action that's barely 5'4" tall. "Looks great!" Liam lies but plays along anyway. He quickly shows them the pictures.

"That's great, Liam, can I have a copy?" Todd asks. He's not the one to takes pictures of them. It was a marriage by a justice in town hall and they spent their honeymoon in a private hotel off the beach. He did promise her a whole weekend in Vegas for a real honeymoon.

"Yes, of course I'll send them to you. I'm sorry I didn't catch your name?" Liam says in his friendly and very charming voice. He uses that same tone for all the pretty ladies that he meets.

"My name is Anastasia. I'm Todd's wife," she answers with broken English, as she smiles and shows straight, bright teeth. She had dental work done the first year she came in America. A lot of Russian people are poor, and they are unable to get good health coverage to take care of themselves.

Liam steps back a little hardly able to believe what he is hearing. "It's nice to meet you, Mrs.…," he says, with a friendly smile. *Son of a bitch! How in the hell do you get one of these? What a lucky bastard!*

"You look very pale, are you sick?" she asks with a look of concern. Her English is not that strong yet, and she knows it's a very hard language to learn but she's trying to be more American. She already loves a double bacon cheeseburger and root beer float to wash it down with.

"Unfortunately, I'm Irish but thanks for your concern," Liam laughs.

"Oh… I see," she says with her continuous smile.

"Liam, I'm hungry!" Sean shouts to his partner trying to get his attention.

"Well, I have to go now. I'll text these pictures to you. It's very nice to meet you, Anastasia! Goodbye," Liam says without taking a breath.

She says goodbye in Russian and waves.

"Thanks, I'll see you after lunch!" Todd shouts back while Liam walks to his car, a Nissan Maxima.

Liam loves his car, and it drives like a pussycat! Both agents get into the car without skipping a beat because they just wasted valuable time during their lunch hour. "When Peter gets a glimpse of these pictures, he's going to fall over! Wait till he sees this pretty young thing," Liam says, as he texts a message on his cell phone with an attachment of pictures of this very odd couple that will be the talk of the town "for weeks on the job!"

Liam gets an important updated text message on his cell phone, "Attention all DEA agents! Within the hour four agents died during a drug bust worth $6 million dollars. The names of the fallen agents will be posted in the main office shortly. Please be cautious and keep your eyes and ears open. Be ready for anything!"

CHAPTER
TWENTY-NINE

*T*he Heidens arrived at the house and everyone seemed extremely tired. The kids went upstairs to change out of their dress clothes, and Keith asked Justine's parents to come by the house to care for Reese as well as anything else that needed to be addressed until they came back from the funeral. They agreed without a fight.

The backyard is adorned with many different flower arrangements. Although Keith is not thrilled with the words, "I'm very sorry for your loss… Is there anything I can do for you?" he does realize that people are offering their warm wishes and kind thoughts. Keith opens the doggie run and lets Reese out. Without a moment to spare, Reese races over to Colin, and they begin to play. The toddler's laughter travels through the flowers like a summer breeze. Colin jumps up and decides to soar over the flowers without a care in the world.

"Daddy! Look at me!" Colin shouts while playing peek-a-boo. Keith stands amidst the flowers as he sees his son freely being himself. Reese is still barking away while his tail wags energetically as he tries to catch up with the toddler. Colin looks very cute with his little black suit and matching clip-on tie.

"Please slow down, Colin. You're going to hurt yourself and fall!" Keith pleads, as he feels very somber. He remembers the time that he went to a funeral for Justine's grandma. Her name was Emma Wills-Anderson and she was from Madison, England. She was buried in her home country that she loved so much. Emma was upset that William was going to live in the states and not live in England where his family was. She was very much loved by her friends, coworkers, and family members. There were a lot of people at her funeral, but Keith couldn't believe how many people came to his dad's funeral. Conrad wasn't a likeable guy. Maybe he changed over the years, but Keith would never know for sure. Keith also was not really sure if he cared one way or the other.

"Okay, Daddy! Can you find me?" Colin shouts, as he puts his whole body behind some flowers.

Peter stands beside his best friend and freely asks, "Should you tell him that you can see his little blond head sticking out of the flowers?" Peter laughs, as he notices that Keith didn't change his clothes. Peter, on the other hand, couldn't wait to get out of his "stuffy" suit. He never feels comfortable in "dress up mode."

"No, I don't want to spoil his fun," Keith answers, as he smiles weakly, but he really feels very numb. He's trying very hard to shake his sadness, but it's not easy. Peter pats Keith's back compassionately, and then he walks into the house to leave father and son alone in their special moment.

"Daddy, can you see me now!" Colin shouts behind a bouquet of red roses that are wrapped in a box container for support.

"Colin, where are you?" Keith shouts, as he plays with the toddler. Colin is growing up so fast, and Keith just wants to hold him at this age and never let go.

"I'm here," he screams, as he waves his little arms in the air.

"I can't see you! Colin, I hear you, but I can't find you!" Keith teases.

Colin jumps up with all his might. "Daddy, I'm here!" he shouts with a huge smile on his face that fills the whole backyard.

A minute later Keith doesn't see Colin running around anymore. He's not at all concerned because he sees his little boy's body on the ground in between a row of flowers. Keith walks toward the toddler and leans down to Colin. He had fallen asleep. Keith picks the toddler up and says gently, "Come on, Colin. Let's take you to bed."

Colin slowly opens his eyes and rubs them. "O...kay," he mumbles and then gives his dad a weak but loving smile. "I fell asleep."

"Really, I didn't know that," Keith smiles, as he picks up his young son.

"I love you, Daddy," says Colin. "Sorry about your daddy. I love you, Daddy."

"I love you too, Colin, and thank you for being you," Keith says lovingly, as he walks to the kitchen side windows. Colin wraps his arms around his dad's neck for moral support, something that Keith needed most of all. "Come on, Reese!" The chocolate lab quickly comes into the house without sniffing one single flower.

CHAPTER
THIRTY

*I*t's now 9:00 a.m. and a white convertible BMW parks in the driveway in front of a house on 2426 Falcon Boulevard in Pacific Palisades. There is a sign on the freshly cut front lawn that reads "California Realtor." Chase Whitman's name and company phone number are listed as well. Although the young woman met Chase on only two occasions, they frequently spoke over the phone. As she gets out of her car, she walks briskly to the front door and opens it with a house key. She anxiously waits for Chase and her client to arrive. You can hear the sound of her expensive shoes echoing throughout the house. There is still no furniture since it was just built six months ago.

"Hello… Chase, are you here?" she shouts, as she continues to walk around the house. The young real estate agent decides to walk toward the backyard. As she opens the sliding back door something terrible stops her in her tracks.

"Oh my God!" she cries and suddenly drops her Blackberry cell phone on the ground.

CHAPTER
THIRTY-ONE

〜〜

The doorbell rings, and Peter opens the door to see the two young agents Liam and Sean just standing outside. "What's up, guys?" Peter asks, as he holds a piece of English muffin in his hand. Both agents walk into the house, as they try not to step on all the toys covering the floor.

"Peter, did you recently get my text message?" Liam asks, as he looks at Peter closely to see his reaction.

"Yes, I did! Can't believe that our tech boy has a hottie!" He laughs with a huge smile.

"Peter, she's so hot that the pavement of the parking grounds was melting around her! She's smoke with fire!" Liam shouts with laughter.

The agents' laughter blocks out the sound of Keith walking through the entrance way. Liam suddenly becomes silent. "Oh, sorry sir; I didn't see you."

"Hi, guys... Peter, do you know if Justine is coming home today?" he asks.

"No, not yet, but I'll make a call today," he answers quickly.

"Thanks," Keith answers, as he walks back out, barely noticing that he didn't say goodbye to the Charlie Brown Peanut Gang just standing around killing time.

"Before I forget, Peter, there's a situation two houses down. Artermis Daly is requesting you take a look at the crime scene," Liam states, as he looks at his cell phone and Peter at the same time. "I really don't know the details, but Artemis just needs you."

"Thanks, I'll check it out," he answers. "Listen, can you guys stay around an hour or two?"

"Sure, Peter," Sean answers, as he starts to clean up the living room. The truth of the matter is he can't stand a messy house, especially a huge house.

"I can't imagine how Keith feels! I bet he's so confused about his estranged dad's death," Liam says out of the blue.

"To be honest, I don't know what he feels. I'm just here to support the family right now and eat all of their food. I think he's trying to hold on the best he can. I know that we have a great relationship with our parents, but it's totally different for Keith. I can't explain it, Liam," Peter states sadly.

"Why did Artermis Daly ask for you?" Liam asks suddenly.

"I guess the man misses me and has the heart to ask me out on a date." He laughs. I'll tell Keith where I'm going, and I'll be right out to join you guys," Peter answers, and without a second to spare he puts the English muffin into his mouth.

The three men walk outside the house to see what the drama is all about down the street. LA police vehicles are parked in front. Serial police dogs are walking around the area and the homicide unit and other business suits are walking in and out of the backyard. The neighbors are looking to see what's going on. Outside the crime scene tape says, "CRIME SCENE DO NOT CROSS!!"

Peter walks away from Liam and Sean as he looks for Artemis. He shows his badge to the officers blocking the crime scene and ducks under the famous yellow tape. He asks a few officers where Artemis Daly is, and then he is directed to the backyard. The sun is shining brightly in Peter's eyes, and he forgot his sunglasses at Keith's house, which doesn't help. The weather is great but not for this poor sucker that's laying on the cement grounds. The victim is not covered yet; he's a huge young man in his late twenties or early thirties, wearing a well-made suit shirt and pants but the suit jacket is not around. There's a name tag, "Chase Whitman," and the company name, "California Realtors."

"Hey Peter," says Artemis Daly, who has brown hair with some distinguishing gray showing on his sideburns. His 5'10" frame and tiger green eyes stop ladies in their tracks! There's a chain around his neck with a golden shield that says, "Los Angeles Detective." Peter and Artemis go way back to their childhood days; they were best of buddies and lived in Calistoga, Northern California. Lately it has been difficult to get together and just get some beers to catch up with life.

"Hey, Artemis, what's shakin'?" he asks with a smile, as he walks over to his good friend. Peter tries to remember the last time he saw Artemis. It must has been two years ago since Peter hung out with Artemis at his sister Adrasteia's wedding.

"Different day same crap! How are you? You want to take a look at this." Artemis announces, as he inches his way towards the dead body. As Peter looks in the backyard, he sees lots of men and women in black police uniforms as well as other LA county workers moving around the yard.

"Okay…just need some more sleep," he answers, as he puts on latex gloves. Peter sees a young caucasian adult who appears to be six feet tall and seems about ten pounds overweight. The crime unit didn't get a chance to work on him to collect any evidences yet, and an autopsy will determine what and how this person died. There's an envelope in the victim's hand. A name is written on the envelope that says, "Agent Keith Heiden."

"Peter, I think the name on the envelope is one of your agents," Artemis says, as he stands next to his old friend.

"Unfortunately, yes," Peter answers, as he rubs his full mane of thick hair.

"If it's okay, I'll go ahead and process this envelope in my department and check out the body completely," Artemis says, as he looks eye to eye at his old friend. Peter has not changed a lot, he looks great!

"Thanks, Artemis, that's fine. Here's my number," Peter says, while he passes him his business card just in case he doesn't have it. "Please let me know if you have anything."

"Sure, Peter, I'll call you. Maybe we can get a couple of drinks and catch up?" Artemis asks, as he puts the business card in his wallet. "The victim worked for a California Realty Company in Orange County. Does that mean anything to you?"

"Well, Agent Heiden's wife works for a realtor office in Orange County. I think they may possibly work at the same office. If you don't mind, can you check out the information? I really have a headache," Peter replies.

"Sure, that's no problem. Are you okay, Peter?" his old friend asks with a concerned look.

"Yeah… I'm fine," he says, as he is really lying. He's not sure if he's helping Keith and the family, but he knows that he needs to try anyway. "If you can help me out that would be great. I think I need all the help I can get on this," Peter requests.

"Peter, I'll keep in touch…and I'll do the same," he answers without a second breath.

Peter heads back to Keith's house and suddenly his cell phone rings. "Hello," he answers, as he tries to walk quickly through the noisy crowd of people.

"Peter, where are you? It sounds loud," the woman asks.

"I'm sorry, I'm working, "he answers. "I'm sorry…who is this?"

"It's Elise," she answers with a friendly voice, "Dr. Elise Sheppard."

"Hello, Dr. Elise. So how's the mind-picking business these days?" he laughs with excitement in his voice as he finally reaches the house and opens the door without anyone blocking his path.

"You're funny, Peter. I'm calling you regarding Agent Heiden. Did he talk to you about the incident between his daughter and me?" Elise asks, as she makes herself a cup of coffee for the tenth time.

"Yes, he told me what happened to you guys," he answers as he waits to hear the real reason for Elise's phone call. "You really like to cause trouble!" he laughs again.

"I guess I do. I really think that this family doesn't like me. I want to give you a heads–up… I have to take action for the stress and anxiety the Heiden family put me through these past few weeks. This Monday, I will file a disciplinary measure against Keith. I'm sorry that it has to be this way. I know you're good friends with the family."

Elise states, as she sits down on the couch. A minute later she is lying down to take a nap.

Peter opens the door to the extra bedroom since he finally can chill, and talk to his soon to be girl. "Oh please, Elise, don't be sorry! Yes, I love them and they're part of my additional family, but Keith has to be punished. It's called tough love!" Peter answers honestly, as he closes the door behind him. "I'm sorry about all of this. Whatever, you feel has to be done do it and don't hold back. Keith is a grown man, and he needs a few kicks in the rear. I know that you will lay down the law. Just be easy on kicking him because I still need him for work." Peter states. "Will this action cause damage for Keith's progress with the evaluation and all?"

"No, because the evaluation is a report for his actions last year not now. I'll make sure the two subjects are separated. Thanks for understanding, and I won't hurt him too much. Just be aware it's not going to be easy for you," Elise states.

"Yes, I know. You don't have to tell me! I have experienced many of the Heiden dramas over the years. I don't need to see reality shows on TV; I have one right here! I'm so happy that you're not angry with me. I don't want to feel your high heels on my Ukrainian, English and Sicilian trunk," Peter laughs.

You can hear the giggles through the phone line. "Peter, you're too much, but also very honest about your feelings That's what a lady wants in a man, honesty not crap!" she says and then the laughter starts.

They both laugh together while ten minutes go by. "Uncle Peter!" Colin shouts from the other side of the door, as his little hands move frantically to get his attention.

"I'll be right out, buddy!" Peter replies, as he looks at the door and sees a tiny hand coming underneath the bottom.

"Elise, you have to see this. Colin is calling my name on the other side of the door." Peter laughs, "and now I'm seeing his little fingers underneath the door wiggling, to tell me that he's there, and to come and play with him!" Peter begins to laugh harder. His body starts to shake the bed.

"That's so cute!"

"Uncle Peter!" shouts the little one, as his hand moves back to the other side of the door.

"Uncle Peter!" he shouts back, "when can we have our real first date?" Peter asks, as he tries to get up from the bed and walks to the door to unlock it. As the door opens and he leaves the guest bedroom he hears a lot of talking and movement downstairs.

"Well, Peter, you can call me later in the week or set the date now. What the hell. I'll go out with you," Elise replies, as she looks at the clutter around her apartment. It needs a cleaning, and she sees a spider's web and dirt that comes out of nowhere. It seems to just creep up in her apartment. She's very concerned that the continuing filth will raise her rent one day!

"That's fine, I'll pick you up at your place at 6:00 p.m. tomorrow night, and we'll go out for a very nice dinner, have a couple of drinks, some laughs and talk about us. What do you think?" Peter asks without any worries on his part. He had asked out many fine hot-looking Californian girls in his day and is very confident in himself.

"It's a date!" she exclaims.

"I've got to go now! I can hear the family downstairs and smell Keith's cooking and that's waking up my stomach! I'll see you tomorrow night at 6:00 p.m. Just don't mess up the patient's mind too much, goodbye," Peter says as he walks downstairs. He sees a huge plate of Keith's famous spaghetti and ground up meat with homemade sauce. Keith lived in a one-bedroom apartment after living at the Andersons. The living quarters were small, but you could always smell the Italian food cooked from upstairs at dinnertime. His landlords were Mr. Alonzo and Mrs. Carmela Amoretti, and they always welcomed Keith with open arms. They treated him like one of their sons, and they already had three in the family. One day Keith had a full day of cooking lessons with Mr. and Mrs. Amoretti. The Italian meals were to die for.

"Peter, do you have my home address?" Elise asks.

"Yes, I do. Remember I drove you home so you could get a clean pair of clothes," he answers without taking a single breath.

"Yes, I remember, okay...good-bye then," Elise hangs up the phone, and suddenly she feels hungry herself. She's not a cook at all... I guess it'll be another frozen dinner in the microwave again.

Minutes later you can hear the sound of the Heiden family ready to eat. "Peter, you always know when to come into the kitchen when dinner is ready," Keith says while he takes the hot garlic bread from the oven to the cutting board. Without a minute to spare he takes one mitten off and gets a sharp knife to cut the bread.

"I love your cooking more than you," says Peter with a friendly smile on his face because it's true! He feels a pull on his jeans and sees the little clone of Keith standing near him. He tries to get that extra love and attention from his favorite uncle.

"Peter, can you please put the plate of spaghetti out on the dining room table? Thanks," Keith requests.

"Uncle Peter!" Colin screams, as he looks up at him.

"Okay, buddy, can you let go of my pants so we can eat?" he states, as he tries to tell Colin to move out of the way.

CHAPTER
THIRTY-TWO

*P*reston Williamson walks into a Star Bucks on Wilshire Boulevard. There are a lot of people coming and going through the coffee shop, as he stands on a very long line during an afternoon work week. At that moment his cell phone rings and the caller ID posts "unknown."

"Hello," Preston says, as he looks at his watch noting the time.

"Hello, Mr. Williamson! I've heard so much about you. Maybe, in my next life we'll meet in person, but for now please listen very carefully. I'm not going to tell you my name. That is insignificant right now. You can ask any questions after I finish. I'm a DEA agent for the greater Los Angeles area. I'm working undercover for the department. Right now, I'm trying to fish out any important information about the Jose Medina's organization. I started working as a mole ten years ago after the case went south from a drug raid. No one knows that I exist, especially Agents Peter Darling and Keith Heiden. They think I'm dead and it has to remain that way because there is a leak in the department. Mr. Medina has a personal grudge against Agent Heiden, and he's trying to destroy his life. Maybe he knows about me as the mole in his organization but can't prove it. So he does the next best thing to get to Agent Heiden," the man exclaims through the cell phone.

Preston walks to the corner and sees a young woman coming towards him. The name "Tammy" is written on her name tag. "Welcome to Star Bucks. How can I help you today?" she says with a friendly smile.

"Hello?" says the man on the other line.

"Just a minute, I'll be right with you," Preston announces, as he tries to hold a conversation with both the waitress and the person on the other side of phone line.

"Sorry, sir, do you know what you want?" asks the lady.

"I'll have Royal English Breakfast Tea venti size," Preston says, as he looks at Tammy.

Tammy smiles at the tall gentleman with a British accent. She's willing to serve anybody that doesn't have a child who is pulling on mommy or daddy for extra attention. Those people make her job harder than ever.

"Right away $2.75, please," the young college student chimes in and she has the change ready for her customer without missing a beat. "Thank you, cheerio!" answers Preston. Seconds later the coffee shop is getting busy and Preston was lucky to find a comfortable lounge chair. He slips into it slowly as to not spill his hot tea with a touch of lemon. British tea has a rich taste. He really misses home. The states are very nice but nothing like Great Britain. They really know how to treat you with style; the fine foods, people, and the great history.

Not realizing that the phone went dead, Preston's cell rings again, "hello!"

He slowly takes a sip of tea before he answers," I'm so sorry why are you calling me??"

"I know that you converse with Agent Heiden. I need to warn you that Agent Heiden's life is in serious danger, and the DEA has a leak inside its department," he exclaims.

"Do you want me to tell him that you are alive? What is your name?" Preston asks hoping he can get an answer.

"Not yet. It's too dangerous, but I thank you for listening. I have to go now." Then immediately you hear the sound of the dial tone.

Preston thinks it's strange that the mole would call him, and how did he get his number?

CHAPTER
THIRTY-THREE

*D*uring dinner Peter is cracking jokes left and right. All the kids laugh but Justine and Keith don't seem to be in a jovial mood. Justine really wants to talk to him, but Keith tries to avoid her all evening. She knows that he's extremely upset and heartbroken over her heavy drinking. Passing out on the family room couch and not being there for him at his father's funeral didn't make matters any better. Justine feels Keith is giving her the silent treatment. It's a deadly method, because she wants to really explain her actions.

Three hours later Keith puts Colin to bed, and then he turns himself in for the night. Peter watches TV by himself in the family room. The other kids are hanging out around the house not really tired, and Justine feels very jumpy and concerned that Keith will not talk to her.

It's now 9:30 p.m. and Keith is sound asleep. You can hear some snoring from time to time, as he lies in bed with the blankets resting on his weak body. She spots a manila envelope that has "Agent Keith Heiden" written on it. It stands on its side between his nightstand lamp and a box of tissues. She walks quietly and slowly as not to wake up Keith. Justine carefully opens the envelope trying not to damage anything. She doesn't want any evidence pointing to the fact that she opened it without permission. For some strange reason she has a strong gut feeling that she needs to open this, as it might be for her.

Justine's eyes become wider, and she desperately tries to catch her next breath without making a sound. There are a lot of pictures with her and her newest lover, Treat Miller. They're having sex in a sleazy hotel just a couple of miles away from her home. Some of the shots are very close up; some are far away and there are shots showing them leaving the crime scene. It looks like a professional photographer's work and he has done the job very well. Suddenly her emotion starts to run away from her. She puts her hands over her mouth and tries desperately not to let out a cry or scream. The overwhelming pain that she has caused her family is too unbearable. She hops on the crutches and rushes quietly to the fireplace. As she tries to get the matches lit and into the grate mantle and fireplace, Justine's hands start to shakes uncontrollably. She is having trouble starting the fire. "Just control yourself, Justine," she whispers under her breath, as she tries to convince herself that this will work. Just take baby steps. You have pulled some good scams in your day and this is not new to you. The sixth time she strikes the match she gets a spark. She slowly opens the fireplace gate and tosses in the pictures of her and Treat Miller. She would like to forget it ever happened, but enjoyed every minute at the same time.

After last year and the Carlos Garcia case there was a lot of stress and tension between Keith and Justine. Now Dr. Sheppard is in the picture, and Justine feels that she's not included in the group. Maybe she's a little jealous subconsciously but she never would admit to that. She knows that Keith would be very angry at her if she did anything to block his recovery process. Keith discovered Justine's first lover, Scott Warren, who she met through the job. The affair ended quickly because Keith beat up Scott within an inch of his life. He ended up with a few broken ribs, one broken arm and nose and lots of cuts and bruises too. Keith made sure that Scott would never step foot in this town again. He agreed on everything and wouldn't tell a soul what had happen. He was very afraid for his life if Keith caught him again. So Justine understands clearly that Keith is extremely dangerous to others if they cross him. She's concerned that Treat will have the same fate that Scott had by her overpowering aggressive husband if he finds out.

Each of the pictures is burning slowly, but the memories are still in Justine's mind for a long time. The pictures were taken professionally and very personally. Whoever took them didn't miss any angles or actions of Treat and Justine. She takes the long fireplace fork to move the pictures around so every part of the evidence burns completely. It's really strange that Keith taught her and the kids to do everything in their power to cover family secrets. Keith has a lot of secrets from his past and now his own family has to stick together with their secrets. Justine is very tired and upset about what she has done to herself and him. Keith moves to his left side and puts the lightweight covers on himself without even opening his eyes. She's praying that he won't get up to go to the master bathroom. At that moment Justine feels a tickle in her nose, and suddenly a sneeze is coming up to the surface. She tries to cover her mouth but the sneezes again and again. She just can't stop. She looks intently at Keith's body to notice if he makes a move to wake up. Her heart beats rapidly; she's thinking how to cover herself. Justine knows that Keith will be very upset about the whole situation. Here it comes, another sneeze and she rushes to the bathroom to avoid any loud noise to disturb the sleeping monster.

Minutes later Justine collects herself and walks back to the fireplace. There are a lot of questions on her mind. Is she as bad as everyone thinks? Is she a total bitch, and a heartless individual who doesn't care about anyone but herself? She knows that she's not perfect because look what she's married to. Her husband that can't stand on his own two feet, with his abusive past is now getting to her and the children. It's just way too much for her to handle. What happened ten years ago and knowing what she knows is hurting her heart. Now last year is taking a toll. She feels trapped in her marriage and Keith hasn't opened up to her in years about his feelings. Now that Dr. Sheppard is in the picture, it only made matters worse. Justine feels that she's sitting on the sidelines watching the game from afar. She hates feeling like she's the third wheel and she knows that Keith still loves her, but does she love him?

CHAPTER
THIRTY-FOUR

*A*s Justine lies besides Keith in her white robe and slippers, she finds it difficult to sleep. She's totally exhausted from working so hard to hide the evidence of her moral crime. Her tears continue to overflow like a waterfall, and her heart bleeds from her sadness. Justine watches the clock on her nightstand as it shows 4:20 a.m., then 5:30 a.m. and finally 7:46 a.m. She sees Keith start to wake up slowly, as he gets up to go into the bathroom. He grabs a clean pair of boxers on his way but never notices Justine. She feels empty inside and wonders if Keith has already seen the pictures and is testing her. It may be one of those DEA skills that he's using on her, as he often does to keep one step ahead of the kids.

The large bags under her eyes are very noticeable, and her frizzy hair doesn't help. That strong drink she had the other night didn't make matters any better. She never thought she'd have an alcohol problem, but the drama of living with Keith and his issues never made things easy for her. Justine's father always said you have to watch your back when dealing with Keith. He still has a bit of an edge about him that you just can't put your finger on it. Subconsciously Justine wants to punish Keith for the hurt he caused her with the Jose Medina and Carlos Garcia cases. These two affairs could make that happen. He already went up the wall when he found out about her first lover. Scott felt Keith's wrath with his fist. What will become of Treat when Keith gets his hands on him?

Twenty minutes later, Keith comes out of the bathroom, walks around the room, and dries himself off with a soft cotton towel. He takes a glimpse of the fireplace and out of the corner of his blue eyes he sees a small piece of a picture, which cannot really be identified. Justine thinks to herself, *Here it comes the emotional roller coaster ride!*

"Good morning, Keith," Justine says with a calm but quivering sound in her voice. She is trying very hard not to give any indication that anything is wrong.

He smiles at her, trying not to show any emotion even though he's highly upset over the pictures that he has seen. It's one of the gifts that he perfected over the course of his life, especially dealing with Justine's father Sir William. Of course Sir William is not his title; he's really Sir Tart William. Keith wishes that this British holier-than thou man would fall off the face of the earth. He has a foul taste in his mouth; that Tart ass father-in-law puts a lot of crazy thoughts into Justine's head.

"Good morning, Justine. How do you feel?" he asks, as he puts on his navy blue shirt and designer jeans that Justine had just bought for him. The truth of the matter is that Keith hates stores and shop-ping and goes to great lengths to say away from them. Keith is a fast dresser. He has it timed just right after dealing with four kids and crazy work hours. He knows you can't waste any time. As he walks over to get his light-weight tan sandals, he automatically puts on his wedding band. For some strange reason he feels naked without his ring on, but at the same time, he can't help letting out a loud sigh. He knows that in a few minutes the road ahead will become very bumpy, as he confronts Justine with her crime of passion. Both of them look at each other waiting for the ball to drop.

"I'm surprised that you would ask me how I feel considering you were the one who just buried your father! Can you please tell me how you feel about the whole thing?" she asks. Justine thinks to herself that he seems extremely calm at this moment.

"Justine, you just came back from rehab. Why wouldn't I ask you? We all missed, love, worried about you and your welfare," Keith announces. He looks in the direction of the fireplace, as she tries to get his attention towards her because she has a strange feeling that he's putting the pieces together. He will realize that the envelope is missing from this nightstand, and Justine will have to play stupid.

She will say, "Keith, I don't know what you're talking about, an envelope… I didn't see one." Maybe he'll forget to ask again or maybe not. He's that kind of person that would keep asking questions until he gets the answers that he needs. Keith suddenly walks into the bathroom to put his wet towel back on the rack.

"How do you feel?" she asks, as she rubs the back of her right leg to get some relief from the pain.

"I'm sorry, what?" he asks, as his voice travels from the bathroom and echoes to the master bedroom. Keith tries very hard not to show any emotion. It's hard for him to forget the image of his wife's betrayal, which will be embedded in his mind for the rest of his life.

"Are you okay? You had to deal with your father's death and see your estranged family," she asks with a sound of compassion in her voice. "Keith, don't you dare begin to play mind games right now."

"I'm not okay, but thanks for asking," he replies. The truth of the matter is he really doesn't know how to feel about the man that gave him a lot of hell throughout his childhood. You can say it's a love-hate relationship that you can't explain, even if you try. Keith really wishes that he had a father like Peter has. His dad, Dan (Peter taught Colin to sing, "Dan the man! Dan can do it like no one can!), is a real father and will do anything for all of his seven children. He has a heart of gold and his kids know that he will do anything for them. Throughout the years, Dan treated Keith like a son. He does call Keith twice a month to see how things are going, and if he can do anything to help out on his end. Dan also asks about the kids and Justine. Keith never really asked Peter if he told his mom and dad about his abused childhood, because they are so nice to him and his family. Or maybe Keith has done a lot for Peter over the years, and they are just saying, "Thank you for helping our son. He really needs it. I mean he really needs it!"

"Can you please tell me how you really feel?" You know burying your dad and all?" she asks, a bit concerned for him. He used to openly tell her how he felt.

"I'm sorry, but I can't talk about my father right now. I'm overwhelmed by it all. I know that you want to help, and I thank you for that. But not now. Please let it go," he solemnly asks, as he walks toward her dresser and looks at himself in the huge mirror.

He feels exhausted and looks it! Keith also doesn't want to deal with Justine's affair at this moment. He knows that his wife is covering up her last stunt. As a DEA agent he can see all the signs both physically and emotionally. As the saying goes, "You become your job." Of course, he hates to say it, but being abused helps also. You must always use all five senses to live. He also must convince himself and others that he has a normal family life and childhood. That's a full-time job all by itself.

"I bet you told Dr. Sheppard!" Justine snaps, as she tries to get up but is unable to because of her injury. She's not very happy about the whole situation with him and Dr. Giggles.

"Justine, I haven't spoken to Dr. Sheppard for over three days now because of the circumstances!" Keith snaps right back to stop his so-called jealous wife.

"You're a liar! Erin told me what happened that morning with Dr. Sheppard! Why did you punish our daughter?" she exclaims.

"You have to believe me. I didn't plan to punish Erin! But under the circumstances, I had to because she threw a dinner plate at my therapist. Dr. Sheppard almost got hit with the dish! That's all I need, more drama!" Keith snaps, as he walks away from Justine. He's very well aware that in Justine's eyes Erin can do no wrong, especially if it concerns his therapist.

"You punished our Erin for that?!" she shouts right back, as she looks with her intense blue eyes at her husband of eighteen years.

"I don't care what you say! The rule stands! Erin is grounded for a whole month for what she did to Dr. Sheppard! I know that you're proud of our little girl, but I'm not. So why do you dislike Dr. Sheppard so much?" Keith asks, as he walks to the lounge chair and lays his body down.

"She called me a bitch!" Justine shouts, as she tries to get out of bed. It's not easy at all to balance yourself on crutches. She hops in the direction of Keith to make sure to get her point across.

"Justine, you know that's not too far from the truth! I already told you that I scolded her for what she said to you. I had threatened to take her license away from her," Keith stated slowly.

"Keith, why would you do a stupid thing like that!" Justine shouts.

"I know it's a stupid thing, but at the time I was fighting for my woman. I have a strong feeling that she'll be telling my bosses at DEA Internal Affairs about the phone call. About your drama the other day, I'm a dead man! You don't care about me, or what I do as long it doesn't interfere with your spoiled rich daddy's little girl's word!" Keith shouts as blood rushes through his abused body.

"How dare you! I'm not Daddy's spoiled rich little girl! My world is not perfect!" she shouts with sounds of frustration in her voice. She pokes at him saying that her marriage to him is not as sweet as apple pie. There are a lot of sour apples in the dessert.

"Blame me, why not? You knew that I was over my head when you received a new BMW for your graduation present from your father. You're daddy's little girl!" Keith rudely laughs, because what he said was truth, not fiction.

"Keith, stop this ludicrous talk, and I'm not the spoiled brat that you think I am!" she exclaims. "I paid my dues in my life! I want more…"

"Really, I don't believe you! Justine, I know you too well!! This is not the fight; it's the warm-up!" Keith shouts. "So let's get started!"

"Keith, I want to tell you why I drank a whole bottle of Russian vodka. I think of all the pressure and stress from what happened ten years ago and now last year too. It's taken a toll on me!" she announces, as she tries to stand. Justine leans on one crutch, but she's afraid that she might fall on her face. She decides to sit right back down on the bed. Keith is not moving an inch to make this easier for her physically or emotionally.

"I know that you'll never forgive me for what I did! I'm sorry! I don't know what else to say to make amends and to move on. Maybe this is the main reason why our marriage is breaking at the seams. We have a lot of crap to clean up," Keith says. "So why don't we start cutting through the layers of the damaged cake!"

"I'm sorry, Justine, you have a disease that needs professional help. I'll support you in any way I can, but that's all I can do for you. If you need to scratch off your skin because you have a fixation to get a solid drink, call your sponsor!" Keith shouts, as he walks through the bedroom in different directions and stops right in front of Justine to get her full attention. "Let me fill in the blanks to get started on this fight. You are always sexy in my eyes, and I guess you really thought that way about yourself, spreading your legs for the Greater Los Angeles area! It doesn't take you long before you go into another man's bed!" Keith shouts with full force, as veins are ready to pop out of his neck and head. He made a promise to himself not to take another drink for the rest of his life, after getting disowned by his family and also he didn't want to end up like his alcoholic parents. But for Justine it's a different story. How does one help her? She's not a heavy drinker, and she only drinks a glass of fine wine on the weekends. "Listen, even the dogs in the neighborhood know you are in heat!" he yells to put another nail in his coffin.

Justine's eyes go back in her head and she say, "you bastard! you saw the pictures already! You set me up!" She was ambushed. Her face turns red within a split-second. Justine thinks to herself that Keith is at his breaking point from all the drama that's coming up to the surface now. It's not going to be easy for her to convince him that she's innocent in all this. She wants to explain why what she did was justifiable.

"You set me up! How dare you! Who do you think you're messing with! I'm not your hobby to play games with!" Justine exclaims while her voice travels, which sends a piercing sound to Keith's ear.

"As you should know by now, I don't like games! You've had an affair with that shit head boyfriend Treat Miller!" Keith shouts furiously. "Hate to tell you he's not good looking at all…so he must be great in the bedroom to fill your needs because I couldn't!"

"You hired a private investigator to spy on Treat and me! You have some nerve! Who do you think you are spying on me!" Justine screams, as she feels her lungs popping out of her weak body. Justine never likes to lose especially to her husband. They need to stop this fighting for their children's sake before it's too late.

"After you had slept with that shit head you have no rights! I bet my life you slept with him more than once! Yes, I hired a private investigator because I had a bad taste in my mouth that Treat was up to no good! I was right and I have proof to put him away for a long time! The private investigator didn't take the pictures, and I don't know who did. When I do find out who did the job, I'm going to buy that person an extra large cup of coffee just to say, "thank you." Keith shouts. He clears his voice for his (capital B) bitchy wife to hear what he's about to say next. "You know what happened to your last lover? I'm going to find Treat Miller and do the same to him! Maybe your first ex-lover and Treat can have lunch together. They can talk about how they received their injuries." Keith laughs.

"This is not funny at all! Keith, you're insane," she roars, as she protests that he has no right to invade her privacy.

"You're a slut!" he snaps right back. They're both acting like two teenagers fighting, but they don't care one way or another if the neighbors hear them or not. It's war!

"Justine, what were you thinking about playing Russian roulette?! You risked your life, mine, and the kids!" he shouts, as he paces like an untamed lion, just waiting to attack. Keith looks straight into Justine's eyes. He's trying to find any compassion in her crystal blue eyes but there's nothing. "I really should sue Treat for Alienation of Affection, but unfortunately in the state of California, there is no law!" This law means that you can sue the other lover who has destroyed your relationship with your partner.

Justine just realizes she's doing it to herself as well as the people she loves. Keith suddenly stops pacing. "Is Colin my son?" he asks with a sharp, clear voice.

"Keith, Colin is your son. He's a clone of you! How can you ask that kind of question!" Justine explains, as she feels overwhelmed with guilt.

"Keith, I really want to explain why I drank, and also the reason that I had two affairs," Justine solemnly requests, as she stops from what she's saying and takes deep breath. "Well... I was alone, and you never give me support."

Keith quickly interrupts her, "I just want to know if Colin is my child or not. You make me sick, and I can't even look at you. Those images of the pictures are still in my head forever! You tell me all the time to take control of my life but what about you? It doesn't apply to you? I'm so sick and tired of trying to please you and your righteous attitude toward me, when you're sleeping around and you're no better! I'll never bow my head down to you ever again! Now that my father is gone, the tension on finding and killing him myself is lifted. I'm saving myself! Our kids need to have a normal life away from you and your wants! I'm making a turning point! Did you ever love me, Justine, or did you feel really sorry for me because I was abused?" Keith asks, as he looks at Justine for a truthful answer.

"I always loved you! I never stopped loving you! Yes, at the beginning of our relationship, I did feel sorry for you but in time I fell in love with you. Even though we don't say I love you as we should," Justine says with tears rolling down her face, but Keith just disregards her water works.

He smirks and says with a sarcastic tone, "You have a funny way of showing it! To say I love you doesn't mean anything if you don't feel it in your hear!" Here it comes again! The voice in his head echoes throughout his whole head. *Keith, just stop shaking! You look like an insane person!! You should know that this will happen! Why are you acting like this especially when it comes from Justine's drama? This behavior shouldn't be a surprise. I can really feel the aggression crawling up through my body. Fuck! Keith, just take long, deep breaths and let the tension release itself. Why are you giving up? She's not worth the time of day! Don't be like Dad! This is not what you want; what Dad did to Mom was unjustified. You're not an abusive person in any way, Keith. You're not your father! You're an idiot to think that! Just stop it!*

CHAPTER
THIRTY-FIVE

*A*gain Keith paces like an untamed lion waiting for the attack. "Justine, I really feel sorry for you. You take extreme measures to find love. I didn't think you ever loved me. I bet you felt pity on me because my family disowned me! It's like picking up a stray puppy. You bring it to your home and give it love, warmth, and attention," he exclaims sarcastically and laughs at the same time.

Keith's sad story is heard so many times; that Justine just wants him to move on. "Keith, you're not a stray puppy!" Justine says, as she turns to wipe her tears away. She feels very tired and the arguments never end quickly.

"I may not be a stray puppy, but you're certainly a bitch!" he snaps back. Suddenly the tears are pouring down Justine's face again.

"Go to hell!" Justine answers back. "How dare you!"

"I'm already there…thanks to you!!" he says maliciously.

As Keith feels his heart ripping from his chest, he gives Justine a final ultimatum. "You have the choice to leave or stay in this so-called marriage. It's up to you!!" He is very disappointed in himself for not seeing the telltale signs of her affairs. The truth is he is very tired from the inside out, and especially too tired to fight with his wife.

"What do you want?" Justine asks uneasily.

"I know what I want. It's your choice! If you stay we have a lot of work ahead of us, like going to therapy. If not, I'll take the kids and raise them by myself. I want to give these kids a happy childhood, which is something I never had!" Keith replies angrily.

"So you'd take everything from me!" Justine shouts, as she gets up from the bed and balances herself with the crutches beside her.

"You never had it!" Keith snaps back with anger and yells directly in Justine's face. "So, tell me, Justine, why did you have two affairs? You might as well tell me all your deep dark secrets now."

"I'm sorry, Keith, I guess… I was really trying to punish you for all that went down ten years ago and this last year as well. I wanted to get back at you, to make you feel my pain. I'm so sorry; please forgive me!" Justine says with a soft voice.

"Who the hell do you think you are? Forgive you after I've seen those pictures! You're out of your mind!" Keith shouts, as he feels a heavy pressure of stress weighing down on him. He can't do this anymore. It's going to kill him before the weekend. Justine makes him this way, and he tries very hard to have control, but he can't make any promises, especially when he's fighting.

"Please, Keith, you have to listen to me!" Justine pleads, as she tries to massage her injured leg. "I really want to explain everything… I love you."

"Did you also love Treat?" he asks, but doesn't really want to hear the answer. Keith can feel his heart pounding. He never thought he would be married and with kids, but a wife having two affairs was not part of the bargain. Keith was blindsided, and he realizes that he never had any control of his whole life. Justine had the wheel and Keith was just part of a plan that never should've lasted this long.

"Yes," Justine answers, as she wipes her tears off her face. How much can one heart take?

"You can't love two people at the same time! You make me sick to my stomach! So while you have been working on your new hobby, I'm working my ass off to prove to you that I'm sorry for all that I've done to you? I don't know how many times I can say that I'm sorry to you! I'm truly sorry, and I don't know what else I can do to change your mind! I deserve the punishment that you gave me but to sleep with someone else!! This is your second lover! Are you starting the hooker business off Hollywood Boulevard because your real estate business is going south?" Keith demands in total frustration.

"Go to hell!" she screams.

"Like I said before, I'm already there!" Keith snaps right back again.

Suddenly, Justine becomes extremely angry. She can't get the words out of her mouth. Without a single sign Justine attacks Keith, but this time he blocks the blow by taking his hand and grabbing Justine's wrist before she had can hit him across the face.

"Keith, please you're hurting me! Please let go!" Justine pleads, as she tries to break free from her controlling and very unstable husband. Keith looks directly into her sharp crystal blue eyes which are now a shade of red and full of tears. He doesn't feel sorry for what he's doing to her. He must put his foot down, claim his life and save his kids from his wife's insane and extreme behavior.

"Please, Keith, what are you doing to me? I'm sorry!" Justine pleads.

"This is the last time I'll be your personal punching bag! You'll never hit me ever again! Just try me, and I'll make your life a living hell!" Keith exclaims, as he is still holding Justine's wrist tightly. It's a gratifying feeling.

"Please, Keith, let me go! I'll never hit you again. I promise! Let me go! You're scaring me! Please let me go!" Justine pleads for her life to be spared, as she tries to break away. Even though he's stronger and more powerful, she still tries her best to release his hold. Justine wouldn't go down without a fight; she's a hardass both emotionally and physically. It might look like Keith's in control of the situation, but he's very unstable. She knows this and she can always use his weaknesses to her advantage. Keith has a lot of guilt on his shoulders.

As Keith continues with his attack on Justine, the thoughts of his horrible childhood creep into his mind. When Keith was seven years old he watched his mother get a beating from his abusive father. He stood motionless, feet glued to the floor and not able to move. What was a little boy to do?

Suddenly, Keith pulls Justine aggressively up from the floor and forcefully rams her against the wall. She screams as she struggles, but she is unable to escape because of his strength. Keith screams into her ear as his body begins to shake.

"Please, Keith, you're hurting me. Let go! Please let me go!" Justine shouts into his left ear, as she spots their oldest son with a gun in his hand, and a look that can kill. "Patrick! Patrick, don't do it!" Justine shouts.

"Let her go!" Patrick shouts, as he holds his father's loaded 9mm Glock and points it at his dad's back. "Let her go! Let her go if you want to see the sun again!" Keith doesn't listen or is blocking it out.

"Patrick, please!" Justine tries to override Keith's screaming in her ears, but their son doesn't hear a word she is saying, "Patrick, no, Patrick, don't! Please, son, I'm really fine!" Patrick's hands begin to shake like a leaf. His mind and vision are blurry. "Keith, please tell your son that I'm all right!" Keith stops the screaming and continues his heavy breathing.

"Hey, Keith! Why don't you face me like a man before I pull the trigger?!" Patrick orders. "Turn around!"

Keith turns his head as per request, but it's too late. The sound of the gun goes off, and both Keith and Justine fall to the ground for safety.

Patrick stands still with the gun in his hand. Luckily the bullet lands in the wall and not into them.

"You guys are assholes!" Patrick yells with anger and then runs away leaving them behind.

He's unable to look back to see if his parents are hurt or not. The truth of the matter is he doesn't care. He storms out of the house leaving the front door wide open. Patrick starts to cry and suddenly realizes what he just did. *I shot my parents!*

Peter sees Patrick rushing out of the house with the gun in his hand. The teenager is beside himself and the agent has an idea what went down. Peter knows it's not good. Patrick stops in his tracks for no reason at all. As he stares into space with a blank look on his face, he begins to turn very pale. Patrick feels like he's going to pass out any minute now, and he doesn't hear any sounds especially Peter walking up to him.

"What did I do?" Patrick screams, as he waves the gun aimlessly in the air. "Oh, my God… What did I do?"

Liam sees the drama unfolding in front of him and quickly gets out of his car. He will back Peter up in any way he can.

"Put the gun down, now!" Liam orders, as he points his gun at the teenager.

He doesn't care one way or another how it came about; all he knows is that he has to disengage this dangerous situation before it gets worse.

"Liam, stand down. I have it!" Peter orders.

"Peter, I have your back!" Liam shouts, as he can feel his heart beating out of his chest; his palms start to sweat from the excitement! "I'm not going to say it again, son. Put the gun down now!"

"Liam, stand down!" Peter shouts, as he gives him a firm look. He tries to override the young DEA agent, but it's not easy to say the least. Seconds later Liam finally listens to his supervisor...even though it wasn't easy.

"Son! You need to put down the gun for Uncle Peter," he pleads softly, as he walks very slowly on a freshly manicured lawn towards the teenager. "Your parents have a shit life! You don't have to be like them. You can change yourself. Just don't give into the madness. So, Patrick, please put the gun down."

"I hate him! Why, Uncle Peter?" Patrick shouts, as he tries not to cry in public. His right hand is waving the gun in the air.

"I don't know, son. Things happen! I don't have the answers to your questions. I'm really sorry, but they mess up your head!" Peter answers with a firm but gentle tone in his voice. He tries not to scare the young lad so he doesn't shoot anything in his path.

Patrick slowly puts the gun down on the ground and Peter carefully picks it up, putting the safety lock on and placing it in his pants. They both walk inside the house, and Patrick sees his dad coming down the stairs. He walks directly in front of him. "I hate you!" Keith doesn't react because he deserves whatever his son dishes out to him. Patrick was just doing his job to protect his mother from harm. His son walks to his mother in the kitchen and hugs her.

"Keith, I have your gun. I'll put it in a different place and tell you the location later. I know you want to keep this incident quiet."

"Thank you, Peter," answers Keith with a soft voice as he hears Colin crying upstairs. He notices that he didn't see the other kids in the house, or maybe he shouldn't worry because it's normal for everyone to scatter when trouble arises. Keith remembers all too well that his family did the same thing. His kids are probably emotionally scarred for life. It's a very sick cycle that really needs to be stopped. But how can you fix something that's been broken for so long?

Peter feels very uneasy and is deeply concerned for Patrick. He knows he must handle this family with caution. He sees the damaged couple both look at each other for support and smile, as if to say, "It's going to be okay."

That evening rolls around, and the family decides to order some Chinese food. Keith walks around the house not saying a word to anyone during dinnertime. He hears his cell phone ring and from the caller ID sees it is Mr. Williamson from Interpol. He doesn't answer it because he's not in the mood to talk to anyone, especially from Interpol.

CHAPTER
THIRTY-SIX

*K*eith arrived at the DEA department ready for work but exhausted from yesterday's family drama. He's happy that no one got hurt at the end of the day, especially where Patrick is concerned. Keith walks toward his office but something stops him in his tracks. A young woman in her mid-twenties is standing behind Jennifer's desk. She wears a light coral-colored blouse and light brown dress pants with a designer belt that matches her business outfit.

Keith has a confused look and says to himself, *is she the replacement because Jenny is out of work because a family member is very sick and she has to go back to China? These days I'm the last person to know anything.* She looks like she's just out of college. She stands about 5'4" or shorter, but you really can't tell from the high heels she's wearing. She has shoulder length brown wavy hair and is thin for her height.

"Hello, you must be Agent Heiden? My name is Nicole Cahill. I'm your new secretary. I'm sorry to say that Jenny's mom is very sick, and she had to return to China right away. I don't know if she's coming back or not. So I'm here to help you with your work and to make things run smoothly," she announces, as she puts out her right hand while holding files in the other. She seems very jumpy from where Keith is standing.

Keith shakes Nicole's hand and smiles back at her. She feels the scars but doesn't flinch even though the feeling is a surprise. "Yes, I'm Agent Keith Heiden. I'm happy that you're on board with the DEA Department. I'll miss Jenny, but I know that you'll do well here. I just want to say up front before we start that I'm a very private person. So can we just keep our conversation about business, and please don't be alarmed if I don't respond to you at first. You can ask anyone, and everyone will tell you that I'm a neurotic piece of work and that makes me a glowing citizen," He laughs. "Can I ask you who trained you for this position?"

This is a very strange way to introduce yourself. "Thank you for giving me the heads up about your disability," Nicole states. "Ms. Kerry Mercy trained me, and I can't believe it has been five months since I was recruited. So here I am! I know about your reputation around here, and I will do my best to step up to the plate!"

Keith smiles at her as he looks over her shoulder to see her workstation. Very organized. Even the dust bunnies have a case file! "That's good. I have to go to my office now. If you need me my door is always open," he answers and doesn't stay around for long to hear Nicole's very long response. He unlocks his office and walks in without missing a beat. Another day at the office! Oh what fun we're going to have!

Suddenly Nicole walks over to Keith and says, "Agent Heiden, please don't go into your office!" Keith walks out of his office with a surprised look. "Agent Jack Forrester needs to talk to you in conference room one as soon as possible," she announces.

"Do you know what Agent Forrester wants?" he asks, as he scratches his head to release any tension. Dealing with Agent Forrester is not a walk in the park from what the government grape vein is saying. Forrester comes out of the woodwork suddenly to become one of the head chiefs of the DEA, and he has only been with the company for about six months or more. He has also made it known that he's a badass, and doesn't care who he steps on to get his way.

"I don't know, but he is waiting for you now," Nicole replies, as she sits herself behind her very clean desk.

"I bet he is," Keith snaps back, as he walks toward his desk to put down his soft black leather briefcase. It was last year's birthday present from Justine; he was heartfelt to receive such a generous gift. Believe it or not this is one of the things that Keith loves about Justine. She tries very hard to find an unusual gift for him, and it isn't easy. Keith likes different items, and it shows around his office. The picture frames come from different countries. They're not bold but stylish to look at.

"I'll be back, Nicole. Do you have enough work to do to keep you busy until I return?" Keith asks.

"Yes, Agent Heiden," she answers with a friendly smile.

"Great, I'll be back soon... I hope," he answers with a concerned look on his face, as he locks his office door.

CHAPTER
THIRTY-SEVEN

〰〰

*M*inutes later Keith walks to conference room #1. He takes a deep breath to collect his thoughts before opening the door. He sees five people in the room who are all government department men and women. They are all sitting around a long conference table. As Keith walks into the room he catches an intense look from one of the agents.

"Hello, Agent Heiden, I don't think we ever met before. I'm Agent Jack Forrester from the main office in Virginia. I started working here a couple of months ago. You may have read a memo about me, or perhaps we passed each other in the halls," he states, as he shakes Agent Heiden's hand. Keith feels the man's cold hand or maybe it's his personality?

"Hello, Agent Forrester. Can you please tell me what this is all about? I have a lot of work on my desk, and I don't really have time for a friendly chat," Keith says, with a concerned look on his face. He doesn't like surprises, especially when someone else seems to have the upper hand.

"Please have a seat, Agent Heiden. You know everyone here, including Agent Peter Darling, your ex-supervisor," Agent Forrester states as he opens Keith's thick case file.

Keith walks slowly and sits down, as he tries to understand what the agent just said. *Why is Peter my ex-supervisor? Is he being fired? It's not a good feeling when you see a water jug with glasses placed in the middle of the table. Hold on tight it's going to be a roller coaster ride!*

"I'm sorry, Agent Forrester, you said ex-supervisor? I don't understand? What's going on??" Keith asks with a confused look. He can feel his airways slowly closing.

Agent Forrester suddenly interrupts Keith using a stern tone. "I'll explain everything to you in a second but first let's talk about a matter that needs to be addressed. I spoke to your therapist, Dr. Elise Sheppard the other day, and she shared some very strange but interesting information… Oh, before I forget, we are all sorry for your loss. It's terrible; I'm so sorry," Jack sighs. He doesn't care about Keith's past. We are here to run a law enforcement business with fewer bumps in the road.

"Thank you," he answers.

"Dr. Sheppard feels uneasy around your family at this point, and this can turn into a major problem! Be mindful that your work schedule starts at 7:00 p.m. and not 8:00 p.m. Agent Darling and I will investigate the error, but be sure to come in at 7:00 p.m. from this point forward. Another major concern for all of us is the disappearance of four case files that were ready to go before the grand jury. Can you please tell me what happened to these files? Think long and hard before answering, Agent Heiden, because your job may depend on it," Agent Forrester exclaims sarcastically.

Keith takes a deep breath. It's going to be a very long day. "I cannot see Dr. Sheppard in her office because I have to care for my three-year-old son. She does understand my situation. I didn't know that my wife and the doctor had a confrontation. She did call my wife a bitch, and I'm sorry that I threatened to take her license away," he quietly states.

That was a stupid mistake. Dr. Sheppard is the key to the future of his job. "*What the hell were you thinking, Keith? You are jeopardizing your job and family?!*"

"Okay! Did you know that your daughter threw a plate at Dr. Sheppard and almost hit her? Can you explain what that drama was about?" Jack asks curiously.

"Agent Forrester, the plate didn't hit Dr. Sheppard," Keith answers, as he squirms slowly in his seat. He takes a look around the room and sees different people including Peter with concerned expressions on their faces. The room is so quiet you can hear Agent Jack Forrester breathing. Keith looks very uneasy. He just wants to jump out of his skin and put his hands around his best friend's neck.

"Please, Agent Heiden, answer the questions as I give them to you. Once again why did your daughter throw the plate at Dr. Sheppard?" Agent Forrester asks sharply.

"I'm sorry to say I don't know. I guess my daughter was upset at the time. I'm not justifying what she did, and I punished her for her actions. She did also apologize to Dr. Sheppard," he answers, as he takes a deep breath.

Keith clears his throat and feels a heavy weight on his chest. It brings him back to when he was a child being degraded in front of his other siblings by his father. He remembers feeling very low. Sometimes, he wanted to kill himself before his father ripped him to shreds.

"Honestly, I don't know why my schedule changed to 7:00 p.m. I wasn't trying to fight the order. I didn't know the change took place. I finished the four cases on time as Agent Darling requested and sent them directly to the people who handle it next. I put my signature on the release forms to the other departments and then sent them on their way!" Keith pleads his case and then looks around at the other people in the room. He knows he's in deep trouble.

"Well, when I went to the departments there was no sign of a signature release form or the files. Where are they?" Agent Forrester asks with a snappy tone in his voice.

"This is very strange. I can honestly say that I don't know! I think I'm being framed and that someone is out to get me," Keith answers.

"This is not professional conduct by any means! You and your family treated Dr. Sheppard in a hurtful and degrading way. Dr. Elise Sheppard is a federal therapist. She and her company were hired by the DEA and other federal departments to oversee the mental health care of our agents. She was not hired to keep you and your family entertained over the summer months. This is your first and last warning to keep your family away from her! Your unprofessional behavior toward Dr. Sheppard stops now! From this day forward I'm your supervisor! Agent Darling can't save you anymore! I'm putting you on a very short leash, Agent Heiden. You'll have lots of work to keep you busy, and you will get calls from me every hour on the hour for updates! You will also have two double shifts this month starting today, and you'll come in on time with no arguments. I must tell you that your field service work is outstanding, and you will continue with it as before. It's just your attitude that needs an adjustment! Do you have any questions for us before we close this meeting?" Jack Forrester asks sternly.

"I have one question. Does Dr. Sheppard have to ask me about my personal life during our sessions, like my marriage and my children?" Keith asks, as he looks directly at Agent Forrester without blinking. He moves his left thumb and rubs the bottom part of his wide round platinum wedding band. It's a nervous tick and a habit that he picked up. Keith doesn't remember when it started. He thinks it's better than punching Agent Jack Forrester's lights out. His blue eyes become very intense as he looks around the room, but directly back at Forrester.

Agent Forrester takes a deep breath before he speaks, "I'll address that matter with Dr. Sheppard. If it's customary to ask personal questions, you must comply with those terms. Personally, I think she needs more information about you to finish her psychological evaluation," states Agent Forrester. "By the way, those questions were confidential. How did you get access to them?"

"I just got the information," Keith answers, as he tries to avoid looking directly at Agent Forrester.

"Well, I must say, that's not the answer I'm looking for. I'd like to get more details from you during my time here. I know you have an attitude problem, and I won't stand for your outbursts. I'm not going to take your crap, and I'll lay the law down as I see fit. Do you understand?" Agent Forrester says, as he quickly looks around the room but focuses his attention on Keith.

"Yes, sir, I understand the terms." He looks straight at his new supervisor with intense blue eyes that can kill.

Agent Forrester dismisses Keith's behavior because he knows that you can't give into the other person's reactions. "I guess we are done here. I have some work on your desk as of right now. You can go," he declares, as he closes Keith's case file.

"Thank you." Keith quickly walks out of the conference room without looking back. He doesn't notice that Peter is right behind him.

Peter receives a text message from Artemis. He says that the realtor agent that died on 2426 Falcon Boulevard in Pacific Palisades was a mule (a person that smuggles drugs by putting them into his/her body and traveling into another country). An autopsy was done and it was found that the deceased swallowed four small bags of cocaine. One of the bags exploded, however, and he also got shot with a .22 caliber bullet through his head. The bullet not the drugs killed the man. There was also an envelope that was addressed to his partner. It contained pictures of him and his family over a two-month time frame. There was also a note that said the agent was being watched. It specifically read, "Be careful what you wish for. As you can see your wish came true regarding your father! You should thank me for ending your father's life. Hope you liked your belated birthday present. Best wishes, Jude Henderson and Jose Medina. PS. We'll be in touch very soon!" Artemis also told Peter he'd be in touch. He has to keep an eye on his partner and his family too. Artemis stated that he doesn't want any more body counts in his district. After Peter read the text message, he says out loud, "crap, I'm not going to have a good summer!"

CHAPTER
THIRTY-EIGHT

"Keith, Keith, hold on!" Peter shouts, as he tries to catch up with his partner. Too late, as the door hits him square in the face. Maybe it wasn't a good idea to speak to Dr. Sheppard ahead of time. Peter thinks you don't mess with a woman's scorn; he knows that full well having four sisters of his own. Pay back's a bitch.

Keith suddenly stops and turns without warning and almost crashes into Peter. It's kind of funny to see because Peter is two inches taller than Keith and he is getting yelled at.

"Do you know anything about this?" Keith asks with a sharp tone. He doesn't look like a happy camper. *Peter, just agree with whatever the man says and don't' blink!*

"I'm not going to lie. I had a feeling something terrible was going to happen, but I didn't know it was going down like this. I'm sorry for that," Peter replies, as he knows more than what he's saying.

Keith starts walking as Peter tries to follow and keep up with his best friend. It's funny because Keith is much faster like a squirrel high on caffeine. They reach Keith's office without a word spoken between them. Nicole gives them a smile, but then disappears because she has a feeling it's not the right time.

"Did I get any calls when I was gone?" Keith asks, as he feels Peter's breath behind him. Peter knows that he's out of shape, and this short walk was not even a mile! What the hell? For crying out loud, I'm a cop!

"No, sir. Agent Forrester just gave me these cases that you need to do right away," she states, as she looks at Peter trying to collect himself. Nicole tries very hard not to laugh at the sight.

Keith sighs. "Thanks. If you need me, I'll be crazy glued to my government chair for the rest of my life!" he says sarcastically, as he tries to let Nicole know we're not in Kansas anymore.

"Keith!" Peter shouts, as he tries to stop his partner from causing any more damage. Suddenly Peter looks at Nicole and says, "I'm sorry, Nicole, for Agent Heiden's behavior. Just believe me when I tell you this is normal. Please don't worry, you're doing a great job here."

Keith quickly unlocks and walks into his office without holding the door for Peter. His ex-supervisor yells, "you're a spoiled brat! Don't be this way!"

"I'm a spoiled brat? What does that mean? I have just been de-clawed by the alpha wolf! Why don't you just admit that you handed me and the responsibility that comes with me over to GI Joe!" he shouts.

"No, Keith, he took you from me! My hands were tied and I didn't have a choice. I don't have any authority to override him!" Peter pleads his case. "That man has serious power and knows a lot of people."

"Peter, are you kidding me! He's here less than three months, and you've been here since the stone age! So don't tell me that you don't have any power to override some government authority! You're really mocking my intelligence!" Keith says and then changes his tone and asks, "I have a question that's been on my mind for a while. Why are you a supervisor? Truthfully, you can't handle the responsibility especially dealing with me!" Keith really wants to ring Peter's neck for this stunt. It's like he's dealing with Patrick, but a taller and older version. He can never get a break.

"Oh, my God. You're so dramatic. I think you've been watching too many soap operas over the years, and it's finally getting to you! Maybe, I wanted to be a supervisor because of their great benefit plan and all the extra overtime money I make!" Peter laughs, as he sits himself down on an office chair.

"Benefits and extra money? Listen, my annoying friend, you just can't handle the workload!" Keith announces. Peter doesn't like paperwork. It gives him a migraine, and he'd rather shoot up some bad guys. He's like the class clown in the department of misfit toys. Peter thinks he does the job very well but not the way other people want him to. He goes along at his own pace and he's happy with that.

"Listen, Keith, I didn't lose four case files, so back off!" Peter shouts, as he sends out a warning. He gets up from the chair and stretches his aching body. He thinks, sitting is not comfortable or maybe it's the conversation?

"As I said before, I don't know where they are!" Keith shouts right back without giving his partner the benefit of the doubt.

"Why didn't you take the supervisor position?" Peter asks, as he walks around the room looking at all the pictures of family and friends.

"You really think I could get the position after what happened ten years ago, as well as last year? I didn't have a prayer! You're sure you didn't know anything about this?" Keith asks with frustration in his voice. "I really have a very strong feeling that you spoke to my therapist!"

"No!" he answers, as he tries to beat around the bush. He was talking to Dr. Sheppard hours ago before the meeting. *Peter, don't look him in the eye! He will bring you down!* Keith is the kind of person that doesn't give up very easily. There are five "Ws" in the English language and Keith can make twenty more. Peter tries hard to keep a poker face without breaking a sweat. "You know, Keith, you really sound like a broken record! I really think you have conduct disorder. [It's a disorder that makes a person act defiant, impulsive and antisocial, and it can be caused by child abuse.]" He laughs.

Keith has a confused look on his face, because many times Peter doesn't make sense. "No, Peter, I don't have conduct disorder! I think I have Peter disorder!"

He laughs, "Maybe... But I think you do have conduct disorder, because you have all the signs!"

"Sometimes you act like Patrick! I think you spoke to Dr. Sheppard recently!" Keith shouts, as he knows that there is something very fishy going on but he can't put his finger on it. However, he'll get the truth out of Peter one way or another. "I bet she told you what was going to happen today."

Peter tries to get comfortable in his chair, but it isn't going to be easy from where he's sitting. He puts his shoes on Keith's desk. "Do you have Spider senses?" Peter asks with a huge smile on his face. All Keith needs to find out is that he spoke to the hot doctor and set up their first date. This information will bring Keith to the edge of his seat and point his loaded gun directly at my head.

Keith pushes Peter's shoes off his desk with force. "What?"

"Oh…never mind," Peter replies, as he gets up from the chair. He walks around the office. *This office is way too clean for my taste!*

"Listen, Keith, there are five Ws, who, what, why, when, and where, in the English language. I really think you can make twenty more from your interrogations! Man you are so uptight! You need to relax and chill. Just get loose and smoke some pot! I know we have some in the evidence room. I won't tell a living soul if you need to," Peter laughs.

"Maybe… But I have to be this way because the people around me are absent minded or brain dead. No one will let me rest for one second! So believe me, don't ask me to change because I can't, even if I tried!" Keith answers and he knows it's the truth.

"Okay…okay, sorry I asked! I'll take it back," Peter replies, because Keith doesn't shut up about his feelings towards the world.

While Peter walks around the office he sees a lot of pictures. There's one picture that especially catches his eye. It was Keith, him, Liam, and Sean on a golf weekend last year in Palm Springs before the Mr. Carlos Garcia case went down in May. Let's say it was a weekend to remember.

"Peter!" Keith shouts, as he knows that Peter is in his own little world.

"I'm here!" Peter answers, as he looks at another text from Carl Woods from the LA Forensic Department.

"Just get the GI Joe jackass off my back!" Keith shouts, as he tries to get his point across without Peter telling a joke or laughing.

Not being able to have a conversation with this individual is stressful enough.

"Don't worry! Uncle Peter will handle the situation. GI Joe jackass, that's a good one! See, you still have your sense of humor," Peter replies with a smile still on his face.

Keith looks up with annoyance. "What? Get out my office! I have a lot on my plate!"

"Keith, listen. Artemis Daly, from the Los Angeles Homicide Dept. left me a text message saying that Carl Woods from the County Forensic Dept. texted him about the murder near your home. The victim was Chase Whitman. He came from Venice Beach and worked at California Realty. I think the house was one of his accounts. The bullet hole in his head had no exit, and there was something in his mouth. There also was an envelope in his chest pocket with pictures of your kids."

Keith stops doing his work. "Did the dead victim have any drugs on him?" he asks.

Peter feels exhausted. "Well, I'm surprised that you're not going crazy because of the pictures. Also this guy worked in the same real estate agency with Justine," he says in-between yawns. Keith nods. "Anyway, Mr. Whitman carried two small bags of cocaine inside his body. The investigation showed he traveled through Mexico by car over the weekend. He brought back a couple of souvenirs from his mini-vacation. I don't think that the cocaine bags killed him; I think the bullet did it. But the autopsy report told us the real story about this poor man's demise."

"Justine will be working closer to home because of California's famous traffic. I think she'll be relocating to a real estate office in Beverly Hills or Brentwood... Wherever the money smells really good," Keith replies and Peter laughs. "Anyway, was the victim a mule? I'm not surprised if he was. The real estate business has been slow lately, and I guess he needed extra cash to pay the bills," Keith answers. "Peter, to be honest, I'm in total shock right now. Please make sure everyone, and that includes Reese, is safe," he pleads, as he starts off reading another file.

"Yes, he was a mule. The autopsy report stated that there were four tiny bags of cocaine in his system. However, it was a .22 caliber bullet through his head that shortened his days on earth," Peter answers. "The police are still on the case. Artemis asked me to watch you and your family closely. I guess he likes you," Peter says with a smile. Artemis told Peter what he really thinks of Keith. He's a bully and a real hothead with no goals in life.

"I'd appreciate any updates you can give me," Keith says, as he sees Peter taking a few more pieces of chocolate from the beer stein.

Keith is acting odder than usual, but Peter doesn't push the subject. "No problem, I can't pass these babies up," Peter says with a huge smile. "See you later!" Seconds pass as he walks out of the office with a mouth full of little chocolates and sees Nicole with a very concerned look on her face.

"Can I come with you, please?" she pleads. "Help me... Agent Darling, I'm scared! I don't want to work with that man. Can I work for you? You really seem like a very nice guy and funny too."

"Nicole, it's very sweet of you to say that, but I'm sorry I can't save you! Have a good work day anyway!" Peter answers politely with a smile. As he walks away you can hear the echo of his laughter as it travels down the hallway. Nicole is left standing like a sore thumb.

CHAPTER
THIRTY-NINE

~~~

*K*eith picks up his cell phone as it rings, "Hello, Mr. Williamson."

"Please call me Preston. Mr. Williamson is so formal. It helps to break the ice if we can call each other by our first names. Hopefully, we can become friends before I leave California," he states, as he sits in a very comfortable chair and drinks fine British tea. Preston slowly drinks as it brings him back to his homeland, England.

"Sorry, I'd rather call you by your last name, and as for us becoming friends, maybe…," Keith answers, as he plays with a paperclip to pass the time.

"Okay, Agent Heiden, I understand. I'm calling you because I received a bizarre call the other day. The party wouldn't give his name but wanted me to give you a message. You and your family are in great danger. He also said that he's working for Jose Medina's cartel. Mr. Medina is retiring and going underground, and a lot of people want his territory and business. I'm sorry to say, but you really have your work cut out for you!"

"Thanks for the information, warning and concern. I know it's going to be a war, but it's not your fight," he exclaims to his new-found Interpol friend.

"I think you're a valuable agent, and I just wanted to warn you," Preston answers, as he takes a drink of the tea that soothes him to his soul.

"Thank you but I can handle it. You don't have to worry about me. Just watch your back," Keith says with concern in his voice. He looks at the notes on his desk and sees one that catches his eye.

"Do you know who put a bomb under your SUV?" ask Mr. Williamson, as he holds a fine cigar and now pours himself a glass of scotch.

"Yes, it was Jude Henderson. He wants to take over Jose Medina's territory and the drug cartel," Keith answers. The note just says, "Call Mr. Artemis Daly." He only knows him from Peter.

"How do you know that?" Preston asks, as he's very surprised to receive a name attached to that horrible crime.

"Because a gentleman with a British accent called me but didn't leave his name. I have a very strong feeling that it's him," Keith says, hearing a beep on his hard-line office phone. "Listen, Mr. Williamson, I'm sorry to cut you off but I really have to go now! I have a lot of work to do and my boss is not a happy camper. He thinks I'm the one that took his personal parking space. I'm pleading the Fifth"

Preston laughs. "I understand, but I must tell you that I heard there's a mole in your department, so beware."

As the other phone line rings it interrupts Keith's train of thought. He feels a little pressure to answer it quickly without being highly rude to Mr. Williamson. "Thank you and please watch your back. I'll keep my eyes open to what's around me. Good-bye," Keith says. Is he ready for the challenge that lies ahead from this new information? It doesn't matter. Whatever comes his way, it's coming no matter what.

CHAPTER
FORTY

As Patrick walks outside of St. Frances Roman Catholic High School, he continues to look for his bus #29.

"Hey, Patrick!" a boy shouts. "Wait, man!"

He turns around to see Frank De Mecca, an old friend from first grade, who catches up with him. Although Frank is a year younger than the Heiden twins, they are all in the same grade. Since the school district couldn't originally place the twins in their proper grade, they stayed home for an extra year. Keith wasn't happy with the whole situation, but it was fine with Justine.

"Patrick, what're you doing after school?" asks Frank. It's been a long time since they hung out together.

"Sorry, Frank, my dad grounded me again. It's one of his hobbies to make my life a living hell. I think I missed my bus! I can't believe this!" he states, as he looks around and tries to find his transportation home.

"It looks that way. I guess you got detention again. Do you know when you'll be available?" asks Frank while he tries to find his bus too.

Patrick laughs. "Well, I'm not having a great month. I'll call my Uncle Peter. Maybe he'll pick me up because everyone else is at work," he says, while dialing Peter's number.

As Peter's cell rings he says with a friendly voice, "Peter here. What's up my surfer dude!"

"Hi, Uncle Peter, it's Patrick. I missed my bus again and this time it wasn't my fault," he explains. "Can you pick me up?" Patrick pleads. It's a long journey home especially, in a polyester school uniform.

"No problem. Where should I meet you?" Peter says through the speakerphone. "Oh crap!" He sees a lot of school buses up ahead. Now it's going to be a challenge to get to his destination before rush-hour traffic starts.

"You can meet me in front of the school where the two huge (Phoenix Canariensis) palm trees are," Patrick replies, as he puts on his sunglasses.

"Okay, that's fine. I'll be there in a half hour or a little more, because I'm stuck behind some school buses. Promise me that you'll stay at that location, so I don't have to search for you!" Peter commands.

"That's fine, Uncle Peter. Thanks! I'll see you soon," Patrick answers.

"Patrick, I have to go now, but we'll hang when you're not under a microscope!" shouts Frank, as he runs down the parking lot toward his bus.

Patrick waves goodbye and walks to his destination at the front of the school. He feels a cool breeze that sends a chill through his school uniform jacket to the core of his bones. According to the weather report, heavy rains were coming early that evening and the sky was already looking very dark. As Patrick reaches the palm trees at the front of the building he notices that the school grounds are deserted.

CHAPTER
FORTY-ONE

"Hey Heiden!" a boy shouts, who appears to be rough around the edges with very old rundown clothes.

Patrick turns around and asks, "Who's asking?" He doesn't recognize the voice, until their faces meet. Patrick's face turns totally white. Duke Stone is not from this school. He is the same age as Patrick, but they're not friends or acquaintances by any means. Duke has a terrible chip on his shoulder about life. Patrick heard a story that Duke's dad went to jail, and he is in the California Federal Prison. He's supposed to be spending the rest of his life behind bars.

"Hey Duke? What's up?" Patrick says. Suddenly, he sees a solid light wood baseball bat in Duke's hand. It didn't take long for Patrick to put two and two together; what's going to happen next?

Duke hits the bat on his hand to show that he means business. "So, Heiden, you haven't called me recently when I called you! So what happened? Why haven't you returned my calls?" he demands.

"Sorry, Duke! I've been very busy, you know," Patrick answers with a quiver in his voice, as he carefully focuses on the baseball bat.

"No, I don't know. You were so busy that you didn't have a chance to even pick up the phone? I know for a fact that you're not handling my business! So I'm here to collect my goods plus interest!" Duke exclaims, as he looks directly into Patrick's crystal blue eyes. Duke can taste and smell Patrick's fear, and he's getting a real kick from this.

"Well, I haven't been a good citizen lately and my grades show it, but you don't need the details on that story," Patrick answers solemnly. *Patrick, hurry up and use your special skills before your head is the baseball!*

"Well, Heiden, so you're not going to tell me why you didn't return my calls! That's okay it's all good! No harm was done, man! We're all friends here!" Duke says and smiles as he walks closer to Patrick. Duke stands at 5'8" and Patrick is almost six feet tall. Patrick can clearly see over this bully's head without any problem but the question is can he fight him off. He has a very bad feeling that no one will ever come to his rescue, like Uncle Peter. This is not my year! Patrick walks slowly backward and suddenly bumps into Duke's two low-life friends that he never met before. He turns his head and says with a smile, "Hey guys." but from their expressions and mannerisms this is not the time to make a friendly conversation.

"Hold him!" Duke commands forcefully. Suddenly the two young thugs take Patrick's arms and lock them behind his back. Duke starts pacing back and forth like a caged wild animal ready to be released and to attack this preppy young teenager. The baseball bat swings from side to side, like a pendulum.

"Duke! Please don't do this! Please listen to me! I didn't mean to ignore you. I was…," Patrick pleads for his life, as he tries to break free from the stronghold of Duke's friends. "Duke, you don't have to do this! I'll give you the goods that you need! I promise that you'll get everything by the end of the day! You don't want to do this," he cries for mercy to the bad boy who lives on the other side of the tracks. But Duke dismisses his pleas.

"You know you're an asshole! I don't care about your life! Your promises don't mean anything to me. It's too late! Now you're going to pay dearly!" Duke shouts, as he hits the bat in the palm of his hand.

"Yes, a lot of people tell me that I'm a smart ass! Duke, I'm truly sorry! Please let me make it up to you! I'll give you the goods, and you don't have to pay for them!" Patrick states. He hid the drugs in his messy bedroom, and he knows that no one in their right mind would enter without getting that uncomfortable feeling throughout their body. Patrick has a very funny feeling that Duke doesn't have money to pay for the goods. It was Patrick's decision not to give them to Duke, and the man (with no name) who hired him will hear about it. But Patrick has a bigger problem right now. "Please, Duke, you don't want to do this! Please, Duke!" Patrick pleads again for his life, but no answer.

"I don't believe you! You know what happens to liars?" Duke shouts as he sends a blow to Patrick's stomach. The air is suddenly sucked out of his lungs.

Patrick tries to get some small energy to say something, but the excruciating pain doubles him over. "Please, Duke, don't do this! Please listen to me! I don't want to cause any problems! Duke, let me go, and I won't tell anyone about this! Please!" He begs.

"Again, I don't believe you, Heiden! You're a liar and you're a piece of shit!" Duke exclaims, as he swings the baseball bat and hits Patrick again. He falls to the ground with a thud.

The two thugs pick young Heiden up from the ground and get him in a standing position. Duke gets ready to finish the job as he swings the bat once more. Patrick falls to the ground again.

"Why can't you guys hold him? He's only one person!" Duke shouts.

"Come on, Duke, finish the job before the cops come!" yells one of his friends.

"Just one more minute, and then we'll play some baseball in the park," he answers.

Duke stands over the injured teenager. "You have my stuff, and I want it now, not later!" Duke yells, as he leans down and spits in Patrick's face. He walks around Patrick feeling very powerful. Duke swings the baseball bat and hits Patrick again and again. Patrick loses count of the blows as he feels his brain bouncing like a Mexican jumping bean. Suddenly he passes out from the shock and pain.

"Get him, Duke, hit him harder! Show no mercy!" shout the two thugs unmercifully.

"Heiden, you're a piece of shit! I want my goods or I'll find you and beat you harder! That's a promise! Where is my stuff, Heiden?" Duke says, but he doesn't know if Patrick can hear him or not. "I'm getting bored… Let's go… Hide the trash and let's play some ball!"

Ten minutes later the boys drag Patrick's lifeless body behind some bushes closer to the school. Hopefully no one will notice that he's there. If it was up to Duke he would like to see Heiden die of his injuries, but only time will tell.

"Come on, guys, let play some baseball in the park!" Duke states to his friends as he kicks the dirt into Patrick's bloody face. Then they all walk away still laughing. As he wipes the blood of his bat, he smiles and says, "Good work, guys!"

Patrick goes in and out of consciousness. As he tries to breathe, the taste of blood and dirt keeps choking him. Suddenly it starts to rain, and the blood washes away from him like a stream. He tries to focus and see if Duke and his boys are around. Then without notice the cell rings and the caller ID displays, "Uncle Peter." Believe it or not his cell phone is not damaged.

He slowly pulls the phone toward his ear. "Hello," he weakly says.

"Patrick, where are you? I'm waiting by the palm trees. What happened to you? Did you meet up with a hot girl in school and forget about me?" Peter asks with a stern voice, ready to lay it on Patrick when he sees him.

A second later, Peter is about to yell some more and then... "Uncle Peter, please help me!" Patrick pleads as his voice becomes very weak from the trauma. He tries to hold onto whatever strength he has left before passing out.

"Patrick, what happened and where are you?" Peter shouts, as he knows that he only has seconds to find the boy. "Talk to me! Come on, son, where are you? I need to find you and get help! Talk to me!" Peter yells, as he frantically looks around for the teenager. Peter is trying to hold it together. He is trained not to show any feelings regarding emergency situations. Out of the corner of his eye he sees half of a body sticking out behind some well-groomed brushes. Peter rushes over to the person not knowing if it's Patrick or some other poor soul that needs aid. Peter's eyes widen and he yells, "Come on, son, wake up! Patrick, wake up! It's Uncle Peter!" He slaps Patrick in the face to wake him up.

"911. What's your emergency?" the lady dispatcher asks with a calm and professional voice.

"My name is Agent Peter Darling from the DEA. I have a situation at St. Francis Roman Catholic High School! I have a seventeen-year-old boy, and he's hurt badly. Please come right away," Peter frantically pleads for help.

"What are his injuries?" the lady asks again.

"I see some scratches, bruises, and I guess some broken bones… I think he has a concussion," Peter answers, as he talks clearly for the emergency operator and for Patrick; maybe the sound of Uncle Peter's voice will wake Patrick up.

"Where are you located?" the lady asks.

"The address is St. Frances Roman Catholic High School, 17 Monroe Boulevard, Pacific Palisades! Please come fast!" Peter shouts firmly. "Patrick, stay with me! Don't sleep!"

"They are on their way!" says the lady.

The ambulance arrives within ten minutes. Two emergency medics race over to Patrick. "Hi, what's the situation?" says a lady whose name tag says, "Tammy S."

"Hi, I'm Agent Peter Darling from DEA. This young man's name is Patrick Heiden," he says trying to keep his cool.

She leans over and says, "Patrick, my name is Tammy and I'm an EMT!. Can you tell me what day it is? Please tell me what happened to you, sir!" she asks clearly but gently as she slowly examines the teenager. "Can you tell me what happened to you? Mr. Heiden, can you please tell me anything so I can help you! Patrick, do you know where you are?"

"School," he mumbles.

Patrick goes in and out of consciousness and finally mutters, "Baseball bat." His vision becomes blurry as his head throbs. He has never encountered this kind of pain before.

"I heard the word baseball bat…and Duke Stone!" Tammy announces to the other EMT and Agent Peter Darling. "Don't worry. I'm here to take care of you!"

She quickly opens her medical bag and gets out an instant cold pack. Tammy squeezes and shakes it, as she puts it on Patrick's head to reduce any swelling. She detects a couple of broken ribs. Then very slowly she puts on a neck brace. The other EMT helps Tammy out and slowly moves the teenager's body to one side and carefully puts him on a flat board. Then they fasten him with restraints to keep him immobile. This is to protect the spinal cord while moving the victim to the hospital. The right arm seems to be broken so an arm brace is put into place until the injury is confirmed. Suddenly the California police arrive to take statements during their crime investigation, but must wait for Patrick's statement until he is stable enough to talk to them. Patrick is rushed to the hospital by ambulance with Peter by his side. He's Patrick's godfather and also his guardian if his parents aren't present.

Patrick arrives at the hospital in less than twenty minutes. He can hear voices all around him but he's not sure where he is. "Mr. Heiden, we are going to take good care of you. You're at the hospital. Uncle Peter is with you so don't be scared," says a young woman. Patrick tries to focus on the nurse's uniform and her nametag that says "Kristene P."

Two hours later, Patrick is set up in a private room in the pediatric section of the hospital. He is laying very still in that hospital bed, with his right arm broken in two places, three broken ribs, bruises, cuts, and a head trauma. He is dressed in a light blue gown with boxers on and is laying on Care Bear sheets!

CHAPTER
FORTY-TWO

*A*s Peter leans against his black SUV for support, his cell phone rings. "Hello, Agent Darling here."

"Peter, what's going on? Justine just chewed my ear off about Patrick! What happened? Is he all right?" Keith asks, as he is ready to jump out of his skin. He is trying desperately not to crack with emotion as his feelings of helplessness bubble to the surface. The fact remains that he couldn't save his son from harm.

"He's fine!" Peter answers, as he tries to interrupt Keith's insane twenty questions. "Keith, please listen to me before you pass out on the floor!" Peter sighs and takes a deep breath to collect his thoughts. Peter hears nothing on the other end of the line. He's not sure if his partner is dead or alive. "He was beaten with a baseball bat by a punk, but he's going to be fine. Thank God that no major organs were damaged during the attack," he answers with a calm voice. "He's going to have a bad headache for a very long time."

"Does he know who hit him with the baseball bat?" Keith asks with a stern but soft voice, as he leans back in his office chair. He rubs his eyes to help release some tension. His stress level is almost unbearable between work and this dreadful news.

"I think so," Peter says, as he looks around the parking lot.

"Peter, don't give me that shit! I know that you promised him that you'd keep this a secret, especially from me! So just tell me before I find you! You know that I will find you! Peter! I can't believe you! You know that you can't promise kids about anything! That's totally unrealistic!" Keith yells in frustration.

"Okay, stop crying like a girl! Please just give me a break! The boy's name is Duke Stone," Peter answers, as he is suddenly distracted by a person from his past walking toward him.

"Duke Stone?" Keith asks, as he looks for a file on his desk. "Stone... Stone that name sounds very familiar. Where did I hear that name before?"

"Are you asking me? I don't know! I really have to go now! Talk to you soon," Peter states while he walks closer to the tall woman with blond hair who is wearing a white doctor's coat.

"Peter!" Keith yells, but he only hears the dial tone. "Peter!"

As he continues to walk closer, he finally says, "Julia! Julia Ulrich! It's me, Peter Darling!" The lady in a white medical coat stops in her tracks and turns around.

"Hello, Peter. It has been a while! When was the last time we saw each other? It has to be almost eleven years ago!" she says in a soft voice with no expression of surprise.

"So you do remember me? Yes, it has been a very long time. How's life been treating you?" he says with a huge smile on his face.

"We were together for many years. Did you ever think of calling me after we broke up?" she asks with a very serious expression on her face.

"Julia, remember you broke it off with me! You made it per-fectly clear not to contact you ever again! Did you know that I was about to propose to you the day that our relationship ended? The engagement ring was inside my coat pocket next to my heart. I was hoping to spend my life with you!" Peter solemnly says, as he studies Julia intently. She really hasn't changed and is aging gracefully as the saying goes. Julia was Peter's first love, and though there were many attractive women in his life she was the only one for him.

"I'm sorry, Peter I didn't know. Are you still working with the DEA?" Julia asks without skipping a beat.

"Yes, I am," he answers with a smile. Peter feels uncomfortable about this conversation but happy at the same time looking at his ex-girlfriend. He's just inches away from touching her soft, silky skin, which was one of the things that Peter truly loved about her. Her smile still makes his heart glow.

"Are you still in touch with Keith Heiden?" she asks.

"Yes, I was just on the phone with him," Peter answers with excitement in his voice. *Damn, you're still hot!*

"Then I was right that you still keep in touch with him. I guess you're the one that brought his son, Patrick, to the hospital late this afternoon?" Julia asks with a sharp edge to her voice as she always hated Keith Heiden since they first met.

"Listen…what's with the twenty questions…… Are you his doctor or something?!" he says.

"Yes, so why don't you tell me what happened to him? Did your partner finally do it…abuse his son, maybe the wife and daughter too? He treats everyone like second-class citizens!" she interrogates without taking a breath.

"Julia, it really sounds like you truly love the guy!" Peter laughs. "Why do you hate him so much? What did he do to you that made you have such a bad taste in your mouth? He didn't do anything harmful to his family. I'm sorry to disappoint you."

"I just don't like him," Julia answers, as she looks straight into Peter's eyes. She really misses him but it could never work.

"What about us?" he asks out of the blue. He has a feeling that he already knows the answer to his question, but it doesn't hurt to ask anyway.

"What about us? It has been almost eleven years! A lot has changed. I'm a doctor, and you're a DEA agent if I'm correct. Half of these patients in this hospital were shot because of you," Julia says.

Peter finally puts two and two together and says, "so you're a pediatric doctor and Patrick's physician." Julia has always been a brainiac, and she always had some sort of medical book in her hands. Peter is not a reader, but he loves books on tapes. It's an interesting way to kill time.

"Yes, I'm his doctor. So listen, Peter, I know that you're a great guy but we never could work out because we are very different people," Julia answers.

"So, you broke my heart many years ago, and you're doing it again," Peter says with a confused look on his face.

"Please don't' get me wrong. I love you and always will. I really have to go now," she answers without giving Peter the time to respond. Julia walks away and leaves Peter again, as she did many years ago.

CHAPTER
FORTY-THREE

*P*eter checks his cell phone for any voice messages that he might have. "Hi, Peter, it's Keith. I need you to do me a huge favor. Please go to my house and look for any drugs that Patrick might have. First check in his very messy room…sorry. We have to find these goods before anybody else does, especially the family. Thank you, Peter, I owe you big time. Please call me when and if you find anything."

A few hours go by as Peter searches Patrick's room. He's very happy that everyone in the house including Reese is sleeping. Finally the search is over! There are two medium size plastic bags of cocaine or crack underneath his very messy bed. These drugs can be worth a lot of money. Peter knows not to arrest Patrick. The word, "brotherhood," means a lot between co-workers like Keith and the family members too. Peter flushes the criminal evidence down the toilet and will never talk about this again.

"Agent Heiden, I'm leaving now!" Nicole says, as her voice travels through the speakerphone. "Thank you, see you tomorrow," he answers.

"Have a good night," she answers.

Suddenly Keith's cell rings, "Hello."

"Hi Keith, it's me… Peter," he answers, as he finishes drying his hands from the crime.

"Peter, did you receive my voice message?" Keith asks with a soft voice. He doesn't want anyone to hear this conversation, especially

Nicole. He sees her walking away from her desk, ending her day at work.

"Yes, it's done. Let me tell you it's not pretty," Peter sighs, as he lays his head on the guest bed pillow. He looks at the digital clock, which says 1:23 a.m.

"Thank you, Peter, I greatly appreciate this. I can only imagine what you found. Is everybody okay?" Keith asks, as he yawns with surprise. "Sorry."

"That's okay; I feel the same way too." He laughs. "Everyone is fine including Reese. I hate to say this, but Patrick is going to stay in the hospital for a couple of days or weeks. Listen, Keith, I have to tell you, he's in serious trouble, and not by the drugs that I flushed down the toilet! My concern is where the drugs came from and who's operating the deals: Do you have Duke in custody?" Peter asks.

"Yes, Patrick's DNA was on the wooden baseball bat that Duke was using at the time of the beating. He's arrested for assault and battery with a deadly weapon and attempted murder. I have a very funny feeling that Duke might be Rusty Stone's son. I can't be sure as of yet, because the computer system is down. Hopefully, the system will be up soon," says Keith. Then suddenly the sound of snoring comes through his cell phone. "Peter! Wake up!"

Three minutes later the response, "What...what?" Peter answers. "Are we finished?"

"Yes, Peter, thanks again, and I'll let you sleep now," Keith says with a smile.

CHAPTER
FORTY-FOUR

*W*ithin a split-second, Keith receives information from the DEA's database. It states that Rusty Stone is Duke Stone's father. Two years ago, Rusty was arrested by Keith and other agents that were working that day. Mr. Stone had three counts of drug possession and also other prior convictions. He also skipped his court dates. Rusty is detained in a Federal Correctional Institution in Northern California for the rest of his life. Home sweet home! Keith doesn't feel that Rusty can give him any helpful information about Jose Medina or his cartel. Rusty is the kind of guy that will die before telling a living soul anything incriminating, especially a cop. Keith finally has three days off from work. He decides that he wants to see Patrick before he heads home. The other kids are in school and Justine is home today caring for Colin.

"Hello," says Keith. A middle-aged nurse with a nametag "Kimberly" walks toward Keith. She wears a designer nurse's uniform with the alphabet drawn on it.

"Hello, sir. How can I help you?" she asks.

"You have a patient named Patrick Heiden who's in the pediatric unit. Can you please tell me his room number, and if it's possible to get his belongings now? I know that he's not yet discharged, but I would like his personal items anyway," he says using his customer service voice.

"I'm sorry. What's your relationship with the patient?" she asks, as she takes a glimpse at the hospital computer searching for the patient's name.

"I'm sorry, I'm Patrick's father. My name is Keith Heiden," he states, as he looks at the clock above. Meanwhile, his stomach is making strange noises, and he realizes that he didn't eat anything.

"Okay, Mr. Heiden, I'm sorry. Why do you want your son's belongings now? He's not ready to be discharged from the hospital from the looks of his medical report," Kimberly asks with a confused look. This is the first time that a family member asks for the patient's belongings before they are released from our care.

"Well, you see, four years ago my wife gave birth at this hospital. When she was discharged her locket was missing. It was in a manila envelope marked with her name and room number. Until this day the locket has not been found. It has a significant personal value," Keith claims, as he tries to remember the details of the locket that he had given Justine on her birthday. He was more upset than Justine was when it was missing.

"I'm sorry to hear that. Let me get your son's belongings. I'll be right back. Please fill in this form, and I need to see your driver's license," she announces and gives Keith the clipboard with a form to fill out.

"Thank you," he says, as he looks at the form and the nurse at the same time.

Ten minutes later someone walks to Patrick's hospital room door. There is a knock on the door. "Come in." says a weak voice. The door opens slowly. "Hello."

"Hey, Melissa!" Patrick says, with a tone of excitement, as he tries to pick up his injured body to get comfortable. He smiles at his girlfriend, as she walks into his room holding a bouquet of fresh flowers and a balloon that says, "get well." Melissa is 5'5" and looks stunning in her lightweight summer sundress and sandals. The blue-green color of her outfit brings out the light green color of her eyes, and her wavy light brown hair beautifully frames her pretty face. Patrick has had a crush on Melissa since kindergarten, but the constant punishments from his controlling father have continuously kept them apart. He really misses her and hopes that Melissa knows that!

"Hi, Patrick," she says, as she walks into the room and puts down the flowers on the dresser near her friend. Melissa takes a chair and moves it towards the hospital bed. She smiles warmly at Patrick as he lays on the Care Bears sheets and pillowcases.

"What?" Patrick asks, as he knows exactly why she has a huge smile on her face.

"Nothing!" She giggles quietly, as she dismisses a conversation that's very funny on her end.

"Melissa, listen," Patrick says, as he really wants to say what's in his heart, but sometimes it comes out of his ass. "I need you! I'm sorry," he pleads with a sad look as if to say, "Take me back!"

"Patrick, I'm just here as your good friend. That's all right now," she says, as she touches his hand. Patrick can feel her warmth and that makes him smile, and he rarely smiles.

"Melissa, please tell me that we're still together," Patrick pleads, as he can still feel a lot of pain even though he has been taking demerol.

"Patrick, I think we should talk about this when you're well," Melissa gently states, as she takes her hand away from him. Melissa's mannerisms show that she's not interested in Patrick that way anymore.

"Melissa, I really want to talk about us now, not later. I really miss you, and I know that I'm grounded for the whole summer but that's not the point. I really want to be a couple. Please, Melissa, let me in your heart again!" Patrick pleads as he feels sadness covering his heart. Deep down inside, he knows he has a better chance of winning the California lottery than getting Melissa back. He really blew it this time.

Melissa is about to answer Patrick's question when suddenly a knock at the door interrupts her train of thought. *No, not now!*

"Come in," he shouts with a look of disappointment. *Why me? I just need a few more minutes with Melissa to plead my case again.* Keith walks in slowly, but suddenly he stops in his tracks when he sees a young teenage girl sitting next to his son. He puts two and two together and then suddenly realizes that he just interrupted a private and personal conversation. *I really feel like a jackass!*

"I'm sorry, Patrick. I didn't know! I'm so sorry!" he says sadly with embarrassment in his voice. He knows how it feels to finally have an opportunity to speak to a popular girl and then get interrupted.

"Dad, please don't leave!" Patrick requests.

"Sorry, son, I'll be outside. Please forgive me!" Keith says solemnly. He walks into the waiting room and automatically sits in a chair without saying a word. Keith wants to give Patrick a few minutes alone with his friend.

Ten minutes later Keith knocks on the door again. "Come in!" Patrick shouts, as Keith cautiously looks in the room to see if Patrick's friend is still present.

"Hello, Dad. You don't look too good. I look better than you!" Patrick laughs a little trying not to hurt himself. Keith just smiles a little bit and looks at the balloons, assorted flowers and the many get well cards that are placed all around the room. I'm trapped in a Hallmark store! Keith tries to walk away from the get well section but a single mylar balloon is following him around. He tries to get away from it but for some strange reason it's not working his way.

"That was Melissa! She gave me flowers, and she also said that she would visit me later on this week. I think that's a good sign that we might get back together... I really hope so."

"That's great, Patrick. I hope it works out for you guys," he answers with a comforting look on his face. Keith realizes that his son almost died. Patrick has a lot of bruises and cuts on his face and a large cast on his right arm. He's taken back to see his son in this condition. "Is the hospital staff treating you well? Do you need anything from home?" he asks in a soft voice.

"I have your personal belongings from the main desk. I'll bring them home for you," he says and feels overwhelmed with emotions. Keith can feel his heart breaking into pieces.

"Thanks, Dad. I'm really fine. Mom brought me all the supplies I need but thanks anyway. The others are coming by to say hello. How are you? Mom told me that you're working almost every day. Just be honest... Were you trying to avoid mother's wrath or were you really working all those hours?" Patrick asks without a second to waste on small talk. He enjoys getting his father upset. It's fun and entertaining at the same time. It's a hobby that he's perfected over the years, but lots of times he gets himself into trouble doing so, but it's worth it!

"What? No, I have a new supervisor now. I have to comply with the long hours. Why do I have to explain anything to you? Remember, I'm the parent and you're the child!" Keith exclaims with a stern voice.

"I'm a man!" Patrick retorts with oxygen tubes in his nostrils. Although he feels pain throughout his body he always has the strength to go one on one with his old man any time and any place! He loves a good rush!!

Keith smiles and says, "Yes, you keep thinking that while you're underneath the Care Bears sheets! It's really helping your masculine image a great deal," he laughs.

"You're way too funny!" Patrick answers.

"I'm sorry that you were beaten with a baseball bat, Patrick, but you brought this on yourself."

"Whatever! I'm a man, and I'm also taller than you!!" he snaps. "Is this your tough love speech?"

"Okay, Patrick, I give up!" Keith snaps back, as he walks around the room to get his old body circling with some blood flow. He's so tired that he doesn't know what day, time or month it is. That hospital bed looks really good right now. If I could just lie down!

Patrick ignores his dad's "when I was young" speech. "Thanks, Dad, for your concern. Now we both have something in common besides sharing the same genes," Patrick says.

"What are you talking about?" Keith asks with a confused look, but he knows very well what his son is saying. Keith will not give in to the game of power. *This kid is way too smart for his own good. Maybe I can sell him on E-bay for a penny? Even though he was cute when he was little, he's now a royal pain in my ass! It's like an itch that I can't scratch, almost eighteen years of pure hell for me. I don't know if Justine has the same feeling, but if so she wouldn't admit it. In her sharp crystal blue eyes, Patrick can do no wrong, but Mitch, on the other hand, is the one that gives her a headache. How can I prove Justine wrong? It's going to be a very long summer.*

"We both now have experienced that same wrath from the base-ball bat," Patrick claims, as he looks at his father and is ready to attack King Lion. "You know after the Carlos Garcia's case was over, Mom was so angry at you she attacked you with a baseball bat in the family room. She really gave you a beating! It's kind of the same abuse you received from your father when you were a child," Patrick announces, as he shows no expression of remorse for his father's experience.

"I don't know what you're talking about," Keith says, as he tries to avoid any interrogation from his son.

"Give me a break, don't lie! You don't have to be ashamed that you couldn't climb a ladder! Do you remember that's what you said to us to explain your injuries? You can't even change a light bulb!! Why can't you just admit it that mom gave you a beating? I know that mom abuses you, and I'm sorry that you can't take control of the situation!" Patrick says, as he tries to adjust himself in the hospital bed to get comfortable. It's a predicament because the gown is rising up on his back, and if he gets up the very thin fabric may cause him embarrassment.

"Think what you want! I'm not going to tell you anything!" Keith snaps back, and then moves his tired blue eyes towards some-thing that catches his attention, the morphine bag! Without a second to spare he walks over and starts to flick it with his fingers; like a cat that plays with a ball of yarn. While the bag swings back and forth Keith smiles.

Patrick looks concerned and snaps, "What are you doing? Don't play with that!! I need that drug to get well! Listen, Dad, I won't tell anyone about the baseball bat encounter; just stop what you're doing before you regret it." He really wants to get up but the pain is too strong. "Please stop hitting the morphine bag; it's not a toy," Patrick orders.

"Relax, Patrick, I'm not going to do anything to harm your precious body," he answers as he stops playing with the bag. "Patrick, since the day that you were born we have always butted heads. Why do you hate me so much?" Keith asks, although he already knows the answer.

"You are always on my case, and I can never breath on my own. I really need some space to become that man you want me to be," Patrick responds.

"I'm highly worried about you and what path you are taking. Listen, this is not the first time you have given me a mini-stroke because of your choices and…it's very scary. Patrick, I don't know but you almost died and it's heartbreaking to see you in this position. I wish you can understand where I'm coming from. I guess maybe someday you will see what I see when you become a parent. Well, I'll see you at home.

"Before you leave, I just want to tell you that mom was bribed by Grandpa a couple of weeks ago. He told Mom to leave you and take the kids with her. He said money was no object…This sounds very serious. What's with you and Grandpa? Why don't you like each other?" Patrick asks, as he knows there is rough water between them, but why?

"Thanks, Patrick, for giving me the information. I guess in life you can't like everyone in the world. It's hard to say, but thanks for your concern. Please get better so you can drive me crazy when you come home," Keith answers, as he knows that he's not William's favorite especially where his princess daughter is concerned.

"Thanks for coming. See you soon," Patrick answers, as he turns around and covers himself with the blanket so he can sleep and get the rest he needs. Keith smiles and walks out of the room.

CHAPTER
FORTY-FIVE

〜〜〜

*K*eith and Liam go to the Federal Correctional Institution. He meets with Mr. Fisher Scott who is one of the wardens from the jail. He has a receding hairline, and from the shape of his body it shows that he has been eating his share of twinkies during his lifetime. But don't dismiss Fisher Scott, however, he has two black belts in martial arts. He could kick ass if he wanted to.

"Hello, Agent Heiden, thanks for coming down. I want to say thank you for sending Rusty to our four-star hotel. He's a total charmer," he laughs at his sarcasm. "Listen, I'm giving you an hour and a half to question him, because I had a great a cup of coffee this morning. However, if I see or hear that you are having one of your tantrums on my playground, you'll be wearing an orange jump suit too. Your new boyfriends will call you, "Sweet Cheeks," announces Warden Fisher Scott (but everybody just calls him Fisher, not Warden Scott).

A few of the correctional officers laugh while waiting for their afternoon shift to begin.

"So, don't mess with my prisoner! I need him for work duty! Just get your statement and leave," Fisher commands.

Fisher has dealt with a lot of characters over the years, and we're not talking about the Mickey Mouse or Donald Duck type from Disneyland. Keith is one of those characters that waves hi to the children as they enter the park with their families.

Rusty enters the visiting room walking very slowly. He's in shackles from his hands connected to his waist and ankles. In front of him is a large metal roundtable that's nailed down or cemented to the floor. Meanwhile, Keith and Liam release their weapons and badges at the jail security booth before being escorted to the visiting section to meet with Rusty. It's a secured room for visitors so they can meet with the prisoners. They're watched at all times with cameras in every corner of the room and prison officers are also stationed close by, just in case things go south.

Over a ten-year time frame Agent Heiden has arrested a good percentage of the prisoners that now live here. A lot of guys would love to give this agent the red carpet treatment. He walks toward Rusty always being on guard and aware of what could happen.

Rusty smiles as he is already sitting and waiting for his company to arrive and have some afternoon tea. He has very sharp green eyes. There's a deep scar near his right eye from a knife fight that happened a year ago, but that's another story.

"Well, Special Agent Heiden, what a surprise! How thoughtful of you to come! Did you bring me a sponge cake with a nail file in it?" he asks with a raspy voice from all the smoking he's done over the years. He doesn't care if he dies from smoking because he's already in hell.

Keith smiles back and replies, "No, but I brought you soap on a rope." He sits himself across from Rusty.

Rusty suddenly laughs. "You're too funny! So what do I have this honor?"

Then his tone of voice change as if to say, "Get out of my yard or else!" He tries to adjust his hands with no luck as he's attached to the steel table. It's going to be difficult to move an inch. His hair is brown with grays showing from his buzz cut. There are a lot of scars and when he smiles you can see that he hasn't been to the dentist in years. This image doesn't help him get a date in the outside world, but jail is a whole different story.

"I want to talk to you about your pride and joy!" Keith answers.

"What the hell for?" Rusty asks with a sharp, nasty tone.

"Duke hit my son with a baseball bat! He almost killed him within an inch of his life!" Keith answers. "So I'm here to collect the answers that I should've gotten two years ago. If I don't get the answers that I want, your boy will be going to jail. Why did you have ten key loads of cocaine in your home? Who was your main drug lord at the time? I'll give you a hint. Does the name, Jose Medina ring a bell?" Keith asks, letting the prisoner know that he means business.

"Very sorry to hear about your son but this is not my problem because my boy didn't do it! You're wasting my peeing and work out time!!" Rusty exclaims, and then he spits on the side of Keith.

The correctional officer takes his nightstick and pokes Rusty on this arm.

"Hey, keep your salvia inside your mouth or the next time you will be licking it off the floor! You get it!" he commands... "I'm sorry, agent. These low lives tend to lose their manners after a while."

"Whatever, you fat ass pig!" Rusty shouts for the whole jail to hear.

"Anyway, I came to tell you that I'm here to collect information from your sorry ass," Keith replies.

"How do I know that you have my son? I don't trust smelly pigs, especially you! I'll never forget that you're the one that put me in this fine shit hole I call home!! Remember that?! So, Heiden, do you have my son or not?!" Rusty shouts, as his voice bounces from wall to wall in the cold room.

Keith takes his cell phone out and shows him a picture of Rusty's son's mug shot from the police dept. The pictures say it all!

"So what do you think Rusty? Do you believe me now? You know that his future is in your hands not mine. So tell me what I came here for and you know I won't leave until I get it," Keith orders, as he looks directly at Rusty. "After this visit I will never have to see your ugly face again....I think you feel the same way. So make it quick. I wouldn't want to miss the lovely Californian rush hour traffic, but wouldn't care because you don't drive anymore and will never experience that again," Keith laughs.

"Come on, Special Agent, please be nice in the sandbox, because I have the information that you need, so remember that, you shit head!! First I need to know something," Rusty requests, as he blinks rapidly, very nervous about something that he would never tell a soul.

"Rusty, you're wasting my time! I'm not here to reminisce about the good old days!" Keith grunts.

"Listen, you drove all the way here just to see me. So let's just talk. I want to know you better.... You know man to man," Rusty says, with a huge smile on his face, as he tries to lean back but can't. Damn these chains!

"You mean man to rat!" Keith laughs, as he adjusts himself on the steel metal stool seat that's not comfortable at all.

"You know that you're very tasty, Agent Heiden," Rusty says, as he gives him a wink.

"Rusty, knock it off!" growls the correction officer.

Rusty shouts, "You're a real cracker, Heiden! You should have gone into comedy because you really suck as a federal agent." He laughs. "I'll answer your questions, but first you've got to answer mine," Rusty commands, as he cracks his neck.

"I really don't have time to play twenty questions," Keith answers with an annoyed tone.

"How did you get the scar on your left ear and hands?" Rusty asks, as he smiles. "Please don't tell me that you got it from your job because that's a load of horse shit!" Keith doesn't answer and it's getting Rusty angry. "Agent Heiden, don't be rude! Answer my questions and then I'll answer yours!" A second goes by and not a word from the agent. "Let me guess, your old man did that to you," he asks, as he cracks his neck again but this time for a dramatic effect.

"Rusty, you're wasting my time!" he snaps with disgust. "I'm not at all surprised that you're someone's bitch, especially in this wonderful place!"

"Agent Heiden, now play nice in the sandbox or I won't talk! This trip can be a waste of your time, not mine!" Rusty laughs, as he gives a smile, showing off his rotten teeth.

Please close your mouth! sighs Keith.

"My father hit me."

"Ouch, Keithie, that hurts like hell!" Rusty shouts, as he makes a painful look on his face and then starts to stare.

"Stop looking at me that way! Don't you dare ask me on a date!" Keith shouts back. "I'm not a freak or exhibit for your entertainment, because the show "Cops" is a repeat episode!"

"Take it easy, Agent Heinie! Please don't go all crazy on me!" he states. "We both had the same kind of childhood! What a small world!" Rusty says with surprise.

Keith pushes a yellow legal pad right underneath Rusty's nose.

"Enough with the small talk. I want all the information, including names, locations and where they might live now. I need to know everything about the drug world that you had dealings with! Don't leave anything out! Believe me, I'll check up on everything you tell me! If it's the truth your boy goes free without a single hair touched on his head," he states, as he looks directly into the inmate's eyes and sees no soul inside.

That's what happens when you're in prison until you depart from this earth. What a waste of a human! I bet he was an altar boy at his local church and helped old ladies walk across the street in his Boy Scout uniform.

"Come on, man. Why can't we be friends?" Rusty requests with his damaged heart on the steel table.

"I don't need friends like you! Just write if you want to save your son from having your same fate!" Keith demands without giving Rusty a second to rethink his decision. *You're trying my patience! I really want to smash your ugly face into the table! I only need five minutes to do the job without people and cameras breathing down my neck.*

"How do I know that you will help my son?" he says, as he's about to touch the pen on the table.

"It's funny…you don't know," Keith answers without blinking. Now he's staring at Rusty to move it along so he can leave and have some lunch. "Are you waiting for me to beg and kiss your feet?"

"Don't have much. My memory is not the same since I've lived here. I'm probably not going to say anything that you don't already know. So, you are wasting my workout time!" Rusty answers.

"Rusty, I want anything you know about Jose Medina's world… you know, just the drug business. You were on the job for years. Do you know any players coming in?" Keith asks. *I'm really tired all of a sudden. Between a mole in the Jose Medina's cartel and maybe a mole in the DEA department, it's very hard trying to keep up.*

"I don't need to write anything down because I really don't have anything. Maybe if you wait another twenty years and maybe…just maybe I will remember what you're looking for," Rusty says with a tinge of sarcasm.

"Sorry, no can do!" Keith answers. "Do you want your son to go to jail? I'm not playing with you, Rusty! You are wasting my time, and I really have a life outside of these walls!" Keith answers as he gets up from the metal seat. "You know that Gloria thinks you're a low life!"

"Come closer to me, Heiden, so I can kill you," he shouts.

"We are done here!" Keith says and walks away.

Suddenly Keith notices something that makes him become calm quickly without making himself look like a fool "Okay…okay… You cry like a little girl." Rusty laughs and starts to write on the pad.

About ten minutes later, Rusty finishes the task at hand. Keith takes the pad and says, "I will see what I can do for your lad, but I'm not going to hold my breath if he gets out of jail or not. But thank you for your help, and I hope I will never get to see you again.

The DEA agents walk away to the exit door.

"Hey, Heiden! I know what you did ten years ago!" Rusty shouts.

Keith turns quickly around and almost collides into Liam. "What did you say?"

"You heard me, you DEA pig!" Rusty answers. "You are going down, Heiden. Mr. Medina is mad as hell, and you are going to pay."

"Listen, Rusty, it doesn't help Duke when you threaten me. Tell me what's going down," Keith demands, as his voice echoes through the first floor. "Or your prodigal son is going to jail! Work with me or else!"

"Don't you touch my son! I have people on the outside that will make your life a living hell!" Rusty screams back. "I bet you have nothing on my boy! Maybe your son did that to himself just to get your full attention," Rusty laughs and without missing a beat. "I know what you did ten years ago, and Jose Medina wants payback!"

"What?" Keith asks again with a shocked look on his face.

"Come on, Rusty, your playdate is over," the correction officer interjects and ends the heartwarming conversation. He unlocks Rusty's handcuffs from the steel table. The officer helps Rusty up from his uncomfortable seat and takes off the handcuff lock on Rusty's waist shackles belt. Rusty begins to walk away from the two DEA agents, and the correction officer then guides the prisoner out of the visiting room.

"Rusty!" Keith shouts back to get a straight answer from the loser prisoner.

Suddenly Rusty stops and turns around. "You can't hear out of your damaged ear! I said, I know, and so does Mr. Jose Medina. He knows what you did ten years ago at the drug raid. He's coming to get you and your family. Payback's a bitch, my friend!"

"Let's go…you have kitchen detail!" shouts the correction officer, as he takes Rusty's arm.

"Don't touch me or maybe you want to finish it in my jail cell?"

"You're not my type!" shouts the officer.

Keith stands alone in the empty room with the steel tables and chairs. He feels as if a two-hundred-pound weight just hit him. Rusty's statement stings worse than a dozen bees!

What the hell happened ten years ago? Why can't I remember? Why can't I remember?

Patrick is in the clear with the drugs that he had at the house, but Keith doesn't know if he has anything anywhere else. Peter or Keith can tell the police that Patrick and Duke just had a huge fight that ended up with a person in intensive care for a couple of days. Criminal charges are being made against Duke by the police, but they don't need to know anything else because there is nothing to prove. Patrick shouldn't get into any trouble…we hope.

Keith has another matter to attend to. He doesn't have a clue as to what happened ten years ago. When he does remember should he tell Dr. Sheppard? Maybe he should tell Reese (the family dog)! He wouldn't tell a living soul what his owner did…if anything! Keith just wants to run away, far away from his problems.

CHAPTER
FORTY-SIX

As Liam walks to the Electronic Surveillance Department his main focus is to find out what's going on with the investigation of Alex Raninsky and his crew of bad guys.

If you have the warrants it is easier to build a case with surveillance equipment then it is to listen to wiretaps for months on end! A sting operation is taking place thirty miles away from Los Angeles in an empty factory. A drug raid should take down twenty ice cream trucks in Los Angeles. You can hear a man speaking broken English through the recording devices. The voice is recognized as that of Alex Raninsky. He's running the crew that will hopefully be interrupted by the DEA. The department needs enough evidence to make arrests and collect the money and drugs which will be worth millions.

"Listen, everyone! In two weeks we'll have our day! About twenty ice cream trucks will be driving through the quiet streets of Los Angeles giving out drugs to little children! We will give out a little here and there and sell cocaine and other drugs along with ice cream. Don't forget the ice cream! We have many different flavors to choose from, and remember the police love free ice cream! Are we ready, my comrades?" The sound of laughter fills the factory, and you can hear the men screaming in Russian which sounds like, "Россия, вперед! [Go, Russia]!"

Todd works on a computer and hears the recording from where he's sitting, Liam walks over to Todd. "Hey, Todd, by any chance did you get the mouse for the computers yet?"

"I put in the request three days ago. Hopefully, we'll get them by today the latest. Thank you, Liam, for the pictures of my wife and me," Todd says, as he looks up at the agent with a tiny smile.

"Good! Keep me posted. We really need them," Liam responds, as he looks closer to see what Todd is working on.

"Hey, do you mind? You're in my space!" Todd shouts.

"Chill out little man!" Liam laughs.

Suddenly, Agent Forrester walks into the electronics department, and all the agents straighten themselves up. The sound of laughter and mindless bull shit conversation comes to a halt.

"Agent Miller, did you get anything?" he asks, as he stands tall with very little signs of exhaustion. Jack has been working many hours on the job, and his paycheck will certainly show that his efforts have not been in vain.

Agent Sid Miller had been working on the job for about three years. He loves it but the hours are a killer, and he barely gets any sleep nor does he have a love life. Very few agents have a family with 2.5 kids and a dog. Sid wants the action and the family, but fighting crime is his thing for now. He's been trained by the best, and that includes Agent Heiden and Darling as well as others. Sid is very grateful that he picked his career, because if it were up to his parents he would have been the family's rabbi.

"Yes, sir, we have what we're looking for! Do you want to hear the recording?" Sid says.

"Absolutely!" says Agent Forrester, as he takes the headpiece and carefully listens to Alex Raminsky.

"Are you trying to kill my computers!" Todd shouts not knowing that Agent Forrester is in the room listening to something. "Oh, sorry."

Minutes later Jack takes the headpiece out of his ears. "Thanks, this is great work, Agent Miller. I need you to collect all the data, and we will start the raid operation tomorrow. I will notify all the agents," Jack adds, as he sees Todd working on the computer. "I also need all the data and hardcopies loaded into my computer before the end of the day."

"Yes, Agent Forrester," Miller answers. He feels a little uncomfortable around his boss.

"Todd, what's going on with the mouses? I was told they were broken and hadn't been replaced as of yet. Is this true?" demands Agent Forrester.

"I guess?" he responds uncertainly.

"That is not an answer! I want you to address the matter and get a new mouse for everyone. Hold the receipt and the department will reimburse you for the cost. This is a direct order with no back talk. I'll call you within an hour to make sure the order is carried out. Do you understand what I've just said, Todd?" Jack directs his command to the nerd with the pen pocket protector.

"Yes, Agent Forrester!" Todd retorts, just to get him off his back. *Why can't I just do my work in peace?*

Jack looks directly at the other agents as they stand around not really doing any work. He becomes a little upset at the situation in front of him. He doesn't like laziness when there is no reason for it. He expected his soldiers in the US Army to move and not waste time staring at the walls. Yes, there is a time for rest and relaxation and there is a time to work. This structured way of thinking goes back to Jack's orphanage years.

"Gentlemen, if you're not stationed to work with Agent Miller on this project, I advise you to move out of this room and find something else to do! If not I'll find something productive for you to work on! Do you understand?" Jack gives an order and his employees jump to his command.

"Yes, sir!" answers one agent. All the agents, including Liam, walk out of the room quietly without backtalk to their boss. Jack Forrester has a very strong hold on them.

CHAPTER
FORTY-SEVEN

*T*he alarm clock goes off at 5:00 p.m., and Peter sees the time from the corner of his eye.

"Elise, I've got to get ready for work. You can stay overnight if you want! There's food in the refrig so help yourself, just try not to make a huge mess," he says, as he rolls his naked body away from his extremely hot therapist. Elise smiles and remembers a great time last night. They spent a lot of time in bed along with drinking an imported wine called "Koblevo," and also eating food from the Ukraine. This is what the doctor ordered.

"Thanks, Peter, I'll stay," Elise answers with that same smile still on her face. She feels like a schoolgirl dating the most popular boy on the football team. She never thought of dating a government agent especially this one with such a fine body. It's all in one package with no return necessary! I guess working everyday pays off. Not that bad at all. She thinks her girlfriends back in Connecticut will be very jealous.

"I'll try to get home early so we can continue where we left off," Peter states, as he leans down and gives Elise a soft kiss on the lips. As he gets up from the bed she watches him walk toward the bathroom and close the door behind him, shutting her off from the view of that gorgeous body!

Elise lies on Peter's side of the unmade bed taking in his scent which is still present on the soft pillows. The sound of the phone surprises her. "Elise, can you please get that and take a message? I'll be out shortly!" Peter says through the bathroom door as the shower water is turned on.

Elise picks up the phone. "Hello. Peter Darling's residence. How can I help you?"

The startled caller asks with surprise, "Dr. Sheppard?"

"Hello, who's calling please?" Elise asks with a friendly voice. She tries to pull the covers up on her naked body to get more comfortable while talking on the phone.

"Dr. Sheppard, this is Keith Heiden. Where is Peter and can I talk to him?" he asks with a sharp tone in his voice. *This is not my year! Keith, you're an ass! Peter has finally done it! What a jackass! I guess that I'm in the same category because I know him! This situation is not good at all.*

"Oh, hello, Mr. Heiden. Peter is in the shower," she says quickly as if she's speaking to the school principal. Elise tries to think of a way to get him off the phone immediately. For some strange reason, he makes her nervous and uncomfortable in her skin. Peter starts to sing and it echoes throughout the bedroom. He's singing the theme song to Winnie the Pooh, as loud as his lungs can travel. He's way off key but he thinks that he has a great singing voice, and no one has the heart to tell him the real truth (not even his mom).

"Who's singing?" Keith asks with confusion in his voice.

"That's Peter," Elise giggles.

"Just tell Justin Timberlake to call me back as soon as he can! Thanks," and suddenly the sound of a dial tone is buzzing in Elise's ear.

"Hello, hello!" Elise tries to get a response with no luck. *It's about time! I thought he would never get off the phone. I'm really getting to like the tone of Keith's voice! Peter is nice but he's not like Keith. I don't know what I should feel right now, and how can I control this overwhelming urge to fall in love with a man that's my patient! Elise, for God's sake, try to get hold of yourself. You can't think about another man, especially Peter's best friend! I really don't know why they're friends. I wonder how they ever met.*

Ten minutes go by as Elise gets dressed in some comfortable clothes. Her navy tee shirt says, "Yale" in faded white lettering, and her skin tight boot cut jeans have holes in the knees. They do show off Elise's best asset, however, which is her firm rear end. But her favorite part of this outfit is her worn out sneakers that Elise purchased with her paycheck during her college years. They hold so many memories for her and have more holes in them then the potholes on the streets! Peter walks out of the bathroom and sees his abs in the mirror. He has been working out a lot at the local gym, and it shows because you can bounce a dime off that stomach of his! He keeps himself in excellent shape. Peter spots Elise standing there.

Peter dries himself off with a tan cotton towel that his mom has bought for him. She helped make his home very comfortable to live in and to visit of course. He smiles at Elise and says, "You look very cute in rags!"

"Thank you," she smiles back at her new man and suddenly they kiss.

"You're a great distraction, but really I have to get to work. Damn, girl, you're too hot for my taste!" Peter slowly pulls away from Elise and starts to collect his work clothes. The outfit for tonight includes black slacks, dress socks, and dress shoes polished and ready to wear. A wrinkle-free designer shirt in a light blue covered the white T-shirt underneath. A thin black belt with a silver buckle completes the outfit. "I almost forgot to ask you who called," he asks, as he continues to look at himself in the mirror.

"Oh, your partner in crime, Keith," Elise says softly, as she looks in the mirror and sees Peter brushing his brown hair. "Don't forget the tie?"

"I'll talk to him when I get to work. Thanks for the message. Sometimes a tie isn't needed when you're already hot. Anyway, the ties are for nerds, not for people like me. Seriously, if I really want to wear a tie I would have joined the FBI!" jokes Peter as they both laugh.

Elise's cell phone rings and she walks over to her briefcase to get the call. "Hello, Dr. Sheppard speaking."

"Hello, Dr. Sheppard, this is Agent Jack Forrester at the DEA Department. Do you have time to talk right now?" he says with his deep raspy voice. Jack taps a pen on his desk to pass the time away.

Elise walks out of Peter's bedroom and starts to talk, "Yes, how can I help you today?"

"Dr. Sheppard, I want you to be totally honest. How is Special Agent Keith Heiden's therapy going? Can you please tell me without giving out confidential information on your case?"

"Well, Agent Heiden, is not getting back to me. We need to make additional therapy appointments. I'm a little concerned," Elise answers, as she looks in the refrigerator for something to eat for dinner.

"I'm sorry. That's my fault as he's been working a lot of hours this week. So if you want to see him during work hours you can," Jack responds, as he leans back in his office chair to get comfortable.

"That will be fine." Peter gives Elise a gentle push to move her out of the way, so he can start dinner for bother of them.

"How about tonight?" Forrester asks, as he tries to avoid a yawn through the phone.

"Tonight," she says with a sharp pitch in her voice as she looks at Peter at the same time.

He smiles.

"Just take it easy and breathe," Peter says softly.

He realizes right away that Elise is very dramatic and this is one of those times. It's kind of amusing to him and a little bit annoying too. He has almost forgotten how expressive woman can be, including his mother and sisters, Justine and Erin. Elise, however, tops them all, especially since she's a therapist.

"Is this going to be a problem for you? Do you have something important to do right now? I don't want to step on your toes, but I know that you have to finish this patient before you get additional new patients. No pressure of course," Agent Forrester laughs. "Agent Heiden's evaluation ends at the beginning of August, and I didn't receive a mid-report on his progress. The district attorney, Chris Lowe, and my other bosses in the DEA Department also want to know the status report. I'm sorry that I sound like a broken record but this is important. Do you have the mid-report on Agent Heiden and the other agents? I almost forgot to tell you that I emailed you the list of names a couple of days ago," Agent Forrester says, as he leans way back in his office chair.

As Jack looks around his office it's obvious to him that there are no personal items to add a touch of home. As an orphan he never had a family to call his own. Jack was raised in an orphanage in upstate New York. He was afraid of rejection, so he never looked for his birth mother. Jack has a few friends but still has no pictures to show for it. He was in the military for most of this adult life, and he did a tour of duty during Desert Storm. After twenty years of service Jack retired from the US Army with a full pension and began DEA training in an Academy in Quantico, Virginia. One day Jack wants to be in Congress or maybe even President. Perhaps in the near future he'll also have a family to call his own.

"Is it possible for me to come in the morning, Agent Forrester? I'm truly sorry…but to be honest, I'm really not in the state of mind to work at this time," Elise states, as she picks on some leftovers from last night's dinner. Peter walks around the kitchen as he makes a plate for both of them. He gives Elise a look to cut the conversation short because dinner will be ready soon.

Agent Forrester suddenly receives a text from his cell phone.

It says, "Let's meet again in the downtown LA park at 7:00 p.m. I've got your money and we can talk. Make sure no one follows you to the location." There is no phone number but Jack knows who contacted him. His name is Eddie Burns and he works for an unknown person but pays a lot of money to get the job done.

"Sure, no problem. You can see him tomorrow morning at 9:00 a.m. and please bring the mid-report. I'll see you in the morning. Have a good night," he says.

"Okay, I will see you then. Good night and thanks." Elise hangs up and hits herself on her forehead. "I'm so stupid!"

"Don't say it if you don't mean it." Peter laughs. "Why are you stupid?" Elise takes a bite of his food with an annoyed look on her face.

"Peter, I totally forgot to do a mid-report on Keith and the other agents in the department. What am I going to do?" she cries, as she chews her food from the Mexican take out that they ordered yesterday afternoon.

"What does a mid-report contain?" Peter asks, as he sits near the kitchen table, and he puts down his plate of food with a glass of coke next to him.

Elise glances at Peter as he continues to smile.

"Come on, Peter, I always given you my mid-report by email or regular mail!"

She walks to the table and sits near Peter to get his full attention.

"Yes, I know, Elise, but can you please entertain me anyway before I go to work?" Peter asks, as he drinks some of his soda.

"Okay, a mid-report is a written document giving you my professional opinion about a patient and what we spoke about in general during our therapy sessions. It just shows what I'm up against and what I need to work on in the weeks ahead," she answers stealing a piece of grilled steak from Peter's plate at the same time.

They really enjoy each other's company and the chemistry seems to be there, but how long will it last?

"Please don't go all crazy on me! I just asked a question," he announces, as he smiles widely and sharply smacks Elise's rear end. At the same time, she tries to get another piece of steak off this plate. Peter looks at close as if to say, "just try to steal another piece of steak! I really don't mind smacking that hot, extremely sexy ass of yours!"

"Peter!" Elise shouts, as she rubs her backside that aches from the firm love slap.

He gets up from his seat and puts the dirty dish in the dishwasher and then turns and smiles justifiably.

"Peter what?" He laughs.

"Peter, you're not well in the head," she replies.

"A lot of people tell me that. Why do I have to go to work again?" he cries, as he walks closer to his newfound girlfriend who looks exceptionally sexy in those skin-tight jeans. Boy she must work out to the max because she has no body fat on her!

Peter has a huge smile on his face, while he puts his hands on her backside and squeezes them like two firm ripe grapefruits.

"I have to go now but, we'll continue this later!" he smiles. Then he gives her a final spank and without a second to spare he walks toward the front door. "Take care, sweet buns!"

Elise laughs as she rubs her rear end. "Bye."

CHAPTER

FORTY-EIGHT

*T*here's a knock at the front door, and Justine opens it without looking through the peephole. A man quickly walks into the house without saying hello.

"Treat, what are you doing here!" she asks with a perplexed look. *How did he know where I live?* Justine thinks, *I never told him or maybe I did? He must have looked inside my wallet while I was in the bathroom. What does he want? Thank God Keith went back to work.*

"I need to speak to your husband! Where is he?" Treat asks sharply with a hysterical tone.

His voice always sounds like he's underwater or has a dreadful cold that won't go away. Treat is 5'4" and wimpy looking. He has light brown hair and bald on the top of his head. His eyeglasses are very outdated, which make his tiny hazel eyes stick out like a sore thumb. There's not enough time in a day to explain his terrible taste in clothes. Treat really looks like a character from one of the cartoon shows that Colin watches on TV.

"Treat, I don't need to tell you where my husband is! It's none of your business! Just get out of my house!" Justine shouts, as she tries to force her low life ex-lover out.

"Justine, I need to speak to your husband! My life is in danger, and I need his help! I don't know where to go!" Treat explains, as he starts to walk anxiously through the house. "These people are after me! They might kill me. I really need to hide!"

Justine follows right behind him. "What are you doing? Treat, who are these people that you're afraid of? Why do they want to kill you?" she asks, as she shouts out twenty questions like fireworks during a Fourth of July celebration. Treat ignores her.

"Get the hell out of my house! I want you out now!" she screams, as she tries to block his path. He's a fast little rat! "I really don't care who's after you! Leave my house or I'll call the police and asks them to bring their dogs!"

"Justine, your sense of humor kills me! Please listen to me. I really need to speak to Keith!" Treat demands.

Suddenly the kids come out of the family room to see what the commotion is.

"Mom! Who is this person?" Erin asks, as she looks straight at her mother.

Erin is very concerned that there is a strange man in the house late at night screaming at her mother.

"Erin, please don't worry! He was a friend of mine until a couple of weeks ago. Please don't worry. Just put Colin to bed because it's getting late," she commands, as she tries to dismiss her daughter.

"Keith, where are you? Damn, Justine, this house is huge! Keith, where the hell are you?" Treat screams which makes Reese get up from his nap outside.

Reese starts to bark as he wants to get into the house and stop the situation right away. Treat at the same time comes back to the kitchen and takes out a gun from his jacket. Suddenly, Treat points the 32 caliber gun directly at Justine.

"What are you doing? I'm calling the police!" Erin shouts, as Colin becomes upset and starts to cry.

Mitch shouts at the strange man, "Hey, put the gun down before you hurt someone! Are you crazy! Erin, call the police!"

"Kids, just calm down! I'm not going to hurt anyone! I just want answers from your mother! Then I'll leave and everything will be normal again," he tries to state his case while still holding the gun. He's never held a gun before and it feels very heavy. Treat begins to shake and tries to focus. He's never done anything like this before; he's an accountant, not a killer. But life points you in a strange directions sometimes, and this is one of them.

"Erin, please don't call the police as of yet!" Justine pleads to her daughter. "I really want to hear what Treat has to say. Let him speak." But at the same time Mitch and Erin look strangely at their mother, as if to say, "Lady, you are off your rocker!"

"Mom, he has a gun in his hand! Are you out of your mind? He's going to kill us!" Erin snaps back.

Suddenly Reese (the chocolate lab) barks aggressively on the other side of the sliding glass kitchen door. He paces back and forth, ready to attack and save the family. Reese's mannerisms say, just let me at him! I'll crush him like a bug with one paw! It's funny how dogs can sense if a family member is in danger.

Suddenly the phone rings and everyone becomes quiet.

"Treat, I have to answer that!" Justine says, with very little emotion.

Keith said to her and the kids one day, if you show any emotion like weakness, you'll be in deeper trouble than you are now. Justine is truly moved that her husband had the time to teach her and the kids about the danger from the outside world. It really helps her when she goes to work and is around strangers that might harm her in any way. Keith is not happy that Justine is a real estate agent because you never know what might happen during the course of the day. He's always afraid for her safety. He wants her to raise the kids full time, but she's not that type of mother to stay home and watch soap operas all day.

"Let the answering machine take it!" Treat commands, as he slowly takes a kitchen chair and sits on it without losing sight of the Heiden family. The answering machine catches the call on the third ring. Keith's voice echoes throughout the first floor of the house.

"Hello, you have reached the Heiden's. Please leave a message, thanks."

Seconds later, "Hello, Justine, it's Keith, are you going to pick up Patrick from the hospital today or is he staying there for a few more days? How are you and the kids? Please call me when you get a chance. Thanks, I'll talk to you soon." He's not aware that his family is in serious danger and might be killed any second by the accountant named Treat Miller.

"Daddy!" Colin screams from the top of his three-year-old lungs. He tries to get away from Erin's grip. "Erin, let go! Daddy!"

"Justine, shut the kid up or I will!!" Treat demands. He never really liked kids; he thinks that they're whiny and spoiled brats. At first he thought that Justine didn't have children of her own, because she didn't seem like the motherly type. Treat was very surprised when he found out that she has four children.

"Treat, you leave my kids alone! What do you want?" Justine pleads, as she tries to hold back the tears. She has to remember to be one step ahead, especially in dangerous situations like this one. Treat must be in serious trouble to wave a loaded gun in her face.

"I want to speak to your husband face to face, not over the phone! I need to be in the witness protection program, and I know that Keith knows some people to make that happen. I owe a lot of money, and they want me killed for the payback with interest! I'm a dead man, and I need Keith to help me in order to stay alive! Please can you help or not?" Treat pleads. "You know, Justine, you owe me big time!" Meanwhile, the gun is getting heavy to hold, so he switches it to the other hand.

"Mom, who is this guy?" Mitch asks. "What an odd-looking man and who the hell are you?"

"I was your mother's lover until recently. I still love your mother, and we would have been happy until your abused father got in the middle! Then everything that I hoped for with your mother went straight down south," Treat declares, as he paces back and forth looking around like a cat high on catnip.

"Mom, is this true? You had an affair with this guy? Does Dad know about this?" Erin asks while she still tries to hold back Colin. She can't believe what she's hearing! Erin knows that her parents have problems but not to this extreme.

"Erin, let go! Let go!" Colin squeaks, as he tries to use all of his little body to break free.

"Yes, but it's over now. Your father knows about Treat and me. He's not very happy about it. We're going to work it out. Please give us the room. It's between your father and me. Please don't worry! Just try to understand," she pleads to her kids to comprehend this situation. What she's really trying to say is I'm human and I made a huge mistake. I really hope in time that you can forgive me.

"Mom, your so-called ex-lover has a gun! What are we going to do? We can't just stand like trees! Let's call Dad, Uncle Peter, or the police!" Mitch yells, as he tries to start something to break this insane drama. He walks slowly to the phone, but Treat notices something is coming down like a ton of bricks.

"Hey, kid, if you want to celebrate your next birthday… I would advise you to stop what you're doing!" he commands. "Justine, you know and let me think!" Treat then looks at his ex-lover: Justine, you know my request. Just get me out of here! I want to leave the country like right now, not later!" he pleads, as he rushes to the phone and picks it up. "Justine, just call Keith! Tell him to come home right away without stopping at red lights! I need to speak to him right away!" He pushes the phone into her stomach to get a fast reaction.

"Please, Treat, I don't want to involve him! Treat, I'm not going to help you!" Justine exclaims, as she walks away from her ex-lover.

"No, you're going to call your ass hole husband! Have him come home now, not later!!!" Treat demands, as he feels his veins ready to pop out of his neck. "I need to get in the witness protection program, and he can help me!" Treat commands angrily, as he fiercely puts the wireless phone right up to Justine's face.

"Treat, I'm not going to help you. You have messed up my life!" she snaps right back with full force.

"Justine, we had sex together! Please don't lie, you loved it!" Treat yells as he waves the gun in his hand.

"Mom! Is this true?" Erin asks, with a surprised look on her face.

Mitch stands next to his sister and Colin once again begins to cry. Erin continues to hold him back but it's a challenge. Treat seems very nervous that Justine is not taking him seriously. He starts to pace back and forth making strange noises, as he thinks to himself what to do next.

Suddenly, Treat points the gun at Reese and orders, "Shut the hell up you mangy mutt or I'll kill you!"

"Stop, Treat!" Justine shouts, even though she's not crazy about animals but to kill one, that's a different story. "Don't shoot the dog!"

"Where the hell is Keith? I'm not playing games with you, Justine. I have a huge headache from your family, and it's getting worse by the second. So tell me, woman!" Treat yells. It's never a good sign to lose your audience.

"Mom, who is this man? Why does he have a gun, and why does he want to talk to dad?" Mitch asks, as he yells to override Treat's thinking process. "Did you have an affair with this guy?"

"I had an affair with Treat and believe me it's over. It should never have happened in the first place. I'm sorry. Please forgive me, kids! I'm sorry that I made a terrible mistake!" Justine cries, as she tries to get forgiveness from her children, but it's not going to be easy to win their trust back.

Treat continues to wave the phone in Justine's face.

"Enough with this soap opera. Call him and tell him to come home right away. Lie if you have to," he shouts forcefully, in front of Justine's face.

"No, I won't do it. You will have to kill me first," Justine answers, as she slaps Treat's hand away from her. He suddenly points the gun in her face to get her full attention. No one takes him seriously and it's really pissing him off, but this will wake them up very fast.

"Believe me, I can make your wish come true!" Treat exclaims.

"Mom!" All the kids' scream in unison and then suddenly the gun goes off. But nothing happens.

"You're a shit head! The gun is not even loaded!" Justine screams.

Treat realizes what he had just done. "I'm so sorry!" He shouts and drops the gun on the kitchen floor. He runs away leaving the front door wide open for the outside world to see. You can hear the sound of the car door slam and not a second later the sound of the tires spinning off.

Justine takes the unloaded gun from the kitchen floor and puts it in a large clear sandwich bag without saying a word to her children who are still in shock. She walks to Keith's office. The family's safe is below the floor panels under the office chair. Justine carefully takes the three panels away, which expose the large safe. It has a high security code, which is only known by Keith, Peter, and Justine. The code will also be given to Erin when she turns twenty-one.

That night Justine sits down with the kids and tries to explain what she did. She states that she'll never do it again and loves their father. She never meant to damage the family. All the kids promise to keep this quiet from their father, and she did make a promise to the kids. She'll tell Keith about the drama but on her terms and time frame.

Justine takes Colin to bed and the others follow upstairs too, while Reese lies on the cool kitchen floor to sleep for the night. The lights are turned off, and all the doors and windows are locked tight.

CHAPTER
FORTY-NINE

When Elise wakes up she doesn't remember where she is. She feels her head on the soft feather pillows and the sheet covering her body. She puts two and two together and realizes she's in Peter's bed without her man beside her. What a great day with Peter! Reading the Sunday newspaper together, eating and drinking and spending time in bed together, which she can't forget! To feel like a woman again is very refreshing. Suddenly the cell rings, she picks up the phone and looks at the clock at the same time. It's now 9:20 a.m. on Monday.

"Shit, I'm late!!" she shouts without paying attention to who's on the other end of the phone line!

"Hello!" the sound of Peter's voice echoes on the line but that doesn't help a bit. "Elise, are you there?"

He looks around the parking lot, shaking his head and waving to a couple of his co-workers.

Elise runs to different rooms in the apartment to find anything to wear that's business clothing not over casual that she likes to wear on the weekend.

"Shit, I have nothing to wear today!"

"Elise! Hello!" Peter shouts to get her attention.

"Hi, Peter, I'm so late! I have to go to your office to see Agent Jack Forrester!" Elise states excitedly getting dressed and having a conversation with Peter at the same time.

Her business suit is at the dry cleaners. Elise didn't realize that she was planning to sleep over the whole weekend, so all she has to choose from is her casual clothing.

"Relax, Elise. Jack will be here all day. Just try to breathe, as I hear you're going crazy as usual. Take deep breaths before you pass out on my floor! I don't want to pick you up from the floor when I get home," Peter laughs. "I'm going to get some breakfast, but I'll be home after that. Will you have lunch with me around 2:00 p.m. at Panera Bread on S. Sepulveda Boulevard in LA?" Peter says, as he sees Keith from the corner of his light brown eyes. His partner in crime is walking towards his SUV.

"Can I call you around 1:00 p.m.? It really depends on my workload," Elise says, as she rushes around to find any other clothes to wear besides her weekend outfit.

"Sure, Elise…can you hold on?" Peter asks, as he walks toward Keith before getting into his SUV. "Hi, Keith, did you have breakfast yet?"

Keith looks at Peter and sees his best friend with a huge smile. He already knows the reason for all his enthusiasm. His friend is now dating his therapist. Keith honestly thinks that the man upstairs is playing a very bad joke on him.

Although he just wants to choke Peter, he tries to bite his tongue, and with a friendly smile he responds, "I can eat."

"Great!" Peter replies, as he puts his cell phone to his ear. "Elise, I've got to go now. I'm going to have breakfast with Keith. I'll call you soon," he announces with a cheerful voice.

"Sure, I'll talk to you soon," she says quickly and hangs up the phone. "I'm so late!"

Elise cries as she runs into the bathroom.

An hour later, Elise arrives at the DEA Department, and a security guard named Davis Jones escorts Dr. Sheppard around the premises. He stands behind Elise as she meets Jack.

They shake hands. "Hello, Dr. Sheppard. I hope Mr. Jones is treating you well?"

"Hello, Agent Forrester. Yes, he's a gentleman," Elise smiles at Davis and he smiles back, as he stands like a soldier. Not even a high gust of wind could bring him down to the floor!

"Dr. Sheppard, I do have some new files for you, but I would like you to continue your therapy sessions with Agent Heiden on a daily basis for now. Of course that doesn't include weekends. You can start with an hour or two today," he states as he looks at the doctor. She's wearing her tight jeans with the holes in the knees, worn out sneakers, and a washed out T-shirt with the word "Yale" barely visible. Elise feels out of place and extremely uncomfortable. It certainly looks like she pulled these clothes right out of the hamper.

"May I ask why?" Elise says, as she looks at Agent Forrester intently.

"Agent Heiden is a special case. To be honest, Dr. Sheppard, I really need him fully active and back on the job. However, don't tell anyone that I said so! He's a hard worker with a great work ethic, even though his behavior leaves a lot to be desired."

"We are always working against time on the job and need all our men and women fully active and ready to go at a moment's notice. It's up to you, however, and how you evaluate Agent Heiden after his last therapy session. Then the board has the final say on his future with the DEA Department. The district attorney has the same opinion about the situation. Anyway, if everything is finished without further delay and evaluation of Agent Heiden can be completed in half the time, you will be able to start work on your new case files before midsummer!" exclaims Agent Forrester, as he feels relaxed and happy to see someone who works outside the office. Dr. Sheppard does look cute in that comfortable outfit of hers!

"Okay, whatever you think is best," Elise answers, but that's not how she really feels.

The truth is she doesn't know what to feel. She knows that her heart skips a beat when she sees her patient. It is a disappointment to her that the sessions will end sooner than expected. In her professional point of view, Elise would like to see Agent Heiden without being pressed for time. She feels that would help her make a clearer and more concrete evaluation, and her final report to the board would truly have closure. At the same time she still may see Keith from time to time now that she's dating Agent Darling. Only time will tell. She knows that their relationship is moving very fast. She really doesn't mind a bit! She needs a cute, funny, goofy character boyfriend to distract her especially these days.

"Dr. Sheppard, please follow me. I'll take you to Agent Heiden's office. Mr. Davis Jones thank you for your services. I can take it from here. I'll call you when I need you again," Agent Forrester states in a friendly voice.

"Thank you, sir…good-bye," Mr. Davis Jones answers with his professional soldier like voice.

With that being said he turns quickly away and walks back to his original station.

They both walk to the reception desk where Agent Forrester spots Nicole's business nameplate.

"Dr. Sheppard, can you please sit here, and I'll call to see where Nicole is," he says with a smile, as he picks up the phone from the desk. He wants to find out if the young lady came through main security.

"Hello, Agent Forrester, sorry I'm late," a young lady says, as she rushes to put down her things. Nicole is ready for another day at work, but her boyfriend wanted her to stay home; someone has to pay the bills, however. They met at college; since then they have been together for over four years and are recently living together. She wonders if he will ever pop the question! Almost all her girlfriends are engaged or married by now. Her mom keeps asking her when and her father says it's fine to wait. She has a great future ahead of her, but she isn't sure what she wants. Nicole really loves Lance Dakota. Well, that's not his real name. He changed his name because he thinks it'll help him become famous.

Agent Forrester puts down the phone and moves quickly out of Nicole's path. She rushes and tries not to look at her boss to avoid any more problems.

"That's fine," Jack says, as he looks at both ladies at the same time.

"Okay, Nicole, please look after Dr. Sheppard, until Agent Heiden comes back. Dr. Sheppard, after you finish your session with your patient please come and see me. I have some more new cases to give you before you leave. By any chance do you have the mid-report on Agent Heiden and the other agents for me?" Jack asks without taking a breath.

"Sorry, Agent Forrester, to be very honest I didn't get a chance yet, but I will get the report to you by the end of the business week," Elise answers, as she sits comfortably on the guest bench made of soft black leather.

"Okay, that's fine. Please, no later than Friday," he says. "Nicole, can you please call me when Dr. Sheppard finishes with her therapy session with Agent Heiden?"

"No problem, sir," she answers while she looks for her silver cross-pen in her desk drawer.

"Thanks, and I'll see you soon, doctor. Thanks again." Then he walks away without looking back.

"Dr. Sheppard, do you want to wait for Agent Heiden in his office? I don't think he would mind," Nicole asks with a friendly smile.

"Okay sure," Elise answers quickly. It will be very interesting to see her patient's office. What kind of design style does Agent Heiden have? She already knows that he's a neat freak! His perfect home showed her that everything was in order! Even Colin looks in order and imperfection is not an option in Agent Heiden's world. A lot of abused people are very anal and strive for perfection and order because of the controlled life they are restricted to. They don't want to cause any more problems than they already have.

"Dr. Sheppard, please don't touch anything," Nicole firmly states, as she unlocks her boss's door.

"Nicole, did he ever yell at you for touching his things without asking?"

"Dr. Sheppard, I don't understand why you would ask me that kind of question!" Nicole says with a confused look on her face.

"Because I'm curious to know if he's abusive in the workplace," states Elise. Of course she already knows the answer to her question.

Nicole walks past the doctor and automatically turns on the light, which gives a little accent to the room. Keith's desk is neat with nothing out of place. There are personal pictures all around the room, and Elise sees one photograph of the four kids wearing similar outfits. Then she remembers the same picture is in Peter's office. This is just great! They're close friends!

"Dr. Sheppard, I did hear a lot of stories about my boss having a very short fuse. I'm happy that I've never had to face his fury yet. I try very hard to keep quiet and sit at my desk. I just do my work as I'm asked. Personally he's not a very friendly individual; he just keeps to himself and only says a few words to me. Just business as usual... Listen, Dr. Sheppard, I don't want to say anything bad about my boss. So please don't ask me any more questions. I don't want to get into trouble!" Nicole states, while she checks some reports on Keith's desk.

"Nicole, we're alone having a friendly conversation. I don't think you'll get in trouble because we're talking," Elise says.

"I'm sorry, Dr. Sheppard. I have to step out of the office for a second to check out something, but I'll be right back. Please don't touch anything," Nicole says, and suddenly she walks out without waiting for the doctor's response. "I'll be right back!" The sound of her voice travels through the glass door and a second later she's gone, leaving Elise to her own devices.

It's another government office like any other. Elise slowly walks around and looks with interest at the items around the office. She gets close to the agent's desk and all at once.

Elise's eyes pop out of her head, as she shouts, "Shit!" and she suddenly falls to the floor.

Keith has a very confused look on his face.

"What the hell are you doing?"

"Are you okay?" he asks with a sharp tone in his voice because he knows very well it's not Nicole behind his desk. *What did I do in my last life to deserve this therapist? Okay, I'm not the best citizen but come on!*

"I'm okay. Thanks for asking," she laughs.

"That's good. We don't want to write up a worker's compensation claim! Dr. Sheppard, do you need help getting up?" Keith asks, as he walks closer to the accident scene. Keith thinks to himself, *personally just observing my therapist she seems a little off or what Patrick would say, what short of a six-pack.* What I did to Mr. Garcia doesn't compare to what I'm going through now.

Elise gets up and puts back the papers that fell off his desk. "Hello, Agent Heiden. How are you?" she says with a friendly voice and smile. Elise dismisses the agent's reaction.

"Dr. Sheppard, can you please step away from my desk right now? How did you get in my office? I know that I locked the door before I left!" Keith says, as he walks past his doctor.

"Nicole, your secretary, let me in," Elise answers, as she brushes herself off from the floor. Now suddenly for some strange reason she feels a little uncomfortable. Elise is not ready for any harsh words to be exchanged with one of her unstable patients. She looks at the special agent wearing a clean-cut black expensive business suit with a white shirt, gray tie and very shiny leather black dress shoes. What a hottie! She loves men that are clean shaven and wearing a business. suit or uniform. It drives her crazy! Like she wants to jump on them right then and there!

"Okay, I'll talk to her later about this. Why are you behind my desk?" Keith asks, not ready for another round of drama especially with his therapist.

CHAPTER
FIFTY

〰〰〰〰〰〰〰〰〰〰〰〰〰〰〰〰〰〰〰〰〰〰〰〰〰〰〰〰〰〰〰〰

"*D*r. Sheppard, you didn't answer my question. Why are you behind my desk?" Keith exclaims.

She's caught off guard with her hand in the government cookie jar. She has to think of something fast, or she'll be in deep trouble.

"I just wanted to see what kind of wood your desk was," she answers.

Keith sighs, "Dr. Sheppard, can you please make yourself comfortable!" Let the interrogation roller coaster begin. He presses the intercom button on his office phone and says, "Nicole, can you hold my calls and take the messages for me? Please tell them that I'll return their calls later today. If it's my family or Agent Forrester please let them through, okay?"

"Okay sir," Nicole answers.

Dr. Elise Sheppard sits down and opens her long yellow legal pad and looks at some notes.

"Thank you," he answers and then releases the intercom button.

As Keith looks at Dr. Sheppard he can't help but ask. "After our therapy session are you volunteering in some sort of program?" Although she looks very comfortable it just doesn't fit her profession.

She laughs, "Oh no. You see my business suit is at the dry cleaners! So that's why I'm wearing my weekend outfit. I'm extremely comfortable in my rags!"

She tries desperately to cover her bare knees that show through the rip holes in her tight jeans, but the yellow legal pad doesn't do the trick!!

"Agent Heiden, I really need to explain something before we start the therapy session," Elise says out of the blue.

Keith stares directly at the doctor and shakes his head. You don't have to be a rocket scientist to know what she's talking about.

"Please don't! I'm not interested in hearing about your new found love relationship with Agent Peter Darling or anything that comes with it! We're all adults and let's just leave it at that. I'll tell you something that's on my mind, because I'm in the mood. This situation is a conflict of interest, however, for both of you. If you pursue this teenage love interest, it's going to bite you on your professional ass!" he exclaims.

"You're warning me?" Elise asks, surprised that this has come to the surface so soon.

"What I'm really trying to do is warn myself! You see Peter Darling is a supervisor in this department, and I guess you already know that he's my best friend. One of his jobs is to give you the names of co-workers that need therapy sessions. You're both way too close to the situation! Dr. Sheppard, people do talk and when they find out that Peter is dating the government's therapist, it's not going to be good. If you have a bad day with Peter, your patients will feel it. It's called the domino effect!" Keith exclaims, as he looks directly into his therapist's eyes.

"I'm sorry, Agent Heiden, I'm still trying to figure out if you're warning me or telling me what's going to happen if we stay together," she asks with a confused look on her face.

"A little bit of both! I'm really trying to save my government butt from any more drama! I already know both of you, and I'm in the middle of this soap opera. I know that I did something terrible to Carlos Garcia, but truthfully I can't uncover my true feelings about the whole situation that went down south. The job is punishing me, and I know that I have to take my medicine like a man. But I'm not going down for this mess between you and Agent Darling that's about to explode very soon. I bet your superior doesn't know about your good news!" Keith announces, as he stops typing and looks directly at his therapist.

"No, he's in Washington, D.C. for a few weeks now, but he'll be back soon," Elise answers in a soft voice. When Jonathan does find out what has gone on during his absence, he won't be a happy camper!

"Do you know my supervisor?"

"Dr. Jonathan Daniels? I never met him in person, but I heard that he's very good at his job," Keith replies, as he sees his young therapist turning ghostly white. Scared shit!!

"Are you going to tell on me?" Elise asks, with a frightened look.

He's surprised that his therapist is pleading for mercy when it really should be him. Sometimes life can be funny.

"Dr. Sheppard this is not junior high school! Believe me, I'm the last person on earth to tell on anybody! I really hate to tell you, but your boss is going to find out and there will be hell to pay. So get ready for a roller coaster ride full of drama! That's my warning to you," Keith answers, as he looks directly at his therapist without blinking,

"O…kay…thanks for the warning, I think?" Elise answers, as she clears her throat and mind to start her job again.

Without warning she asks, "Can you please tell me what happened to you ten years ago on the Jose Medina case?"

As she passes the case file to her patient, she is well aware that he knows the case from start to finish.

It was a drug raid that lasted less then three hours. Jose Medina's men ambushed the DEA Agents, and when the shooting stopped a lot of men were dead on both sides. It was a total bloodbath and as close to hell that a person could encounter. Only Keith and Peter lived to witness what really went down, and both of the agents were never the same since then. Keith blocked everything out for his own sanity and safety.

At times he really wanted to ask Peter, "Is this real or a horrible nightmare that will never go away?" Whatever he did it's coming back to haunt him instead.

"Okay, I'm game. What am I looking at?" Keith asks, as he sees Elise sit straight up in her chair.

"I want to know what happened in this case, ten years ago. Can you tell me what's behind the black marks that are noted in the report?" Elise asks, as she puts the case file on his desk to talk about the matter.

"Dr. Sheppard, I'm not at liberty to talk about what happened in the Medina case. This report will be open to the public once the case is finally closed. These black marks are concealed over words that are confidential. Even if I could tell you, I wouldn't, so this conversation is over," he answers, as he adjusts his chair. "Listen you're assigned to the Carlos Garcia case and what I did. You know you've wasted twenty minutes that I will never get back, and also touched upon a subject that's none of your business! Dr. Sheppard, if you don't have any other questions regarding my harsh behavior toward Carlos Garcia, I advise you to leave my office. I have a lot of work to do!" Keith exclaims with exasperation.

"What are you afraid of? It was ten years ago. What are you hiding? I know that you have something to share. I'm a very good listener!" Elise replies, as she tries to calm down her patient.

"I really don't want to have a heart-to-heart conversation, especially about what happened ten years ago. I think you should drop it, or I'll have to call security," Keith threatens.

Keith knows it's a waste of time because he can't remember anything. He does know he gets a huge stomach ache when he tries to remember the events of the day! Is his body trying to tell him something? Maybe he is guilty of something, like a crime that he committed? Deep down inside he's afraid to ask Peter what really happened that day. Keith is starting to remember bits and pieces of his childhood but not the drug raid.

"I'm not letting it go as of yet. So, Agent Heiden, what did you do?" Elise asks.

"I have a right not to answer any of the questions that relate to the Jose Medina case, and what I did or didn't do," Keith answers quickly.

"Agent Heiden, you are a hard person to crack, and you don't make my life easy. I'll drop the subject for now. But I really think you blocked your childhood years until the Jose Medina case came into play. You never went to therapy until now. So now you have to deal with your past and the present at the same time. I know it hurts to think of both at once," Elise says, as she takes a bottle of water.

Suddenly she smiles as she sees an 8 by 10 picture by her patient's shoulder. Keith glances at the doctor with a confused look on his face. He doesn't understand, why she is smiling.

"Are you okay, Dr. Sheppard? Have you been smoking something recently?" he asks with distress.

She giggles and answers, "No, I'm looking at the picture of you and Colin. It's so cute!"

Keith turns his chair to see what Elise is looking at.

"Thanks. Yes, it is a cute picture. Colin loves to take pictures. He's a real ham," he answers with a smile on his face.

Colin has a very special place in Keith's heart, which is hard to explain. He doesn't favor one child over another. They are all special in their own way and also very different. Keith never thought about being a dad, but after the shock wore off he was happy about it! It's harder then being a DEA agent.

"Agent Heiden, may I ask you a personal question?" Elise asks.

Keith shakes his head and snaps, "Dr. Sheppard, you've been asking me questions about my personal life since the first day we met!"

"Oh, how silly of me! You have a lovely home, and I can't help but notice that both your incomes don't appear to fit your lifestyle," Elise says. "I'm sorry if I sound out of line."

"I'm not at all surprised you asked that question. Actually, I was waiting for it. Our incomes don't afford us the luxury of living in a gated community or sending our children to private schools. What you don't know is I made a lot of money in the stock market. My father was a stockbroker and very good at his job. I learned about his work from the books that he had in his office," he says with a smile on his face. "I used to sneak out of my room and take books from his office. I would read them from top to bottom and then bring them back. I guess he didn't mind because his office door was always unlocked," Keith answers. "I got my brokerage license when I was in my twenties."

"Thank you for that information. Before I forget, I'd like to say that I'm truly sorry about the loss of your father. Why did you go to his funeral? How did it make you feel seeing your distant relatives?" Elise asks without missing a beat.

"Thank you for your kind words. Well, I guess I went to my father's funeral because he was my dad and he gave me life. I have very mixed feelings about him. Just seeing him buried six feet under made me happy and sad at the same time. It's very hard to explain," Keith answers solemnly. "I'm not going to lie. It was also very difficult to see my family. Well…my mom cornered me, and I guess she had enough nerve to talk to me. She pleaded with me to come back to the family. It was my father's wish to disown me, not the wish of the whole family. My mother also asked me if I had the heart to forgive every one. It's just too hard to digest all at once. She said that they really miss me, and that she never stopped loving me," Keith says, as he takes a deep breath while he continues without losing his train of thought. "It was too much for me to handle for one day."

"It was very brave of you to go to the funeral. Maybe you wanted answers that day. I'm very surprised that you didn't show any harsh behavior towards your mom and siblings. You apparently have a love-hate relationship with your father. I know you have anger management issues that stem from your abuse, but you seem to have a handle on it most of the time. So why couldn't you control yourself when you tried to arrest Mr. Garcia? You told me in our first session that you blacked out, and that this was something that happened throughout your childhood," continued Elise, as she crossed her legs and tried to cover her bare knees! *Oh well, just another sticky situation!*

What a moron!

CHAPTER
FIFTY-ONE

Instantly, Keith stops what he's doing and looks directly at the doctor.

"That's very interesting. I think you're way off on your mind picking theory!"

Dr. Sheppard stops writing on the notepad and uncrosses her legs to get comfortable.

"I don't think so. Let's continue. Agent Heiden, during your childhood did you have a support member in your family, because I know that you couldn't survive without any help." Elise states.

"Well, my sister Jennifer and brother Christopher, who were twins and also one year older than me, helped me a lot. Jennifer was like a mother to me, and Christopher was like a father. They taught me a lot and Christopher really helped me when puberty kicked in," Keith states, as he types on his computer system again.

"Were you interested in men or women? It must have been very difficult because of your sexual abuse by your father," Elise says, as she looks directly into her patient's blue eyes. With a perplexed look on his face, Keith thinks. Is she out of her mind??

"What are you talking about? I was never sexually abused! I was physically and mentally abused but not sexually! Where the hell are you getting your information? You must be mistaken!" Keith answers. What a moron! "Are you reading my case file or someone else's?"

"Agent Heiden, I know what I have in front of me!" Elise answers.

"Well, Agent Forrester notified me that I have to answer your questions to the best of my ability. I want to say something before you continue our therapy session. Thank you for putting my family and me in our places after the last situation. We didn't try to hurt you in any way. I hope you know that," Keith says, as he adjusts himself in his chair. "I'm sorry and so is my family…"

"Okay. Did your father sexually abuse you?" Elise asks without a second to spare.

CHAPTER
FIFTY-TWO

*S*uddenly, Dr. Sheppard has a terrible feeling! She needs to stop this therapy session before she loses her concentration completely and whatever respect she has left. She tries to collect her thoughts but nothing is working.

"Agent Heiden, can you please give me a second!" Elise requests, as her mind starts to go blank. It's like someone has erased every thought from the chalkboard. "So... You...weren't...sexually abused?" she says again.

"Dr. Sheppard, are you smoking weed or inhaling meth these days? I'll only say this once more and only once. I've never been sexually abused by my father or anyone for that matter. The only abuse was physical and emotional, and I think that was more than enough to endure," he exclaims, as he feels very uncomfortable. "I really think you've opened the wrong case file!"

"Are you sure, because I know I saw something here!" Elise answers, as she turns rapidly through the case file and out of nowhere another patient's name emerges!

"Oh God! I'm so, so sorry! It's a different patient! Can we forget what I just said?" Elise asks. *I'm screwed!*

"You just busted my government balls over nothing," he shouts. *Can I shoot myself now?*

"I'm really truly sorry!" Elise pleads, as she can't imagine what will happen next if Jonathan finds out about this episode. Let's just say it wouldn't be pretty. "I'm a real ass!" she announces freely.

"Yes, you're an ass, but I'm a bigger ass because I know you, and you're my therapist!" Keith yells. *Maybe I should start drinking again and just maybe it will make a lot more sense to me then.*

Keith takes a long drink of water, as he tries to collect his thoughts. He finally has the nerve to let go of what just happened but knows he must be extremely cautious from this point forward.

"Dr. Sheppard, do you have other patients that had the same kind of childhood experiences?" Keith asks.

He wouldn't be surprised if she says yes to the question, because they're a lot of cases of abuse in this country. You hear horrible stories in the news or newspaper and now the internet. It's truly sad that abuse is taking place right under your nose.

"No, you're the first. To be honest, Agent Heiden, you're the only one that has so many problems from your past to the present. In my professional opinion, I think you need therapy for the rest of your life. This is the first step in your healing process. I can see so much hurt in your eyes from all your painful memories, and it truly saddens me," Elise states as her voice begins to crack.

Keith smiles at her response and he's very touched that his therapist does care, but not surprised because she's a sensitive woman and certainty not like his wife these days.

"Thank you for caring," he answers.

"Why didn't you get therapy earlier?" Dr. Sheppard asks without skipping a beat.

"Well, my job ordered me to get some serious therapy or serve jail time. I'm not a stupid man. I picked the therapy. To be honest, this is more torturous than being in solitary confinement for a month in the big house. Please don't take this personally, but talking to you about my past is not a walk in the park for me," Keith announces, as he leans back in his chair and sees a picture that catches his eye.

It's a picture of Justine and Keith sitting together at a restaurant table in front of a huge palm tree. It's about two years ago on their sixteen anniversary. He remembers that the day was very clear and they had a wonderful time together without worrying about the kids or other responsibilities that life can bring. After lunch they took a long drive up the coastline not really going to any specific destination, but just enjoying the California scenery. From time to time, Justine put her hands out through the sunroof just to feel the wind. She begged Keith to stop at different shops along the way. Justine enjoyed herself and it showed in her smiles and laughter. Keith wished the day would never end. He had quality time with his wife, and he knew that deep down inside this happy feeling with Justine wouldn't last long and he was right. Keith wished he could get it back.

"Anyway, when I was disowned by my family, I had to shut down completely and grow up quickly. I didn't have a choice in the matter. To be honest, I didn't think anyone cared. My friends helped me the best they could. They were all going to college. The other way was to kill myself, and that didn't work as you know. It was very difficult, but I did it. I needed a job and place to live right away. Time goes very fast! I got married young, and the twins were born the same year. I was going to college and starting a career with the DEA department and with a brand-new family by my side. I guess I wasn't thinking about myself at the time. I was living my life without blockage from my past," Keith announces, as he rubs his neck to release some tension.

"I think you were very selfish because you didn't get therapy early in your life. The truth is you needed to take care of this problem. It consumed your existence for a long time before you started your new life. Agent Heiden, you couldn't give your full attention towards your family or your real feelings because you never sought the help until now. I can tell by your mannerisms that you're not a happy man because of your sad childhood. To solve this major problem is a challenge, to say the least," Elise explains.

"Dr. Sheppard, why are you yelling at me? I didn't do it intentionally!" he snaps back quickly.

"I'm upset with you for not taking charge of your life. I think a lot of people tell you that you have this attitude and you feel that people owe you because of your troubled past. Well?"

"Yes, I admit that I'm very hard to deal with! I'm angry!" Keith shouts.

"Why are you angry?" Elise asks.

"Because my father is dead, and I didn't get the answers that I was looking for. Why me? Did he ever love me? Did he ever stop and hear my cries? Was I so bad that he had to do these things to me? Did he really want me to die?" Keith cries. "Did I really deserve what my father did to me?"

"Agent Heiden, that's not true! You speak like a victim of abuse. Your father was a very sick man. There was no good reason for his madness. I think one of the reasons that your father attacked you was because you weren't a twin. That's why he picked on you because you didn't have anyone to protect you. Your father thought that he was above it all," Elise claims. "He tried with all his might to put you down physically and emotionally, and I would say that he did a wonderful job!"

"Just like a pack of wolves! The alpha wolf always smells out the weak one in the pack. He'll put the other wolf in his place by degrading him in front of his peers. The weak wolf will bow his head to the alpha wolf and will be the last in line when traveling and also to get the food. I understand now, I was the weak wolf, and I didn't respect the alpha wolf and got punished for it." Keith smiles, as he now understands what Dr. Sheppard is saying and it makes sense.

"No, you weren't the weak wolf. Your father thought you were the enemy," Elise announces.

"Why do you think that?" he asks with a confused look on his face.

"I think because you were smart and nice. It made him sick to his stomach that he couldn't break your spirit but he died trying," Elise answers, as she gets comfortable in her seat.

"I don't know about that one...being smart and nice. You can ask anyone that knows me how they really feel about me. You'll get a huge percentage that will give you a dramatic response without saying a single word, and it won't be pretty!" Keith answers honestly.

"Agent Heiden, you don't think highly of yourself, do you?"

"No."

Elise moves some pages in her notepad. "I know that I asked you about your scars on your left ear and hands. What I can remember from our first or second therapy session is that you stated they were presents from your father on your thirteenth birthday. Can you please tell me what happened? How did you get those scars?" she asks solemnly.

He looks up at the doctor and with a smart-ass sarcastic remark he says, "I really love to be interrogated like this! I have a great idea! We should do this kind of therapy, just to get to know each other better. It'll break the thick ice quickly so we can become really good friends!"

"Agent Heiden, can you please tell me? Please don't be angry with me. I'm only doing my job. If I understand your past, then maybe I can understand what went on with Mr. Garcia. Remember him? You almost killed him and this is the reason why you're here having therapy sessions with me. It's because of your choices that fateful day."

He clears his throat and takes a deep breath to answer, "I took some icing off my birthday cake." Keith remembers all too well that horrible event, like it was yesterday. It plays over and over again in his head; even though he tries to shake off the memory from his mind, it's still there as clear as day.

Elise has a devastated look on her face. She's heard a lot of troubling things that people have gone through, but this tops all the other stories by far. She shakes her head and tries to concentrate on the next question that she has to ask. Elise looks at Agent Heiden with tears in her eyes. He calmly looks at something on his desk not paying attention to what his doctor is doing at this minute in time. Elise looks around to see if any tissues are available. Damn it!

"Excuse me, Agent Heiden. Do you have any tissues?" she asks.

Keith looks up and sees his doctor crying, and he shakes his head in disbelief. *What the hell! My therapist is falling apart!* He gets up from his office chair and walks over to the closet and gets out one box of soft tissues. He takes a very deep breath and hands her the box, and then heads back to his seat without saying a word. Keith tries not to get upset with her reaction. *I think that my therapist needs a therapist, not me.*

"Dr. Sheppard, let's get something straight! You asked me about how I received my scars and you're crying? I don't understand! I know that you have additional questions to ask me, and it's not easy for me to tell you my Hallmark story! So before we continue our therapy session, I really need you to nip your emotions in the bud! This isn't easy for me to talk about!" Keith exclaims. Besides working a double shift for Mr. Happy Go Lucky (Agent Jack Forrester), now I have to deal with an unstable therapist to top my day. This is one of those days that I wish I called in sick. Someone upstairs is testing my patience!

"I'm sorry, Agent Heiden. I'm just a little emotional today," Elise says, as she takes the box of tissues and places it on her lap.

She wipes the tears off her face. Elise didn't have time to put on any makeup; she barely made it to the shower this morning!

"I don't understand women. I have two at home and I still don't understand them!" Keith states. *What did I get myself into? Can someone shoot me now! I think I have my gun, and I hope it's loaded. This is more painful than a hangnail!*

"Agent Heiden, I'm really sorry that you have to see this. I'm not really like this. I can't explain. Maybe, it's a woman thing," Elise says softly as she continues to wipe the tears away.

Keith leans back in his office chair and rubs some of this tension from his stress-filled eyes.

"Dr. Sheppard, I don't need this drama! You are a professional, so act like one! You speak to people all the time about their problems! I don't understand why you would break down over my problems! Can you explain to me why?"

"I'm just emotional right now," she answers, as she looks at her patient. *Why do I have deep feelings for Agent Heiden? Maybe I'm attracted to that bad boy image! Or I feel very sorry for him because of his terrible childhood. Why am I still crying?*

"Dr. Sheppard, you're wasting my time! If you can't keep your feelings to yourself, and you don't have any more questions to ask me I really think you should leave! I have a lot of work ahead of me, and my new supervisor is on my case. So what is it?" Keith snaps back, as he looks directly at the doctor.

"I have a question for you," Elise says, using a high pitch tone to control the emotion in her voice.

"Oh, what a surprise! Are you sure you can handle my answer?" he says sarcastically.

"Yes, I'm sure," she answers, as she sits straight up in her chair with a notepad on her lap. Elise is ready for anything that comes her way. I didn't get my doctorate for nothing! "Can you please tell me how you received the scars on your ear and hands?"

A minute goes by, and Keith finally stops what he's reading. He tries to think through what his therapist has just asked him. He feared that this day would come, when he had to admit the truth to himself, to save his job and maybe his marriage. I tried to scream for help, but no one came to my aid, because they were afraid of the same fate. In the past, people would ask him about his scars. To be honest he never really gave anyone an answer. The story goes by the saying, "What you don't know won't hurt you!"

These therapy sessions are worse than having a root canal!

"After I took the icing off the birthday cake my father flew into a rage. Suddenly he took the strap to me in front of the whole family. I tried to scream for help but no one came to my aid, because they were afraid of the same fate. My family just stood there and cried for me. All of a sudden, I lost my balance and I fell to the floor! I tried to protect my head with my hands, but the belt caught my left ear and it started bleeding heavily."

Keith gets up from his office chair and takes a deep breath. He tries to choke back the tears. "Dr. Sheppard, are you happy now?" he snaps. "It was the worst day of my life! If you don't mind can you keep this under wraps?"

"Agent Heiden, I'm not happy that I know the truth about your thirteenth birthday, and I'm truly touched that you told me. I'm so sorry that you had to go through that. What was your father's reaction to the whole incident?" Elise asks as she anxiously waits for Keith's answer.

"Well…let's just say he was more upset about the blood on the floor then my mangled ear!" Keith snaps. "Touching, isn't!"

Elise dismisses the agent's smart remark, because it's a typical reaction from a person who has been abused. It's another way to release stress.

"Agent Heiden, I'm very sorry for all that you had to endure. As you know our conversation today is totally confidential," Elise announces. "Please believe me! I guess from the tone of your voice you don't like birthday celebrations."

"I never had great memories."

"Thank you, Agent Heiden. I know it was very hard for you," Elise solemnly says, as she chokes back her tears again. It's heartbreaking to hear about the sadness in people's lives.

Keith takes a deep breath and says in a soft voice, "To be honest, Dr. Sheppard, I wish I had a happy childhood like Peter Darling's. Now that you're getting to know him you'll meet his lovely family. I'm a little jealous, and I know that it's childish because I want what Peter has. His family always gives him unconditional love, and they'll welcome you with open arms, and make you feel that you're a part of the family," Keith says wishfully.

"Thank you for your honesty," Elise replies.

This therapy session is running the way I want it to now. If only I was dressed in my proper attire!

Elise's dad would have been very disappointed to see her not dressed like a professional businesswoman. She remembers how he threw her favorite sneakers into the garbage, and she saved them before they were gone forever. Elise loved her sneakers even though they had lots of holes and barely had soles. She loves her comfortable clothes but knows there is a time and a place for everything!

CHAPTER
FIFTY-THREE

"Do you think it's childish of me to think this way?" Keith asks, with a perplexed look. This is not the first time that he's feeling confused.

"No, you're not selfish. You want something that you can't have. You try very hard to fill that void, and it's still not enough," Elise answers without blinking her attractive hazel eyes.

"Maybe you're right," he answers.

"You know it's not your fault! You have to stop blaming yourself. You didn't deserve to be abused!" Elise exclaims.

He slowly sits down in his chair and says softly, "I guess." Keith is not realizing that he sounds like a victim, not a fighter.

"It was your birthday cake, and you had every right to eat it whatsoever!" Elise explains.

"Dr. Sheppard, I can't turn off my abusive behavior like turning off a light switch! I was my father's personal punching bag. He did a magnificent job, don't you think? I still don't know what you want of me!" Keith answers with an angry tone.

"I really want you to let go of the past and take control of your destiny! I'm not going to lie to you! You have a lot of baggage that you need to deal with. Only time will tell if you'll fully heal or not. But first, I need you to comply with what I'm asking you," Elise says with a cheerleader tone of voice.

"I'll sure bet it was humiliating to be abused in front of everybody?" Elise says, as she tries to focus on Keith's answer.

"Yes, it was humiliating," Keith says, as he opens a piece of mail from the private investigator, Paul Lauren.

Keith reads the letter and doesn't notice that Dr. Sheppard is talking up a storm. He zones out for a moment. The letter says, "I'm sorry, Mr. Heiden, that I didn't get back to you sooner. I found some very fascinating information about the investigation against your wife. The purchase for the hotel visits for Justine Heiden and Treat Miller was from William Anderson's credit card. If you want me to investigate even further, please let me know. If you have any other questions or need other services, please feel free to contact me. Take care, and I'm sorry again."

CHAPTER
FIFTY-FOUR

〰〰〰〰〰〰〰〰〰〰〰〰〰〰〰〰〰〰〰〰〰〰〰〰〰〰〰〰〰〰〰〰

"Agent Heiden, you have post-traumatic stress syndrome," Elise states while she writes down something on the pad and then looks at her patient.

"What? Excuse me!" Keith says in exasperation as he feels his heart beating faster.

Keith feels like he's getting a heart attack and falling from a high cliff with no parachute. William dislikes Keith, and it shows. Now it's war!

He gets up from his chair.

"Dr. Sheppard, I think we should stop this therapy session and continue another day," Keith announces, as he opens the door for her to leave.

"I'm sorry. I'm not going until you tell me what's in the letter!" Elise states. "I know there's something bothering you, because you've turned as white as a ghost!"

"I don't know what you are talking about! Anyway, you are the last person that I would ever tell. Please leave and have a good day!" Keith says rudely.

Keith is so angry right now that he really wants to drive to Sir William's expensive overpriced home and twist him like a hand towel.

"You're not going to leave? That's just great!" Keith shouts and slams the door.

Elise suddenly takes the letter from Keith and quickly reads it without him being aware of what happened. He's blindsided with hurt and betrayal and can't think straight.

"Who is William Anderson?" Elise asks curiously.

"Excuse me! What the hell do you think you're doing?" Keith shouts as he takes the letter out of Elise's hand.

She licks her paper cut and begins to understand why he's acting this way. It all makes sense. She can help a lot if he lets her.

"Please let me try to help you!" Elise says, as she continues to lick her paper cut.

"It's none of your fucking business! So, if you're not leaving my office, I guess we can continue this so-called session," Keith says, as he desperately tries to calm down and focus. She's still there!

Both the agent and therapist sit down at the same time and continue the session from where they left off. For some strange reason this therapy session doesn't seem to have a time limit! That's not always a good thing!

"As I was saying, Agent Heiden, my diagnosis for is you post-traumatic stress disorder," Elise states.

"I'm sorry. Don't soldiers have that problem when they come home from the war?"

Elise stops her writing and says, "Are you asking me or telling me?"

"Both. I'm not a soldier and never went to war. So you really can't put me in the same category as a soldier who's going through a terrible ordeal." Keith states while he rubs the back of his neck.

"Agent Heiden, you were in a war from your childhood days and even now. You need a lot of intense therapy for the rest of your life. You kept your abuse inside you for many years and now it has exploded in front of you, your family and your job. You need to take full responsibility for your actions," Elise announces.

"Do you know that you are way off base and out of line with this theory?" Keith replies, as he looks straight into the eyes of the woman who can save his life and keep him out of jail too.

"No, and I don't care. Since day one I told you that I would help you in any way I can. But you have to meet me half way, and also answer my questions. It's an important step to recovery. You are stuck in your job and home life!

A minute goes by and Keith doesn't answer Dr. Sheppard.

"Agent Heiden, please answer my question. Do you want to claim your life back or not? Your father is dead, and he can't hurt you anymore! What do you want to tell me?" Elise says, as she tries to push the patient to the edge of the cliff. He decides to drop the past and think of his future.

"What happened ten years ago? Agent Heiden, I know you want to tell me. Let me help you. We are friends here. This conversation doesn't leave this room," Elise pleads, but she doesn't know if it's working or not.

CHAPTER
FIFTY-FIVE

*K*eith takes a deep breath and slowly drinks some of his water. He tries to collect his thoughts; he can feel his heart beating faster than ever. It's only a matter of time before his heart jumps out of his chest and attacks his therapist.

"Listen, I'm not very happy about what I did ten years ago. So here goes! I physically hurt my wife, the way my father did to my mother," he says, as he feels an overwhelming sadness.

It was a horrible day for the Heiden family, and everything changed from that day forward.

Keith leans back in his chair and says, "Before the Jose Medina case began, you know the drug raid, Justine and I fought hard. The yelling and screaming was endless. The fight never really ended because I came home after two straight days of being debriefed, and we continued from where we left off. We fought long and hard. I think we did better on this subject then making love. Hours went by, and we were still fighting, and I didn't notice where the twins were. This was before Mitch was adopted."

"Go on, "Elise says, as she starts to write on the legal pad.

Keith doesn't know what she's writing, and he wouldn't be able to understand it anyway because it's in shorthand.

"Well, my wife continued head-on with her yelling and stood right in front of me. She wouldn't let me out of the room and really wanted the answers to her questions. Believe me, I pleaded with her to stop, but she wouldn't let go until she was satisfied. I became extremely angry and suddenly I took her and pushed her against the wall just to shut her up!" Keith explains.

Keith's mind is running in high gear; he's trying to think of everything that happened over ten years ago. He doesn't know if the events happened or he watched a very bad movie.

He tries to drink the water again, but this time his hand starts to shake. Keith is trying desperately to hold it together, and not to show Dr. Sheppard that he's breaking apart at the seams.

Elise is acting very calm about the whole situation; she's just writing on her pad and looking at her patient from time to time.

"Anyway, we were physically fighting. She's tough as nails. Justine punched me, and I took..." he replies.

Keith stops himself. He knows very well not to tell the therapist that his wife attacked him with a baseball bat. Keith can make himself go down the river without paddles.

She looks up at her patient with concern and asks, "Agent Heiden, what did you take? Please tell me. I won't judge you," Elise says with a soft voice. "Please, Agent Heiden, I want to help you."

In therapy you have to feel the pain before you can start the healing process. Elise believes that all patients can be healed in some way or another. It's only a matter of time.

"Oh God!" Keith exclaims with despair in his voice.

He leans forward in his chair and desperately tries to avoid looking at his therapist.

After a few moments he begins to pull himself together and quietly says, "I'm sorry. I bet this is the first time you've seen an agent break down in front of you!"

Elise feels touched that Agent Heiden is explaining his feelings to her. It takes a true man to show his emotions.

"No, I've seen worse," she says sympathetically.

"That's sweet to say," Keith says with a weak smile and glimpse at his therapist.

He clears his throat before speaking further. Keith truly doesn't like being questioned about his actions, because he feels they were justified at the time.

"I took all my strength and hit my wife the way my father hit my mother. My God!" Keith shouts, as he sees Nicole stand up. "I can't believe that I'm the monster that I claimed I wouldn't be. Why can't this thing leave me alone and let me live my life in peace?"

Thank you, God. Nicole can't hear anything through Keith's office walls and glass windows. He'd be screwed otherwise.

Keith thinks back to his horrible past that clouded his whole life.

"I couldn't help my mother!" he exclaims as he feels overwhelmed with emotions.

Keith just keeps talking, not aware that he's giving very critical information to his therapist. This agent's evaluation case file is going to be very heavy; you'll need a crane to carry it out of the government office.

This is what Elise is waiting for! She's getting ready to hear what the core of the problem is! She's very excited but tries not to show it.

"Agent Heiden, you're doing a great job. You can't stop now. You must move forward to claim your life. You have a right to be happy! You've been on your own since the day your father and family disowned you! You were only eighteen at the time. You didn't have any money in your pocket and only the clothes on your back. It wasn't easy and I'm sorry," sighs Elise.

"Thanks... I think,"

"How old were you when you first witnessed your father hitting your mother?" she asks knowing that the questions are going to get harder. *Elise, don't break under the pressure! You're almost there!*

Her job is not easy and it doesn't help when she carries her emotions on her sleeve. But she's sworn by a code of silence not to give out any information.

"I think... I was seven," Keith answers solemnly.

No child should witness a horrible event of any kind. Your home and family should be your safe haven.

"I'm so sorry to hear about this terrible event." Elise sighs.

The truth of the matter is Elise doesn't need to know any more details about her patient's terrible childhood. She can see it in his eyes and mannerism.

What Elise does need is more information on why Keith's violent behavior is coming to the surface after all these years. The patient stated that he blocked out his childhood and made up a new one to cover up his demons. He did it very well to get this job, to adopt his son Mitchell, and to have the family he has.

What broke the camel's back was Agent Heiden's attack on Carlos Garcia. Something extremely troublesome must have happened for Agent Heiden to run wild. It's not going to be easy to break down this patient and get the real truth. Dr. Sheppard really wants to know what happened ten years ago, not last year! She knows that's where her answers lay, she has to be very patient for Keith to open up.

"I'm sorry, please continue," Elise says, as she holds her pen tightly.

"Well…my son Patrick came into the room and saw me beating his mother. He attacked me, because I told him and Erin many times in the past to protect their mother at all times. Patrick listened to me and suddenly bit me on my leg. So I took him, threw him on the floor, and started beating him. I had this uncontrollable aggression inside of me! Then I realized what the hell I was doing, and I suddenly stopped and quickly ran to the bathroom and threw up. Hours went by and Justine sat at the kitchen table until we were ready for a serious talk. She looked troubled and bruises were forming on her. She was extremely calm. I didn't say a word. I just let her talk. I didn't see Patrick anywhere that day. She told me that she spoke to him and it wasn't his fault. Now I know why he's hated me all these years. He has every right to hate me!"

"I'm so sorry! Did you get therapy after your abusive outburst?" Elise asks, as she tries to make herself comfortable in her chair.

"No," he answers without hesitation.

"Why not?" Elise asks with a very surprised tone in her voice.

"Well, Justine and I agreed to keep this problem under wraps," Keith answers, as he gets up from his chair to take something out of his file cabinet.

He uses his keys to unlock the cabinet. Elise looks up to see what he's doing, and she decides to say something that she really wanted to say since the therapy session began.

"Don't you think that was stupid?" she says.

Keith looks at her with annoyance as if to say, "How dare you!"

"You had an abused childhood. I don't think your wife should have given you that huge mug with hot coco to console your pain," Elise replies. "I believe that it was selfish on her part and yours for not seeking help when you needed it the most. This is my honest and professional opinion!"

"Listen, I know you both don't get along! Maybe it's a woman thing?" he says. "Dr. Sheppard, I'm not going to go off like a crazy person. I know deep down inside your pretty head you have an intelligent answer to cover your smart ass statement."

"I'm not going to take back what I said!" Elise replies, as she can feel a fight brewing. Bring it on!

"Dr. Sheppard, do you think that my wife is blocking my healing process?"

"Maybe. Did you have a heated argument with your wife before you went to Carlos Garcia's apartment and the Jose Medina raid?" Elise asks.

"You're getting on my last good nerve! I don't understand why you're asking about two different events in my life. What does that have to do with what happened one year ago?" Keith snaps. "Dr. Sheppard, you're confusing the hell out of me. You know I feel that I'm on the hamster wheel during this therapy session, and it doesn't look like I'll be getting off anytime soon! Get to the point!"

"I'm trying to put the pieces together to complete my puzzle about your life at home and work. So did you have a heated argument with your wife before going to see Mr. Carlos Garcia? Yes or no?" Elise sharply asks, as she looks directly at Agent Heiden for his full attention.

Don't piss me off!

"Okay, maybe I should ask nicer," Elise says, as she clears her throat. "Sorry…let's start over."

"Yes, both times before I went to work. So what are you getting at Dr. Sheppard?" Keith asks impatiently.

"Dr. Sheppard, you won't leave my office until I answer all your questions, right?"

"Now you know how I work," she says with a friendly smile, as she crosses her legs showing off her naked knees. How embarrassing!

Minutes later, Keith says, "Yes, I had recent episodes. I'm not proud of my actions." *I'm not going to tell the doctor what happened because I'd be a dead man for saying it! I think she has enough information.*

"Agent Heiden, thank you for being honest! It really helps you with the healing process. I think your episodes started ten years ago, but why? Do you remember what you and your wife fought over?" Elise asks.

She has a strong feeling that he knows that true answer to her question. But will he give in and tell her what made him go bananas?

"Agent Heiden, from what I'm observing I don't see you as an abusive husband and father. I don't have to report that kind of criminal behavior to the police and your job. You know what you are up against. So how can you start fixing this major problem? Your secret came out, and you didn't plan to let it out in the first place. My question is what hit the cord to make your nightmare come up to the surface and have you finally realized that you need professional help?"

"I don't know," he sighs.

"I bet it started ten years ago during your first heated argument with your wife and from that day forward everything fell apart. Agent Heiden, your huge secret is taking over your whole life and not telling anyone is eating you up inside. Why don't you tell me what the letter said? Your wife's name was on it and a man named William Anderson," Elise states.

"I think you have enough information about me for your evaluation! To be perfectly honest, Dr. Sheppard, I rarely go to confession at church. Please explain to me why I should to plead my soul to you?" he snaps.

"Agent Heiden, we're almost at the core of your problem. So please work with me!" Elise strongly requests as she takes a deep breath to collect her thoughts.

She's almost at the top of the hill to solve this patient's case. Elise can taste victory, and she's getting her professional opinion ready to close this file.

"Can we try to overcome this obstacle?" Elise asks, as she prepares to write a lot on her legal pad; hopefully her sterling silver cross pen won't run out of ink.

She can feel the rush of adrenaline running throughout her veins, as her heart beats faster. Elise clears her throat to make sure That she can speak clearly.

"My wife had two love affairs, one ten years ago and one a year ago. I guess that brought out my good side while I was on the job," he answers.

"Good this helps put the pieces of the puzzle together. I'm sorry but we have to look further so can you please tell me what happened when you were seven years old? Everything begins and ends. I want you to go back to the beginning of your abuse and work on closing this chapter of your life and move on to what you want in life. You need to feel safe in your own skin and trust people who love you," Elise answers.

Keith's blue eyes become watery and red, and he has his hands folded tightly. His fingers are turning ghostly white from the lack of circulation.

To deal with major problems head-on is difficult by any means.

"When I was seven years old, I'd witnessed my father raping my mother," Keith answers. "I think I raped my wife like my father did to my mother."

Elise tries to hold back her tears while her heart drops twenty stories.

"Agent Heiden, is that why your father started abusing you?"

"I guess to make me shut up. I had become my father's personal punching bag," he answers.

"Did you ever ask your mother what happened? Are you sure that you raped your wife? It would be a terrible crime. If you did this horrible thing was this ten years ago?"

She thought she heard it all. She tries to give her patients a little hope, and can trust therapy to take their pain away for good.

"Yes, to both your questions. I think I raped my wife, but she didn't say anything about it...But I can see it in her eyes and her behavior too. I know what I did, and I can't take it back, and believe me I really want to!"

"Do you want to take a minute and rest before we continue?"

"Why stop now? We're having a great time!"

Dr. Elise Sheppard takes a deep breath and continues.

"What did your mother say?"

"What do you think she said? It's like all other abused wives. She stated that nothing happened. She tried so hard to avoid answering my questions. My mother said, "help me make some Irish Soda Bread," and that was the end of the conservation!"

"Agent Heiden, if this was true did your son witness you raping your wife?" Elise asks with a huge lump in her throat.

"I don't remember! I guess I blocked it out. You have to believe me! I don't remember!" Keith exclaims, and then suddenly his body starts to freeze up.

Elise quickly walks to his aid, "Agent Heiden, you're going into shock! I need to call someone in medical!" She bends down to rub Keith's arms to break him of the shock. He can feel the warmth of her hand on his arm. Keith is not fully in shock, but he's on that path. He wonders if this is the first time the doctor has seen a patient go into shock. She's getting her money's worth.

Suddenly, no words are exchanged. You can only hear the sound of deep breathing.

"Dr. Sheppard, please don't call medical! Just give me a minute to collect myself," Keith answers, as he suddenly gets up from his seat and walks around his office to get himself back in control.

Keith takes a quick glimpse at Dr. Sheppard, as she sits herself down and waits patiently to continue with the therapy session. She then starts to write something on her legal size notepad.

"Maybe it's good that you blocked out the event," Elise continues. She really wants to say, "You're lying through your government teeth!"

Elise doesn't have the strength right now but in due time she will regain the courage to say what she really wants to say to her patient.

"Maybe that's why my son hates me so much," Keith states with a calm manner.

"I don't think your son hates you," she answers with a soft smile.

"Dr. Sheppard, I don't know if you met my oldest son, the golden child, Patrick. He has that look that can kill! I think over time that he killed millions of people. Of course that's a figure of speech," Keith says. "What do I do? Should I ask him? Did he block out the terrible event like I did when I was his age? How do I go about this, Dr. Sheppard? I guess I can't remove this problem with a bowl of Rocky Road ice cream," Keith says.

"I love junk food! That's my downfall!" Elise answers.

"Yes . . . It's good," he says with a smile.

"This is my professional opinion. I think that every time you have a heated cat-and-dog fight with your wife, you feel guilty so you bow down to her every need. There is your key! You transformed your father's abusive behavior into your wife. She takes control of being abusive and you're still that abused child," Elise states, as she gets up from the chair and walks around the room.

"Excuse me! You're telling me that the circle of abuse never changes! It's the person who's controlling the wheel. Well, I'm not surprised. I have to admit it's interesting. But how did I transform my wife to be the abuser?"

"I think it started ten years ago during your first abusive fight and has progressed since then. You were deeply hurt and maybe you still are. You can't be in control of the relationship so you gave it to your wife. Even though you discipline the kids, she wears the pants in the family."

"Interesting, but I think our time is up," Keith states.

"Not yet... I think I know that question you might have, but you can't say it. In order for your wife not to be abusive towards you anymore, she'll have to go to therapy herself. Would she be willing to start therapy?" Elise asks in a professional voice.

"What makes you think that she's abusive toward me?" Keith asks.

"I guess you want an apology from me," Elise says, as she sees her rainbow socks showing through the holes in her sneakers. It's really embarrassing to look like a welfare case.

"That would be nice," Keith replies with a sarcastic tone.

"I'm sorry, Agent Heiden, that I called your wife a bitch. That was very unprofessional of me to do and again I'm truly sorry," Elise announces but she wants to say this. "Even though I'm truly sorry for calling your wife a bitch, you have to admit without a doubt in your mind that she is a bitch and gives the word a new meaning. Do you think?"

"I know it isn't easy to apologize and I thank you for saying it. Justine won't go. She'll say that she doesn't have a problem. I know that she's punishing me for my actions over the last ten years. Justine will forgive in time but won't forget. She's just like me. I married myself but with blond curly hair. A couple of times I did ask her if she wanted to go to therapy, but she declined on each request. Dr. Sheppard, it's not going to be easy convincing her that she should talk to someone," Keith states, as he leans back in his seat to get comfortable.

"Well, all I can say is to keep trying, if you want your marriage to work and you want to save your kids at the same time." Elise looks at her watch and says, "Now the time is up. I guess we'll continue to have our therapy sessions in your office because my office is... Well, let's just say it's under construction at this time."

"Dr. Sheppard, can we make it at 7:00 p.m., Thursday night?" Keith asks.

She picks up her briefcase and pocketbook with a friendly smile.

"That's fine, Agent Heiden. I'll see you at 7:00 p.m., Thursday night. Have a good day. I'll let myself out," Elise answers.

She really needs that large cup of coffee. It's been on her mind all day.

"Before you go, Dr. Sheppard, here's my daughter's apology letter that I promised you," Keith says while he looks directly at his therapist. He has a white business envelope in his hand.

"I'm sorry?" Elise says with a shocked tone in her voice. *You've got to be joking!*

"Dr. Sheppard, please take my daughter's apology letter before you leave," Keith requests, as he keeps waving the envelope. "Have a good day!"

"I'm sorry, Agent Heiden, but your daughter verbally apologized to me. I don't need a letter from her," Elise replies with a firm voice.

"Dr. Sheppard, it's not a bomb! Please take it!" Keith says with an annoyed look on his face.

"Did you read the letter?" Elise asks.

"No, Dr. Sheppard. I know that she put her heart into it, and I trust her judgment. So please take the letter and then you can leave. Please make sure you give back your security pass to the security guard up front," Keith said.

Minutes go by and there is no answer or movement from the doctor.

"Dr. Sheppard!"

"Yes!"

"What are you waiting for? Please take the letter and leave!!" Keith shouts forcefully. *I feel like I'm dealing with one of my kids! I should've called in sick today!*

"I'm sorry once again. Please leave and take the letter! Read it or rip it up, I really don't care!!" Keith retorts impatiently.

Elise walks closer to the patient's desk and slowly takes the letter from the agent's hand.

"Thank you," he says without looking up at the doctor.

"See you soon, take care," says Elise.

CHAPTER
FIFTY-SIX

After work on Monday, Todd leaves the DEA parking lot and drives his brand-new silver and blue 2007 Toyota Prius Hybrid toward home. He dials his wife's cell phone and puts the receiver on speaker so he can drive with two hands on the wheel.

"Hello, Anastasia, it's me Todd your IT honey bunny," Todd says with pep in his voice.

"Hello, my dear, how was work today? Do you have any good stories for your love?" she asks with excitement in her voice.

Anastasia lies on a lounge chair on the sand in Venice Beach. She tries desperately to get that California sun to tan her fair Russian skin. She takes a bottle of a strawberry wine cooler from her six pack.

"Yes, you'll love this! The DEA is going to do a drugs raid within two weeks. There will be twenty or more ice cream trucks delivering drugs to children in the LA area. They are loading up a lot of drugs so they can begin the summer season with a buzz. The DEA office has been planning this moment for five months. The drugs are worth over $220 million. How sweet is that? The ringleader of this operation is Alex Randinsky from Russia. Did you ever hear of this man back home?" Todd asks. What are the odds for Anastasia to know Alexander Randinsky?

"Love your story! You'll get a little surprise for giving me a taste of excitement. I'm at the beach but I will be home when you arrive. No, I never heard of this Alex Randinsky. He must be a very powerful man. Did you ever see a picture of him?" Anastasia asks, as she drinks some of her wine cooler.

"I never thought of looking for a picture of the guy. Sorry, but I'll try to get you a copy of one soon! I really have to be careful, my precious. I will be home soon." Todd answers with a huge smile.

For some reason or another he's one happy tech nerd and he's proud to show off his trophy wife to every citizen of California! They will get jealous and say, "Man, why can't I get me some of that! Or I should've done better before I said 'I do!'"

"Todd, what time will the raid start?" she asks out of the blue.

"Oh…at 12:00 p.m.," Todd answers, as he turns into Park Ave toward the Santa Ana Freeway.

He loves listening to the oldies on the radio even though it's a drive to his home because he's hitting morning rush hour traffic. Todd really wants the shift, so he doesn't have to play catch up on much-needed sleep.

"Anastasia my darling wife, I have to go. I'm heading toward the highway, so I'll see you at home. Love you, my Russian princess!" Todd exclaims.

"Good-bye, my love, and thank you for all your juicy job stories. You are my handsome nerd!" she replies.

"Before we hang up please say something to me in Russian. I love when you talk foreign and dirty to me!" Todd replies.

Todd wishes that he could speak another language other than English and Hebrew. He needed that to make his Bar Mitzvah. But it would be great to speak Russian.

"Okay, but I have to go and catch up on my sunbathing." she exclaims. Anastasia says in Russian, "I love you to the end of time [Я люблю тебя до скончания веков!]."

"Oh, mama . . . you know how to get my blood pumping!" Todd shouts, as he gets all excited. "Thank you, my love! See you at home."

"Anytime…see you soon!" she says.

They both hang up their cell phones at the same time.

Suddenly Anastasia makes a call. "Hello."

She begins to speak in her homeland language of Russian.

"Hello, Anastasia, what is wrong? Is that little monkey mistreating you? I will break every bone in his wimpy body!" Alex yells and then laughs.

"No, no, Alex, I've something important to tell you. Todd, my little man, said to me that the DEA is planning a raid on you and your Russian friends for drug trafficking, "Anastasia says with concern in her voice.

"I love you, Anastasia! Please keep me informed on any other activities that the DEA might have planned. I had a feeling those pigs were after my crew and me. But it won't happen as long as you're on the inside of the operation and keeping a look out! Just don't get caught, especially with Todd, the whiny nerd." Alex says, as he laughs and his friends join in. "Make sure that no one knows that you're my cousin and that we came into this country to make a huge fortune from America's pain because they take our drugs. Anastasia, please don't worry your pretty young head over it. I'll handle it and these pigs will never get us because we've got you on our side. Let's do dinner sometime. Please take care of yourself and watch out," Alex exclaims with a mouth full of Borsch soup.

Then he takes a drink of vodka from a very dirty glass. A little dirt doesn't hurt a living soul. It helps put hair on your chest and it gives you character.

"Yes, we'll have dinner," she answers, as she walks toward the edge of the ocean to get her feet wet. "I'll be very careful and keep you updated. Be careful yourself!"

CHAPTER

FIFTY-SEVEN

*I*t's a Tuesday as Keith parks his new black SUV in the garage. He rubs his tired eyes and yawns at the same time. Minutes later he walks into the house and hears the family in the kitchen. Colin walks out of the kitchen and sees his dad out of the corner of his little blue eyes.

"Daddy!" Colin says, as he charges into Keith's legs.

"Take it easy Colin! You're going to hurt me. How are you?" Keith asks, as he leans down and rubs his son's blond hair.

"Fine, Daddy!" he screams with a huge smile.

Erin walks into the living room and sees her little brother wrapping his arms around their dad's leg. It's very sweet to see! Keith has no chance in hell to get out of the lock. He smiles as he sees his little girl; she's now a young lady without braces. Keith remembers like it was just yesterday having those many tea parties with Erin and in the company of her stuffed animal friends. They had great times together. Patrick, on the other hand, is a different story.

Erin walks over to her dad and gives him a hug.

"Dad, you're finally home! I thought you were going to live at work," she says, as she breaks away from him.

"Me too, but I'm home now and I'm happy to see my crazy family again," he answers with a smile as Colin continues to hold on to his leg. "I have a new supervisor, and he wanted me to work extra hours."

"I thought Uncle Peter is your supervisor. What happened?" Erin asks, as she sits herself down on the living room couch.

"Sometimes, Erin, you really sound like your mother and that's pretty scary. Colin, can you please let go of my leg? I want to sit down and talk to your sister for a minute," Keith says, as he gives him a friendly pat on his tiny blond head.

A second later the half pint releases his grip and runs towards the back of the house. Keith finally gets a chance to talk with his beautiful daughter before the toddler monster comes back with his sneakers that light up.

"To be honest, Erin, I really don't know why Uncle Peter is not my supervisor anymore," he answers, but he knows the real reason why.

Erin cares so much Keith doesn't want to upset her with his work problems.

"I guess someone doesn't really like me at the office, but please don't worry your sweet head about it," he responds, as he makes himself comfortable.

"Dad, what do you want to talk about?" Erin asks with a concerned tone in her voice.

"I really want to talk about your boyfriend and why I haven't met him yet. Everyone else in this family including Reese has had the opportunity," Keith says with a calm tone of voice.

"Well, Christopher does want to meet you but…," Erin answers slowly, unable to put her thoughts together quickly.

"But what, Erin? Please tell me," Keith replies, as he knows what she's going to say. "Dad, you're not a people person. Someone dating me while holding my hand is not good."

"He's afraid of you," she answers.

"He doesn't even know me! How can he be afraid of me if he never met me! Did you put stories in his head to think otherwise?" Keith asks getting a little upset with his princess.

"No, Dad! We were on the phone one day, and he overheard you yelling at Patrick! It scared him. That's the reason he didn't meet you yet," Erin answers as she begins to feel uncomfortable.

"Oh, please. I yell at Patrick almost every day, and it's like me brushing my teeth in the morning. That's just a cop-out. Before you see him again I would like to meet the lad. You know the family rule." Keith exclaims.

Colin is now jumping aimlessly around the living room to burn off excess energy. Just watching this toddler is getting Keith exhausted.

"Erin, do you understand what I'm asking of you?"

"Yes, but it's not going to be easy, because you really scared him when you were yelling at Patrick!" Erin exclaims.

"Poor, baby. That's not my problem. I still want to meet him before you start going out again. Erin, please don't fight me on this rule."

"I think it's a double standard!" Erin says, as she knows that her dad never really met Melissa, Patrick's girlfriend. "I bet you never met Melissa!" Erin says.

Sometimes Erin feels that her father doesn't listen to her because Patrick takes up so much time and energy. It's not easy to be in this family full of boys.

"I did meet Melissa at the hospital while she was visiting Patrick. It was kind of sweet to see." Keith answers.

He doesn't have the energy to fight with any of his kids because the truth of the matter is he never seems to win the battle.

"Melissa seems nice. Can I please meet with Christopher? I just want to know that the lad you're dating is on the up and up with my daughter," he says with a calm voice.

"Okay, Dad, but please promise me that you won't hurt or kill him," Erin pleads looking at her dad with very soulful eyes.

Erin always melts his heart no matter how old she is. She is Keith's little girl forever.

"Okay," Erin answers.

"That's great to hear," Keith replies as he kisses her forehead. "Where's your mother?"

"She's upstairs."

"Thanks, Erin. I just want to talk to your mom, and I'll be right back," he answers.

"Take your time. I'll take care of Colin."

"Thanks, Erin!"

Keith is about to go upstairs to see Justine until Colin meets up with his dad. *Damn! I got caught! I was almost there!*

"Daddy, where are you going?!" shouts the little monster.

"Listen, buddy. I want to talk to your mommy. I've got a lot of catching up to do. Erin is going to take care of you and play with you," Keith answers.

"I want Tabitha!" Colin shouts like a bullhorn.

Tabitha is Colin's playdate, who he sees once a week.

"Come on, Colin, play with me. We can play with blocks," Erin says as she tries to lure the little man away from her father.

Keith smiles at his daughter. "Erin, I think you'll be a great mom one day."

"Thanks, Dad, that's nice of you to say," answers Erin, as she gives Colin a loving hug because he come to her without a fight.

Keith remembers the close, loving relationship he had with his sister Jennifer. She was a mothering figure to him. He also bets that she's a great mom now and maybe a teacher too. *I guess it's a gift to have such patience.* It's certainly something Keith doesn't have. Erin really reminds him of his sister. She has a lot of her mannerisms, especially when dealing with Colin. Keith really misses Jennifer and her twin brother Christopher. You can say that Jennifer was the mother and Christopher was the father figure to Keith. The twins are one year older than Keith but very mature for their age.

"Thanks for watching Colin for me. Love you both," Keith says, as he rushes up the stairs.

He hears Colin screaming from the bottom step.

"Daddy, I want Tabitha!"

"I want your mommy!"

"Daddy!" Colin shouts with his little hands on his hips. "You come down here, young man!"

Erin laughs. "Colin, you're too much!"

Keith finally enters the master bedroom and sees Justine. By the looks of what she's wearing he can tell she's going to work today.

"Hi, Justine. I guess you're heading to work. When are you going to transfer to your new office in… Beverly Hills…or Brentwood?" Keith asks.

"Hi, Keith. Yes, I'm going to work, and I'll be moving to the office in Brentwood. But I didn't tell you that I might be working for my father in his international real estate business. I would be selling commercial business buildings which would be big sales.

"Why are you going to work with your father? Why do you want to do a crazy thing like that? You'll have to travel out of the country just to make a commission of what 30 percent or 40 percent on the sale! You're crazy! I think your curls are too tight for your head! You're not thinking straight!" Keith exclaims.

Not to mention the fact that her father paid not once but twice for her way into someone else's arms!

"I'm not really sure of my future plans yet. However, I'll definitely let you know because you feel like telling me the pros and cons about this issue! You do know the final decision will be mine," Justine replies as she puts on her earrings that cost her a pretty penny. Only the best for Justine as she must remain at the top of her game in the real estate business.

"Once again, thanks for giving me your two cents that go against what I think!" Keith says as he makes his move on Justine.

Keith is not a romantic guy, but when he tries, Justine always shoots him down. He suddenly kisses her neck on her favorite spot.

Justine is taken back with Keith's quick behavior.

"What the hell are you doing? I don't have time for this. I have to go to work. Remember we need money to keep up with the Joneses!" Justine says, as she tries to back Keith away without success.

"Listen, Justine, I'll let go of the past, and I'll be that man who forgives but can't forget. You know what I'm saying. Please let me back into your heart! I know my name is floating somewhere. I love you, Justine, and no one else… Please, I want you!" Keith pleads. *Boy, public speaking is a piece of cake compared to getting Justine into bed! I should've called in sick today!*

"Keith, will you stop it! I really think that you're one of the kids sometimes. Sorry, I stand corrected, all the time! That's why I need to talk to real adults, not a toddler like you!" exclaims Justine.

"I love you but not your insane curly hair that has a mind of its own. You just want to fight, not to make love to me. Do you remember the husband that you married eighteen years ago? God forbid should that matter to you in your pretty little mindless world," Keith replies.

The truth of the matter is Justine and Keith love to fight; other couples love to hold hands and walk on the beach right before the sunset. Not these two! They remind me of two alley cats fighting because they're both in heat. Deep down they love each other in a very strange way.

Suddenly Keith gently holds Justine and starts to kiss her the way she used to be kissed before any drama occurred. It's a great feeling to be loved again.

CHAPTER
FIFTY-EIGHT

*W*ednesday morning comes around and Peter leaves work early to beat rush hour traffic and see Elise before she heads to work. Peter's cell rings.

"Hello!"

"Agent Darling, can you come back to the office? We need to talk about the four files," the sound of Agent Jack Forrester's voice echoes through the phone.

"Oh that!" Peter says, as he stops in his tracks, turns his body around and makes a face as he looks at the DEA building. "Listen, Forrester, I just finished my work, and I'm leaving to see my sweet hot girl. Can we talk tonight? I know that you've a lot to say, and I'm proud of you for using your words rather than violence. You're growing up so fast. Your man and I love you so much!" Peter says as he tries not to bush.

"Real funny, Peter. I'm very serious. We have a lot to talk about and I don't want to put it off any later than you already have. I truly understand that you need to release some stress. That's fine. I don't want to rain on your parade, but you have to be an adult about this. So, Peter, promise me that you'll come to my office, and we'll have that one-on-one talk."

"Okay, Jack, we'll talk tonight... Scouts honor!" Peter answers quickly just to get him off the phone.

Without warning Jack starts to talk again.

"Jack, I'm losing you. What're you saying?" he smiles as he hangs up the phone.

Peter laughs as he spots Todd with his mail-order bride, Anastasia. He walks towards the lovely couple.

"Hello, Todd."

"Hi, Peter! How's everything?" Todd answers back with a friendly smile. He's beaming because he has Anastasia by his side. She is pure candy and fantasy for most men.

"I'm fine. How about you? This must be your lovely wife," Peter says using all his charm.

Anastasia smiles back. She missed that class about never talking or taking candy from a stranger. The Peter charm has never really left the building! He never gets bored doing something on the outside, like swimming, running, rollerblading and playing volleyball. But his most popular sport is getting that girl that every man wants.

"Okay… They make me work on stupid things. Once again, no one is taking me seriously. My talents are wasted on mindless stuff. I don't know if you know that I'm highly educated!" Todd claims.

"Yes, little man, you have major issues and there's no therapist to help you," Peter answers, as he knows that Todd can get off the bandwagon very easily and there's nothing in the world to stop him.

"Who's this pretty lady in front of us?" Peter asks, as he knows very well who she is by the picture that Liam sent to him.

"Peter, this is my pretty wife, Anastasia. She's from Russia."

"Hello, Anastasia, it's an honor to meet you."

She's very attractive. Why on earth did she pick a geek like Todd? He makes good money but not enough for a woman like Anastasia!

Peter can't control himself and says something funny in Russian to Anastasia. Minutes later they start to laugh uncontrollably. Todd starts to get upset because he doesn't know the language, and he thinks that they're talking about him.

"Hey, guys, what's so funny? I hope you're not laughing at me for your entertainment! Peter, whatever you said in Russian, I hope you're not asking my wife out on a date! Right?" shouts Todd.

"Todd, don't get your pocket protector upset." He laughs. "It's harmless. I have to go now. It's nice to finally meet you. Take care, Todd. See you tonight!" Peter replies as he walks away.

Anastasia says goodbye in Russian.

CHAPTER
FIFTY-NINE

"Keith, wake up! You have a phone call!" Justine shouts, as she tries to rock her sleepy husband back and forth.

"What? Did something happen? Is there a fire?" Keith shouts.

"Keith, you have a phone call! I really have to go to work now, and I can't miss another day, or someone else will get my commission. Oh, before I forget, my mother and Jocelyn [Justine's younger sister] agree to take turns to have Colin and Mitch sleepover for a couple of days. Erin will be home with you. She has to write some papers for college. Patrick is still in the hospital but he will be home any day now, and they will call me to pick him up. Mitch is getting himself ready for the trip," Justine answers.

Keith yawns and rubs his tired eyes at the same time.

"Okay, whatever you say sounds good to me," he answers back.

Then Keith picks up the phone from his nightstand and almost drops it in his sleepy state.

"Hello," Keith says, as he hears the other phone line hang up somewhere in the house.

"Hello, is this Keith Heiden?" asks the caller.

"Speaking," he answers, as he puts his head back on his comfortable pillow.

Keith closes his eyes, hoping one of his organs can sleep a little, while the others are still working.

"Keith, this is Christopher, your brother! I'm sorry, did I wake you? I really need to talk to you in person," says the caller.

Keith doesn't recognize his brother's voice and why would he? It has been twenty-two years since they last saw one another. Keith looks at Justine getting undressed. Just to see her flawless smooth bare-skinned body makes him smile from ear to ear. Then she enters the master bathroom and closes the door behind her. Keith wishes that yesterday would last forever. She's still hot!

"I'm sorry, who are you again?" Keith asks as the image of Justine totally naked still travels throughout his brain. She has a kicking body.

"Christopher, your brother! Do you remember me?" he asks. "Is this a bad time? I can call back later when you come home from work."

"Half the time I work nights, and I'm lucky to have a couple of days off. Please don't mind me if I sound tired because I am. I'll be home all day with my daughter" Keith yawns at the same time. "Sorry!"

"It's important that I talk to you in person."

"Well, I'm our Mom and Dad's family lawyer, and I need to talk about Dad's will in person. I have papers that you need to sign. What's a good time to meet you?" Christopher asks, as he looks at some papers in front of him on his very expensive desk.

"Okay, only got your name and to be honest anything else you just said is a blur. How about this afternoon? I'll make lunch and bring your swimming suit with you," Keith says.

"Are you okay, Keith? Did you just say to bring my swimsuit?" Christopher asks with a surprised tone.

"Can you swim?"

"Yes. You don't have to give me your home address. I have it. Can I meet with you earlier? I've got court, and I can't stay too long. But thank you for the invitation about swimming in your pool," Christopher answers.

"How about noon time? I'll put your name at the front security gate. Thank you for calling; I really need some more sleep. Good-bye. See you soon," Keith answers.

"Good-bye," Christopher replies, as he knows it's going to be a very interesting visit.

CHAPTER
SIXTY

A message comes up on his PDA (personal digital assistant) that's on his nightstand. Keith picks up his PDA without knowing that there is a message. He walks outside, sits on the patio chair, and puts his hot coffee on the table. He presses the button to retrieve the text message.

"I want to warn you that you have a leak in the department, and I know that Mr. Preston Williamson from Interpol has told you too. So listen carefully and don't piss off anyone or act like an asshole. This is valuable information and might save your life. Don't try to be a hero. If you and the department try to get Jose Medina, he will retire sooner rather than later and go into hiding. Jude Henderson wants to take over the business, but Alexander Raninsky also wants Jose Medina's drug cartel, business, and territory. Please be careful if you want to stay alive. I'll be in touch within a couple of days. If I get any updates, I'll send them your way. Please don't trace this message. You won't be successful trying to pinpoint my location. Good luck, Agent Heiden, because you really need it!"

Keith puts down his PDA, drinks his coffee, leans back to his chair and takes a deep breath while rubbing his eyes once again.

His PDA beeps again. Keith picks it up quickly. "A couple of days ago Treat Miller came to your house and asked your wife about you. He wanted you to get him into a witness protection program. I guess you know the state of California's attorney general in person! Treat Miller was hired by Jose Medina and Jude Henderson to get your wife into his arms but the plan backfired because he had sex with her. That wasn't the plan and now they want their money back. It was over a million dollars for the job to be done right. He might contact you in person or die on the streets of LA. Please note your family might be in extreme danger. I'll be in touch soon. Take care and keep your eyes and ears open. Please note that Jude Henderson hired your son Patrick. They want to get their goods back from your boy very soon. Please keep your son on a short tight leash at all times. I can help you with this very important matter. They already have you right where they want you in your job, but I think you already know that."

Justine took Colin and Mitch to her sister Jocelyn's house (she lives in Culver City) for a couple of days and then to their grandparents' house (Beverly Hills) for another round of sleepovers. I guess the boys will be back in two weeks or more after they have fun with Justine's relatives from England and Germany. They are spending the summer in the states to visit Gertrude and Sir. William and the other Anderson family members, Justine and her siblings, Jason, Joshua, Jocelyn, Jennifer, and their spouses and the kids too.

Erin didn't want to go with her brothers to see the relatives because they are all coming to Colin's fourth birthday party within weeks from now. She really has a lot of college pre-work to do to get into the colleges of her choice. She doesn't have the heart to tell her dad but mom knows that she wants to apply to colleges on the east coast. Erin loves the West Coast and with good reason. She was born and raised in California, but she wants to spread her young wings into new adventures. She wants to get into Yale, the college that Dr. Sheppard went too. She also has an interest in Princeton and Cornell.

Erin is doing her work at the kitchen table as Keith walks in.

"Hi, sweetie, what are you doing?"

"Hi, Dad, just doing a lot of pre-entry work for the colleges that I want to get into... I hope."

"That's great, honey. What colleges? Are you applying to the colleges that your mom and I went to?" Keith asks, as he walks closer to his daughter.

Keith is always excited and shows interest in what his kids love or want to do. Any activities with the school, sports or hobbies hold his interest. Just to go into their minds and pray that none of them end up on the streets is vital to him. He's so amazed how the kids love different things in their own way. He never pushes them to do anything that they can't do, or handle at the time. He always says, "Just try it once. If you don't like it, you don't have to do it again. Just try it. You might be very surprised." Keith's mom always encouraged her children to reach for a goal in life because life is very exciting. Also never to look back once you find your happiness. Keith's dad was the total opposite! He would laugh in your face in front of others about your ideas. See that rock on the ground? It's smarter than you!" Keith and his siblings were very confused about what to do and how to find their way.

Keith finally realized in life that it's not just about best DEA agent in the department or the best husband, it's about being the best for the kids. All they need in their life is full support and someone to be there for them no matter what. To Keith this is still very new to him, raising kids the way he wanted to be raised. It's a challenge every day not to become his father. He knows that Justine pushes him to the edge of that cliff. She knows that he can snap. Does she want him to do the unthinkable or does she want to help Keith not be the father he had?

Is Dr. Sheppard right in her psychoanalysis that Justine has taken over his father's position as an abuser and the circle of craziness never ended? Maybe she's right for once in that coffee brain of hers.

"I didn't want to tell you, but I'm applying to colleges on the East Coast," Erin answers.

"Why the hell do you want to do that? Don't you love us anymore?" Keith asks with a surprised look.

He puts his PDA down and gets a fresh cup of coffee, shaking his head at the same time.

"Erin, don't you love your daddy anymore? What did I do to you that makes you want to live three thousand miles away from me? I'll take any punishment away…just stay home. You're the only normal member of this family. The truth is… I really can't take your brothers, "The Three Stooges" and your mom too. Listen, I'll pay you to stay in California and go to college here!"

"Dad, I love you no matter if you punish me or not. It's something I want to do! I want to live on the East Coast. I will feel so alive feeling the winter season! I've never seen snow, and I want to see it! I want to feel the cold through my body! I know it'll make me feel so alive!"

"Okay, I'll take you on a trip to NYC during a winter blizzard. That will change your mind very quickly!"

"Sometimes, Dad, Colin makes more sense than you!" Erin laughs.

"Maybe you're right in that area." Keith laughs. "I just love you! I really need your full support, because I think I'm on my own and it's not very good. Please, Erin, stay home!"

"Dad, don't you want me to grow as a young lady and explore new adventures in my life?" she asks with a confused look. "You tell us all the time to reach our goal and get that pearl in life. Also to never look back when you find your happiness. Didn't your mom used to say that to you, your sisters, and brothers?"

"Boy, I really have to stop talking to you, because it's biting me in the ass!" Keith laughs.

"Dad, you're too funny! Listen, I'm not going to jail for the rest of my life. I'm just going to college for four years or maybe longer if I get my masters. I love you dad, I want to do things! Don't you want me to be happy?"

"Yes, happiness is the key factor in living a long life and also having all the kids out of the house. Why can't it be Patrick? You are my pride and joy! Erin, I always want you to be happy, but it's just...I'll miss you terribly, and this home will not be the same without you here," Keith says.

"I know, Dad, and I love you, too, but you have to let me go someday," Erin answers as she hugs her dad tightly.

Keith kisses Erin on the head. He's so blessed to have great kids especially a daughter who makes the world look so bright.

"I did and thank you for being you and don't ever change for anybody especially a boy! And there's no more punishment for you... I think you learned your lessons," Keith says softly.

"I did and thank you. I won't change for anyone, Dad. I have to get back to work before I decide not to do it at all," Erin answers, as she sits back down in her chair.

"I understand. I get that feeling all the time. Erin, is your laptop slow?" Keith asks, as he puts his hand in a paper bag that was from the drug store.

Suddenly Keith is holding a prescription receipt for Justine Anderson Heiden for prenatal vitamins. His tired blue eyes become wider because he can't believe what he's seeing. He's getting too old for any more shit in his life especially Justine's extracurricular activities. Keith thinks to himself, *Will this hamster wheel ever stop moving?*

"Oh shit," he shouts with a horrified look. Keith says to himself again, "I just want to go to sleep and never wake up from this nightmare!"

Keith break's Erin's concentration from her school work as she picks up her head with a concerned look.

"What's wrong? Are you hurt?"

Erin runs to his father's aid. Keith is in shock but that's nothing new. He tries to think but how can he reason something that he's unable to explain to himself or others especially.

Yes, Keith knows the birds and the bees very well. It's never a good thing to play with Mother Nature because it will come right back at you with full force. People get many diseases when playing too hard. It's a chain reaction that will never go away!

"Please, Dad, tell me what's wrong? You're turning as white as a ghost!"

"Prenatal vitamins?"

Erin backs up with her hands up and makes a solid statement.

"That's not mine!"

"I know it's not yours because it's your mother's." Keith sighs, as he sees the prescription receipt and pills too.

"Congratulations, Dad! You're going to be a father again!" Erin says, as she tries to hug her dad, but he's as stiff as a board.

Keith breaks off the hug because he's screwed big time.

"I'm not the father!"

"What are you talking about? Then who's the father? Oh my God! Treat Miller is the father!" Erin shouts and thinks to herself at the same time, *How can Mom do this to Dad and us too? She's evil in many ways and no one can stop her!*

"Boy, Erin, you really don't need to go to college," Keith replies, as he feels sick to his stomach.

"Dad, I'm confused. How do you know that you're not the father? Nothing is final without the proof of a DNA test from the unborn child and the parents," Erin replies.

"You really have to stop reading mystery novels. It's killing your brain. Shit!" Keith shouts.

Keith is so angry; he doesn't know what to do at this point. Justine had two affairs and to make matters even worse her father paid for these relationships. This whole situation makes Keith want to throw up. He can't wait to put his hands around Treat's and Sir. William's necks and twist them like a hand towel.

Keith's father was a real womanizer in his day. There were a lot of phone calls from different women across the country that always wanted to talk to Keith's dad (Conrad). His mom (Megan) used to cry herself to sleep every night. She knew deep down that she was lost, stuck in a loveless marriage and with a lot of kids to take care of. Her family back home in Ireland never really had the money to save her. They always told her to come home. They really missed and loved her. Is Keith in a loveless marriage too just like his mother was? How can you break the circle of madness when it's all you know in life?

"Dad, how do you know that Treat is the father?"

"You're a real woman with all these questions. It's killing my brain cells. Can you please stop the twenty questions!" Keith replies.

Before Colin was born, Keith had gotten a vasectomy. He didn't want any more children.

"Now I know where Patrick gets his attitude from," Erin snaps back. "The apple doesn't fall far from the tree."

"Sorry, honey, I'm really not in the mood for anything. Let's just say I know and leave it at that," Keith answers and then gives Erin a loving kiss on her check.

"Okay, Dad. I have to finish my work, or I'll never get into any college," Erin says, as she quickly goes back to her workstation. "I hope everything works out for you and Mom."

"Me too. I'm going to take a swim...You can come in and join Reese and I."

"Maybe. Just give me a couple of hours, and then I'll come into the pool."

Keith walks over to the kitchen counter and turns off his PDA. He knows he needs to relax and be smart. Reese gets into the pool with Keith. They enjoy each others' company. Both dog and human love spending time especially together in the pool. Reese learned to swim before he was housebroken. Keith loves the pool; he thinks that he's a fish, not a man at times.

CHAPTER
SIXTY-ONE

*M*inutes later Keith and Reese are enjoying the pool; they are just cooling off in the hot summer heat. Reese loves to play fetch with his owner. He can play ball for hours without getting tired, but it's different for the person who's throwing it. Keith swims some laps in the pool when suddenly he sees a long dark shadow of a man standing near the edge.

"Hello, Keith?" says a tall man about 6'3" with a slim build.

He's wearing a light summer material gray suit with a white shirt underneath. A silk tie finishes the outfit off. He looks like a taller version of Keith.

"Keith!" the man shouts again.

Keith finally comes to the surface and responds to the man who's been calling his name. He just wants to enjoy the whole day with Reese. Keith hates being interrupted from his time of relaxation.

The man takes off his dark sunglasses and says, "I'm Christopher, your brother. Remember we had spoken on the phone this morning?"

Keith is a little taken back, because Christopher looks just like their dad but with their mom's Irish skin tone.

"Oh. Hi!"

He gets out of the pool and dries himself off without saying a single word.

"I'm sorry. What do you want?" Keith says.

"I'm Mom and Dad's family lawyer, and I'm here because of the business of Dad's will…"

Keith looks up at Christopher because of his height. He's not in the mood to listen to this man who won't go away. You would think that since Conrad Heiden is dead and buried it would be over and done with, but I guess not.

"Christopher, you seem like a nice guy, and I don't want to be rude, but I have no choice. You can put the check where the sun doesn't shine!"

"I guess you're not in a good mood. I understand… It's one of those days that you want to put the covers over your head and hide. But we have to talk about Dad's will. You have money coming to you, and it's not loose change. It's a pretty large amount of cash that you might want to put in your children's college fund," Christopher says.

He's not surprised at his younger brother's behavior. Believe it or not he's used to it, because that's Keith's distress mechanism. He acts like a real smart ass which can get him into major trouble. Christopher wouldn't doubt it if Keith has a son who acts just like him.

Christopher remembers all too well the many physical fights that Keith and their dad had. One time Keith dislocated their dad's jaw. His father left him alone after that until the huge fight that ended their relationship forever.

"Christopher, I don't need his poisoned money! I'm doing fine without it! Just give it to Mom."

"You didn't even get a chance to look at the check in order to make that final decision! Mom is set for life, and she lives with Jennifer and her family in Oak Park about 35 minutes away from Chicago. She's very happy that she's finally free of Dad…even though he changed a lot after you left the house. He was hurt that he did that to you, and I didn't know how to have your back. Dad was very stubborn as you know," Christopher says, as he sits himself down on the patio chair and opens up his briefcase.

Keith looks annoyed about this whole sorry tale of a story that he can give a rat's ass about.

"I don't want his money or to listen to his side of his story! I'm sick and tired of this shit!"

"Keith, you have to understand that I'm in the middle and their lawyer as well. I'm sorry that I'm not a therapist so I could help you."

"I guess I understand what you're saying, but why didn't you contact me sooner?"

"Dad changed a lot. He did a one-eighty in his way...stopped yelling, hitting, drinking, smoking, and being a womanizer. He was paying for my college in full, and all I had to do was not get in touch with you," Christopher answers, as he takes off his suit jacket at the same time.

"Well... I'm surprised, but that doesn't explain why you couldn't have contacted me, especially you and Jennifer!" Keith shouts. "I thought we were best of friends... Shit! I looked up to you in many ways!"

Christopher tries desperately to get a word in edgewise, but it's difficult.

"Keith, you really have to calm down and let me explain before you have a major heart attack! I'm here now. Doesn't that count for anything?"

"I guess so... So Dad put a hold on everyone. Boy, he didn't change one bit! What a shit head!"

"Are you done yet?" Christopher snaps back.

Keith becomes quiet and listens to what his long lost brother has to say.

"I'm very sorry for what happened to you. I really wished I could've stopped Dad."

"Christopher, you were just one year older. What were you going to do, beat him up? Dad was the same height, as you are now, and we were all helpless. But thanks for thinking that you could've done something to make the situation easier. Anyway, why are you here again?"

"I'm Mom and Dad's family lawyer, and your name is in Dad's will. I have a check that has your name on it, and I wanted to say hello in person," Christopher responds.

"Hello... Now get out!" Keith demands.

"No, I won't leave until I give you this check. It's for you and no one else. Please take it so I can go to court! I have to meet with my clients!"

Christopher puts the envelope on the patio table for the owner to open.

"Listen, I don't want the check… Give it to Mom… I think she needs it more than I do!"

"As I was saying before, Mom already has her money, and she's set for life. Keith, don't give me back talk. Just take the money and let's move on!"

"You know you're the only one that I'll listen to!" Keith says rudely.

Keith sits down, takes the envelope, and opens it. In wide-eyed amazement, he exclaims.

"You've got to be shitting me!" This startles Reese who is napping under the table.

"No, Keith. It's a legal check and ready to be deposited by you," Christopher responds without missing a beat, since his check was for the same amount.

"Okay, is this a Monopoly check?"

"It's real and it won't bounce if you deposit it in your bank. I have to go now, and we'll talk soon," Christopher says, as he gets up from the comfortable patio chair and takes his briefcase.

Keith gets up from his patio chair and shakes his brother's hand. He's very touched to see Christopher who hasn't really changed over the years. It's kind of funny in a way that a person can age so gracefully.

"Well, thanks for coming, and I'll walk you to your car."

"Thanks, Keith, but I can walk myself out. I'll call you soon, and maybe we can have dinner or something. I'm happy that we had a chance to catch up," Christopher answers.

"Maybe we can meet sooner. You're welcome to celebrate my son Colin's birthday party with us. It's on Saturday, June 30th at 12:00 pm. You're welcome to bring your family with you. Do you have one?" Keith asks rudely.

"Yes, I have a family!" Christopher answers and tries to dismiss his little brother's rudeness.

Christopher has been married over thirteen years now to his beautiful wife, Savannah Morgan, from Taylor, Georgia. They have two amazing children. His son Dale Christopher is ten, and his daughter Sarah Jennifer is eight.

The older brother turns his head and then laughs.

"Do you know that your dog is rolling his body in dirt, and didn't he just get out of the pool?"

"Yes, I know," Keith answers, as he knows very well what a mess Reese is making. It's a real pain to clean him. "So bring your swimsuits and the family to the birthday party. I know that Colin would love to see you guys."

"Okay, I will. Goodbye, Keith. See you soon."

Christopher walks away from his brother, but this time it's totally different. He can finally relax and breathe on his own terms. He's pleased to meet Keith finally, and he realized he changed a bit.

As Christopher walks away, he thinks, *maybe Keith is right that their dad hadn't really changed. He just put on an act for the public. Dad wouldn't let anyone in his family contact Keith over the years. But the truth of the matter is my siblings, Mom, and I really enjoyed Dad when Keith wasn't around. But when Dad got very sick, his medical needs were too stressful for Mom, and she couldn't care for him anymore.*

Will Keith open his arms to his whole family, or will he move on?

CHAPTER
SIXTY-TWO

//

*P*eter walks into his apartment just as his cell phone beeps. He doesn't notice that Elise is not there. The text message says, "Please don't try to trace this message, and I'm not in the radius to be found. Agent Peter Darling, I've been working for the DEA Department for over fifteen years now. I'm a deep undercover mole for the DEA working for Jose Medina's cartel. I was there ten years ago, and I remember all too well what happened to you and Agent Heiden during that terrible raid of Jose Medina's drug mob. We were ambushed and lost a lot of agents including our supervisor Agent Will Fields. It was a terrible day. If you don't remember who I am my name is Frankie De Luca."

Peter gets into the elevator and presses the button to the first floor without skipping a beat. He types an instant message to the person that claims to be a good old friend named, Frankie. "Please tell me more about you if you're Frankie De Lula. How many years have you been in the DEA department? Other agents and I like to play jokes on our co-workers on the job. I'm going to give you a date and time when this joke happened and where it took place. It was December 24th and the time was around 3 a.m. The joke was on Agent Keith Heiden."

Peter walks outside the elevator through the main lobby and into the outside parking lot. The sun is shining brightly, and you can feel the dry heat. It's going to be around 97 to 100 degrees, but it feels hotter. Southern California now has water restrictions in effect.

There are mini blackouts from time to time as well. Anything to save money!!

Peter drives on the Santa Monica Highway heading towards work. An hour later he reaches his destination. During that time his cell phone continues to beep with new text messages. Peter parks the car and reads the text from the so-called friend, Frankie De Luca.

"December 24 at 3:00 a.m.? Give me a minute. Okay, you told Keith to open the company closet to get something. I don't remember what but it was not too important. When he opened the closet, Deon and I jumped out dressed in reindeer costumes and scared the living daylights out of him! Keith jumped out of his skin! He punched me and Agent Deon Jones, and we ended up in the hospital during Christmas healing from our injuries. We came back on the job after the New Year. Until this day, Keith never said sorry to us. We never pressed criminal charges or discipline action against him because we started it. Don't forget, my friend, you were a part of this too. That was a great moment! Do you want more information on me?"

"Peter, I want out! But I want to help you and Keith before I see the world again. You have to keep this secret from everybody including your partner. No one knows I'm alive. You know that Keith and his family are in great danger. I don't know anything about a man named Treat Miller, but he was hired by Jose Medina to get Justine Heiden into his arms. He was paid over a million to do the job, but the plan went down south very fast because he wasn't supposed to sleep with Mrs. Heiden. If Keith finds out, Treat is a dead man! Also Jose wants his money back right away or he'll put an end to Treat. You have to keep a very close eye on your boy because there will be hell to pay if you don't."

Peter answers quickly, "I won't tell a soul. I'll watch Keith and his family for their safety. Please keep in touch if any other information comes your way. Be careful and thanks again."

CHAPTER

SIXTY-THREE

〰〰〰〰〰〰〰〰〰〰〰〰〰〰〰〰〰〰〰〰〰〰〰〰〰〰〰〰〰〰〰

*A*n hour later Peter walks into Keith's office.

"You called me?" Peter asks, as he sits down on the chair.

"Yes, Peter! I received a notice as you did too, from the Defense Department. They're going to cut DEA all across the board about 20 percent or more. Each department head has the right to make the call where to cut. Unfortunately, our department might be cutting the field agents by 10 percent, as well as the other sections too." Keith answers.

Peter jumps up from his seat and shouts back.

"Wait a minute! They can't cut us off at the knees! We need all the field agents out there!! So, what can we do?"

"We need a very big break, like the ice cream raid! I want Alex Raninsky on a silver platter. We are talking over $4.1 million worth of drugs, guns, and other elements from the information that I received just an hour ago," he answers as his voice echoes throughout his office.

A minute later there's a knock at the door.

"Come in!"

Nicole peeks her head through the door and says, "Sir, is everything okay?"

"It's okay. You can take your break if you want to. Can you please hold my calls?" Keith says.

"No problem. Do you need anything before I go?"

"No, thank you. Do you want something, Peter?" Keith asks.

"No," Peter answers, as he sits back in the chair while reading the report that was on Keith's desk without blinking an eye.

Nicole smiles and then walks back to her desk.

"Peter, you didn't tell me that you found the four files. You know I was about to go straight to jail for misplacing them. Where did you find them?" Keith asks.

Peter hesitates for a minute.

"I found them underneath my Archie comic books in the office drawer," he says sheepishly.

"Were you going to tell me before they put me in handcuffs?" Keith exclaims. "If Jack didn't tell you to clean your shit out of your office, those files would have been lost forever!"

"Keith, give me a break! Don't start!" Peter shouts back. "Man, you should go to yoga classes or something! Maybe some green tea. You need to calm down, man," he says with a Jamaican accent.

"Listen, you jackass! I know you're dating Dr. Sheppard! Now I know why I was transferred to supervisor GI Joe, because you want to make your Peter moves on my therapist!"

Peter laughs, "No, that wasn't my first intention but you do have a point there. GI Joe that's a good one!"

"Peter, there are a lot of beautiful women that live in California. Why must you pick my therapist? What's wrong with you? You really need the therapy," Keith snaps, as he tries not to break a major artery.

"I'm getting some," Peter replies and winks with a huge smile. "Her hips are dangerous!" Oh, memories!

"Jackass! You know I'm doing a lot of your work. You can't seem to handle the responsibility of being a supervisor. Tell me something, Peter. Do you ever do any work?" exclaims Keith.

"I've thought that I don't want to be supervisor anymore. I want to be a fulltime field agent," Peter states.

"Peter, you're thirty-eight years old! I really need you to think like an adult for me. Can you try for an hour time frame!" Keith shouts, as he tries to get through to his childish partner's mind.

"Just rub my age in my face, why don't you!" Peter shouts back. "Listen, Keith. I don't care what you're trying to say. It's going to work in your favor anyway!"

"Listen, moron! You can't be a fulltime field agent after being a supervisor more than five years! You'll get the pink slip, and I'll be selling maps of the star homes on Hollywood Boulevard, because I know you!" Keith exclaims.

"Keith, you're very funny. That's one of the reasons why I love you so much! Your imagination runs away with you!" Peter laughs, as he slips his hand through his dark brown hair.

"Sleeping with the doctor and jeopardizing your job puts my job on the line too. You know that your co-workers will talk about your new love relationship! Listen, if you have a bad day with her my evaluation will be flushed down the toilet! I'll never get a job in this town again! Also your job is to give Dr. Sheppard names of other agents that need therapy. They'll have mixed feelings all the way around! You need to stop this love affair roller coaster!" Keith announces.

"Keith, you're a drama queen! I'm not going to stop my relationship because you're my best friend and love me and all of that! I know what I'm up against! I wasn't born yesterday."

"You're an ass! You don't know what you're doing! I need you here! We have a huge raid on Alex Raninsky coming up within days! I want to get these guys and their goods too! Stop thinking below your belt for once in your life! Did you see your assignment for the raid?" Keith asks.

"Yes, I received the assignment a couple of days ago. I'm not going to answer to you, especially where Dr. Elise Sheppard is concerned! She's the best thing that's ever happened to me! It's my business not yours! You have no right to tell me what to do in my private life! Who died and made you king?"

"Are you finished yet?" Keith asks sarcastically. "It's my business because she's my therapist and you're my best friend. It's a conflict of interest! If you love birds have a very bad day, the DEA Department will be affected by your outcome. So yes, I have a right to tell you what to do, because I'm in the middle of it!"

"Oh please!"

"Did you get a chance to tell Agent Jack about your newfound love that's blossoming?"

Keith walks past Peter and really wants to smack him on his head for being so stupid.

"No, I didn't tell Jack as of yet, but I will. Go ahead have fun telling me what I should or shouldn't do in my life! I know that you have concerns but Uncle Peter can handle it! Please don't worry and I love you for caring," Peter answers, as he leans back in his chair with a huge smile on his face.

"Uncle Peter, you can't even balance your checkbook! How are you going to handle this? Are you chemically imbalanced? You're not a teenager anymore! Just grow up!"

Peter laughs. "That's good, chemically imbalanced. I've got to use that line one day! Keith, I'm not going to Sin City to tie the knot with the doctor. We're just having sex and I'm going to ask her to live with me… Oh crap!" *Peter, sometimes you're so stupid and this is one of these times! I really hope my gun is loaded and ready to use it on Keith if he jumps on me.*

"What?"

"Listen, try not to break a vein as of yet, because it looks like one is about to blow any minute now!" Peter pleads, as he looks for the exit door to flee from the scene before a crime is committed.

"I know that you're sleeping together but living together? Peter don't you dare ask the doctor to live with you. It's not good at all. You should really rethink what you're doing in your life and get crap straightened out! I need you, and we have a lot of work to do! I want you to be the raid commander of this field operation on the ice cream raid and Liam will be your wingman. Can you handle this responsibility or should I get someone else?" Keith exclaims.

"Keith, you're so dramatic! You should get an Emmy for your performance!"

"Peter, can you take me seriously for once in your life!" Keith snaps back at his insane partner. He's just not normal.

"Keith, you have to calm down. You're going to have a heart attack or something because of your erratic behavior. Boy, Keith, your father really did a number on you! I can handle it! Why are you giving me an order? I'm the supervisor, not you!" Peter responds with a confused look on his face.

"Because Jack feels that I'm more responsible than you are right now! This department needs a break, and I'm sick and tired that we're the laughing stock of the FBI. I want to get Alex Raninsky and his men!" Keith exclaims.

"That's fine! Don't worry; we'll get him and his merry men too! So, you said that I could be the raid commander…so that means that I can be a field agent from now on?" Peter asks as he stretches in his chair.

"Yes, Peter, only for this time."

"Seriously?"

"Yes, Peter! This is the only time that you'll be raid commander because no one else is qualified for the position. Just really practice your shooting and the plan of action before you tell your friends in the sandbox," Keith answers sarcastically.

"Okay, temporary boss. I'll study the work of the raid and practice at the shooting range.

Peter gets up from his chair, and he's about to open the office door and walk out. Then suddenly he turns around to ask a question.

"Hey, Keith, do you know Dr. Sheppard's first name?"

"What does that have to do with the job and your future here?" Keith asks with a snappy tone.

"Nothing…just play with me! So do you know her first name?" Peter asks with a huge smile.

."Why do I need to know this information?" Keith asks. *If I spend too much time with Peter, I'm going to have to shoot him between his eyes. Did I load my gun today?*

"Just in case you have to write a personal check to her." Peter laughs.

"The job pays for my therapy you moron!"

"Come on, Keith, don't get upset. I'm not holding it against you if you don't know her first name!" Peter states, as he rolls his eyes at his best friend.

"Peter, as always you're wasting my time! Just get ready for the big day and practice your shooting. I want to get these low-lives!"

"Her name is Elise. Do you like her?"

"She's my doctor," Keith snaps back.

"Keith Patrick Heiden, you're not playing the game! Do you like her as a friend or something else?" Peter laughs.

"As I said before, you're wasting my and the company's time!" Keith exclaims.

Peter decides to mess with Keith's head some more. He places himself back in his chair.

"I'll take that as a yes. That really sounds good shooting some bullets. Do you want to go a few rounds with me?" Peter asks, as he puts his feet up on Keith's desk.

Peter wonders how long it will take for Keith to notice that his feet are up on his office desk again.

"I would if I didn't have to do your job," Keith snaps, as he tries to focus on his work, but it's not easy seeing and hearing Peter's juvenile distractions.

"Okay then, I'll see you later. I have to do public speaking in different schools in the Los Angeles area. It starts in September. I really need your help on public speaking," Peter says, as he sees his partner getting flustered.

"This is your punishment because of the four files?"

"Yes, Keith. It's my punishment by Agent Jack," Peter answers with a friendly smile. "Please help me, buddy. I'll be your best friend."

Keith gives a stone-cold look at his partner and pushes his shoes off his clean desk.

"Can you please take your smelly feet off my desk? You're asking me to help you with your public speaking after what you put me through? You're a real jackass!"

"Right back at you! Do you know that your love warms my heart like Christmas morning," he announces and laughs at the same time. "Thanks for volunteering your time to help me. I know that I can count on you when I'm in a jam. I'll get the information for you as soon as I get it myself. Also, I'll look at the raid information carefully," Peter says, as he gets up from the office chair. "Be honest, what do you really think about Dr. Sheppard?"

"Well, she's a clumsy, absent-minded, compassionate, professional person," Keith answers in a signal breath.

"I love it!" Peter laughs.

"Peter, just leave, or I'll shoot you where your royals are! My gun is loaded!" Keith announces with a smile.

"Keith, we found two bags that looked like cocaine and heroin underneath Dr. Sheppard's car. She wasn't arrested because it wasn't drugs. But she did accidentally bump into a fine well-dressed English man. She didn't catch a name, but I bet it was one of Jude Henderson's guys!" Peter ponders.

"Well, that makes a lot of sense from all the pictures that were developed of the doctor, me, and now my family." Keith answers.

"It's going to be an exciting summer," Peter answers, as he leaves the room.

CHAPTER
SIXTY-FOUR

*A*lex walks around the ice cream factories near a secret location in southern California. He looks at his friend Victor from grade school.

"Hello, Victor, are we ready for Friday?" Alex asks in Russian.

"Yes, yes, Alex, we are ready," Victor answers back in Russian, as he hits his hand on a truck. "We're set for the huge job. Some of our Port and Customs Authority Police are on our payroll, so it was easy to get the drugs from Mexico. Also, there will be a good amount of cash in the end. Now we just have to pack it in the ice cream trucks and travel all over California. We have to be very secretive about our plans or we will all die."

Alex spits on the ground because he feels like it.

"I received a strange call from Anastasia. She stated that the DEA is ready to move in and destroy our plans. We have to change our time to make it sooner, not later. The new time is now a day ahead of schedule. We will go before the American pigs get us. Everything is set and we will get our money at the end of the job. Jose Medina's organization is giving us the green light and the goods to do it. Russia will hit America and hit it hard!

"Great Alex, I'll tell the men. Don't worry the job will be done with no problems. Mother Russia will be proud!" Victor laughs and shows a very toothless mouth! "Please, Alex, let's drink! We have a lot to celebrate!"

"Yes!" Alex takes a bottle of Russian vodka off the table and grabs two dirty glasses. "We toast to good fortune, health and to Mother Russia!"

"Alex, how many ice cream trucks are going out on Friday?" Victor asks, with a concerned look on his face.

"Twenty trucks will go out to sell drugs in the Los Angeles area, as well as other cities across the state. We need to get six more trucks. that will drive in other directions so the pigs can't find us quickly. If the plan runs smoothly, we will work for a long time and take Jose Medina's business territory and the power that comes along with it.

"Should we relocate everything to another area because of their watchful eye?"

"Yes! We will have a meeting outside the radar and make sure no one follows us. We'll do everything one day ahead of schedule, but we'll make believe that everything is following the same plan. They think they have the upper hand, but they don't know about our inside source, information from my beautiful cousin Anastasia," Alex answers, as he takes a cigar from his pocket and lights it up. "Sorry… I'm so rude! Do you want one?"

"No… No!" Victor answers. "So what day do you really want to leave and do the job so we can get out of here?"

"Victor, you're like a spoiled American! Take, take, take and never give back to your community! Thursday will be our launch date and the time will be 11:00 a.m., not Friday at 12:00 p.m."

Alex and Victor start to laugh harder. While Alex laughs his ashes start to sprinkle all over the ground.

"Alex, I'm a little concerned about Anastasia living with that nerdy American. What if something terrible happens to her?" Victor asks, as he waves the cigar smoke away from his face.

"Sorry, Victor! Both Anastasia and I came from nothing. We had to sell our bodies for money on the streets of Russia until our very dear friend Vladimir…may he rest in peace…saved us from hell. We worked for him, and he gave us the money to put in long years of planning to come to America and get their money. Anyway, our plan is to get total control and take over Jose Medina's cartel territory, but Jude Henderson from Britain wants it too. It's going to be a western showdown of power! Who's fit for the position of control? You see, Victor, Mr. Medina gave Jude and me a test to see who will take over by the end of the summer with more money and spread the love of drugs to the streets of America. I really don't know how Jude got a head start in the game of getting full control of Medina's cartel, but it won't take too long until we catch up to the British limey bastard. We will prevail and win the battle! We just have to get clean-cut men to look like ice cream men, not like us!"

They both laugh, because it's so true.

"Very well, Alex, we will make it happen. The men will do anything for Mother Russia and for you, because you'll make everyone very rich!"

Victor pours more Russian vodka for his friend and himself.

"To Russia!" they toast and smile showing the very few teeth they both have in their mouth!

CHAPTER
SIXTY-FIVE

The sound of a beep comes through the phone line.

"Yes, Nicole," Keith says.

"Agent Heiden, Mr. Williamson is here to see you."

"Thank you. You can send him in," Keith answers, as he sees him near Nicole's desk.

Then a second later Nicole escorts Mr. Williamson to Keith's office.

"Good Evening, Agent Heiden. I hope I didn't take you away from anything too pressing?" Preston asks while he shakes Keith's hand.

"No, not really. We weren't scheduled to see each other today. I thought our first visit was our last?" Keith asks.

"I know, but I have some information that will be very helpful to you," Mr. Williamson answers as he hands a file to Keith.

Suddenly without skipping a beat, Keith walks behind his desk and sits down on his chair. "Please, Mr. Williamson, have a seat. I guess you've been busy with Jude Henderson."

Preston sits and looks at his watch. He doesn't want to miss his flight back home to England. He has four days off, and then back to work again. He's going to Italy this time to find another international criminal.

"Please call me Preston. It's my job, and I want to tell you that I finished with Jude Henderson's case at this time. I hope you can find him before he's off running into the sunset."

"I still feel better if I call you by your last name. Thank you! This is very helpful for our case against Jude."

"Did you get any other surprises by him?"

"Well, it's a long story, and I don't need to bore you with the details," Keith answers, as he knows it's too long to explain. "Please, there's nothing to worry about but thank you for your concern."

Preston gets up from his seat.

"Okay, I really hope it's nothing major. Well then, I have a flight to catch!"

Both businessmen are ready to say their goodbyes.

"Thank you! Please have a safe trip back home."

"I will! Agent Heiden, I want to say thank you for telling me about all the different tourist attractions in California. You know this is my first time in this state! It's very lovely and exciting too," Preston says with a smile.

There's no doubt that America is one huge tourist attraction and Preston loved every bit of it!

"I'm happy that you enjoyed California and all its beautiful sites," Keith says with a friendly smile.

"You're a very interesting person, and I'm happy to know you. It would be an honor to have you and your wife stay at my cottage home if you ever visit England." Preston gives Keith his business card.

"I have been to Scotland and Ireland. We were in England for my wife's grandmother's funeral. It's a lovely country. You're too generous to give my wife and me the time of day, and especially to stay at your home. We'll see what happens," Keith answers with a friendly smile. "You're very kind. Believe me, you won't forget this."

"Agent Heiden, I wouldn't take no for an answer. Just please give me a month ahead of time, and I'll give you guys a royal tour of England. I would love to share my country with you! Here's my business card with my personal cell phone and home number on the back. I'm proud to call you my friend."

Keith takes the business card from Preston and feels overwhelmed with gratitude.

"Thank you. Please have a safe trip home."

"I wish you luck, Agent Heiden. I'll call you within a month to see how things are going."

Keith answers with a smile and a nod.

Having a friend from Great Britain is indeed a nice feeling!

CHAPTER
SIXTY-SIX

*I*t is 1:20 a.m. California time; Preston Williamson checks in at the ticket line of British Airways. His flight is at 2:00 a.m. and he has time to use the men's room before he goes on the plane. The flight will take at least ten or more hours to get to London International Airport. It will be a very long day for Preston. He doesn't mind as long as he gets home to sleep in his bed. He really does miss the feel and smell of his homeland. Preston did get some California sun, and he's very surprised that he tanned during that time period.

Preston walks into the men's restroom near gate 17. He knows it won't take long at all.

A few minutes later Preston is going about his business unaware that he's not alone in the men's room. Another man dressed in a gray uniform and baseball cap walks into the other stall and then gently takes a garrote loop (it's like a very strong and sharp piano wire) from his belt. This man quickly stands on the toilet and leans over the wall. The garrote loop wraps around Preston's neck, and the man pulls it up high with all his might, as he jumps off the toilet. It only takes a minute to finish the job, as Preston's head is quickly cut off from his body.

The man stuffs his bloody garrote loop into a plastic bag, puts it in his pocket and gets out of the stall. Less than a second later he leaves the men's room and quickly walks away. A murder has been committed without anyone's knowledge.

Preston's head falls to the floor like a broken doll and hits the stall door. His body is still half naked on the toilet with blood flowing down the wall and pooling across the restroom area.

The man in the gray uniform walks outside the airport quickly and gets into a dark foreign car that was waiting for him.

"Jude, is the job done?" Jack Forrester asks as he sits behind the wheel of the car.

He's also wearing a gray baseball cap, which covers most of his face.

The man takes off his baseball cap and answers, "Yes, it's done. Let's get out of here!"

"Very well, sir!"

The shiny black car quickly drives away, after the Interpol agent has been murdered by Jude Henderson.

CHAPTER

SIXTY-SEVEN

The time reads 2:39 a.m. on Artemis Daly's watch. He walks around the crime scene and sees a witness talking to an officer. The Crime Scene Investigators are in the men's room taking in all the pieces of evidence. Artemis gives everyone room to do their job. He's just there to supervise from afar, and everyone knows that he's in charge of the night shift homicide department.

Artemis is very much aware that he and his crew have a lot to do because his beeper keeps beeping. His girlfriend Kristin (he's in the relationship for three years now) keeps on hiding his beeper because he won't take a day off!

The Crime Scene Investigators have a lot of work ahead of them. The crime scene is a bloody mess (not an English thing) because the victim lost his head. Pretty soon the body will be bagged to travel to the LA County Coroner's Office for an autopsy, just to rule out if decapitation was not the factor that killed the poor soul.

It's going to be a long day at the office again.

Every minute that goes by another murder is committed in LA. This either involves gangs, drugs additions, dealers, sellers, prostitution, domestic violence or drive by shootings. People go crazy when the full moon is out.

"Artemis, the gentleman named Engel Wells has just given me his statement. He said he found the murder victim on the toilet seat with his head on the other side of the stall. You know the sad part about this is that Mr. Wells was assigned the seat next to the victim on the airplane back to London," says Dante Francese. He's a young homicide investigator that has worked in the business for a year now. He's still not used to the dead bodies, even though working in this department looked great on TV.

"Who was the murder victim?" Artemis asks.

Dante looks at his notes in a mini notebook.

"His name was Preston Williamson from Britain, and his ID card in his wallet said that he worked for Interpol. There was another thing in his carry-on bag. It's his appointment book that shows a meeting with a gentleman, Special Agent Keith Heiden, from the DEA. It was before he was heading back home. I guess this was the last and final meeting ever," Dante laughs.

"God, your jokes are getting old very fast! Can we please stick with the job?"

"Boy, you're never a happy dude!"

"No, I'm a very cool dude and everybody loves me including the dead ones," Artemis laughs. "Interesting Interpol! Why does a British dude come to the States? We have the internet and phone to get the foreign criminals, so why does he need to see an agent in the DEA? Very strange!"

"I'll keep asking anyone questions to try and get some answers."

"Thanks, Dante. I'll follow up his plan book," Artemis says while chewing a very tasteless gum. "Also, I'll need a fifty mile radius of video footage cameras around this area. Maybe we can get the guy or guys before he strikes again, and we have a headless city!"

Dante gives Preston Williamson's plan book to Artemis.

"It's going to take a lot of time getting every footage from the video cameras, but I'll see what we can come up with," answers Dante.

"Thanks! Keep me posted on any updates on this investigation."

"Will do, Artemis."

Dante and Artemis part ways.

CHAPTER
SIXTY-EIGHT

〰〰〰〰〰〰〰〰〰〰〰〰〰〰〰〰〰〰〰〰〰〰〰〰〰〰〰

*T*wo days later, it was confirmed by the County Coroner's Office that the deceased was Preston Williamson. There were no other findings of drugs in his system; he was killed by decapitation caused by a garrote loop device. His family from England was contacted and will be bringing Preston home by the end of the week.

Artemis did call Keith to notify him of the event and to ask him a few questions. How do you know Preston Williams? Was it a personal or professional relationship? Why would an Interpol agent come to see a DEA agent? What kind of case were you working on together? Artemis wanted to rule out Keith as a suspect. Hours later, Keith is cleared because his statement is confirmed by Peter.

Keith decided to reach out to Preston's sister Penelope Watson and they talked for an hour or two. She's touched that Keith, an America, would give up his time for Preston, and she would be happy to have him come to the wake and funeral to say his good-byes. Keith can only fly in and out within a four-day time frame, which is what his job and Justine would allow.

The drug raid against Alex Raninsky won't start until Keith is back from England, so it seems like a plan.

For some strange reason Jack Forrester is nowhere to be found; he hasn't been to work for at least four days straight. The Human Resource Department called his house more than once but got no answer. A couple of co-workers went over to his house to see if he was home but no luck either. He seems to have disappeared without a trace! Peter filed a missing person's report with the LA police; maybe they would have better luck than the DEA. They have narcotics sniffing dogs, not missing person sniffing dogs to do the job.

A day later the DEA Human Resource Department found out that Jack put in his papers and is not coming in anymore because he retired from the position. He gave his two-week notice, packed his stuff, and got his last check. But no one knows that Jack is working for the other side now and his boss is Jude Henderson.

CHAPTER
SIXTY-NINE

*I*t was a long flight to England, but Keith knew he had to do it. He wanted to pay his respect to Preston Williamson. His family was pleased and grateful that Keith came for Preston. The wake service was full of friends that knew him, but the funeral had many people from various walks of life. I think everyone in town came to pay their respect, including the town's mascot, Barney, the tan and white-colored English bulldog. Keith had a difficult time understanding half of Preston's friends and family. They had very heavy English accents, but they loved to drink a lot and eat to make you feel welcome. A variety of people wanted to know about America and if Keith liked living there. They hear so many stories and sees a lot of American shows on the tellie (British term for TV).

Preston's family and friends loved celebrating Preston's life, and they will miss him terribly. Their stories about Preston will keep him alive in their hearts forever.

Keith was happy to return home after his four days in Great Britain. He was glad to be able to understand the American English language again fully!

CHAPTER
SEVENTY

〰〰〰〰〰〰〰〰〰〰〰〰〰〰〰〰〰〰〰〰〰〰〰〰〰〰〰〰〰

*I*t only takes a few days for Keith to adjust back to Pacific Time. He has Treat Miller's home address and wants to say hello in person.

It's around two in the morning and Keith can't sleep. He has a lot on his mind. The fact that Treat Miller came to his home and almost killed his family was the last straw. Keith quickly gets dressed without waking up Justine and quietly walks downstairs. He turns off the house alarm and opens the front door.

Suddenly the door slams shut in front of him. There she is, the wife, standing behind Keith with an angry look that he knows is for him.

"What the hell are you doing?!"

"I'm going to work. They called me to come in at the last minute," Keith answers with a poker face.

"I don't believe you! I can't tell if you're lying to me or not, but I know, that you're not a field agent anymore. Field agents are on call 24/7 but you're not. Where are you going, Keith?"

"I've work to do."

The truth of the matter is that Keith doesn't care what Justine says.

"You're lying! You're going to beat up Treat Miller!" she screams. "Look at me when I'm talking to you!"

Keith eyes are on her and he answers, "yes, I'm going to give him what he deserves! That's what I do best!"

"Keith, please rethink what you're about to do before you make a terrible mistake! Remember what you did last year. It wasn't pleasant for all of us!" Justine pleads. "Listen, Treat is an accountant who collects foreign money, and he has a pet Bearded Dragon named Spot. He's only 5'4", and you've no right to bully a petite man!" she exclaims.

Hopefully it will stop her aggressive husband from doing an insane thing that he can't take back once it's done.

"Good! I don't have much to beat down on then!" he laughs.

Justine puts her hand on his arm, "Please, Keith, listen to me for once! Do you want more trouble than you already have?"

"Please? Justine, you're already in trouble! You're carrying his unborn child," Keith snaps back.

"Who told you? Patrick?"

"No, your prenatal vitamins that were in a paper bag from the drug store, and they were laying on the kitchen counter!"

"You're insane! I don't believe you!" Justine screams. "I have a feeling that Patrick told you!"

"Believe what you want! You're the insane one, not me! So what do you want?" Keith asks with an annoying tone in his voice.

"I know that I can't change your mind, but please promise me that you won't get caught because we can't afford bail money. We need that money for the kids' college fund," she pleads. "Please don't kill him."

"Okay, I'll try my best not to get caught with my hand in the cookie jar! I can't promise not to kill him," Keith answers with a smile. *Another beat down, how sweet is that?*

He opens the front door and walks out of the house without a second thought.

Even though it's very early in the morning, Keith has the strength to take down anyone that's in his path. He's angry at himself, his wife, and especially Treat.

It's only been a half an hour, but the journey seems endless to Keith. By using the GPS (Global Position System) to the condo complex where Treat Miller lives he finally arrives. As he reaches his destination and slowly parks his black SUV, he's keenly aware of the silent neighborhood. It's 3:15 a.m. as Keith quickly walks to Treat's door. He knocks on the front door and it suddenly opens. Keith is very cautious using all of his senses. He takes out his 9mm Glock from his holster and moves slowly into each room of the condo. He listens carefully so as not to be surprised by anyone on the other side of the walls. Keith doesn't hear anything and the moonlight shining through the windows of the condo is his only light. He finally walks into Treat Miller's bedroom and sees an image of a body lying on the bed.

"Treat, get up! Come on you little bastard. Get up!"

Keith grabs Treat, and he doesn't like what he's touching. It feels like liquid or something gooey. He turns on the nightstand light. Keith can't believe his eyes. Treat is laying face down on his bed in a pool of blood; it seems like he was shot several times in the back and once in the head. Keith finally realizes that's he's in the room with a dead man.

Damn it! Someone did the job for me!

Keith walks backward and suddenly a wire of some kind wraps around his neck. Luckily it doesn't touch his throat to cut his breathing passageway, because Keith quickly uses his hand to block it. Within a split second Keith fights back by pushing his body weight against this man wearing black, pinning him to the wall. He keeps bouncing back and forth and Keith's gun falls out of his hand while trying to fight for his life. The killer reaches quickly and tries to fight back but doesn't let go of the wire. He doesn't want to give up that easily. Keith's never been a quitter by any means and loves a good fight.

Keith's left-hand starts to bleed, and he knows that he needs to escape this entrapment.

Minutes later the man in black releases the wire and tries to escape from Keith so he can get to his gun that's fully loaded and ready to be used. They both exchange punches; Keith can take a lot of blows without blinking an eye. The man suddenly takes his 9 mm gun out of his back and points it at the DEA agent. Then without a second thought, Keith punches the man's right arm in his ulner nerve, and he screams in pain.

"Bloody hell!" he shouts with a British accent.

Keith doesn't see what's happened to the gun. Both men are looking desperately for their guns. The man in black finally gets his gun back and points it at Keith.

"That's it!" the man shouts with a British accent.

But Keith, not thinking that his life is in danger, slaps away the gun from his hand and grabs his throat. The man suddenly fires a gunshot but it misses the target. Both Keith and the British man struggle to kill each other. They don't notice that they're now near the edge of the stairwell. It doesn't take long for them to fall down the stairs like tumbleweeds in the breeze.

It's amazing that the loaded gun is still in the man's hand. Keith tries to get the gun out of his grasp by biting him like an aggressive dog. The man breaks free and retaliates by pulling on Keith's badly scared left ear. He sees stars! Finally, both men break out of the hold and stand up at the same time, still wanting to fight and pulsing with the energy that you see in video games. Neither one of them wants to give in and die. Keith kicks the gun out of the man's hand. The man tries to get it, and Keith takes the man's good arm and twists it like a pretzel. Suddenly, Keith takes his right knee and jams it into the man's chest right into his sternum. Then there is another hit and another until the man falls to the floor. Keith rushes towards the gun but falls to the floor again because the man has Keith's ankle. The unmarked man starts to choke Keith forcefully. At the same time Keith grabs one of Colin's toys out of his right jean pocket and jams it into the man's throat. Suddenly the man lets go of Keith's neck and starts to choke himself. Keith gets up, and another man comes from behind and hits him in the head. But Keith doesn't do down. Instead, he turns around and punches the guy where the sun doesn't shine.

Unexpectedly shots are fired.

"Freeze! LAPD! Put the gun down slowly. Now!" says the police officer in uniform.

A flashlight shines into Keith's eyes and blinds his sight. He wouldn't dare disobey the officer's orders.

"Listen, I'm a DEA agent. I'm one of the good guys on your side," Keith answers but he doesn't think the officer cares.

Keith still has the gun in his hand.

"Sir, please, put the gun down slowly to the ground where I see it! Do it!" the officer orders.

"Okay…okay"

Keith slowly puts the gun down on the carpet that is redder then tan because of the blood redecorating the condo. He just realizes that it's the gun! He was holding the other man's gun that might've killed Treat. *Shit! I'm a dead man!! Keith, don't say anything that will put you in the paddy wagon to the big house!* He knows that he has very interesting "friends" that are waiting for him in jail. They will give him the red carpet treatment. We're not talking about the Hollywood scene!

"Please listen, my name is Keith Heiden. I'm a DEA agent!" he says again as he tries to override the officer's commands.

"I don't care who you are! Slowly, put your hands on the wall and spread your legs!"

Keith listens to the officer without a fight. He knows the routine very well. The officer pats him down for any other weapons or guns that he might have hiding in the mix. Then he takes out Keith's wallet from one of his pockets.

"Let's see what we have here," says the officer and looks at the identification card. "This is very interesting claiming that you're a DEA agent. That's some stuff!"

"Can I get out of this position?" Keith asks, as he feels very uncomfortable.

The cop laughs a little. Then other police officers in dark uniforms walk into the condo as well as homicide detectives wearing business suits. You can't really start "the party" after a murder without the Crime Scene Investigators.

"It's very odd that you're the only person that's alive in this condo! Why is that, Agent Handel, right?"

It's a normal reaction for that person to get upset if the other person is making a joke, reading, and saying your name wrong.

"Sorry, it's Agent Heiden," Keith answers as he tries to bite his tongue; what he really wants to say to the officer is "no, I don't know why I'm the only one alive. I guess it wasn't my day to die."

"You know being a smart ass gets you in jail," the officer snaps back.

"Thank you for the warning. Can I sit down? I really got beat up from these men with no names."

"Sure, but I'm watching you like a hawk." The police officer puts handcuffs on Keith just in case it goes south.

The young officer looks like he just came out of the police training academy. He's a typical Los Angeles police officer, wearing his shiny new uniform. He's standing tall and proud. Even at the height of 5'4". I wouldn't doubt it that his mommy polished his badge and pressed his uniform because he still lives at home. He must also get his lunch made and gas money every day before heading off to the mean streets like Skid Row (name of the streets where low income people live in LA).

Keith sits down slowly and shakes off the excess stress from this event. He tries very hard to focus on his future in jail that might happen after this day ends. He really wants to go home and sleep this nightmare away for good, but that won't happen because Artemis (It's origin is Greek and it means "god of the hunt.") Daly comes into the condo with a strained look on his face.

"Shit!" cries Artemis.

He really hates his job. He should've worked with his Uncle Chrysostom (his mom's brother) in the family business deli in Astoria, Queens, New York. But Artemis wanted something better. What he didn't know was that being a homicide detective was going to be a full-time job that had a lot of challenges both physically and emotionally. At this rate, he'll never get married to his girlfriend (Italian & Jewish) and him (Greek & Irish) to have little ones. His mom really wants grandkids. Every year on Mother's Day Artemis has to put on the card in Greek, "Sorry, Mom, maybe next year you will have some grandkids. I love you, Artemis."

Artemis is standing on the other side of the living room; he's trying to analyze his surroundings while giving Keith the evil eye. It's as if to say, "Don't worry, I'm coming to you very soon." Artemis really wants answers from the agent; it's going to be a very long night.

"A criminologist did a study that shows a large percentage of murders are committed by someone who knows the victim personally. It can be your lover or ex-lover, a friend that you owe money to and so it goes down the line." The Crime Scene Investigator says to Keith as she checks him for any injuries and takes pictures.

"I didn't know that," Keith answers, as he stands to make the CSI officer's job a little easier.

"Artemis, you have to look at this," shouts another officer standing by the staircase.

Artemis walks up the stairs without saying a single word.

"Artemis, this looks like a confession signed by Treat Miller," says the officer.

The letter is enclosed in a plastic ziplock bag. It's clear enough to read. Artemis takes the plastic bag and reads the letter. He's very interested in what it has to say.

> Dear Agent Heiden,
>
> I'm genuinely sorry that I caused pain between you and your wife. I didn't mean to fall in love with Justine and have sex. It just happened, and now I know I'm paying the price for my actions. You see, Jose Medina and Jude Henderson paid me to get your wife into my arms but not to bed until they said so. However, it was too late in that department. They paid me over a half million dollars for the job before I even pursued Justine. Both Jose and Jude were not happy, and they wanted their money back. Unfortunately, I already spent it by paying my student loans off. I loved Justine, but I knew they were going to kill me if they didn't get their money back soon. Once again I'm sorry. I really hope there are no hard feelings.
>
> I know many names of people in the drug crime family. Everything you need to know is in the envelope attached to this letter. I know

that will help in your investigation. Please keep this information in a very safe place. If this gets into the wrong hands, you will start a blood war against Alex Raninsky, Jude Henderson, and Joes Medina's cartel. They all want the LA territory for the drug sales. The one who gets it first is the winner! I guess you already know that part.

Please take this information and use it carefully, because I will be dead by the time you read this.

Sincerely,
Treat S. Miller

"Very interesting but I really need to have the handwriting analyzed to confirm that it is Treat Miller's writing. Collect all the paperwork of the deceased's handwriting in his condo to be analyzed," Artemis states to the officer and the Crime Scene Investigation team.

Peter walks into the condo with his photo identification saying that he's with the DEA department to a police officer, to let him through the yellow tape. Seconds later Peter sees Keith sitting on the couch and Artemis coming down the stairs ready to start asking questions of the only survivor from this messy situation.

"Okay, Keith. Please help me and fill in the blanks. There are three men murdered, and you're the only one that's alive," Artemis says with a concerned look.

"I guess it wasn't my time to die."

Artemis clears his throat and tries very hard not to get angry at Keith. He needs all the information that the witness might have. So if he has to get nice and friendly to get the job done quickly, so be it.

"I just found a fascinating letter from Treat Miller. It was like a confession or something. But we have to take it to the lab to get it analyzed to see if the letter came from Treat. Until then maybe you can help me fill in the blanks, because the truth of the matter is, I'm stuck." Artemis takes another breath and continues. "What I read from this letter is that he, Treat, and your wife were having a love affair that went on for a year or so. Is this statement true?"

"Sorry, Artemis. I really can't help you, because I might be a suspect in three murders, and I don't want to say anything that might incriminate me. So I want to talk to my lawyer."

"You're an ass, Heiden. You are not arrested as of yet, but the way you are talking to me and co-workers it might happen. Believe it or not, I want to help you not hurt you. We've something in common. We're both good friends of Peter's. You know he's in the middle of this sticky situation."

"Go to hell, Artemis!"

"Okay, we'll play it your way for now but believe me I'll get what I want!"

Artemis walks away leaving Keith alone with the young officer in the living room. He walks toward Peter, who's standing like a sore thumb with a look of confusion.

"Talk to your maggot friend before I bring him downtown," orders Artemis.

"Artemis, you have to listen to me! Keith wouldn't kill anyone without a good reason for doing so. I have a strong feeling this was self-defense, not murder. I'll talk to him but he might not talk because he knows his rights and he'll stick by them," Peter replies, as he feels that he picks up all of Keith's messes.

"I really don't care how you get the answers. Just get something so I don't look like an ass in my department!" Artemis shouts.

He really can't stand stupid of any kind. This includes poor, rich, or middle-class people. Artemis and Peter watch Keith strip down to his boxes because the forensic team wants to collect evidence to build a case for the district attorney's office. The CSI officer holds a very large bag so Keith can put his clothes into it without problems. Another CSI officer takes blood and gunpowder from Keith's hands.

During this time three body bags are taken out on hospital stretchers. The bodies are escorted out to the LA coroner's office so they can start the identification process and perform autopsies.

"Okay, Peter, I'll get all the answers from you instead of your annoying friend," Artemis answers, as he sees Keith from the corner of his tired eyes.

He's getting dressed in medical scrubs to go home. The CSI took everything except his boxers for evidence.

"Okay, fine. What do you want to know?" Peter snaps back.

"Well, my childhood friend, why was Mr. Heiden at Treat's home at three in the morning? Don't you think it was a little early to say hello?"

"Listen, Artemis, Keith and Treat were not best of friends. It's hard to explain but not everyone on this planet likes each other."

"Okay, did Treat have a love affair with Keith's wife?" Artemis asks.

"Yes… I guess they were together about a year or so. I really don't know why Keith would come to Treat's place and say hello at this hour. I know I don't get paid to babysit him," Peter answers.

"Peter, I need you to be honest with me. Do you think that Keith killed Treat Miller in the name of revenge?" Artemis asks.

"No," Peter answers but he's really lying.

"Listen, I'll find out the truth one way or another. Just get out of my way," Artemis states.

Artemis walks away from Peter leaving him alone in the hallway.

"All right, Heiden, you can go home but don't leave town," Artemis orders, as he knows that he doesn't have anything to hold him or until the evidence shows otherwise.

"Artemis, they took my sneakers! I don't have anything to wear on my feet! I can't walk anywhere until I have something for my feet!"

"Well, you have a problem on your hands now, don't you?" Artemis laughs at the situation.

He looks around to find shoes for Keith and comes back with doggie slippers.

"These might fit. Try them and see how they feel. Don't worry, I'll clear these slippers from evidence."

"You're a pal, Artemis! I don't know what I'd do without you and your merry men!" Keith snaps, as he tries to put on the smelly slippers. "You've got to be kidding me!"

"Listen, leave my area so the police and I can work. We'll be in touch real soon."

"Fine," Keith answers, as he gets his keys, cell phone, and wallet from the coffee table.

Keith walks out of the condo, trying to avoid any laughter from the nosy crowd, or any newsmen on the scene who are waiting to get the hottest story in LA!

CHAPTER
SEVENTY-ONE

*K*eith comes home around 6:00 a.m. and quickly gets undressed. He falls fast asleep and doesn't even realize where Justine is.

Justine turns on the TV, and the news come on about Treat Miller's murder.

"Oh my God!" Justine shouts and wakes up Keith from a deep sleep.

"What?!" he asks with surprise.

"You killed Treat! Oh my God, you killed him!" She shouts.

Keith jumps out of bed like the house is on fire. He puts his right hand over her mouth and whispers in her ear, "Shut up, woman! I didn't kill the little bastard! Someone killed him before I got there. You've got to believe me!" Keith blinks rapidly. "I'm going to let go now. Don't you dare scream for mercy and wake up the kids. I'm going to let go. Do not, I mean, do not yell."

Justine shakes her head up and down. She agrees not to make a stupid move because she's dealing with an unstable man. He gently takes his hand off Justine's mouth.

"You killed him!!"

"Listen, shut up before the police come knocking on the door and take us both away in white straightjackets. I didn't kill your lover."

Keith takes a deep breath and says, "Please tell me the truth about your relationship with your father."

Keith can't believe that Sir. William would go all out to destroy his daughter's marriage. Most of all Justine has damaged Keith's heart. It feels like a sharp knife has gone through it, because it hurts so much.

"What does that have to do with killing Treat?" Justine asks with a snappy tone and confused look.

"Now everything comes in full circle! I'm a jackass for not knowing what's under my nose this whole time. You didn't have one affair but two affairs! It kills my heart! Is your dad your pimp? Because I know your daddy paid for your affairs, and he doesn't even realize this is wrong on any level! Especially being pregnant with Treat's child or maybe someone else's! I don't want to know anymore. I can't look you straight in your eyes. I guess I wasted about twenty-three years of my life building a relationship and falling in love with you. Now having a family together makes it more difficult to break up with you without feeling guilty in the end."

"Keith, you don't understand the true story about what happened," Justine pleads her case once again.

"Oh, my God! I finally realize why your dad did what he did, because you told him about our huge fight ten years ago. Payback was the only answer Sir [not his real title] William knew. He was trying to get me out of the picture for good. I can't believe that you agreed with this crazy plan. You guys are a lot alike in many ways and it's very scary," Keith says, as he knows that he's not likable to many people, but for his own family not liking him is very hard to digest.

"Yes, he knows what happened ten years ago because he had a feeling that something bad happened between us," she answers.

"Sir William bribed you not once but twice to leave me. I guess he and your mom would've helped you raise our kids without me. Everything makes sense now. I'm the subject that has to be taken care of," Keith replies.

Out of the blue, Justine starts to cry, but it's not because she got caught in a sick game. She's crying because she really loved Treat and can't believe that he's gone forever. Keith killed him, and it's doesn't make the situation any easier.

"I can't believe you!" Keith shouts with a confused look. "You're crying over the tart! You don't give me a chance to plead my case that I didn't kill him, but you have a second to cry! You've some nerve. You'll never change! You're like my father, a cold heartless individual! You make me sick to my stomach!" Keith shouts.

"What do you want from me? I'm so confused! I'm not that cold, heartless bitch that a lot of people think I am!! I love you and I want you to understand!" Justine pleads, as she gets a couple of tissues from her nightstand.

"Oh, please, Justine! I'm so tired of your shit! I didn't kill Treat but I have a bigger problem. I think that Jose Medina's men killed Treat. He's after my blood and it's going to be war."

"Are you telling me that Jose Medina's men killed Treat Miller because of you?"

Keith sits on the edge of the bed and takes a deep breath.

"Treat Miller was hired by Jose Medina. They had Treat lure you into his arms but not to sleep with you. That wasn't the plan. They paid him a lot of money to do the job and mess with my personal life. So they wanted to destroy my life! Treat didn't do the job right so they killed him. He confessed everything in a letter. Also there's important information needed to take the drug lords down. I know that you don't believe me but it's true," he solemnly answers, as he looks at his wife that still has her mouth wide open.

"Oh my God. It was a set-up?" Justine says, as she starts to sit next to Keith on the bed to comfort their pain together.

"Yes, I'm sorry but what I'm telling you is true."

"Why are you saying sorry to me?" Justine asks, as she puts her hand on his hand.

"I don't know. I guess because I got you into this mess," Keith solemnly says.

"I'm sorry, Keith, that I let you down, but I'm not going to apologize for having feelings for Treat," Justine states, as she walks in front of her husband.

"So we are back to square one! That's great, Justine! What's the point of our marriage? You're incredible!" Keith announces.

"Sorry, Keith. You have to give me space, and please understand what I'm going through!" Justine pleads.

Deep down inside she's very much in love with Treat and Keith, but in different ways. Treat used to console her needs with emotional support, but Keith provides for her financially. The sad part about it, however, is that she needs two different men in order to get what she wants to make her happy.

He pulls away from his very controlling wife.

"You've got to be shitting me!" Keith shouts, as he's never shy about cursing out loud to get his point across. "You're out of your mind like everyone thinks you are! Don't talk to me!"

"Keith, please listen! It's going to take me some time to believe that you didn't kill Treat. Is there evidence to prove this? Keith, do you hear me?" Justine exclaims.

"I guess I don't have a choice. Have you heard of Artemis Daly? He's Peter's friend. Well, he's heading the investigation, and I'm not sure if I'm going to jail or not. But he did warn me not to leave the state. I'm exhausted from all the drama, and now I'm going to bed," Keith answers, as he doesn't care one bit what Justine thinks.

Keith doesn't really want to fight anymore; he's physically and emotionally tired. It's sad that this family is falling apart because they are so dysfunctional.

CHAPTER
SEVENTY-TWO

~~~~~~

*T*eams from different departments of law enforcement (DEA and ATF agents, LAPD and LA SWAT) have their instructions and have been debriefed to take down Alex Raninsky and his men. There's a warrant for their arrest on ten counts of drug and gun trafficking, sale, and supply on the streets. If the raid is successful, the estimated amount of contraband taken off the streets for this one deal is about three million dollars.

The teams (LAPD and LA SWAT, DEA, and ATF agents) are surrounding the factory just waiting for the ice cream trucks to leave the building. Just business as usual!

"Peter, what are we waiting for?" Liam asks while he looks at his watch that says 9:37 a.m.

"Agent Gallagher, just hold your pez!." Peter says, as he sees the action through his binoculars. "Liam, what is your location??"

"We are near the rear of the building just waiting for the go ahead. I really have a funny feeling we're behind schedule."

"Why do you say that?"

"Because it's too quiet!"

"Listen, I have my orders from Agent Bailey and Ross. Let's just wait a little bit and see what happens," answers Peter. *Where the hell are you guys? Come out! Let's play!*

"That's fine, but something smells bad," Liam responds. "What happened to Agent Forrester? I heard from the government grapevine that he retired and didn't say goodbye to his co-workers. Is this true or did I get the wrong information from the wrong grapevine?"

"Sad to say but it's true. He left without giving anyone notice. I just found out from the Human Resource Department a couple of days ago that he's gone. He didn't even get to eat his good-bye cake. I guess he wanted to go to DC and become that congressman or senator for the state of California," Peter answers, as he waits for some action to begin. "He's a very odd bird."

"That's a true statement! It would be very sad if Forrester is our next president." Liam laughs.

"If that happens, I'm moving to Canada or Europe! Somewhere out of here!" Peter laughs as he continues to eye the building in front of him. "If I go to Mexico, I think the people will smell me out as a DEA agent!"

Suddenly without warning the factory garage door opens.

"GO!!" Peter shouts. Flashbang grenades go off.

The LA SWAT team is fully armed and protected. They enter the building quickly.

The call of "Police!" shouts out from all corners of the warehouse as officers burst in.

SWAT, DEA, ATF, and LAPD teams all enter the building. They have their Glock pistols, Beretta 92, and other military assault weapon just to be one step ahead of the bad guys on a good day. The flashbang smoke clears in less than a minute; shots are firing. You can barely hear conversations coming from the different radios, as everyone in the law enforcement team has to be on the same page or this raid won't work in their favor.

One officer says, "Take cover!"

Raninsky's men are fighting hard and saying things back and forth in Russian.

Another officer says, "What's your status team B?"

"We are near the ice cream truck but there's nothing to report that's unusual," says an LAPD officer, as he looks inside and sees nothing but empty containers.

Raninsky's men reach the second floor level in the warehouse. Now they're shooting below and getting clear shots at the law enforcement pigs. Alex's men love a great fight and will die rather than go to prison. Their only concept of prison is a Russian gulag.

In less than thirty minutes many of Alex's men are dead while others are alive but pretty shook up. Peter finally shuts the operation down. The Russians are handcuffed with plastic zip cuffs.

"It's over, gentlemen. I think you know the drill," he says in English and then in Russian just in case they didn't hear him the first time.

Peter orders his men by walkie-talkie to close up shop and get ready to leave within the hour.

"No problem, Agent Darling!" answers an officer.

An hour passes and the DEA and LA police find nothing to incriminate Raninsky. A grim day for the DEA Department. A lot of agents are packing up their gear heading back to the department. Agent Darling walks out of the building and sees a lady standing in the middle of the road wearing a light summer dress.

Julia Ulrich? Peter says to himself. Then he finally realizes that his mind is playing tricks on him. She has been on his mind a lot lately, especially after their recent meeting.

CHAPTER
SEVENTY-THREE

*P*eter's cell phone rings in his tactical uniform black pants pocket and takes it out to answer it.

"Hello."

Then out of the blue he hears the sound of a voice from the past. "Hello, Peter. It's me, Julia Ulrich."

"Hello, Julia. How did you get my cell phone?"

"You gave me your cell phone number when we last met," she says as she lies through her teeth.

Justine gave Julia Peter's cell number while they were having a lovely lunch at the Santa Monica Pier, but he doesn't have to know the details.

"Lately I was thinking about you. I just wanted to know if you want to meet again…maybe for coffee or something," Julia asks like a shy teenager, as she stands in her living room which overlooks the Pacific Ocean.

She has a great view as she looks out the window of her million dollar house.

"Peter, I just want to tell you up front that I still love you and have never stopped loving you. Even though our lives are different now and we have nothing in common, I think we are made for each other. You've heard the saying that opposites attract. I know you have feelings for me, because I could sense that the last time we meet… Peter, I finally realize that I was a fool for letting you go, and I will never forgive myself for that. So what do you think? Can we try again??"

Peter walks to the company SUV and sits in the driver's seat. He can usually talk to anyone about anything, but now he is at a loss for words. Peter can't believe that he's talking to his long-lost ex-girlfriend. He turns on the SUV and puts his cell phone on speakers as he drives away.

"Oh well, Julia, you're putting me up against the wall. I did have feelings for you but it has been over ten years since we broke up. I'm sorry, but if you remember you broke it off with me. You made it perfectly clear that we had no future. So I've moved on, and I'm in a new relationship. I'm sorry," Peter replies.

"Please, Peter. We have a history together. I really think we can work it out. Please rethink what you're saying," Julia pleads. "I love you, and I never stopped loving you."

"Julia, you're great and I love you, but it has been over ten years. You broke my heart, and I've never been the same since. I'm sorry, Julia. Good-bye and I wish you all the best." Peter cries, whiles he feels a pain in his heart.

"I know you were sad because Justine told me so," she states, as she sits on the patio chair and watches people passing by on the beach enjoying the great California weather.

"What did you say? Justine... Is her last name Heiden?" Peter sharply asks while he sits straight up in the driver's seat.

"What does her last name have to do anything?" Julia asks sharply.

"Her last name is a major factor in this conversation because you brought it up."

"Peter, why are you getting angry?"

"Because Keith is my best friend and Justine is his wife. You just put me in a sticky situation. My life is not an open book to you and a conversation piece at the dinner table. So what was said between you girls? Julia, you have no right to play with my feelings!"

Peter is angry, and he has every reason to be.

"Yes, Justine Heiden is still my best friend. There I said it! I don't think there's any harm in it. Justine tells me updates about your life. I'm just concerned, and I still love you. Anyway, I finally realized I made a terrible mistake. Please, Peter, understand. I'm sorry for everything. I want you back! Please don't be angry with me because I want you, and I know you want the same thing!" Julia cries, as tears run down her cheeks.

"Julia, I can't do this right now! Please don't... Listen I have to go. Good-bye," Peter says sadly, as his heart hurts the same way it did ten years ago.

CHAPTER
SEVENTY-FOUR

*H*ours later Peter is debriefed. He takes a long overdue hot shower at the company's gym. An hour later Peter walks up to Nicole's desk and sees her working like a busy beaver.

"Hi, Nicole. Is your boss in the office?" he asks softly while he pops another Pez candy in his mouth.

"Hello, Agent Darling. I'm sorry, but he just stepped out for a minute, but he'll be back soon. Is there anything that I can help you with?" she asks while writing something on a hot pink post-it note.

Before he can answer Nicole's question, Keith walks into the office without giving Peter second a glance. Peter follows his partner.

"Keith, I need to talk to you about your wife!"

"Why do you want to talk about her?" Keith asks, as he sits himself down behind his desk.

"Justine recently spoke to Julia Ulrich about my relationship! Julia wants to rekindle our love that she broke off ten years ago!" Peter shouts, as he stands waiting for an answer from Keith. As he well knows he'll be waiting for a very long time.

"Oh. How is Julia Ulrich?"

"Remember my ex-girlfriend from ten years ago? Now she's Patrick's doctor at the hospital!"

"Oh that. Sorry I wanted to tell you that she's Patrick and the other kids' family doctor. Sorry again for not telling you and also that you're having problems in the women department. Honestly, I really don't know anything about their (Justine & Julia's) conversations. Yes, they're best friends and that never ended because your relationship was over a long time ago. They might go out to lunch or dinner from time to time. This is all I know," Keith announces while he starts to type his reports. "It's very sad but women talk and they talk about everything that's on their pretty little minds, and believe me I know! I have two of my own at home!"

"Oh please! Why didn't you tell me that Justine and Julia are friends?" Peter shouts.

"Why does it matter? Your relationship was over a long time ago. You know how women are! Also you should know by now that I have no control over Justine! Please, Peter, I have a lot of work to do. I bet your work is on your desk waiting for you," Keith answers, as he looks at his partner with concern.

Peter rolls his light brown eyes at him and says, "Please, Keith, I really need you to understand that my love life is being played with and I want answers! Why did Justine do this? Did you tell Justine about me and Dr. Sheppard dating?" Peter asks with a sharp tone.

"What?" asks Keith as he stops typing and looks directly at Peter.

"Did you tell Justine about me and my newfound love?" Peter asks forcefully.

"I guess, I don't remember! You're wasting my time as always! I have a lot of work to do," Keith answers, as he starts typing on the computer again.

"Fine! I'll talk to Justine and get my answers out of her," Peter states as he walks toward the door.

"Peter, you're asking for trouble but go ahead if you want to, I wish you luck!" Keith laughs because he knows all too well what Peter is up against dealing with Justine.

"I can handle Justine. It's Julia that I'm worried about," Peter answers. "Are you going home tonight?"

"Peter, I just started work! You know that I have the night shift! I'll leave in the morning."

"Okay, I'll talk to you later."

Then suddenly out of the blue Keith says something that quickly stops Peter in his tracks.

"Peter, you know it's not your fault. You were ambushed at the ice cream raid. This is why you didn't get all the goods and Alex Raninsky's head on a platter."

Keith stands up and sees Todd from his office glass door window. Todd is talking to some co-worker, and Keith doesn't know the other person's name.

"Did you ever hear the saying 'loose lips sink ships'?"

Peter makes a strange face. "Yes, and why are you asking a silly question like that?"

"Because I know that the agents didn't leak any information about the raid but the office staff is a different story all together," Keith pounders.

Peter slowly walks up to Keith.

"Keith, what are you saying? That the staff in the DEA leaks out information? It sounds interesting but can you prove it?"

Peter thinks to himself that Keith has had crazy ideas in the past, and they worked for him. It's a surprise how this agent boy thinks.

"I think I can prove it. What's Todd's wife's maiden name?"

"How the hell should I know? You know Todd's wife is the leak just because she's Russian, and Alex came from the same country?" Peter says.

"Preston Williamson from Interpol said that there might be a leak in the DEA Department and he was right! I have a strong feeling that something is going to happen, and it's not good but DEA is ready for a challenge and won't go down without a fight. Do you know Todd's wife's maiden name? Can you get that information to me as soon as possible without anyone knowing about it? If the information is correct we have to close the leak before it is out in the open," Keith says without taking a break to breathe.

"How would I know about Todd's wife's maiden name? Todd and I talk by passing in the hallway, but I don't think that he can tell stories to anyone especially his wife. Yes, there are a lot of Russians that live in America, but it's a very slim chance that Anastasia and Alex are related. Keith, you're getting rusty in your old age!" Peter laughs as he leans back in a comfortable chair.

"Todd wants so bad to be that federal agent that tells stories on campus and at home to his wife. I really don't trust Todd. He's little and angry," Keith exclaims because he's very close to the core from this major setback in the department. They lost the bad guys and the goods that were worth millions of dollars.

"Okay you win. I'll try to get you the information about Todd's wife and Raninsky, but it might take a while," Peter answers, as he can hear Todd's little nerdy voice shouting.

He says through the glass office windows, "No one is taking me seriously! You know without me you guys would be screwed. I'm giving you fair warning! Don't mess with my department or me."

Todd is standing like a sore thumb, and people are looking but walking past him at the same time. It's like he's a crazy man on the city street.

"Now I'm interested to see how this plays out," Peter says as he sees the little nerd waiting for someone to hug him.

"It's going to be very interesting, that's for sure," Keith answers with a smile, as if to say I'm on to you! It's just a matter of time!

"Okay, I'm going!" Peter shouts.

"I have a huge problem on my hands, and I don't have an easy answer to fix it," Keith says as he takes a deep breath and says for the first time out loud, "Justine is pregnant."

Peter suddenly turns his body away from the door and says, "Come on, man! I was almost at the door!"

"Congratulations!"

"Thanks, but the baby isn't mine," Keith answers as he can feel the sigh of pain in his heart. He needs to talk to someone, and sadly it's Peter at the moment.

"Damn! Are you sure it's not yours?"

"Yes, I'm sure. Let's leave it at that."

"What are you going to do now?" Peter asks with a concerned look. He's thrilled that he doesn't have Keith's life.

"I don't know. Justine claims that she's in love with both Treat and me."

"Well, the problem is fixed, Treat's dead and you're still alive. So, right now she's in love with you not the one in the county morgue," Peter answers.

"Thank you for clarifying the situation. I've been playing with my lawyer's business card all morning. I'm fighting with myself to call him and to have him file divorce papers. My mind is telling me to do it but my heart is saying no. What should I do? I'm so confused!" Keith says with a stricken look on his face.

"I'm sorry, Keith, but I don't have answers for you. What are you going to do?"

"Boy, I must be fully damaged, because I still love her from the day I asked her to marry me. Peter, I made major decisions all my life, some worked out in my favor and some didn't. I'm so confused. I don't have any answers. I'm really stuck," Keith answers honesty.

"Listen you know you can't stay married to Justine because of the kids' sake. They are tough as nails. They have yours and Justine's DNA flowing. The question is, what do you want regarding happiness?" Peter asks.

"Well, Dr. Sheppard got into your mind. You're thinking like a doctor that handles mental health problems, or you drank really great coffee this morning?" Keith says.

"Maybe a little bit of both," Peter answers with a laugh.

Peter doesn't want to see Keith's family fall apart, but it's not his call to make. It's Keith's decision. There's no happy answer to this situation.

"Whatever you do, Keith, I'm behind you to help you if you need me," Peter answers.

"Thanks, Peter, it means a lot. I know that you love Justine and me too. I really don't want you to be in the middle of my drama if I decide to end the marriage."

"Keith, I'm a big boy! I can handle myself and hustle any situation especially your family. I really want to be there if the kids need me, especially Colin," Peter honestly answers as he can feel the sadness that's coming out of Keith.

"Thanks, Peter, I still don't know what to do. If we stay in this so-called marriage, we need to see a therapist. He or she, the doctor of mental health, will get their money's worth dealing with us. Justine is so stubborn in her ways it's hard to get anything out of her, especially fixing our marriage. She did more damage than me, and she won't admit that she did anything wrong on her part. It makes me sick that I feel like a hamster on the spinning wheel and can never get off," Keith says, as he feels a lot of pain in his heart and a couple of aspirins won't be able to fix it.

CHAPTER
SEVENTY-FIVE

Out of the blue Todd starts yelling, and it's getting louder. Keith and Peter look in the direction of the drama that is unfolding through the glass window.

"There's something very wrong with that guy," says Keith.

"He has little man issues, and no one takes him seriously," Peter laughs, as he sees Todd waving his arms with emotion as of he's ready to fly into the air.

Keith looks at Peter and has an idea that just came to his mind.

"I will get the information," Peter answers.

"Listen, the reason why the raid went south was because they were tipped off that you and other law enforcement agents were coming. I bet that they left a day or two earlier to make their move and get away," Keith answers.

"Okay, if that's the case, why haven't we heard any news of people keeling over from the drugs that were sold on the street from the ugly ice cream man!"

"Maybe they changed their plans at the last minute. Maybe they sold it outside of the Los Angeles area. We're checking into it as we speak. I think they're going into hiding because plan "A" didn't work out for them and plan "B" was the only option they had right now. They really don't want to get caught by the cops, because they can taste victory at the end of the race. What do you think?" Keith asks, as he knows things happen for a reason and it makes sense.

It's like playing chess; you have to be one step ahead of your opponent to live another day.

"I guess. So when do I find out about Anastasia and Alex? What do we do next?" Peter asks because he's still confused.

"Anastasia might be related or had a run in with Alex in the past. So that's why you need to get additional information about her last name and her history."

CHAPTER
SEVENTY-SIX

*T*wenty ice cream trucks finally reached their hiding place but it took a lot of planning to get everyone safe and not caught by cops. They drove to an underground drainage tunnel to hide the vehicles. Alex Raninsky comes out of one of the ice cream trucks while smoking a very smelly cider. He's so pleased with the job that he and his men pulled off, that he can't stop smiling and laughing out in the open. He walks with a slight limp, but it doesn't stop his happiness of fortune and power that he has the upper hand in the race against Mr. Jude Herrendson to get Jose Medina's cartel and territory. It wasn't easy at all to win the game but now it's done. Jose will be very happy and pleased that this business will carry on with his name still in play as the big guy from Mexico.

Alex shouts in Russian, "Gentlemen, we did a very great job! You should all be proud of yourselves, and we sold the drugs in less than an hour time frame. We did it! The job is successful with a few men dead but it's all in a days work! To Mother Russia!" He takes a bottle of 100 percent pure vodka and raises it in the air for the world to see that they are the badasses of Russia.

"To Mother Russia!" All the men shout out loud as the sound echoes throughout the tunnel.

Alex's cell phone rings, "Hello."

"Alex are you okay?" Anastasia asks in Russian.

"Yes, my dearest cousin. It's a great day for Russia! We should be proud!"

"Good we must celebrate," Anastasia states, as she sees her nerdy husband walking down the block and heading towards their one-bedroom apartment. "Alex, we must quickly talk because Todd is coming home any minute now."

"Anastasia, don't forget to kill your husband before you leave for good," Alex says.

"It will be done. Anyway, I'm sick of looking at his nerdy face. He thinks he's all man, but he's a sewer rat." She laughs and Alex laughs too. "Don't worry about me, just get out of this country. I'll go dark until Jose Medina gives you the key to his business. Don't forget to kill Jude once you have the drug business in your hands."

"Yes… Yes, I know! Please meet me at the safe point by tomorrow morning. Join us and celebrate our huge victory! I love you, Anastasia. Please be careful and watch your back especially for cops. Also cover yourself after killing Todd."

"I'll watch my back and see you tomorrow. I'll call you when I'm near you," Anastasia answers, as she packs up quickly, ready to leave town for good and never look back.

"Honey, bunny I'm home!" Todd shouts.

He notices something strange; Anastasia's suit case is in the hallway. Suddenly she walks out of the room and faces Todd for the last time. She takes out her 4mm gun from between her sexy long legs. Todd sees the barrel of the gun, and he's unable to talk to fight for this life.

She says something in Russian as one tear runs down her smooth cheek. She pulls the trigger and suddenly Todd falls on the wooden floor with a bullet straight between his eyes. They are open, lifeless, and she walks over his head without a second thought. Anastasia takes any money that he has in his wallet.

Hours later Anastasia has meet Alexander Raninsky at the secert location.

"Welcome please come in! Alex is waiting for you!"

"Anastasia, did you kill Todd before you came?" Alex asks.

"Yes, Alex, and I took care of the body too. Don't worry there's no traces coming back to me," Anastasia states.

"Good, you're safe here, and no one will get you. We are family and will die for a cause!" Alex kisses Anastasia on the cheeks. "Let's eat and celebrate out good fortune! To Mother Russia!"

"To Mother Russia!" they all shout out loud.

CHAPTER
SEVENTY-SEVEN

"Keith!" Peter says as he almost passes by him in the hallway at work.

Keith stops in his tracks, turns around, and looks at Peter without saying a single word.

"Here's an update on the news about Todd. I'm sorry to say he was murdered, and his wife is missing. I also found out that Anastasia and Alex are cousins on their mom's side. It seems like Anastasia killed our little tech man and then went underground with Alex," Peter states. "We've sent out an APB [all points bullets]. Hopefully, we can find them before they go back to Russia. Unfortunately, many people got sick from the drugs that were hidden in the ice cream trucks. By the time the police arrived, everyone was gone."

"Yes, I heard the news. I'm not surprised about Todd and Anastasia. I knew that something was not right. I'm sorry to hear about Todd. He was odd but knew his work inside and out," Keith answers with a sigh.

"Did you get a chance to call your lawyer yet?" Peter asks.

"No, not yet. Justine has terrible morning sickness from her pregnancy. I don't want to put the subject of divorce under her nose right now. She's already down. The kids are staying at my in-laws for a few days so she can rest, because she really has it bad. I'm having a difficult time just watching her go through this again."

"That's bad?"

"Yes, very bad. During her pregnancies, her cravings have always been dill pickles and vanilla ice cream together."

"Oh my God! That's gross! How can you kiss that?" Peter makes a strange face.

"I don't."

CHAPTER
SEVENTY-EIGHT

〰〰〰〰〰〰〰〰〰〰〰〰〰〰〰〰〰〰〰〰〰〰〰〰〰〰〰〰〰〰〰〰

*T*wo hours later, Keith leaves work and starts to drive on Highway 101 as the traffic is getting heavier. It's always a common thing in California. Finally, Keith picks up speed and reaches sixty-five miles per hour (the speed limit for this state). It doesn't seem like there's any gridlock ahead.

Twenty minutes later the traffic slows down, but for some strange reason Keith's SUV is not slowing down in speed. His right foot is way down on the brake pedal, as he can feel the numbness creeping up to his brain. Keith has to think quickly, or he's a dead man. Thank God he has the company's government SUV; he turns on the lights and sirens, but nothing seems to work. It's never a good sign when things don't work in your favor. Someone must have tampered with the brakes, lights, and siren. Keith should start to pray to the man upstairs because no one down on earth is helping him now.

"Shit!" Keith shouts as he can feel his stress level reaching the danger zone.

He is now zipping through traffic, on his left, to the right, trying to avoid any accidents along the way. Then out of the blue Keith looks in his rearview mirror and sees what no driver in the world wants to see. However, this may be his saving grace! California Highway Patrol Officers are tailing Keith's SUV and their flashing lights are on.

"You, in the black SUV pull over now!" the police officer orders through the intercom.

Keith is still in the same sticky situation as before with no brakes. He would love to pull over to end this nightmare.

How will Keith get the officer's attention without being shot in the process?

Minutes later, Keith's cell rings. He presses on the speaker button. "Hello!"

"Hello, this is Office Banks from the LA Highway Patrol. Is your name Agent Keith Heiden from DEA?"

"Yes, I have no brakes! I can't stop!"

"Okay, let me go in front of you, and I'll try to stop your vehicle!" answers the officer, as he can feel his heart beating faster. "Stay on the line! Don't hang up! I'll talk you through this situation!"

"Okay!"

The police car speeds up in front of Keith and then slows down to match the SUV's speed. Thank God the vehicles are letting the officer pass by so he can make his job easier. But it's the gas tanker that's a mile ahead of them that should be a concern. Suddenly three other police cars join in. Two of them are on the side of the SUV and one behind.

The SUV collides into the back of the police car with full force. The young police officer tries to press on the brake pedal, as the police car's tires are burning rubber which you smell a mile away. Keith's knuckles are turning ghostly white from holding onto the steering wheel with such force.

"Hello!"

"Is the SUV's speed going down?" the police officer says.

"Not yet!!"

"Okay. I think it will take a couple of minutes for the speed to slow down. Try to stay in the lane the best you can and enjoy the ride," the police officer answers nervously.

The police officer can feel the car making funny noises, and that's never a good sign. The huge gas tanker is coming closer. Suddenly four other police cars speed by and pass Keith and the officer. The patrol cars are trying to make a lot of room in front of Keith. To make matters worse there is a police helicopter in the air covering the scene. Once again it looks like one of those famous Californian car chases.

Suddenly Keith's SUV starts to slow down and gradually stops. The SUV and patrol car are still stuck totally together at the hip from bumper to bumper. Then out of the blue, the SUV lights and sirens turn on and surprise the two men.

A couple of days later Keith is still shaken up. He has to be strong and shake off the uneasy feeling that he was almost killed!

CHAPTER
SEVENTY-NINE

*P*eter and Elise finally move in together. They have also agreed to live in his place because it's bigger than her apartment. It's also closer to where she works. Elise will really miss her friends but will try her best to keep in touch. They all have a special place in her heart. She left her family and friends back home in Connecticut to follow her dream on the West Coast and become a successful therapist.

Elise's phone rings. "Dr. Sheppard."

"Hello, Elise. It's Jonathan. Remember me?" he asks with a happy voice.

"Hello, Jonathan. How was D.C.?" she asks while she puts on her old sneakers. Peter looks at her with a smile as he passes by with another box that says odds and ends written in black magic marker. He puts down the box and out of the blue spanks Elise on her rear end because he wanted to, and she's wearing those tight jeans with holes in the knees. Elise can turn Peter on.

Elise gives him a stern look and a smile at the same time; what she's really saying is "This isn't the time!"

"Elise, are you there? What was that sound?" Jonathan asks.

"Sorry, Jonathan… It's nothing… What were you saying?" Elise asks, as she once again rubs her backside that must endure Peter's playfulness.

"D.C. was fun but hard work at the same time. Elise, the reason I'm calling is to ask you to come into my office before you start work tomorrow. I really need to talk to you about something, and it can't be done over the phone," Jonathan says with a calm voice.

Elise's complaint file against Agent Heiden is in front of Jonathan. He wasn't pleased after reading it. He was only gone a few weeks and all this drama happened while he was away on business. This makes the department look bad. Jonathan is so tired from speaking with Congress and telling them how mental health care is important. Congress wants to cut the mental health department by 20 percent and that's not good for Jonathan and the staff. This problem with Elise is going to affect everyone in the office.

"Jonathan, can you please tell me a little bit about this meeting?" Elise asks.

Peter walks around the apartment while looking at Elise. He listens carefully and tries not to make any noises.

"We will talk when you come into the office. Come at 9:00 a.m. tomorrow. Please don't be late," Jonathan orders. "I'll talk to you soon. Have a good day."

She starts to pace back and forth throughout the living room..

"Elise, please stop pacing and talk to me. You look like you're going to explode any minute now! What did he say to you? Do you have any idea?" Peter asks, as he puts down another moving box on the carpet and walks over to Elise.

Peter hugs Elise as he knows very well that she's about to cry. It's like clockwork.

"Peter, I think your best friend called Jonathan about the events that happened. I'm in big trouble, and I don't know what to do!" Elise cries.

"Are you sure? Did he tell you that? Are you just guessing? Elise, I know that being dramatic is part of every woman's DNA, but you need to breathe before you pass out!" Peter laughs.

Peter guides Elise to the couch, as he tries to console a professional doctor who handles mental health problems for a living. It's only a matter of time before she'll be wearing a snow white straight jacket.

"Peter, I really don't know what to do! Jonathan didn't tell me exactly what he wants to talk about. I bet it has to do with Keith

Heiden and his family. The next topic is our relationship! You know for a fact that meetings never end well," Elise answers hoarsely.

"I think you're taking this whole situation out of the ballpark. I bet he just wants to see you and give you some extra work or something like that! I think I remember you telling me that he still has a crush on you! But there are no openings in the love department. I also think that he's a lonely middle-aged man that likes you a lot but never got to first or second base with you or any other girl for that matter. Jonathan is the kind of guy that's married to his job because he's not married with kids. It's sad but it happens to a lot of people. As for me I'm not the kind of person who wants to care for little people of my own. I just need a girlfriend beside me and to live life to the fullest," Peter states.

"Maybe marriage down the road?" Elise tactfully hints.

"Maybe… Listen, please don't sweat the little stuff in life. Everything has a meaning, and we're made for each other. Maybe it's a good thing that Jonathan knows. Maybe you can break the rule that you can separate personal from business life. As for me I can handle myself and keep both job and personal life separate. I know it's going to be hard but it can be done," Peter answers. "What do you think? Do you think we can change these stuffy government people and make the rule go away?"

"Peter, thank you for your positive words, but people still won't understand our relationship especially our bosses. Remember, Peter, it's a solid rule from both departments. We're not to date agents or therapists!" she retorts in frustration.

"Yes… yes, I heard it all, but I still believe we can turn this rule around because we're happy and we're not hurting anyone in the process," answers Peter.

"I know what you're saying, but Agent Heiden warned me. He said it's like a domino effect."

"Keith is an ass to even talk to you about this! Just do me a favor and stay away from that boy. What a jackass!"

"Really, Peter, it's okay. He was just giving me friendly advice."

"I bet, to protect his own government ass, not yours or mine for that matter!" Peter answers, as he still wants to choke his best friend.

"Well, it's done, and I have to face the music somehow. I knew it was coming sooner or later. I'm going to bed now, and maybe if I get my needed rest, I will be sharp enough to save my job and keep my pride!"

Elise kisses Peter and walks to the bedroom and closes the door quietly behind her.

CHAPTER
EIGHTY

*T*here is a knock at Jonathan's office door.

"Come in!" Jonathan answers.

Elise walks in looking very professional in her expensive business suit.

"Hello, Jonathan. I'm happy that you're back!"

"Hello, Elise, thanks. Please have a seat….. you're late," he says with a smile.

Jonathan is not surprised that she's late; if she was early then he would be highly worried.

"What do you want to talk about?" Elise asks with a concerned look, as she knows very well what the conversation will be.

Elise can't read Jonathan's face. He's just a low key guy who's relaxed about life; nothing really rattles his cage, especially working with patients that have major mental health problems. Jonathan's method of life is that everything can be fixed with a lollipop or candy cane (if it's the holiday season).

"Okay, you want to get to the point. You had a dramatic altercation with your patient's wife. Can you explain to me what gives you the right to call this lady a bitch? You know what patient we are talking about, Agent Keith Heiden. Also why would his daughter throw a plate at you? What got Agent Heiden so angry that he had to threaten to take your license away from you? Can you explain these events to me?" Jonathan asks tensely with a very confused look on his face.

"Can I first ask you how you heard about these allegations?!" Elise asks quietly.

She hopes that Jonathan will be open to answering her questions since he's so easy going.

"I know that you're curious. I found out because you filed a complaint against Agent Heiden a couple of weeks ago, and I have a copy of it in front of me. I'm not too happy with your behavior. You're a therapist for God's sake! Are these questions that I had to ask you true or not?" Jonathan asks vehemently, as he leans back in his seat still looking directly at his friend and co-worker.

"Yes, the allegations are true. I'm not going to lie. I did call Mrs. Heiden a bitch. If you met this woman you would know why I said it. This is my professional opinion. Because I called his wife a bitch, Mr. Heiden was upset and angry with me and threatened my license. Agent Heiden's daughter did get angry with me, and I don't know why but she threw the plate in my direction," Elise explains uneasily.

"Elise, what the hell were you thinking? I don't care if Mrs. Heiden is a bitch! You're a highly intelligent woman who knows better! Agent Heiden did have a right to fight for his wife! You weren't asked to go to the house on the day of Agent Heiden's father's funeral. Why did you go there?" Jonathan's demands, as he can really feel his blood pressure is rising.

"No. It was my choice to go to his house. I wanted to help and support the family in any way I could," Elise answers, not telling the real story. She desperately wanted to see Keith for no reason at all!

"I still don't understand. It's only if the family member makes a special request. It wasn't in the log book that we received a call from the Heiden house." Jonathan sighs and takes a minute to collect his thoughts.

"We have an important responsibility to treat mental health for the different government agencies like DEA, FBI, FDA, FTA, and other departments. You and I can't afford to play childish games, especially the one that you pulled recently. Elise, you're not just assigned to one agent. Please don't forget what we do and why we are here. Can you explain to me why you are dating Agent Peter

Darling, a supervisor of the DEA Department?" Jonathan asks with disappointment in his voice.

A mental health problem can be a serious illness that people shouldn't take lightly. Jonathan's mom was mentally unstable all of her life. His whole family struggled for years to get her the care that she needed. She died not knowing that her family was beside her hospital bed. It broke Jonathan's heart that he couldn't save his mom from the pain that was controlling her mind. That's when he decided to help people who had mental illnesses.

"How do you know that?" Elise asks with a very surprised look. She had a terrible feeling for a long time that he already knew, and it was only a matter of time before he was going to talk to her about her new love.

"Elise, please answer the question!" Jonathan says sharply.

He's not at all surprised that she found another man younger than himself. Jonathan and Elise never went out on a date but the thought did cross their minds more than once. Jonathan really hates himself for not making a move before it was too late.

She hesitates before answering her boss, "Yes… I'm dating Peter Darling."

"That is a conflict of interest! This is unprofessional behavior! Now to top it all you're dating a DEA agent. Listen, Elise. I have no choice but to suspend you for two weeks without pay. Your future with this company is in your hands, not mine. Please think long and hard about what you want to do. If you decide to work here, you have to break off your relationship with Special Agent Peter Darling. I'm pulling you off the Agent Heiden case. If you decide to leave the job, you could keep your relationship. I really don't want to sound like a nasty boss." Jonathan sighs but continues to speak his mind. "Elise, you really put me up against the wall. I have to do something about this before you can really damage this company."

Jonathan stops and sighs again and then continues. "Do you know, Elise, when I was in D.C. I was trying to fight for mental health and the problems we are facing in our government world? Do you understand where I'm coming from and that I have no choice in the matter? It's really out of my hands." He sighs once again.

"I'm sorry, Jonathan. I don't understand. How do you know about my relationship with Agent Peter Darling? I never told any-one...especially this office! I know that you're upset that we can't be a couple, and I'm truly sorry about that. I wish it were different, but it's not, and I'm sorry!" Elise exclaims while tears start running down her face.

"Yes, I'm upset that we can't be a couple, but I know that you're in your thirties and I'm in my fifties. Besides the age difference, you never were attracted to me. That's fine. I came to terms with it. I hope that we can still be friends. I had to shorten my trip to D.C. because of all your drama. Let's just say, I learned about your new relationship with the agent, and truthfully, I'm not happy with it personally. Believe me, Elise, this is not my rule. It's the job and you know that. I also know that you have a love interest which another agent... Agent Heiden. Elise, I know you so well even more than you know yourself and it's very sad. Please take off your blinders and look at what you're up against."

Jonathan passes a box of tissues to Elise. Seeing anyone cry espe-cially someone that he holds dear to his heart hurts him to the core. He didn't want to tell her the bad news but that's part of his job.

"Jonathan, I still don't understand! I'm starting a new life with Agent Peter Darling now. I just moved out of my old apartment into his place. I'm sorry but can you change your mind about suspending me from work and also change the rule?" Elise pleads as she tries to wipe away her tears.

"I'm very sorry, Elise, but these are the rules. I'm not making this up. This department has very strict guidelines that we have to uphold. You need to break it off. I'll send out a general voice mail message to all your patients that you're taking two weeks off. They don't need to know the details. Please let me know by the end of this time frame what you decide to do. You can collect whatever personal items you have in your office. Please leave all the case files on your desk. If you have some at home I need them by tomorrow. Don't keep anything that has to do with your patients," Jonathan states, as he hands her a few papers to sign. "I need you to sign off on this meeting and that you are willing to comply with the terms of your two-week suspension without pay."

Elise takes the papers but she can't focus because she is still crying.

"Do you have a pen?"

"Sure."

Jonathan passes a silver cross-pen to her. He feels very sad about the whole situation and for her too. He doesn't want anything to happen to his good friend but things happen for strange reasons. She passes the papers back to Jonathan, but can't look him in the eyes. Elise is so embarrassed about this whole thing. All she wants to do is to leave his office quickly. Elise really wants to be alone until next year when she can show her face in public again.

"I'm sorry, Jonathan, and I wish I could take it all back but I can't," she says softly.

"Me too! I really hope that we can still be friends." Jonathan says quietly as he feels heartbroken about the whole thing. She's a great friend but her behavior has spoken.

"Hey… I guess we can still be friends. Well, I must go," Elise answers.

"Elise, if you want to know, I didn't have a good time in Washington. I have a hundred dollar gift card from Dunkin Donuts that I want you to have to pay for your coffee fixation," he replies, as he gives Elise the gift card.

"You're lying about Washington and thank you for the gift card," she whimpers as she takes the gift card from his hand.

"I was trying to make you feel a little better. I hope to see you soon. I'll give you a call when the two weeks are up for your answer," Jonathan says, as he walks to open his office door..

"Thanks, Jonathan, and I'll seriously think about our conversation," Elise answers sadly, as she slowly walks out of his office. Her cell phone rings and of course it's Peter Darling.

"Hello."

"Hi, Elise, so what happened at work today? Did you get the famous pink slip?" Peter asks as he plays golf with some of his buddies from work.

Elise is totally shocked, and she can barely walk down the hallway to get to her office. She really wants to hide underneath a rock and never come out. Elise tries very hard to hide her tears from her coworkers.

"Elise, are you there… Please talk to me!" Peter says with a tone of concern, as he walks from his golf game leaving his friends behind.

"Peter, what are you doing? We have a game here!" yells one of his buddies. "Talk to your girlfriend another time! She'll still be mad at you when you get home!"

"I'll be right back… Just give me a minute… We just started… Everyone here is not playing well anyway. So what's the rush?" Peter answers as he flips a bird to his friends. They don't care one bit that his girlfriend is having a nervous breakdown.

"Can you please tell me what happened? I'm worried about you!" Peter says to Elise.

"Peter, can you please give me a minute. I… I just want to get into my office and lock the door behind me before I continue speaking. I don't want my coworkers to know my business especially what I'm about to say," Elise answers as she finally reaches her destination. Boy, what a long hallway!

The sound of her door locking is the best sound she ever could hear right now.

"Yes, Jonathan spoke about my behavior, and he wasn't very pleased that we are a couple. He made a decision right then and there. I'm suspended for two weeks without pay because of my actions with the Heiden family.

"Elise, please calm down! Try to tell me everything and maybe I can help you," Peter calmly says, as he can see his friends getting annoyed with him. They want to use the golf club on him instead of the ball.

"Peter, I have to call you back," Elise cries.

"Elise, please don't hang up! Please talk to me! So what's your punishment?" Peter asks, as he gives a sign to his buddies, just one more minute and I'll be right there to play golf.

"Peter, you didn't hear a word I said to you!" she shouts into the cell phone.

"Listen, Elise. I don't really have to play golf with the guys. I can come home and comfort you. We can talk about what to do next. What do you say…is that a plan?"

"Peter, I can't. I just don't know what to do!"

"Elise, just come home and then we'll talk! Please just come home and I'll meet you!" Peter cries.

"Peter, I really just want to be alone for a while. Please don't worry about me. Enjoy the lovely day and your golf game. I know it's very important to you to play with your goofy friends and to de-stress from your job. I'll call around 5:00 p.m.," Elise answers, as she knows where to go to talk about life in general with her great friend Miguel.

"Okay… Please call at 5:00 p.m. because I'll call you if you don't."

"Okay, Peter, it's a deal… Thank you." Elise smiles because he's very kind to her needs. It's sweet.

CHAPTER
EIGHTY-ONE

𝒯he time is 6:30 a.m. and Keith just arrived home after many hours of work. He quietly walks into the house trying not to wake anyone including Reese. He's about to make some morning coffee when his Blackberry beeps. The messages says, "Agent Heiden, please be aware that something terrible is going down very soon. Please keep your eyes and ears open." The message doesn't have a sender phone number. This is very strange, but Keith is very thankful for the warning.

The afternoon rolls around, and Peter walks into the Heiden's house. He's part of the family of crazy and he also has a key.

"Hi, Uncle Peter. What's going on?" Patrick asks, as he lies on the living room couch reading a boring history book at the same time.

"I'm fine but my friend is having problems at work, and I need to talk to your dad. Where is he?" Peter asks, as he peeks in the kitchen.

"Did you mean Dr. Sheppard? Is she in trouble at work because of what she did to this family? Or what Erin did to her with the plate?" Patrick asks with a smart ass tone.

"Patrick, don't start with me. I'm not in the mood! Where is your father?" Peter snaps back.

"Uncle Peter, do you really love the therapist? She's kind of a messed up doctor," he replies.

"Listen, you little brat, back down, or I'll give you a wedgie for the rest of your life! Just try me!" Peter laughs because it was done to the Heiden boys before. "I have to talk to your father, and I don't have time to play twenty questions with you! Where is your dad?" Peter asks as he is now getting upset with the teenager.

"Please, Uncle Peter, why can't you answer my questions? Listen, if Dr. Sheppard did something to my family, it's my business to get involved," he states. "So why don't you tell me!"

"Now I finally figured out why you're grounded for the whole summer! It's because of your big mouth. So, I'll give you some mentoring advice, shut up or else!" Peter answers, as he looks around the house for his best friend.

"Uncle Peter, you're too funny for words! Dad is sleeping and I suggest you don't wake him!" Patrick warns the man that has all the right answers about life.

"Patrick, you are all heart!! I can't imagine what your bad side is," Peter laughs.

Keith walks downstairs because he can't sleep with all the noise that's coming from the first floor of the house. Peter zones in on Keith's every move.

"Keith, did you call Dr. Jonathan Daniels?" Peter asks as he follows his best friend to the kitchen.

"Hello, to you too. No, I didn't call Dr. Daniels. Oh, let me guess! Dr. Sheppard is in trouble because she's dating you," Keith states as he looks into the refrigerator to get some food to eat.

"Maybe... Are you sure you didn't tell Dr. Daniels everything about Dr. Sheppard and her unprofessional conduct toward your family?" Peter asks as he stands tall not backing down from Keith.

"I guess your brain is not working right today, because I'll say it again so you can understand it for the second time. I didn't tell Dr. Daniels anything about Dr. Sheppard or that she's dating you right now. I guess she wrote a report against me that Dr. Daniels had on his desk, and he wanted to have a talk with her," Keith answers as he makes a tuna sandwich for himself.

"I don't know about that! All I know is that she's suspended for two weeks without pay! Are you sure you didn't call Dr. Daniels, because I smell something bad and it's not the cheese!" Peter says, as he looks at Keith directly. "Dr. Sheppard has to decide whether to keep her job or her relationship with me. So, Keith, did you tell Dr. Daniels about our relationship?"

"I'm not going to have this conversation again. You're wasting my time as usual!"

Keith is not surprised that Peter would blame him. He never forgave him when his relationship with Julia Ulrich ended so harshly.

"I'm sorry, Peter, but I didn't call Dr. Daniels about Dr. Sheppard. The truth of the matter is that no one listens to me or what I have to say. Reese is the one that you should talk to on your life's advice. Also, you should know that we as DEA agents have to hold up an oath to keep our mouths shut at all cost! Sorry, Peter, but I did tell you that people in the government do talk. I warned you both about your teenage love relationship and how it's going to get very sticky."

"Okay, if you didn't tell Dr. Sheppard's boss then Justine told on her," Peter says as to give Keith a clue that his wife is dangerous and very powerful if no one tries to stop her.

"Sorry to rain on your parade, but Justine has had very bad morning sickness. As of right now, she can't even pick her head up off the toilet to even talk on the phone," Keith answers.

"Okay. I don't believe you but that's okay. I'll find out one way or another!" Peter replies.

"Whatever!" Keith answers like a teenager.

"I think that you're lying through your teeth, so you don't get into deeper trouble. You pulled a fast one and turned people's attention towards my girlfriend. Also do you know that she might lose her medical license because of this? You're damaged goods, and you don't care who you bring down with you because you're an unhappy person!" Peter continues, "I know that Dr. Sheppard has a thing for you, and I warned her that it wouldn't be wise to go that path even though you're having marital trouble that might end up in divorce court."

"Wow, Peter! You have all the answers now, don't you?" Keith snaps back because I guess it was due time for a fight and why not now!

"You're an ass!" Peter shouts as he tries to make everyone in the house come into the kitchen and see the fight first hand.

"You're an ass too, because you shouldn't get involved with a doctor or mental health especially if she works for the department. I'm very sorry that she's going through this terrible time, but you both put yourselves in this position, not me! So back off!"

"Keith, are you threatening me? Believe it or not, I can bring you down in a second."

"Please don't make me laugh. I'm having a shit year! But thanks for entertaining me when I'm down." Keith smiles because he's not afraid of Peter whatsoever.

Mitch walks into the kitchen and sees Uncle Peter and his father arguing. It catches the men off guard, and they stop right away. They decide it is pointless to continue the fight.

"Hey, Mitch!" Peter says with a friendly smile.

"Hi, Uncle Peter. What are you guys fighting about? I can hear you down the street."

"We're talking about politics again." Peter laughs as he knows that the lad isn't going to believe him.

"Mitch, did you grow again, because you look like you shot up at least an inch or more."

"I guess I grew, Uncle Peter."

"How tall do you think you're going to be?" Peter asks.

"I don't know."

"How tall is your father?" Peter asks.

"You mean John!" Mitch snaps back at Uncle Peter.

Mitch doesn't want anything to do with his birth father or mother, especially after what he went through as a young child. John Paul Pollack writes to Mitch every month, but Mitch doesn't reply back. Keith decided not to get involved. If Mitch wants to have a relationship or not with his biological father and mother, it's really up to him, not Keith. Keith will back Mitch up and support him in whatever he chooses to do with his relationship with John and Faith (his real mom).

"Sorry, Mitch," Peter says, surprised at his reaction.

"That's okay. Dad, can Tommy come over?" Mitch asks, as he sees his dad walking over to Colin to give him his lunch.

"Sure, Mitch. Do you want lunch?" Keith asks.

"No thanks, Dad. I already ate."

"I'm sorry, Mitch. Who's Tommy again?" Keith asks.

It's very hard to keep up with all of the children's friends. Keith starts to make coffee because one cup won't do it for him.

"You know, Tommy that lives down the street. His father is a fireman and his mother is a doctor," Mitch answers.

"Okay... I guess I remember. That's fine for him to come over," Keith answers and smiles at the same time. He's very proud of Mitch and how he is becoming a great young man in his own way. He's great at hockey and hopefully he will get a scholarship to a college of his choice one day.

"Keith, what should I do next?" Peter asks

"Sorry, Pete. I don't have any words of advice to give you. All I know is that I'm your best friend but I'm failing in my job. Listen, just wait it out. Maybe it will blow over," Keith answers before drinking his fresh coffee.

"Blow over? What the hell does that mean?" Peter snaps back. "Keith, you didn't listen to me! It has already blown over and Elise is now using my clothes for her tissues! I have to go! Thanks for nothing!"

"Listen, drama queen, I didn't cause this avalanche! You guys did it on your own. As a friend of yours I did my duty and warned you both of what would happen, but no one listens to me. I'm only saying this from the bottom of my heart."

"Listen, yesterday, Elise wouldn't let me out of my apartment because she was overly emotional! All day she talked to me, screaming, cursing, and your name was mentioned many times!" Peter exclaims as he looks at Keith straight in the eyes.

Keith grunts and makes a face at the same time.

Keith is still trying to get his mind wrapped around the fact that Dr. Sheppard has a first name.

"I'm sorry, Peter. I don't know what to say. Yes, Justine yells, screams, curses, and I do the crying."

"I can see that happening." Peter laughs. That made his day.

CHAPTER
EIGHTY-TWO

hat evening Keith stands near the dresser mirror as he gets ready for work. Justine walks into the master bedroom and sees Keith. She quickly closes the bedroom door behind her. Then she takes off her slippers, sits at the edge of the king size bed, and looks into the mirror. Keith looks through the mirror and sees Justine behind him. She looks upset and concerned at the same time. He knows another serious talk is coming.

"What's wrong, Justine?"

"Have you spoken to Patrick?" Justine asks.

"Yes," he answers, as he takes his yellow silk tie and starts to put it around his neck.

"Did you talk to him?"

"Yes, Justine, I've spoken to Patrick. He's not too happy that he's grounded for the whole summer. As I said before, he'll have the whole summer. He'll be a very busy beaver taking driver education classes and doing chores around the house. I'm fine that he hates me for the rest of my life. I'm used to it," Keith answers, as he puts his business shoes on and then his marriage ring.

At this time Keith wishes that things were very different between Justine and him. He still has the divorce lawyer's business card in his wallet. He just doesn't have the nerve to call and make it legal to end the long, painful marriage that both parties are not happy with. Seeing Justine in her pregnant state is killing Keith. It's not even his baby but he feels very responsible like it was his. Justine is cold as ice, and she doesn't care about anyone's feelings. Keith doesn't want to grow old with Justine, but it's hard just to look at her especially becoming a mom again. It's very hard for Keith to look at Justine straight in the eyes and to see her as a human that has motherly or loving feelings toward others.

"How much trouble is Patrick in?" Justine asks.

"Justine, I'm not going to lie to you. Patrick is in deep trouble. He got himself into a hole that he can't get out of. He was very honest when we spoke. I believe he's telling the truth, and that he doesn't know anything else other than selling the drugs he was given. He just wanted to do the deal and get the money at the end during the business transaction. He has a lot to think about during his time home," Keith answers.

"What if he breaks the rules again? He's very stubborn and only listens to what he wants to hear not what you say to him! His behavior has to stop right now!" Justine exclaims.

"Yes, I know all too well that Patrick is extremely stubborn. He has our DNA in him. That's a dangerous mixture. I am well aware of what I'm up against. Listen, I have Patrick on a very short leash. Don't worry your pretty little head over it. He'll listen. It's funny, the other day I was watching TV and this story came on. It was a man who was a sergeant in the police department from a state on the East Coast… I forgot what state he was from. Anyway his two boys got into some terrible trouble so the man took them on a family field trip to the city morgue," Keith says with a smile.

"No," Justine shouts. "I'm not going to let you take Patrick on this insane field trip!"

"I was thinking about bringing Patrick with Mitch and Erin."

"Are you out of your mind? You're insane!"

Keith laughs. "Thank you for noticing my special gift."

"Did you hear me?"

"Yes, Justine, I can hear you. How can I not?!"

"How can you not be emotional in this situation?"

"Because you're the woman and I'm the man." Keith laughs. "Listen, I see this situation differently. Patrick is in deep trouble in the drug world, Mitch is going to be thirteen in October, and Erin is going to college soon. So these situations are up in front of me. This is the real world!" Keith answers.

"I know you see the world differently because you're a cop."

Keith shakes his head with disbelief.

"Justine, you've got to be kidding me! From day one I had to discipline the children. You come and do a hundred eighty on me. You are yelling and lecture me on everything I do wrong in front of the kids. No wonder the kids don't respect us! We are crazy people, not parents to them. You never support me or believe in me. Until you can give me an intelligent reason why I can't bring the kids to the morgue, my rule stands," Keith answers.

"I don't have an intelligent reason, but I'm afraid that they won't like you."

"Justine, they don't like me now, so why stop there?" Keith laughs.

"Will you buy them lunch?"

"Yes, after our lovely trip is over," Keith answers with a smile.

CHAPTER
EIGHTY-THREE

Four hours have gone by, and Keith is working away behind his desk. He tries to get his paperwork done before another vast pile lands on his desk and soon Keith won't be able to see the door to his office or see Nicole working at her desk. He opens an envelope with a letter from the department that tells him he's getting a new therapist. Then a return name and address on another envelope catches his eye. It says Mrs. Megan K. O'Shaughnessy Heiden from Oak Park, Illinois.

He opens it quickly without giving it a second thought that it might be a bomb or something.

> Dear Keith, my son,
>
> I was happy to see you after all these years. I know that you are hurting; I want to say that I'm deeply sorry for what we did to you.
>
> I came across this picture. It was you on your fourth birthday. You received a red bike that we bought you. You were so cute and very happy that day. A picture was taken of you and your father; it was a very touching moment. He was teaching you how to ride the bike with training wheels attached. It was a beautiful day. It was like yesterday when you were born into the world, and I remember holding your tiny little body in my arms. I miss that and you. Please try to

remember the happy times with your dad if you can.

Enjoy the pictures! If I come across any more, I'll mail them over to you. Don't worry I have copies. I'll keep in touch from time to time, and I want you to know that you're always in my thoughts and prayers.

Please take good care of yourself. I miss and love you always!

> Best wishes and love,
> Your mom or Megan
> xoxo

Keith leans back in his chair and starts to feel a little sad, as he looks at the 4x6 picture of him and his father. He finally realizes that his dad was a very sick man, and that he wasn't to blame for his father's madness.

CHAPTER
EIGHTY-FOUR

///

It's June 30th and the time is 9:17a.m. Colin runs into the master bedroom and stops in front of his dad. Keith is sleeping in his comfortable bed but not for long. Colin is wearing a white polo shirt, shorts, and sandals. He looks like he's ready to go to the Hamptons on Long Island for the weekend.

"Daddy, today is my birthday party! Daddy, it's my party today so wake up!"

Keith opens his blue eyes slightly as he knows this kid won't go away anytime soon.

"Dad, can you please wake up!"

"Come on, Colin, leave your daddy alone and let him sleep!" Justine exclaims to the four-year-old. "Colin William!" She walks over to her stubborn son and takes his hand.

"Come on, Mom, I need to talk to Dad!"

There's a lot of activity going on throughout the Heiden's house just to get ready for Colin's fourth birthday. There will be about fifty people coming over and lots of them are Colin's play friends and family of course. Two hours later, Keith walks toward the kitchen and sees Justine and Erin setting up the party food.

"Hello, ladies," Keith says, as he brushes his blond hair back and feels the tension building up in his head. He doesn't like parties with a lot of people around.

"It's going to be a very long day," Patrick says as he shakes his head back and forth.

"Oh, Patrick, you're not helping matters. Make yourself useful or leave this room!" Justine shouts, as she pushes her son.

"Hi, Dad! Are you ready for a lot of Colin's friends?" Erin asks with a friendly smile.

"Well, let's say it's going to be a very interesting day and leave it at that."

Keith takes a large mug and pours coffee for himself. Peter comes into the house with lots of plastic bags full of alcohol.

"Keith, are you wearing that outfit?" Justine asks as she looks up and down at her husband. Keith gives a very strange look right back at her. "What's wrong with my outfit?" He's wearing a light white shirt, khaki pants, and sandals.

"I'm not going to change because you say so," he exclaims, as he takes a drink of his coffee and smiles at his daughter as he looks her way. "I know that you want to pick a fight but it's not going to work."

Erin smiles back as if to say, "Sorry, Dad. I really can't help you with this one, but good luck anyway."

Justine looks around her to make sure that Colin is out of sight before she says what she needs to say to Keith.

"Did you build Colin's bike?"

Justine walks out to the backyard, which is decorated with different shades of green balloons blowing in the summer wind. Party plates, cups, and hats are on the tables. Keith follows his wife outside. He has a confused look on his face but tries not to show it.

"What's with the color green?"

"The party theme is Teenage Mutant Ninja Turtles. Keith, the bike?" she asks, as she finishes the final touches for the party. The weather is great for a four-year-old's birthday party. The temperature is going to be around eighty-seven degrees with very few clouds and a blue sky.

"The bike is in the family room, and it's covered with a blanket. He wouldn't know it's there. If someone tells him, like Patrick, then that's a different story. I'm not responsible if that happens," Keith answers, as he drinks his much-needed coffee.

"Hey, I heard that! I take that remark personally!" Patrick says as he stands behind his dad.

"Please, you'll live!" Keith answers with a smile as he looks at his annoying son.

Hours later the party is just getting started; Justine's family and Colin's friends arrive. Here come the little pre-scholars who are having fun with music playing, and it's amazing that the balloons are still on the party tables. Peter is behind the bar making drinks for the kids but especially for the adults. Uncle Jason (Justine's brother who's the same age as Keith) is cooking hot dogs, hamburgers, sausages, corn on the cob, shrimp and other food on the barbeque. Mitch plays with the kids, while Erin takes pictures. Justine and Keith are enjoying the party and talking with their company. Throughout the backyard, you hear a lot of laughter and talking. It's a great sound to hear especially from this family. Colin is really enjoying his birthday party and he loves the attention.

"Dad," Colin says, as he pulls Keith's khaki pants to get his full attention.

"Yes, Colin."

"Daddy, I want to see Jo Jo the Monkey!"

"The monkey is coming soon," Keith answers, as he knows this monkey is not the greatest idea, but he never got a chance to say anything on the matter.

Colin starts to cry, and Keith leans down to aid his son.

"What's wrong, Colin? Don't cry. The monkey is coming soon. Please don't cry."

"Okay," he answers, as he wipes his tears from his face and then runs away to join his friends.

Time is now 1:00 p.m. and the entertainer with Jo Jo the monkey comes into the backyard. Colin sees them and quickly runs for the monkey. Keith sees his son charge toward the animal and blocks him from getting hurt or bitten by the monkey. "Colin!"

"Daddy, Jo Jo!" Colin tries to get away from his dad; he's very fast on his feet. It's not easy for Keith to keep up with a four-year-old.

"Hello, Mr. Heiden. My name is Tommy Smith, the entertainer. We spoke last week," he says as he shakes hands with the birthday boy's dad. "This is Jo Jo the Monkey. He's four and a half years old. He's very friendly, and he loves kids too!"

Jo Jo puts out his hand paw to shake Keith's hand. He wants to show that's he's a friendly monkey, not like King Kong.

"Thanks, Jo Jo, but no thanks. Well, Mr. Smith, do you have papers to prove that Jo Jo has all of his shots and that you are certified as a licensed entertainer in the state of California?" Keith ask as he tries to block Colin from getting to the monkey. Erin quickly helps her dad by escorts Colin away from JoJo.

Tommy Smith passes the certified papers over to Keith.

"Mr. Heiden, Jo Jo has all his updated shots, and he has never bitten anyone. I raised Jo Jo since he was a baby and he's fully trained to use your toilet if he needed to go do his business."

"O…kay!" Keith answers with a confused and surprised look. He looks at the paperwork carefully to make sure there are no bumps on this road. Keith wanted a magician or a man with a few dogs that ride bikes.

"Mr. Smith, the papers look okay. Please promise me that Jo Jo won't bite the kids because I have a loaded gun and so do my friends that I work with. Son, do you understand what I'm saying?"

"Yes, Mr. Heiden, I fully understand where you're coming from. Jo Jo and I are professionals, and we make a living entertaining kids at birthday parties. So please don't worry too much because I have been doing this line of work over four years now," Tommy answers.

"Can I give out my business cards after I finish my show?"

"Sure, before you start, I have to put my dog in his run, because I don't want Jo Jo riding on his back."

Tommy smiles with excitement in his voice. "He does that trick too."

"I bet he does!" Keith answers and then walks away quickly to take care of business.

"Thank you! I'll get ready for my act. Come, Jo Jo, we have to go to work," Tommy says, as he takes the monkey's hand. Jo Jo is wearing a tuxedo with a bright red vest that you can't miss.

One hour later the monkey show was successful, and everyone enjoyed the entertainment. Keith was too stressed out to enjoy the show that could have been an accident waiting to happen. Justine realizes that they are running out of ice in the freezer and three huge coolers. She walks over to Keith while he is eating a hamburger.

"Keith, it's your turn to get the ice."

"Already! Let me finish eating my food and then I'll go. How many bags of ice do I need to get?" Keith asks.

"About six bags or so."

"Okay... I'll get them in a minute."

Keith goes to the bathroom before he heads out to get the ice. Then without a minute to spare he collects his car keys, his cell phone, and a black wallet with forty dollars inside.

He walks towards Justine and says, "Justine, I'm leaving now. Do you want me to get you anything else besides ice?"

"No, I just need the ice," Justine answers, as she picks up her wallet to pay for Tommy and Jo Jo.

Colin's blue eyes get very wide when he sees his dad walking over from the backyard and heading towards the gate.

"Dad, where are you going?" Colin asks with a concerned look on his face.

"I'll be back. I just have to get some ice, and I'll be right back!"

"Okay, Daddy. Gummy Bears?!"

"Thank you, Colin," he answers with a smile and eats a red and green gummy bear as per requested.

"Come back soon, Daddy! I love you," the youngster says, as he runs away leaving Keith alone with his thoughts.

"I love you too," Keith says with a smile, as he sees his little boy growing up so fast.

CHAPTER
EIGHTY-FIVE

*T*en minutes later Keith arrives at the local mini-market/gas station to get gas and bags of ice too.. He pumps gas into his SUV. Then he parks his vehicle near the ice cooler to get the ice.

"He's going into the store right now. He's going to the store right now. When he gets to his SUV, then we will grab him," says a British man who's talking on his walkie-talkie while sitting in his black Lincoln Town Car. "Just keep your eyes open and get the job done. Make sure you don't get caught because Mr. Henderson and Mr. Medina will be very upset. They want Heiden on a silver platter without any questions, or they will doubt that you can do the job right. You have to think of the big picture and the money we're getting!"

"Bloody hell! He's a federal agent, and we can get the death penalty if we kidnap him. What do they have here? There's the electric chair or lethal injection. I don't know about this plan. We might get caught or killed by the cops. They can smell a crime taking place a mile away!" answers the other British man sitting in an adjacent car.

"This state has the gas chamber or lethal injection! So stop flipping your pie hole and let's get the job done!" retorts the other British man.

"Okay…okay, don't get your knickers in a knot!! I'll do the job, but I'm just giving you fair warning. I have a very terrible feeling about this job! Why are we working with Jose Medina's men? They don't understand a word of English!"

"Stop whining and belt—up [means shut up in British terms]! No wonder you haven't gotten yourself a love mate by now. Jose Medina's men wouldn't understand us any way because we're from the United Kingdom. We already speak 'funny English' to the people that live in the states. So mate we're out of our league on this one, but money is money, and we have a job to do! We have to make both bosses pleased and kidnap the DEA agent! We can't show our faces until we bring back this agent in one piece."

"Fine, but I don't like the feeling that I have in my gut!"

Minutes later Keith pays the cashier and walks out of the store. He opens the trunk door and puts the bags of ice in the SUV. Suddenly two men wearing all black and ski masks surprise Keith from behind. Keith doesn't go down without a fight.

"Bloody hell! Hold him!"

The two men finally lock Keith's arms behind his back, and the third man uses a stun gun to bring down the federal agent. In less than a second the deed is almost done. The two British men tie Keith's feet and hands and gag him. They quickly put Keith into the trunk of the black Lincoln Town Car. They ride away leaving the SUV trunk door open, and the bags of ice are starting to melt away from the summer heat.

CHAPTER
EIGHTY-SIX

*P*atrick's cell rings. "Hello?"

"Hello, Patrick. Remember me?" asks the man with a British accent (Jude Henderson).

"Oh. Hi... Hey... What's up?" Patrick responds as he knows getting this call is not a good sign.

Patrick walks toward his father's office where he can have a private conversation. He closes the door and locks it too. He can feel his heart beating fast before the conversation has even started.

"Well, Patrick, we didn't have a chance to talk about our business transaction last month. You were in the hospital healing from your injuries... Oh, by the way, how are you feeling?"

"I'm fine. I still have the cast on, but it's coming off in a couple of days. I'm sure you're not interested in small talk."

"I really need answers! Why didn't you do the job? Why did I have to hear that you were beaten with a baseball bat? Boy, you Americans like to fight dirty! I'm very upset that I didn't get the money from the business transaction. Why is that, Patrick? Please tell me because I'm confused. Please, Patrick, enlighten me with your charm!" retorts Jude Henderson.

"Well... Sir... I really didn't catch your name. I guess you're not going to tell me anytime soon," replies Patrick.

"Please go on, Patrick... I'm waiting."

"Well, at the time I felt that the person I was dealing with was not telling the truth. But I had a bad feeling about it. Unfortunately I was right! He never had the money on him," Patrick answers.

"Okay, you made that choice, and it's done. Patrick, I know that you're very young and you're new in the business. But you need to get the job done no matter what you're up against," Jude says as he smokes a Cuban cigar. "Do you understand what I'm trying to say?"

"Yes, sir!" Patrick answers.

"I'm happy that we're on the same page. Now, where's my cocaine? Do you have it or did you finally sell it to someone who had the money up front?"

"Well…well, you see I don't have it," answers Patrick as he can feel his body going numb.

"Bloody hell, Patrick! Where the fuck is it?"

"I don't know! When I came home, it wasn't there. Someone took it. I'm sorry!" Patrick pleads.

"Patrick, can you find it?"

"No."

"Patrick, where's your dad?"

"What?" asks Patrick as he begins to get sick to his stomach. "Why the hell do you want to know about my dad?"

"I've kidnapped him! It's only fair that I take something of yours because you took something of mine! Now, Patrick, I think we're even! I'll never call you again. Enjoy your freedom and I'll enjoy making your dad suffer slowly. Maybe you will see him one day in a body bag, but for now, he's all mine... Have a good day and enjoy your brother's fourth birthday party!" Jude says, as he continues to smoke his cigar.

"Wait! Wait… You did what?" Patrick asks desperately, as he thinks his hearing is playing tricks on him.

"This is a joke, right?"

"Listen, Patrick, please don't tell me that you didn't want your dad gone. I know your type very well, so please don't lie. I guess that's why you get into trouble a lot, because you can't stick to the game plan. So I did you a favor and made your wish come true. Your dad is gone forever!" Jude answers. "I didn't hear you say thank you!"

"No, I'm not going to say thank you! I never wished this on him! Bring him back home!" Patrick demands, as he feels his chest getting tighter. Patrick thinks he is going to have a heart attack right now.

"Sorry, no can do! You never really loved your father or liked him for that matter! Patrick, why don't you be a man and tell the truth for once in your life! Good-bye, Patrick!" says Jude, as he looks at his next plan of action.

"Please don't hurt him! I'll do anything! Just please don't hurt him... What do I have to do to get him back alive?" Patrick yells but he knows in his heart that it won't help.

"Oh, Patrick, Patrick. I think it's best if we parted ways. Please let me do the job that I was paid to do. Oh, before I forget, please tell Agent Peter Darling that Jose Medina says hi. He knows what I'm talking about," Jude says, as he sees his dinner coming into the room. "This is an answer to a terrible deed that was done ten years ago!"

"What did he do that you had to kidnap him?"

"You made my final decision, but if you have to know, ten years ago your dad killed Jose Medina's nephew with a loaded gun. The young man didn't have a gun on him. Please ask Peter what really happened, and maybe he'll tell you the truth because he was there too."

"Listen, you don't know for sure that my dad killed Jose Medina's nephew. He's an agent, and he only kills to protect the law, not go against it!"

"You'll get your answers if you ask your Uncle Peter."

Suddenly without warning Patrick hears the phone line die. His heart skips a beat as he tries to catch his breath.

"Hello! Hello! Sir, can you hear me? Please answer me! Don't kill him! Please! Please!" Patrick cries for mercy, but Jude is already off the line.

CHAPTER
EIGHTY-SEVEN

*S*uddenly Patrick runs into the bathroom and throws up in the toilet. What's happening to Keith right now makes Patrick have a lot of guilt inside of him.

The numbness consumes his body, as he gazes at the partygoers who have no idea of his father's predicament.

Patrick can't tell his mother because of her condition and grandfather will be so happy that his loser son-in-law is gone forever.

He slowly walks out to the backyard and looks for Uncle Peter. Seconds later he sees him dancing like crazy with Colin and his little friends. It's not going to be easy.

"Uncle Peter, can I talk to you alone? It's very important."

"Sure, let me get my drink and then we can talk in the house!"

"I really think you should just drink water. You'll need a clear head for what I'm about to tell you," Patrick answers solemnly.

"Ok…ay!" Peter takes ice from the ice cooler. "I hope your dad comes back with the ice, because it'll be water soon. "Damn, it's hot today!"

"Uncle Peter, Dad is not coming back any time soon. The boss that hired me a month ago just kidnapped him. Remember I told you?"

"Wait. What? Are you telling me that the men want interest because you didn't do the job? So now they have your dad?"

"Yes!"

"Shit!" Peter shouts as the company looks at him strangely. "Sorry, guys!"

Peter quickly walks past Patrick and talks to Liam and Sean. Then he walks back to Patrick to fill him in on the plan.

"I think we should go inside and talk. I need all the details," Peter says, as Liam and Sean wait behind him for instructions. "Let's make it fast because we don't have a lot of time to find him."

Minutes later, Patrick fills Peter in on all he knows including the comment about Jose Medina. Peter chooses to keep that information to himself for now.

Peter calls for backup. He remembers that there is a local gas and store station a couple of minutes away from the house. So he'll check that location first before anything else.

CHAPTER
EIGHTY-EIGHT

*K*eith suddenly wakes up an hour later with a throbbing pain throughout his body. He's in total darkness and very disoriented. It takes him a few minutes to realize that he's been kidnapped and in the trunk of a car. Since very little air is coming into the trunk, he must conserve his energy. He tries not to pass out from heat exhaustion because it's extremely hotter than outside. His hands are handcuffed and tightened behind his back. Also, his feet are cuffed and a gag in his mouth. He tries to calm himself down and think of a way out of this situation. As the car begins to slow down, he decides to break a tail light.

Keith was caught off guard and surprised from behind. He has no idea how many men he is up against. As a federal agent, he should know to watch his back at all times. He got careless.

Keith can barely breathe…. He has a sheet tied tightly around this head to prevent him from yelling for help. The sweat is pouring down his face like spring rain. He never thought he'd be in a situation like this!

He pushes all his weight against the trunk before the car starts to move again. Damn! Nothing budges! Back to plan A. He'll break the tail light and hope a cop will pull the car over.

Here goes nothing!

Keith finally breaks the tail light with his feet, and he carefully turns his body so he can breathe fresh air from the hole that he just made. Only time will tell if plan A works.

An hour goes by and Peter, Liam, and other California police officers arrived at the scene. The security tapes show Keith but not the kidnapping taking place. They see a black Lincoln Town car driving quickly away. They scan for fingerprints from Keith's SUV as every minute counts.

The sun is going down within two hours, and the Lincoln Town car is still on the road. The location is unknown, and it doesn't help Keith who is tied up in the truck for hours. He has to go to the bathroom and he can't hold himself any longer.

Keith can smell the exhaust through the broken tail light and the fumes are making him sick and angrier by the minute. He can't wait to get out and smash some heads in.

He doesn't know where his wallet and cell phone are. Maybe it fell out of his pocket during the scuffle.

Suddenly he hears the sound of sirens from a California highway patrol car. The Lincoln Town car slowly pulls over without a fight.

Praise the Lord... Now get me out of here!

"Don't say anything and be calm. It will take a couple of minutes but we'll take care of this," says a British man that's in the drivers' side.

"Fine, make it fast!"

The driver's window goes down, and the British man looks at the California Highway Patrol Officer through the rearview mirror. He slowly walks up to the car and sees the left tail light missing. The officer first puts his fingerprints on the trunk as evidence that he was here, just in case something happens to him. If this car were to be impounded by the police they would find evidence that Officer Storm Morgan's fingerprints were on the car.

Officer Morgan sees the hole where the tail light used to be and takes his flashlight. He leans down to take a closer look to see clearly what he's up against, as he hears a good deal of noise coming from the trunk. The light shines directly on Keith's blue eyes that are looking back at him!

"What the fuck!" Officer Morgan exclaims and pulls out his gun. Someone is in the trunk! The officer calls in for backup on his walkie-talkie and records what he's up against. He realizes that this is not a routine traffic stop.

"Sir! You in the driver seat, get out of the car slowly and put your hands high in the air where I can see them!"

The British man gets out of the car with his hands up in the air as ordered by Officer Morgan. However, the passenger gets out at the same time.

Officer Morgan has a shocked look on his face and firmly says to the passenger. "Sir, please get back in the car, and I will deal with you very soon. Get back in the car!"

"Bloody hell! What the fuck!" The passenger shoots the officer in the head right between his eyes.

"No!" Keith shouts, but the gag stops him.

"Let's go before the backup comes. Open the trunk and put the cop in with Heiden. He can now have company for the ride," orders the British man who was driving (Number One as they call him). "Number three, drive the police car and then burn the damn thing until there is no evidence. Call us, and we'll pick you up and bring you to the safe location."

"That's fine, Number One," answers Number Three as he gets into the police car. He speeds away from the Lincoln Town car to take care of business as per requested by Number One. Burn the mother fucker!

The trunk opens quickly, and the man says, "Heiden, you're a piece of shit! Here's some company for you during your travels. Cheerio for now!" says the British man named Number Two as he pushes the dead officer into the trunk.

"Now we'll have to drive off the main road just in case other cops are around! We'll call Number Three to see how it's going on his end," Number one says to Number two.

"Very well, Number One!"

They quickly get into the Lincoln Town car and drive away without headlights on to attract attention.

Keith can smell death creeping into the officer, and now he really can't breathe. Soon the smell will be overwhelming.

CHAPTER
EIGHTY-NINE

*T*he time is now 7:00 p.m. and finally the Lincoln Town car has reached its destination. The location is not on any maps on GPS.

Finally, the trunk door opens, and one of Jude's workers takes out the fallen officer, leaving Keith alone. "Hello, Agent Heiden. Happy that you can join us. We have a lot of catching up to do!" Two men get Keith out of the trunk. "You smell like urine. Clean him up! Then put him in the room!" orders Jude with a smile on his face. His men, not Jose's men, did very well in capturing the federal agent without any bumps in the road.

Jude's plan is in play. He is moving to get full territory from Jose before Alex gets his hands on it first. Alex was successful with the ice cream trucks. So Jose can make his final decision who has his business for the next three years or more. That is if you can live to enjoy the wealth and fame of being a drug cartel dealer in Mexico, Europe, and now the United States.

Jude has a major job ahead of him. He has to make Agent Heiden admit that he killed Jose's nephew out of anger. It's not going to be easy. But Jude will try his best to break a man that has dealt with a lot of his own anger. It's going to be a challenge for both parties (Keith vs. Jude) to stand their ground.

An hour later Keith is undressed and cleaned up. Since he was drugged he is unaware of what's going on. He's placed in a room very much like a prison cell. It has four cement walls, a bed, a sink, and a toilet.

He tries to analyze the drugs they put into him but no luck because his mind is not clear enough to think straight.

Keith finally realizes as the night-time becomes daylight that they injected him with Ketamine nicknamed Black Hole. It makes him not see right or walk straight. Keith feels like a drunk who didn't drink.

There're a lot of questions that Keith is thinking about. *What do they want from me? I'm a nobody! Why can't I go home to my boring life?*

CHAPTER
NINETY

〰〰〰〰〰〰〰〰〰〰〰〰〰〰〰〰〰〰〰〰〰〰〰〰〰〰〰〰〰〰〰〰〰〰

A knock sounds at the door. "Come in!" Justine answers, as she lies on her bed. Her doctor ordered Justine to get enough bed rest because she's in a fragile state and needs to control her stress level.

Christopher walks into the master bedroom with a tray of freshly made pancakes and an extra large orange juice. He quickly closes the door behind him with his foot, so Justine doesn't hear the crying from downstairs.

"I hope that you're hungry because you need your strength for you and the baby," Christopher says with a weak smile. He knows very well what the family is up against, and Keith's situation seems very grave.

"Why don't you be honest with me and tell me you don't care about the baby or me?"

Christopher is taken back with Justine's response. However, he'll let it go because he was informed about her behavior from Peter. He knows what he's up against.

Christopher says to himself, *Just don't pay attention to her childish behavior; maybe she'll change her attitude once she eats.*

"Where can I put the tray?" he asks.

"You can place it on my nightstand," Justine answers without giving in to his kindness.

"Listen, Justine, I'm only here to give you your breakfast and that's it. I'll leave your home if you want me to. Just say the word!" Christopher answers with a calm voice.

"Christopher, do you know that Keith has an emergency fund just in case he was kidnapped or worse yet, killed on duty?" she says. "I really don't know why I'm even talking to you about this. He's a stranger to you!"

"Yes, but you talking about him helps me know him better," Christopher answers as he knows what he says is the truth.

Justine feels that she's going to cry again, but she has no more tears. She feels lost without Keith, and she finally realizes that she does love him and never really stopped loving him. He has always been in her heart.

Justine sighs and says, "Thanks for breakfast, but I'm not in the mood at eat. But thank you anyway for trying... I'm sorry. I really can't look at you because you look so much like Keith. You're confusing me. Can you please leave my home?"

"I'm very sorry, Justine. You're dealing with a lot right now. I wish I could make it go away but I can't. I really wish I knew Keith as you do. Justine, please try to hold on to happy memories of him until he comes back home. I have a strong feeling that he'll be home soon."

"I really don't know what to think at this point. I'm scared for him."

"Listen, Justine. If it means anything, Keith was trained at a young age to endure lots of pain. Believe it or not, he took it like a man and never gave up hope. That's why I love him. Not only because he's my younger brother but because of what he stands for. He's not afraid of life. I'm amazed at how he turned out, and how he has a loving family that stand by him no matter what. Don't get me wrong. I know that he needs a lot of therapy from all the pain that he has bottled up inside. But overall, he did an amazing job. He got to where he wanted to be in his life."

"Okay, but what do the kids and I do until then?" Justine asks sadly.

"Well, you hope and pray hard to the man upstairs!"

"Okay, thanks, Christopher. I really need to rest so can you leave my room now? You're welcome to stay with the kids until you have to go somewhere else. It seems that they like you a lot and they're very happy that their dad's brother is here to finally see them."

"I'm happy too!" Christopher answers, as he has a touching moment with his newfound sister-in-law.

"It's hard for me to look at you but I'm trying," Justine replies.

"Whatever you feel comfortable with. I understand either way and thank you for your honesty. Before I go, I must mention that Dr. Elise Sheppard is downstairs."

"What the hell! Why is she here?" yells Justine, as she feels a terrible headache coming on.

"Justine, please calm down. Listen I'm just the messenger. Peter called her as a favor to the family. He thought that you all may need a professional to talk to now," Christopher answers quietly.

"I thought she'd lost her job and that was the end of seeing her ugly face! I really need a break from that loon!" Justine screams.

"It sounds like you like the doctor!" Christopher laughs and says, "Justine to be honest, all I know is that Peter wanted someone here just to listen that's not part of the family."

"I'll never want to talk to that psycho bitch ever again!"

"O…kay that's my cue to leave the room! That means that she needs to leave your home," Christopher replies, as he doesn't want to be on Justine's bad side.

"Yes! If you can, that would be great… Thank you, Christopher."

"You're welcome, I think! I want to say that if you need a professional to talk to, she's right downstairs. But it's your choice and your home. I'm only a guest here," Christopher replies.

Justine laughs and shows that she's relaxed again. "Thanks for making me laugh and for your input on the situation. The kids and I'll be fine without a therapist, especially that one. My dad will be coming up shortly to visit me, so that I won't be alone for too long. Thanks for keeping me company. I think I'll eat my breakfast now."

Christopher gently puts the food tray on her lap.

"It looks great! Thank you, Christopher!" Justine says with a friendly smile.

"Enjoy, and I'll take the tray down when you are finished," he smiles back.

"So will you tell that doctor to leave my home?" Justine asks with a winning smile that she flashes when she wants something from a handsome man. It always works in her favor.

"I guess I don't have a choice in the matter. I'll tell Dr. Sheppard thanks but no thanks."

Christopher leaves the master bedroom but is not sure how the doctor will take it, or if she will leave without a fight.

About ten minutes later Dr. Sheppard leaves the Heiden's house. She's upset and angry, but since she's not getting paid for her services, she'll leave the home without a fight. Peter owes her big time for this one!

Erin closes the front door behind Dr. Sheppard. She's not herself at all, and from time to time she cries, but she tries to hold back for Colin's sake. Erin loves her father so much and wishes she could take his place.

Patrick is too strong to show any weak emotions like crying for someone. He's the man in the house, not Uncle Peter. If Patrick doesn't see his father's body, then there's no reason to cry. Patrick never thought that his father would be kidnapped especially in the daytime.

Mitch feels very sad inside for the dad that saved his life. He really misses, love, Keith and is proud to call him dad. Mitch is also happy to carry the Heiden name; it suits him. He knows that his father will come back and is not worried at all. Because he knows he will fight hard to live and see his family again.

Colin is crying and keeps asking everyone, "Where is Daddy?"

Reese knows that Keith is gone, and he whines for his owner to come home.

The family misses, love, Keith but does his job wonder about him?

CHAPTER
NINETY-ONE

*I*t has been a couple of weeks now since Keith has been captured by his kidnappers. He looks very weak and unable to move much. He lost a lot of weight and is drugged too. Ketamine is a drug used in humans and vet medicine for general anesthesia. This drug relaxes a person so much they can barely walk! It is making him very sick, and he's not thinking clearly as an officer of the law. His blond shiny hair is now dirty. Keith is growing a beard, and he smells very bad from not showering. He does remember that a couple of men helped him take a shower. There's an ugly, smelly towel and sink next to it that makes it a perfect five-star hotel minus their very soft robes.

A man that is 5'9" with dark brown hair and brown eyes unlocks the door to Keith's room and walks toward the man lying helplessly on the mattress. He leans down to the sleepy victim and whispers, "Agent Heiden! Agent Heiden, wake up." He speaks Spanish, so he doesn't damage his cover and let on that he's really a DEA agent working as a mole. He wants to keep his cover secret as long as he can. Keith's blue eyes open slowly, as he tries to focus on who is in front of him calling his name like they know each other.

"Hi. Do you remember me?" the man asks, as he wears green cargo pants and a black T-shirt. "Agent Heiden... Agent Heiden... It's me Frankie De Luca."

"All right..." Keith slowly picks himself up and leans his weak body against the dirty cold cement walls. "Frankie," he says in a soft voice and smiles back. "Is it really you?"

"Yes, it's me. You don't look too good, but really you never did." Frankie laughs still speaking in Spanish. He, Keith, and Peter applied for the jobs in the DEA Department at the same time and spent many hours studying together.

Keith says in Spanish, "So you're the mole. Can you please tell me how? Because the last time I had saw you, we were dealing with Jose Medina's men and raiding their compound, and you ended up dead on the cement floor like the rest of the agents. That was almost eleven years ago. We were ambushed. I really thought you were dead. Peter and I were the only agents that survived the mission."

Keith tries to move his arms to get some circulation, but he feels very weak. He continues, "Wait a minute. I don't think we should talk. The devices above my head might be on and recording this heartwarming conversation." Keith rolls his tired blue eyes toward the direction of the cameras.

"Don't worry, Keith. I have a device that will override the main panel that's recording this conversation from the upstairs room. I also have some men to help us with your escape. Listen, we don't have enough time to talk. The bosses talked about me being a mole like the others, but they never made it more than five years tops before Jose's enemies killed them. The heads of the DEA Department spoke to me months before the raid. They wanted me to be assigned to be a mole from the inside to bring down Jose Medina and his cartel. I had to fake my death to enter into the drug world. (It wasn't easy leaving my family, friends, coworkers, and even my dog Petie behind.) It wasn't an easy decision, but I did it. Do you understand?" Frankie answers.

""Yes, I understand fully. You were just doing your job. So you were the one that gave me juicy information all these years?" Keith asks.

"Yes, I did," Frankie replies.

"Thanks but what do you get out of all this being secret and having a double life?"

"I have no life besides being a mole, and I promised to do my best to get these bad guys. I'm very sorry about your father," he says.

"Thank you, Frankie, for the kind words. Do you realize that you know more about the outside world than I do? So did you know that Jude kidnapped me? If you did, why did it take you so long to get here?" Keith asks with the feeling of a shooting pain traveling throughout his body.

"I was in Mexico for a month, and I just came back to the states. I was surprised when I heard you were kidnapped. They picked the wrong guy to get the information out of. You're a hard ass to break!" Frankie laughs because it's true.

"How can I trust you after all these years? You have been in this organization for almost eleven years now. What makes you think that you're not one of them?" Keith asks, as he tries to move anyway, but it's not working in his favor. It's just making it worse.

"You were never the one to trust another person... Don't talk. Listen, you can trust me, Keith, or you can die in Mexico!" Frankie exclaims.

"I'm in Mexico?"

"No, not yet, but within days you will be, and they don't like DEA's! They can smell you a mile away!"

"I don't want to go to Mexico. I will be killed for sure!"

"Yes, that's why I'm here to save your ass and bring you home to your family."

"Frankie, what's the DEA code?" Keith suddenly asks, as he looks at Frankie or is that his real name? It has been a very long time.

"What are you talking about?" Franked asks with a surprised look.

"Every mole from the DEA has a code to identify themselves from the bad guys. Do you know the code or not? How can I tell if you're Frankie De Luca? You know it has been many years now," Keith announces, as he tries once again to walk around the room. He doesn't want his legs or other parts of this body to become numb. He tries very hard to shake off the feeling of the drug but no luck. It's really not his year.

"Well...let me think for a minute," Frankie answers his drugged friend. He gets up and stands near the smelly mattress.

"Don't worry I'm not going anywhere." Keith laughs, as he tries to rub the tension from his head with both hands. This feeling was brewing from the first day being captive. Now it's been a couple of weeks, and he knows that he smells like a homeless man on the streets. Keith never let his appearance go; he tried to grow a beard, but he didn't like it. He loves to be clean-shaved and get a haircut every two weeks, but this is beyond his control.

"That's funny," Frankie says, as he leans against the wall. He rubs his brown eyes, as he tries to remember. "Okay, I think I got it. The code is, if I remember correctly, 17479gh. Am I right?"

"It's close enough. I'm all drugged up," Keith answers.

"You were always an ass. Listen, I'm giving you a day and we'll get out of here for good. Are you ready?" Frankie asks.

"Okay… I guess I don't have a choice. What floor are we on?" Keith asks.

"You are underground. There are about fifty men at the work-station, and you can't handle your escape alone," Frankie anwsered. "I have given Peter the location to get you out before you get deported to Mexico forever."

"Peter might come but don't think that our coworkers will help because DEA doesn't work that way," Keith answers because it's the truth. He and his job that he did for the department doesn't mean anything without the order from the government. "Frankie to be honest with you, I really don't want to live if I have to go to Mexico. So be it."

Keith is mentally and physically throwing in the towel about saving his life. Also, he feels strongly that no one from any law enforcement will come and save him from hell. He'll die in this room.

"Listen, seeing you doesn't make me warm and happy inside. I want you home, and I want my life back. I need to retire from this job. I'm young enough to have the family that I always wanted and never could have for some reason or another, but it happened."

CHAPTER
NINETY-TWO

$\mathcal{P}$eter is trying his best to keep his personal feelings of his best friend being kidnapped inside. But the truth of the matter is he's breaking apart at the seams. His cell phone beeps and gets a text message.

It reads, "You have three days or less to save Keith. I think they're planning to bring him to Mexico. I only saw him once a couple of days ago but he was transferred recently to another part of the compound that I don't know about. So if you want him, get him now, not later. I'll keep you posted if I know anything. Here are the directions to the compound. Hopefully you're not too late to save your partner."

Peter is in total shock and sits slowly down in Keith's office chair and stares into space. He thinks to himself how the hell is he going to get the manpower to save one DEA agent from disappearing from the face of the earth? Mexico is a huge country and the people don't really like Americans in their territory asking questions. Once the people find out that Keith is a DEA from America they're going to torture or maybe kill him. Keith's chances of surviving are very slim.

The DEA department doesn't want to find a missing person; they're fighting the war on drugs. The head bosses want to have the police or the FBI handle getting Keith back safely. They will say, "It's their duty to find missing persons, not ours. So get back to work or you'll be on the unemployment line!" Peter can't do it all. He really needs the manpower in order to take down Keith's kidnappers and maybe Jose, Jude, and Alex in the process.

Also, it's not a great sign that the department wants to use Keith's office because he's not using the space at this time. They have a lot of work to do, and they don't care where. Peter is not too happy at all; he's angry that the DEA department is dismissing Keith. They're really trying to say, "We're very sorry, but it's part of the job. This shouldn't be a surprise at all."

CHAPTER
NINETY-THREE

*L*ater that day Christopher and Peter go into the Heiden house at the same time to see how the family is doing. They see Patrick crying, sitting on the couch in the living room.

"Are you okay?" Christopher asks with a concerned look.

Patrick quickly wipes his tears, as he tries to hide that he's highly upset and doesn't know what to do with himself. He's waiting for a terrible phone call that his dad is dead and it's all his fault.

"Sorry, Uncle Christopher, can I talk to Uncle Peter alone?"

"Sure, no problem, but if you need me I'm close by," Christopher replies.

"I'll keep that in mind. Thanks Uncle Christopher," Patrick answers with a weak but soft smile.

A few minutes later, Patrick and Peter sit down for a heart-to-heart talk that Peter always loves to have.

"What's up, Patrick?"

"Uncle Peter, it's my fault that Dad is kidnapped!" Patrick got up from the couch because he can't sit for a minute.

"As I said before, it's not your fault that your father has been kidnapped. Things happen that are beyond your control. Try not to beat yourself up. How is your mom doing?" Peter asks, as he feels sad about this whole thing.

"She's okay I guess. Grandpa and Grandma are here caring for all of us. Also many of the aunts, uncles, and their families have been keeping us company to show their love and support. But at the same time Grandpa puts his two cents in about my dad. Grandma always

445

corrects him. She's a real German. That shuts down the British man in a heartbeat. It's pretty funny when you witness it," Patrick says with a smile. He wishes he had a camcorder at that moment.

Patrick's mode of speech changes and he says "Uncle Peter, it's still all my fault that Dad has been kidnapped because I didn't do the drug transaction!"

Patrick doesn't feel that he deserves the Heiden name. His father is proud of the name even though his grandfather treated him like yesterday's garbage. The last name stands strong.

"Patrick, please keep your voice down. There are people in the house that don't know what your situation was, and we should keep that under wraps forever. Do you understand where I'm coming from?" Peter ask with a sharp tone in his voice that he means business.

"Yes…sure Uncle Peter. I understand."

"Listen, I know for sure that you didn't cause your dad's kidnapping. I think the people who captured your dad planned this many months ago before your business went south. Your father is a DEA agent and has a lot of enemies. So he's a walking target like I am. Please don't put blame on yourself! I really hate to say this, but overall, you're a good son with rough edges in the package." Peter laughs to release some tension.

Patrick smiles a little." I guess, Uncle Peter. Thanks for talking."

"Okay anytime. I'll let you get back to your homework."

"Uncle Peter, can you get Dad and bring him home?"

"Listen, son, I'm not going to lie. You're old enough to understand what I'm up against. The DEA doesn't want to search for Keith anymore. They really want the police to handle the matter. The department is paid by the government to work to fight against drugs on the streets. They really don't have time to find one single DEA agent when they have bigger fish to fry." Peter sighs. "'This is what I'm up against, and I can't find him myself. I need solid evidence so DEA can get involved in the search and get Jose Medina and his cartel."

"Yes, I heard of that man before over the years. Boy, he's hard to catch."

"It's going to be hard, but I'll find him with some backup. Somehow it will work. I just need a break or something," Peter answers.

Peter didn't have the heart to tell Patrick that his dad is being deported to Mexico for good. Just the thought of this plan being real is making Peter sick to his stomach. What if the mole is wrong about the address and he gave Peter the incorrect street where Keith is staying? Peter really has to think fast and try to get the DEA department to be on his side and search for the agent. Keith spent many hours on the job and risked his life for the sake of fighting against drugs on the streets and homes.

Peter is going to have a long summer.

CHAPTER
NINETY-FOUR

An attractive young businesswoman walks into one of the rooms of the funeral home. She gently places an assorted array of beautiful flowers on the table next to the coffin and fixes them before she leaves the room. The coffin is open to the public as well as family members, friends, and coworkers to say their last good-byes. The casket is made from an expensive mahogany wood. It holds a peaceful-looking man in his early forties. Suddenly an older man walks over to the casket and leans over it as he takes out a large cigar. He begins to laugh!

"Please don't get up on my behalf." The old man laughs while the ashes fall on the body. "Oh, sorry about that." He continues, "So why the hell did you have to die? You gave up so easily! You were a total loser from the day you were born! Very sad. Well, you did it to yourself, and you have no one else to blame but yourself. When will you ever learn from your mistakes? Listen, don't you blame your past. You caused this not me! What the hell." He flicks the ashes into the coffin just because he wanted to. He leans forward and shouts, "If you want to live, wake up right now!"

Keith suddenly wakes up! He realizes that the old man in his dream was his father. He also understands that he killed Jose's nephew in cold blood. The details of the whole event are coming back to him. There was no mercy during that time; Keith just wanted to get his point across.

It happened ten years ago during the Jose Medina drug raid with the DEA, the LA police, and ATFs. The raid ended in a bloody mess with both law enforcement and bad guys killed. Everything happened so quickly, but near the end, Keith picked up the young man's gun and ordered him to get on his knees. He placed the gun into the man's mouth and said something in Spanish, "Decir hola al infierno!" (Say hello to hell!). Keith pulled the trigger and the boy's brains exploded onto the back gray-colored wall. Jose's nephew was in his early twenties. This was cold-blooded murder.

There was no evidence to prove that Keith murdered the young man because the boy's body was carried away by Jose's men. They worked quickly, leaving nothing behind before Keith and Peter came back to the room.

Keith doesn't know if Peter witnessed what he was doing. They never talked about the sticky situation. But Peter and Keith were never the same after that. Peter and Julia broke up after many years of being together. Peter blamed Keith for the breakup. Keith and Justine had a huge fight too, and Keith ended up raping her during the fight. No one talked about anything that happened during or after the Jose Medina drug raid.

"Oh my God! What've I done?" Keith cries, at his voice echoes and bounces from wall to wall in his cement-walled room.

He feels terrible about the whole thing and knows that he'll never see his family again because of the choices he made ten years ago. As of right now, Jose is the police, jury, judge, and executioner, and he's going to make Keith's last hours on earth a living hell.

CHAPTER
NINETY-FIVE

*P*eter's cell phone rings. "Hello, Peter," a man's voice says without giving Peter a chance to say hello first. Then all of a sudden Peter says to the person on the other line, "Frank!"

"Yes, listen. I really can't talk for long. I just want to tell you that Jude Henderson and his men were hired by Jose Medina to kidnap Keith," he says quickly, checking over his shoulder to be sure he won't get caught. "Jude Henderson and his men are running the compound and Jack Forrester is with them!"

"What do you mean with them? Did Jose order Jude to kidnap Jack too? I should stop before I know the answers to my questions. Are you sure it's Jack Forrester? You never met the dude in person!"

"Yes, it's him. Jack Forrester is working with Jude. I saw them briefly… Peter, you really have to shut your mouth and listen because I don't have time to talk about your golf games! I don't need anyone finding out what I'm up to. It will be bad for all of us working on this operation! Keith is in an underground location, and there's no real address. I can find out where he is, but you'll have to give me time. It's all driving instructions, but I'll get it for you. Once you get the location, I know that you will come quickly, but you need a heavy backup before you enter the underground compound. There's a lot of men with weapons, and they're not shy to use their new toys. I don't think Keith will be at this place too long… Jose is planning to move him to Mexico," Frank whispers, as he tries to keep his cover from blowing. "I'll text you the directions once I get them. Then come quickly or you will never see Keith again."

"How do you know that Keith is really at this location? Did you speak or see him recently? It might be a trap, and I don't like getting caught," Peter exclaims, as he sees Justine and Colin having lunch together in the kitchen.

"Listen… I saw Keith the other day, but they might have moved him from the last spot. Peter, don't ask so many questions just get here fast before it's too late! I have to go now… I'll get back to you. Just keep your cell phone on… I'll be in touch. Be careful," Frank says quickly, as he looks around to make sure that no one heard his conversation with a DEA agent.

"Wait! Wait, Frank, what about Jack? Are you really sure that he's one of them?" Peter asks briskly.

"Peter, I've seen him with my own eyes and he's working for the bad guys! It's not too pretty because he was the mole! I have to go now before I get caught in something I can't get out of," Frank answers rudely. Suddenly the sound of a dial tone is heard.

Peter feels alone, confused, and angry at the same time. He can handle a lot of situations that are extremely bad, but this is throwing him off. Once he gets the information from Frankie, Peter knows that he needs that backup to save Keith from hell and get the bad guys all in one trip. The question is how is he going to do that without additional information. Frankie told him everything he knows, and Peter doesn't feel that he's lying to him. Peter desperately needs solid evidence, like now. If this doesn't happen, Keith will die or be gone forever.

CHAPTER
NINETY-SIX

*A*fter the FBI saw the video footage of the kidnapping at the gas station/mini market, they decided that they would be handling the search for Special Agent Heiden. The FBI, DEA, and the police departments agreed that they don't want this news to leak to the press. That's all they need for the public to know that one DEA agent is kidnapped during broad daylight. This whole situation would be a pure embarrassment for the law enforcement world.

Peter is not at all happy with the updated news. Now he really feels helpless! He wants to save his partner but he's only one man. He has weapons but no extra manpower. He's exhausted from the waiting and hearing the bullshit that the FBI is giving him about finding Keith. The waiting part is the killer, especially dealing with a kidnapping situation. Peter is afraid that Keith is already in Mexico or any another South American country.

All of Peter's bosses have been saying. "I'm so sorry, Agent Darling, we can't do anything. It looks like it's out of our hands. As you know, the FBI is handling the search for Agent Heiden. We have bigger responsibilities, like fighting the world on drugs which seems to get stronger each minute that passes. Our priority is getting the highest drug lord from America's Most Wanted list. Sorry, Peter, we're not the search and rescue department! That's the police and the FBI's job, not ours. But I really feel your pain. If you need anything else please let me know. Happy to help out any other way I can!"

A week goes by, and Peter is getting more worried than before. Each day that passes will be harder to find Keith. He's also concerned because he can't reach Frankie (the mole). He doesn't answer his messages or texts. It's never a good sign when your informant is not getting back to you! Peter is really stuck in a deep hole! Frankie is the only one with inside eyes and ears to the operation. What can Peter do? He might as well throw in the towel!

Just the thought of not saving his best friend is killing him inside. Peter can't sleep, eat, or take a hot shower for that matter, and he has not been home with Elise since Keith was kidnapped. He's staying at Keith's house with his family because Justine asked him to, and he doesn't feel right leaving the family alone. Elise calls Peter from time to time to hear how he's doing. But the real reason is that she's not allowed to come to the Heiden's house as per Justine's rule. The doctor ordered Justine to get a lot of bed rest. She's in the first tri-semester of her pregnancy and that, along with her fragile state of mind during this trying time, is putting her close to the edge.

Peter won't talk about his actual feelings. He's fully trained not to take any case personally, but this is different. His best friend's life is on the line, and they are like brothers. He wishes that Julia Ulrich would call him again. He really misses her, and she can make things better especially with his state of mind right now. Julia gets Peter in many ways that Elise can't, especially after being together for over ten years. But after the Jose Medina raid, the love they had for each other fell apart very quickly. It was Peter's first love, and that's why it hurts so much. Believe it or not, Peter never deleted her cell number from his phone. I guess he needs the closure that his relationship with Julia is really over. The last time that they spoke, he told her that it would never work out because he had someone else. Peter is the one that pulled the plug, not her. He also knows that Julia is more of a doctor than Elise could ever be, but he will never verbalize that. Peter knows that he will break down like a little child if he sees Elise, and it's best to have a clear mind. He wants to be the head of the operation that recovers Keith back and the bad guys too.

Once again, Peter is sitting alone in the dark behind Keith's desk. He's playing with a video footage of the kidnapping on the copy DVD on Keith's TV screen. As he presses the rewind button, he still has no answers. Peter wants to make sure the bosses (the head chiefs) of the DEA department did get a chance to see the video. The DEA has a code of brotherhood like an officer of the law! They are not alone in any situation and that also includes kidnapping. Does that code still apply? Do the bosses that work on the higher floors of this building still use the system too?

A half-hour later Peter knocks on one of the doors of his bosses. "Come in," says the lady on the other side of the door. Peter walks in slowly; he has only met this person once during his years on the job, and he thinks she's the one that signs his paycheck. She's also highly attractive, which is in her favor too.

"I'm so sorry to interrupt you, but do you have a minute?" Peter asks, as he holds the video DVD in his hand like it was his best friend.

"Hello, Agent Darling. I'm happy to finally meet you again! How can I help you today?" the lady asks using her business and friendly tone at the same time.

Rebecca Johnson is a very successful African American woman that worked very hard to climb the business ladder of the DEA. She now has twenty years under her belt and loves her job! She put a lot of hours in the field and didn't get this far overnight. It was a man's job but she proved everyone wrong in the end. She's book smart and very quick to use her gun if need be.

"I'm here because Agent Heiden is missing and the FBI isn't coming up with anything. I was wondering if we, as DEA agents, if we have the manpower and the bullets for the mission," Peter requests, as he feels very nervous asking for help because all of his life he did everything by himself.

"Listen, Agent Darling, you seem like a nice guy, but our hands are tied. Anyway, I want to show you this before we continue our conversation," Rebecca says, as she puts a case report on her desk. Her mannerisms are telling the story, and it's not good from where Peter is standing. Peter quickly opens the case file and starts to read.

"Agent Jack Forrester wrote this report a week before he left. What did you do to deserve this kind of evaluation from him?" Rebecca asks in a calm voice. "You must have upset him for some reason or another."

Peter keeps on reading. "What the fuck?" He says freely, "Agent Keith Heiden is mentally unstable and unable to handle any situation for this department. Agent Peter Darling, that's me, is lazy with his work and it's never on time. Agent Liam Gallagher is a follower, not a leader and never will be, and Agent Sean Tierney shows no interest in being a DEA agent. He seems lost on the team," Peter shouts with a confused look.

"I really don't know the guy personally. He's not my drinking buddy. I only talked to him maybe a few times. The conversations were only about work and nothing else. Jack had it out for Keith, for no reason at all. Agent Johnson, this report is not accurate at all. It doesn't make sense! Did you know Jack?" Peter asks.

Peter doesn't understand why this person would make up lies about him and the people that he works with. We all are like family. "If ex-agent Forrester didn't like us, he should've told us to our face, not behind our backs."

"I know him professionally, not personally. He wasn't the kind of guy that you could really talk too. He was in the army, and it was in his blood. He was a soldier through and through. Get or give orders, that's who Agent Jack Forrester was. I don't know why he left DEA. He was doing a great job and very professional for that matter. I don't understand. No one really knew what his game plan was. It felt like he just left, and he never said his good-byes. His secretary Mindy was very surprised that he was leaving. She knew nothing. She sat inches away from the agent! So my final thoughts are that his case report told us that your team is messed up. The DEA department is not going to search for Agent Heiden because you say so. This is my final answer on this matter," Rebecca states firmly.

"Wait! Wait! Did you get a chance to look at the video footage of Agent Heiden's kidnapping?" Peter asks with a spark in the tone of his voice.

"Yes, my coworkers and I looked at the video footage and it's very sad to see this crime taking place. But I'm sorry to say that the decision to save Agent Heiden is not mine alone to make. The other coworkers have decided not to go ahead with it," Rebecca says.

"Is there a mole that's working for us inside the Jose Medina cartel?" Peter asks, as he feels that he has a lot of questions and a fire in his stomach.

Rebecca's dark brown eyes open wider. "What are you talking about? I thought you're concerned with getting Agent Heiden from his kidnappers, whoever they might be. I'm sorry, Agent Darling, you're not making any sense."

"Please listen to me for a minute! It was ten years after the Jose Medina drug raid and the DEA assigned four agents to become the mole working for the department. They agreed, and during the past ten years, three of the four DEA moles died. Also their secret died with them. Right now one is still alive and working for us. At that time the bad guys knew something was up, because many of the jobs were going south."

Peter continues, "Todd wasn't the mole working for Jose. It was for Alex Raninsky's cousin Anastasia, who was married to Todd. He didn't know he was doing her dirty work because he was madly in love with his Russian wife. Todd fed her information about the job, especially regarding Jose Medina's next move. The mole told me that Jack Forrester is working for Jude Henderson and Jose Medina. Agent Johnson, I really don't have any proof about Agent Forrester's plan or why he left this department. All I know is he didn't like us or the job. I guess he's showing off now."

Rebecca sighs. "Thank you, Agent Darling, for giving this some thought, but as you know I need solid proof that Agent Forrester is working for the bad guys."

Peter sits down in a chair because he's tired but not finished talking as of yet. He thinks to himself that maybe Agent Johnson can help because he's stuck with no answers in sight.

"Yes, I guess so, but something doesn't fit right. I might be the clown in this department, but I do my job the best I can. Also, my team is the best, especially with what we're up against. Now, Agent Forrester is out of the DEA just a week before Agent Heiden was kidnapped. We can't locate him. It's as if he just dropped off the face of the earth. It just seems very strange how the two might be related, but I don't know how or why. What do you think about all of this,

Agent Johnson?" Peter asks, with a look of concern and worry on his face.

"Yes, but Agent Darling, you have nothing to back up your statement that Agent Forrester is working for Jude Henderson or Jose Medina. Or you can't find him. I'm sorry, but I really think this subject and this investigation is dead…until you have solid proof to go and get Agent Forrester and the people he works for we have nothing to talk about… Except what you may be having for lunch today?" Rebecca replies, as she tries to sympathize with his pain.

"Okay, why would Agent Forrester write those terrible things about my team? I really think that he didn't want us to search for Agent Heiden from the start. He wanted us to believe that Keith was a loose cannon and the DEA is wasting their time trying to find him. He doesn't play by government rules. But why would he write a report?" Peter snaps because now he's angry. "I smell something not right and it's not bad cheese. It's very strange!"

"I'm so sorry, Agent Darling, I don't know what to say. I'm sorry about your partner. I hate to say this, but the whole department feels that Agent Heiden is a loose cannon who never really played by the rules. He has to save himself in this situation." She sighs and takes a minute to collect her thoughts before she continues. "Please let yourself out of my office. I have a lot of work to do and need to finish it before the day is up," she answers apologetically but to the point.

"I think it's important that we go after Jack Forrester!" Peter says emphatically before heading toward the door.

"Agent Darling, in this department we play by the rules. As I've already said we need solid proof before we even move forward. If you can get me information, then we can talk," Rebecca replies, as she feels really terrible for Agent Heiden but there's not much she can do from where she's sitting. Right now it's totally in the hands of the FBI.

Minutes later Peter walks out of his boss's office. He's not at all happy. Then suddenly he receives a text message from the mole, Frankie. It gives the directions to Keith's location and the knowledge that Jose, Jude, and Jack are there too! Peter turns back to Rebecca's office with a huge smile on his face.

CHAPTER
NINETY-SEVEN

~~~~~~

*S*uddenly a large, muscular British man who works for Jude, pours ice-cold water over Keith's head. He wakes up from his drug-infested state and coughs trying to catch his breath while not drowning from the water. His arms are tied to an uncomfortable wooden chair. Someone must have changed him into clean dark green-colored medical scrubs. He can't move his chest, hands, and legs because they are tied with two inch thick rope. It's slowly cutting off his circulation throughout his body. Keith feels totally helpless and alone in this sticky situation.

"Wake up, Agent Heiden!" says a short Spanish man well dressed in expensive clothes and groomed.

Keith's blue eyes become wider as he sees the devil himself.

"Jose!" Keith never really met Jose in person, but there's a lot of pictures posted at his job on the list of America's top ten Most Wanted. He's one of the most dangerous drug cartel lords in the world. Jose made trillions of dollars throughout the years and killed more people than you can imagine.

Jose starts to talk to Keith in Spanish and seconds later he says something that makes Keith extremely angry. Keith's body tightens, ready to fight. His mind and body, however, are not up to game.

Keith answers back in Spanish, "¡Vaya al diablo Jose!! ¡Va a pagar matar a mis compañeros de trabajo y amigos durante los años!" (Go to hell, Jose! You're going to pay for killing my coworkers and friends over the years!)

"No, Agent Heiden, you're going to pay for killing my men but most of all my nephew! Do you remember? If you don't remember you're going to when we're finished!" Jose answers back in his native tongue. "You're also leaving the states, and we're heading back to Mexico."

"Jose, I don't want to go to Mexico! I don't remember killing your nephew! It was ten years ago. I don't know what day or time it is! How the fuck would I remember what I did ten years ago?" Keith answers in Spanish.

"Believe me, Agent Heiden, you'll remember! You'll also tell me the name of the mole that's working for the DEA," Jose shouts, as he flicks the ashes from his Cuban cigar onto Keith's lap.

"Shit!" Keith exclaims as the ashes burn his skin.

Suddenly Jude and his partner walk into the cement room. Keith is more surprised than ever. This is not his day.

"Jack! What the fuck! What are you doing here?"

"Hello, Keith! I guess from all your questions that you really missed me. You speak perfect Spanish. I didn't know that you were highly intelligent, especially speaking three languages. That's very impressive! I bet your mom is proud of you!" Jack says with an evil smile on his face.

"You think that you…know me…by reading my file. It doesn't constitute knowing me! Todd wasn't the mole that leaked DEA information out. It was you!" Keith yells, as he can feel the blood rushing through his veins as he's ready to attack Jack. "I never liked you… from the beginning and now… I know why, because you're a traitor to the DEA…and to our country!"

"Think what you want! I love this country and I have risked my life more than once just to fight for freedom. I'm not going to justify myself to you because you're a prisoner not a friend." Jack continues, "The people who I work for have the upper hand as do I! Who's going to stop us? No one, because they are not here! They don't care if you're dead or alive anyway. Todd's wife was working for Alex but not for us. Poor Todd didn't ever have a chance to live on this earth. He didn't even know that his wife was the mole or spy for Alex Raninsky, her cousin. Let me tell you a story because I can, and you can't leave the room." He laughs because he told a joke and it's true. "Two years ago, Jude offered me a huge business deal that I couldn't pass up, particularly where the money was concerned. He explained to me that Jose wanted the drug cartel, but he had to prove himself. I would be very handy if I could get juicy information from inside law enforcement ahead of time. Oh, before I forget, I took these pictures of you, your family, Dr. Sheppard, and I can't forget Justine and her lover, Treat Miller, the accountant. I hope you like them as I took great pride in them. Photography is one of my favorite hobbies! The great thing was, I got paid for my crafty work. Sorry that I'm bragging, Keith, but I can't help it! You have to give me credit that I also messed up your SUVs…not once but twice. Sometimes I surprise myself," Jack says with a huge smile on his face. "I hope you enjoyed your recent ride!" He laughs and the other men laugh too.

Although Jack changes his mannerism to business mode, he still has a lot more to say to Keith. "I'm sorry to say but I don't take credit for killing Mr. Preston Williamson from Interpol. That was Jude's handy work. Before I continue, I didn't hear you say thank you to Jude or me on a job well done." Jack says while using a voice like a parent talking to his child in public.

"When hell freezes over! What I can say is fuck you!"

Jack just smiles as bad guys do. He's not at all surprised by Keith's reaction. It's kind of entertaining from where he's standing. To watch a full grown man tied and drugged up. The prisoner is not with us half the time. Jack never really cared for Keith in the first place. He deserves everything he gets. Karma is a bitch.

Jude says, "I'm sorry, Keith, that you feel this way but you're already in hell! Oh, before I forget, I also killed your father. I know that you will be happy about that. I think you didn't care one way or another if he was a dead or alive."

Keith snaps back, "Whatever!" He goes back to giving Jack his cold deadly look.

Suddenly he feels really light headed. It feels like he sucked all the helium out of a very large balloon. He can't imagine what kind of drugs were put into him because he's so out of it. He wants answers but with his state of mind, it's going to take a long time to ask his questions.

"Jude...why would...you kill... Preston? He didn't do...anything to you," Keith asks, as he tries to shake off the feeling of the drugs in his system, but it's not working out in his favor. It's only making matters worse. He feels like he's on a bad carnival ride that won't stop.

"Well, if you must know, old chap, Officer Preston Williamson was a thorn in my side for years, and he was blocking my path on the plans that I had. On the story of your dad, well let's just say it was a Christmas gift to you... Thank you, Jude... Welcome, Keith, anytime!" Jude says in a firm but friendly voice with a satisfied smile too! "I guess if I'm talking...too crazy, then I'm going to get crazy... Answers from a crazy one!" Keith says, as he still tries to shake his head. "What...what about... Alex? Does he know...about your plans teaming up together as college buddies, or is it a secret?"

Keith feels like he's had too much to drink. The last time he was drunk was over twenty-three years ago. It was the day he was disowned by his family.

"Well, you know how the saying goes, what Alex doesn't know won't hurt him! Besides, you know how bad guys play dirty. We're bad to the bone!" Jude laughs. "So do you have answers to Jose's questions? Did you kill his nephew because you felt like it? Also who's the mole that's working for Jose's cartel but really working for the DEA?"

Jude walks closer to Keith, then squeezes his face like an orange. Keith spits into Jude's face telling him that he doesn't like what he's doing to him. Jude lets go of Keith and wipes off the saliva with a handkerchief that he has in his pocket.

"We can't hurt you because your past already damaged you, but we can get your family!" Jude says.

"Don't you dare touch my family! I will break you!" Keith shouts as he tries desperately to get out of the thick ropes. "I don't remember killing Jose's nephew or anything about a mole!"

Keith is lying about what he knows, because he honestly feels if they didn't hurt or kill his family by now they wouldn't do it. They have him and that's all they wanted in the first place. Keith is the main target and no one else. It's only a matter of time if he tells anything to the bad guys so he can go home and see his family again. But only time will tell.

"Enough with the talking. Just get it over with!" Jose orders as he sits comfortably watching the show from afar.

"I want to get back home before night falls!"

"Okay, you heard the boss!" Jack replies, as he walks in front of Jude to get the job done.

Keith spots a very long needle. His blue eyes become wider, as he still tries desperately to wiggle his way out of the ropes.

"What the hell is that?" Keith shouts.

"It's sodium pentothal, and you know it as the truth drug. This will help you to remember all about what happened ten years ago. Especially what you did to Jose's nephew. Also we need the mole's name that's working for the DEA," Jack answers calmly. "If Jose is satisfied he will let you go home unharmed."

"I don't know any mole...primarily working for the DEA! I don't remember what happened ten years ago, about what went down during the raid against Jose! So why don't you kill me because I'm not going to tell you anything since I don't know!" Keith answers, as he feels exhausted, and he doesn't have the strength to fight for his life.

He won't be able to see his family ever again. Keith doesn't realize that he's just given permission for the bad guys to kill him with no regrets whatsoever. Not a great move on the agent's part.

"Well, it's up to Jose, if he is going to kill you or let you live in Mexico and suffer the last years of your life on earth in hell," Jude answers and spits in Keith's face to return the favor.

Keith can't see him but he senses Jose is behind him. Jose is just relaxing and enjoying the show that's playing in from of him while sitting and smoking a Cuban cigar. The smoke travels in the air making Keith sick to his stomach. He really hates when people smoke cigarettes of any kind, because the smell reminds him of his father.

"Jose, tienes que creerme que no recuerdo nada pasar diez años matando especialmente su sobrino! Por favor, Jose, tienen un corazón déjame ir y haría cualquier cosa para venir a conseguir. Usted puede salir del país en paz con todo el poder que usted gana en el proceso."(Jose, you have to believe me that I don't remember anything that happened ten years ago, especially killing your nephew! Please, Jose, have a heart! Let me go, and I won't do anything to come after you.)

Jose is sitting down in the back of the room just listening to the conversation and smoking a smelly cigar. He laughs and answers Keith in Spanish. "¡Muera el hijoputa de la madre!" (Die mother fucker!)

"Hold him down, so I have a direct shot!" Jack orders the two very large British men standing on each side of Keith.

"Jack, you don't want to do this. What about your future in the government sector? What happened to that dream of yours that you'd always talk about in the office?" Keith asks, as he tries to not be a target of entertainment in this sideshow.

"Keith, shut the fuck up and let me do my job!" Jack snaps without warning. Keith's eyes are focusing on the three-inch needle that's coming closer to him. "Now hold still. This will only take a minute!"

Keith spits into Jack's eye.

"Son of a bitch! Hold him down!" Jack shouts as he rubs his eyes.

The British men hold the prisoner down forcefully with their bodies.

Keith's face turns beet red and he angrily shouts, "Get away from me!"

Jack collects himself from the assault by the DEA agent. "This will only take a minute and then you can have lunch afterward," Jack says with a smile.

"No!"

CHAPTER
NINETY-EIGHT

〰〰〰〰〰〰〰〰〰〰〰〰〰〰〰〰〰〰〰〰〰〰〰〰〰〰〰〰〰〰〰〰〰〰

*T*he DEA now has enough evidence from Frankie, the special agent and mole. There's a warrant for the arrest of Jude Henderson, Jack Forrester, and Jose Medina too. Hopefully, Keith will still be there and not in Mexico by the time the good guys arrive. Peter is having bad luck trying to get Frankie on the cell phone. I guess he went undercover until the law enforcement agents come to get him. Frankie is itching to get out of the drug world and spend the rest of his days in the witness protection program somewhere in the world.

Two hours later the DEA, the police, and other law enforcement reach their destination. They come with full force, lots of weapons and equipment to fight the bad guys. They are all wearing protective bullet-proof vests and now are advised to wear their gas masks on site. The K-9 police are also there for extra backup.

One San Diego SWAT officer quickly puts an explosive charge on the doors that enter into the underground compound. The officer goes back into formation with his task team without a second to spare. The explosion blows the doors wide open. At the same time shots from four tear gas containers launch from the guns of two SWAT officers, creating a screen of pain and confusion within. The SWAT team enters in two lines, one on each side of the tunnel entrance. They're aware of their surroundings and know that danger can come from any direction. The entry to the underground compound where Jose Medina, Jude Henderson, Jack Forrester, and Special Agent Keith Heiden are (hopefully he's still there) is camouflaged with shrubs and dirt to make it look like another hill in the dry forest of California. It's only a couple of miles away from the Mexican border.

After a quick pre-raid briefing all the teams of the law enforcement agencies, San Diego SWAT, FBI, CIRG's Tactical teams and the DEA task force enter into action. Then suddenly without warning shots are fired back and forth. Peter comes further into the compound to try and find Keith; he has no blueprint to follow or any memory of what to look for. It's like a massive maze with no end in sight! Which way does he go? Peter sets his mind to the task and then orders the Squads! "Go turn this place inside out!"

The smoke from the tear gas makes it hard to shoot. The noises echo and bounce off the cement walls. Peter will have to remove his head gear and use all his senses to the end of this journey. He does have the upper hand, however, because he and others are wearing gas masks and they can see their target easier.

Peter desperately looks everywhere with caution to find his partner but still no sight of him, Jose, Jude, or Jack for that matter. He listens carefully to any noise that might be an enemy around the corner. Peter is having a hard time seeing through his mask because the smoke is very thick, and he's having difficulty breathing too. He opens the doors quickly with his fingers locked on his gun. Peter is ready to shoot if necessary. He's getting highly worried about Keith and his welfare. He's afraid that he will open one of the doors and find Keith dead on the cement floor with a bullet between his blue eyes. Peter hears from his walkie-talkie that the cops are saying clear and secured at their station. Finally Peter reaches the last door to this long hallway.

He opens it quickly and says, "Police!"

Peter's eyes are wide from what he sees in front of him. Keith is tied to a chair and passed out. He's not very sure if his partner is alive or dead.

Then suddenly three men come running into the room without taking notice of Peter. It's Jude, Jose, and Jack.

"Police! Stop right there! Don't move!" Peter orders as he feels his heart pounding against his chest. He can't believe that they're all in front of him.

The smoke gas has disappeared, and Peter takes off his gas mask because it's now safe to breathe freely.

Jude and Jose are carrying weapons themselves and are not going down without a fight.

"Put down your guns now!" Peter orders. He'll never put his gun down, and he's an expert shot!

"Put down your guns, or I will make this situation very messy!" Peter orders again with a firm, clear voice.

Peter might seem soft and childish at times, but when it comes down to business he's very serious.

"Put the guns down, NOW!"

One by one like clockwork the three men take off their masks. It's now safe to breathe freely. But for how long?

"I guess you'll have to shoot us, Agent Peter Darling, because we're not going down without a fight," shouts Jose with a smile showing no fear whatsoever about dying.

Then out of nowhere shots come from Jack's gun, but Peter, without even blinking, pushes Keith over and drops down on this knee in front of his friend. Peter shoots back with his tactical MP5 full automatic machine gun. He shoots the three men at the same time. Jack in the chest, Jude in the leg, and Jose directly between the eyes. The only one that is still alive is Jude. Both Jack and Jose are dead.

Jude doesn't care if he's hurt; he's trying to reach for the gun that he dropped. Peter gets up from his position and quickly clears all the guns away. He shoots Jude's hand and Jude screams from the pain.

"Enough!" Peter shouts, as he puts the other gun on safety lock and into the back of his pants. He immediately picks up Jude from the floor like a helpless animal. Peter places Jude on the chair where Jose had been sitting. He cuffs him to the chair and tell him his rights.

Liam, other agents, and police are coming down the hallway now to see the damage that Peter has caused. Peter rushes to Keith's aid. Then suddenly he checks his partner's pulse, but it's fragile. Maybe talking to him will help at this point.

"Keith! Wake up! Are you okay?" Peter yells.

"We need medical attention now!" Liam orders through his walkie-talkie.

"On our why!" answers someone that responds to Liam's cry for help. He sees Peter starting to break down.

"Peter, we can pick it up from here. I think you need to get some air. I'm not asking you, I'm ordering you to leave this room and let us do the clean up."

It's time to collect the bodies of the bad guys as well as the drugs, money, and weapons that are worth over a million dollars. It's a really good day for the good guys!

Jude Henderson is arrested along with his men that were still in the building. Jose Medina's cartel dies along with him. Can't forget Jack Forrester who died as a criminal, not a hero to his country that he said he loved so much.

Six hours later Keith is treated at the hospital for dehydration. He's very weak from not eating and needs time to detox from any drugs that are in his system. He will live another day.

More good news for the good guys! Later that week the police from Death Valley find Alex Raninsky and his crew along with Todd's wife, Anastasia. They are all arrested.

The DEA mole Frank De Luca is now under witness protection and living the life that he always wanted. He's no longer a DEA agent or a mole under another drug cartel. He's thrilled being retired, with a new name, a new black lab named Petie, and a new life. He lives where no one knows his location, and he loves it that way.

CHAPTER
NINETY-NINE

A lady in her early forties walks into the hospital room that says number 213. She sighs as she opens the door.

"Can I help you?" a gentleman in a business suit says to her. The room is filled with people, and she stands out like a sore thumb. He sees the lady look a little pale. "Miss, are you okay?"

"I'm sorry! I think I have the wrong room number," the lady answers with a look of surprise and embarrassment. She tries to leave quickly, but suddenly a man's voice exclaims, "Jennifer!" She'd not recognize that voice but has a feeling it is her long lost little brother.

"Jennifer!" The people make a pathway so Keith; who is lying in the hospital bed, can see who's in front of him. "Agents, this is my sister!"

"Sorry, Ms. Heiden!" answers one of the FBI agents. "Well, I think, we're done here. If you have any questions, please call us." Keith and the federal agent shake hands. "Good-by, we're happy that you're alive and back with DEA."

"Thank you, Agent Ross," Keith answers with a smile.

Jennifer walks over to her little brother while the agents walk away quickly and quietly to let the brother and sister have alone time.

"Hi, Jennifer!" Keith says with a huge smile. Jennifer is the only person that makes him very nervous. It doesn't matter if it was two decades ago since they last saw each other; the feeling has never left him.

"I can't believe that you remember me!" she says in surprise.

"How can I not? You're my favorite sister!"

"You're very sweet to say that! I'm happy that you're alive and well. But, before I forget, Mom is outside, and she wants to see you. She's talking to an old friend in the hallway, but she'll be right in to visit with you. Is that okay?" Jennifer asks.

"That's fine… What are you doing here? Don't you live in Chicago?"

"Yes I live in Oak Park near Chicago. Mom lives with me and my family. Anyway, Christopher called me and told us what happened and said that they found you. We took the first flight to California."

Jennifer looks at her brother and notices that he didn't change one bit. Besides the after effect of the ordeal, Keith is aging gracefully and not that bad looking either!

"How long has Megan been living with you?" Keith asks, as he tries to get comfortable in his hospital bed, but it's not working out in his favor.

Jennifer understands that Keith wouldn't call their mother mom. She decides to bite her tongue so she doesn't say what she really wants to say to him.

"Well…let's see. It has been at least five years since Mom put Dad in the nursing home. Enough about me, how are you doing?"

"I'm fine, I guess… Just trying to get the drugs out of my system. I'm happy to say that I wouldn't be addicted to the stuff," Keith answers honestly.

Jennifer has to say something or she'll explode. "Do you want to see Mom? Because she's outside…"

"That's fine…tell her to come in," Keith answers without thinking what she asked of him.

"I'm surprised that you wanted to see her after your huge fight with Mom… Do you remember that fight on the cemetery grounds? Do you know that you made her cry!" Jennifer says upset at her little brother.

"I'm sorry. I was angry at the time!" Keith snaps back. He never saw it coming from her.

"I know that you are angry from all the years of hardship, but she's our mother! Believe it or not, Keith, she was in the middle of Dad's madness and had nowhere to go!"

"Okay… Okay! Jennifer, enough! I'm not really in the mood to fight with you on the subject… Please leave it alone! I have my reasons… So please drop it," Keith requests loudly.

Jennifer quickly changes her attitude because she isn't getting anywhere.

"I'm so confused," he sighs.

"I know, Keith… It's sad to say, but you'll never get the answers to your questions that you want desperately from our parents… Please try to let it go and move on with your life," Jennifer says with a word of encouragement and wisdom that comes from being the big sister. She puts her warm soft hand on his for comfort.

"I really hate it when you're right!"

Jennifer laughs, and seconds later Keith smiles from her reaction. He suddenly realizes that Peter is not the only one that has talent to make people laugh… *Beat that, buddy!*

"I always remembered your laughter, and it hasn't changed after all these years."

Megan walks into the room and Keith is a little stunned at her presence. It caught him off guard.

"Hello, Keith!" she says with an Irish accent and smile. "This is for you! Hopefully, this will help you recover faster." Megan puts the assorted flowers that are in a vase on the nightstand. Attached to it is a get well card.

"Thank you!" Keith says with a memory of Megan getting all excited when she gave presents on a birthday, at Christmas, or any other happy event in the life of their family.

Megan is so relieved that her son is alive and that she's finally talking to him in person. He looks weak from losing a lot of weight, and he also has a pale complexion. She can't imagine what Keith went through.

"Do you know that I prayed very hard for you to come home safely?" Megan says as she touches Keith's hand.

Keith is very touched that his mother cared so much about his well being. He can now see and feel her love. Her blue Irish eyes say it all.

"We're finally back together! I love you and always will!" Megan says with happiness in her voice as she holds his hand for warmth and love. She starts to tear up, but in a good way! Finally, she has her family back, and husband can't stop her from loving them the way she always wanted to. It's a great feeling.

"Thank you for caring, so much," Keith answers, as he quietly wipes his tears away. He never thought he would ever get this feeling.

"Did you ever get a chance to read the letter that your dad gave to you? You know, the letter that I'd personally handed to you?"

"Yes, I remember, and no, I didn't get a chance to read it as of yet," Keith answers.

He doesn't know where the letter is. Knowing his luck Justine might have thrown it away because she felt like spring cleaning for the hundredth time. He thought he was a neat freak but Justine is worse than he is on many levels.

Megan looks at her watch. "Oh my God! Sorry Lord!" She looks up to the heavens. "Jennifer, I have to take my pills with food… Remember?"

"Okay," Jennifer says with a confused look. "Keith, is there a food court or café close by?"

Megan releases her grip on Keith's hand. She automatically gives him a kiss on his forehead like he used to get when he was little. It was a happy memory that he never really forgot. Keith smiles at her for the kind gesture.

"Keith, I'm sorry. Is the food court close by?" Megan asks, as she rubs his clean blond hair

"I think it's on the first floor where the main information desk is… You can ask the hospital staff members," Keith answers in between a yawn. "Sorry about that. I guess I need more sleep."

"That's okay, my love, we truly understand," Megan answers with a motherly voice.

Suddenly Megan changes her tone and says, "Okay, Jennifer, let's go. Keith needs his rest. We'll be back in an hour or two, and then we can catch up talking about the years we've missed."

"Okay, that's fine… Have fun!"

The picture of the two of them is a funny sight. Jennifer, who's almost six feet tall being pushed out quickly by Megan who's only 5'1" in height. It makes Keith smile because there's no fire in sight to make them leave so quickly.

"Thank you! Get some rest. We'll be back!" Megan says.

CHAPTER
ONE HUNDRED

A minute goes by and Keith is out like a light underneath his covers. His head is lying comfortably on a pillow that's not soft at all but it is good enough for now. He just wants to get that needed rest before he heads back home.

Suddenly without warning laughter fills his room. Keith wakes up from a deep sleep.

"What the fuck?" Keith shouts, as he sees a woman standing by the dresser. "Dr. Sheppard, what are you doing here?" He says to himself, *I really wish I had my gun right now!*

Caught by surprise, Elise turns around quickly and knocks off all the get well cards that are on the dresser. It's like an avalanche that's hard to stop.

"Oh my God… Sorry for the mess… Boy, you have a lot of get well cards! I guess you're liked."

"Dr. Sheppard, what are you doing here?" Keith asks. For some strange reason his blood pressure goes up quickly when he encounters her presence.

"I just wanted to say hi," Elise answers. She has a concerned look on her face. It's hard to see a grown man lying in a hospital bed. It doesn't help if the patient has lost weight and his complexion is ashen too. Elise never visited anyone in the hospital before. Her two sisters and brother asked her many times to see her new nieces and nephews when they were born in the hospital. She gets sick to her stomach when she sees the sight of blood and IV (intervenes). It took all of her might to get into the room to see the patient. She says to herself, "Elise just take baby steps, and you might surprise yourself!"

"You could have called," Keith says and gives her a clue that there is a phone beside his bed.

"I could have, but I was concerned. I wanted to meet you in person," Elise answers.

"Dr. Sheppard, thanks for coming and I'm really fine... I'm very tired and I need my strength before I go home. So if you don't mind, you can let yourself out of my room... That would be great. Thank you for coming!" Keith replies, as he pulls his covers closer to his head.

"I'm not going to leave as of yet!"

"Good God, why not?"

"Because I have something to say, and I don't think I have the courage to repeat it."

Keith looks around for the nurse button to press so someone will come and get this doctor out of his room... But it's not going to be easy by any means.

"I want to tell you that Peter Darling and I are still a couple. I picked my new found love over my old job. So I'm not your therapist anymore. I really hope you understand," Elise announces... I really want to say something that's been on my mind for a while."

"Dr. Sheppard, please stop! Listen, you seem like a very compassionate lady that cares a lot about what you do. As you know, you have to stand by a code of ethics that you swore an oath to from the day you started your career. So under the situation we can't be friends," Keith says as he feels a little uncomfortable. Maybe it's the conversation or the bed he's laying on.

"I know what I'm up against... I'm not going to lie. I did pick Agent Darling over my job, and that's my first love, and it always will be," Elise states. "Agent Heiden, you already know that without me saying it."

"Dr. Sheppard, I bet you like to take chances in life! Like bungee jumping off a high cliff to celebrate your twenty-first birthday," Keith says with a smile.

"Something like that," she answers with a look of confusion.

"Dr. Sheppard, you came to see me for a reason and you won't leave my room until you get it. So, let's get started. Dr. Sheppard, come closer!" Keith commands, as he looks straight into Elise's hazel eyes for a quick response.

"What?" she says, but she has an idea what he may be asking for. Elise is getting closer.

"Come closer to me!" he commands.

It's taken a little while for Elise to figure out what the agent wants her to do.

"Agent Heiden, I really don't think this is a good idea! What if someone comes into the room unannounced and sees us?" Elise asks with that confused look on her face.

Keith laughs, "Yes, that would be a very sticky situation right then and there. Listen, Dr. Sheppard; it's a simple command! Come closer to me!" he says with a stronger tone that he means business.

"Okay," Elise says, as she can feel her heartbeat coming out of her chest.

Elise says to herself, *This is not good but is it? It's going to happen finally... Elise what are you waiting for, just do it! You have been dreaming of this for a long time, ever since that first day you laid eyes on him. I think he finally realized what's in front of him.*

"Close!" he commands, as Elise is still working her way towards the final destination. "Closer!" he says again.

Keith smiles showing that's he's up to no good and says, "Dr. Sheppard, now kiss me!"

"Excuse me!" she asks with a sound of shock, but she knows what she's up against and continues to play the game.

"Kiss me!" Keith requests.

"Agent Heiden, I really don't know what you want from me! I really feel very uncomfortable about this whole situation! I think we should stop before you and I regret this for the rest of our lives," Elise exclaims.

"Dr. Sheppard, my sister and Mom are coming back in a few minutes. I know what you want, and so do it. What are you waiting for? I'm not going to say it to you again. There'll be no strings attached. I know for sure that I won't tell my wife, and I know you won't tell Peter. So kiss me!" Keith says with a little bit of annoyance in his tone.

Suddenly the doctor stops arguing with the man. Elise kisses her unstable patient on the lips. Then suddenly an extremely high energy feeling comes through Elise like a bolt of lightning hitting her full force. What a feeling! She was waiting for this feeling for a very long time, maybe from the first day they had met. Okay, she's in love with her patient but how does he feel about her? Does he have any feelings for her? She has to stop this crazy roller coaster before it gets out of hand. She breaks away from the kiss and gazes at him with her soft hazel eyes looking deep into his blue eyes. He's a great kisser and she's in love with him!

Elise fixes herself, and with a feeling of embarrassment she picks up her Gucci pocketbook and starts heading for the door.

"Please don't leave!" Keith pleads, as he takes his hand and grabs hers. "Dr. Sheppard, please don't leave because I really don't want you to go."

"I must go...but I want to say something that's been in my heart for a while....I love you!" Elise responds back with a soft friendly smile.

"I know that you love me, and I love you too but...," he answers, as he feels a huge lump in his throat. Keith desperately wants to have an affair like Justine has had many times. He hates himself that she has the upper hand in every situation of their marriage. But that's going to change forever!

"But what's your delay?

"Well, it's confusing and also a very long story," he answers with a smile.

"Okay...okay, I get it..." Elise interrupts the agent.

"Please don't get me wrong, I'm flattered but...," he honestly answers. "I really wish it was different but..."

"But what... I know you have feelings for me!" Elise says using a tone with a bit of an attitude.

"Yes… I do love you, and I still have strong feelings toward my wife. I know that I can't love two people at the same time but how can I not?" Keith honestly says from his heart.

"You can have a better life with me, and you know that…but I'm falling in love with your best friend," Elise says. Then she walks out of the room without saying goodbye.

CHAPTER
ONE HUNDRED-ONE

*P*eter walks into Keith's new office and looks around. "The executive office, how sweet is that!" he shouts louder than usual. His voice echoes throughout the whole room and makes Keith look up quickly.

"How did you get into my office?" Keith asks with a confused look.

"Front door," Peter answers, as he walks toward his best friend. He suddenly notices something different about his long-lost friend.

"Where is Nicole?" Keith asks as he tries hard to focus on any movement on the other side of the glass wall.

"I don't know... How are you?" Peter stops in front of Keith's desk. "You look different today. I know that you got a haircut but there's something else that I can't put my finger on. Can you help me out because I'm at a loss here."

"I have to use reading glasses." Keith sighs because he doesn't want to get old. He just realized that Peter is acting more boisterous than usual this morning. "Peter, why are you so damn loud so early in the morning?"

"Well, I had three cappuccinos before I came here. Please remind me to use the bathroom before I leave the building today. You look like an adult with your reading glasses on. Anyway, this present is for you. Be careful. It's very heavy," Peter announces, as he hands over a substantial package wrapped in Sponge Bob Squarepants wrapping.

"That's heavy?" Keith asks, as he feels the present. "You finally did it! You're giving me your dirty underwear in a box!"

Peter laughs. "That's really good but no… Do you like the wrapping paper?"

"Yes, it's all you, Peter! Sponge Bob Squarepants."

"How do you know this cartoon character?" Peter asks with a surprised look. He can't believe that his partner knows what's hot today.

"Peter, I have kids and he's a demented sponge," Keith answers, as he rips up the wrapping and opens the box quickly like it was Christmas day. He suddenly has a surprised look and says, "Okay… okay…rocks, you've given me rocks! This is my gift?"

Peter walks into Keith's office bathroom and laughs, "All you need in this bathroom is a man wearing a tuxedo with white gloves folding your hand towels for you!" He continues between laughing because he can't help it. "Good morning, Agent Heiden, would you like to use the unscented towels or not?"

"You're so funny, and that's why you're on the main floor of this department, and I'm on the top floor!" Keith answers with a smart remark.

"I have to tell you, Keith, that your sense of humor makes me want to know you more," Peter laughs harder.

Peter continues, "You have to look through the rocks to find your real present."

"Oh dear God!" Keith answers with attitude. As he opens the gift completely he finds a gift certificate to a golf resort.

"Everyone pitched in for this present," said Peter.

"Thank you. That was very kind," says Keith. It's a membership to an expensive golf resort and spa.

He places the gift on the table and without another thought sits himself in his office chair.

"How are things at home? Did you have a heart-to-heart talk with your lovely wife?"

"Yes, she told me that she's carrying twins!"

"Oh my God! I'm happy that I'm not you!" Peter shouts so loud that people from the outside of the office look inside to see what's the drama about. "Pretty soon you'll need to buy a bigger house with these kids that will be living with you."

"Thanks, Peter, for telling me. I don't know what I'd do without you. Now get out of my office before I call security!"

"I need to say something before I go. Do you know that you and Justine look alike...like you're brother and sister? So when the twins get older, you don't have to tell them you're not the father because your likeness is very similar to Justine's. If they don't want you to take a DNA test, you or Justine can tell them the truth before they turn five if you want." Peter answers.

"Yes, this is not the first time that I was informed Justine and I look alike..." Keith answers with a tone of frustration, because this situation can't be fixed with a lollipop. "Unfortunately it's not my call. It's Justine's decision to tell the kids the truth. Peter... I don't know what to feel, especially when the kids are born."

"If you don't tell them they won't know that you're not their baby daddy!"

"I guess you're right..."

Peter's face is showing that he's thinking too hard, and his brain is starting to harden...It's like drinking an ice-cold drink too fast and you get that famous brain freeze.

"Peter! Justine and I are not brother and sister!"

"Right...not...brother and sister! Whatever you say, boss! But here's a thought... What if the twins look like Treat... You know the real baby daddy?" Peter says with energy in his voice.

"If the kids look like Treat then we have to deal with the situation when it comes," Keith answers. "I don't know if Treat knew that he was going to have kids with Justine before he died."

"Is Justine going to tell Treat's family about this wonderful news?" Peter asks with the same energy kicking in.

"I don't know...It's her decision, not mine," Keith answers, as he feels tired of this same conversation that's not going anywhere.

"Before I forget, I'm a brand-new owner of a house in Santa Monica!"

"Wait! Wait! Are you telling me that you're going to pay a mortgage each month? Who's your co-signer because you don't have a great credit rating?"

"Oh...that! Please don't worry your pretty blond head about that. Your Uncle Peter is taking care of this huge adult responsibility... I know that you care and love me because you have to worry. That's why you're my best friend! I love you too!" Peter mentions. "Dr. Elise Sheppard is my co-signer, and she's also living with me."

"Oh... Well, I wish you the best... But seriously how can I not worry about Peter Richard Darling? Look at yourself... You're a feather in the wind. Just flying by with no care whatsoever, living on this planet," Keith says, as he gets up and walks to Peter. He puts his hand out to shake the hand that saved his life

"You're joking! Come over here!" Peter requests and gives Keith a huge loving hug. "I love you, but you're still a pain in the ass!"

Keith quickly breaks away, but the brotherly bond they have is very strong.

"Right back at you, "Keith laughs and gives him a loving punch on the left arm because he wants too.

CHAPTER
ONE HUNDRED-TWO

〽〽〽〽〽〽〽〽〽〽〽〽〽〽〽〽〽〽〽〽〽〽〽〽〽〽〽〽〽〽〽

*T*he digital clock says 9:49 a.m. and as always Dr. Elise Monique Sheppard is late once again. This is not surprising to Ms. Debra Jones, her secretary, who has worked for her the past month now. They worked together at the Mental Health Department in a Los Angeles hospital. Debra is a forty-six-year-old single mom raising three kids on her own without the help of her loser ex-husband. She wishes all the time that he'd just die, but with her luck! Without any warning, he left the family to claim his love for a younger woman half her age. Unfortunately, the kids like her but Debra wants to run her over any chance she gets.

"Good morning, Debra… I'm sorry I'm late," Elise says, as she tries to catch her breath while holding onto her things along with her precious third cup of coffee.

"Good morning, Dr. Sheppard. Believe it or not…you're early… Are you sick because this is not like you," Debra says as she gives her boss a friendly smile.

"Debra, you're too cute but thanks for your concern. I'm really fine," Elise says with a smile.

It took a whole month to get a secretary after it had taken three whole months for Elise to make that important decision to fill this particular position. Her bosses were breathing heavily down her neck to make her mind up now, not later.

"Dr. Sheppard, before you get started on your business work schedule, you have a huge gift," Debra says, as she picks up the gift from the floor next to her desk. She tried to put the present on her desk. It blocked her from seeing the phone and computer.

"Oh boy!" Elise says with a surprised look. There's a huge oval wooden basket with lots of different coffees (from around the world) and assorted cheeses, crackers and cold cuts inside. It's covered with a clear plastic wrap.

"Do you know who sent this to me? Is there a name from the sender?" Elise asks.

"The only thing I know is what the delivery man said." "So sorry, Dr. Sheppard, apparently the sender wanted to remain anonymous, but he or she seems to know you very well...because you do love coffee," Debra says, as she passes the doctor her phone messages to start off her day.

"Yes, I really want to drive myself into coffee land and be done with it," Elise laughs and Debra joins in too.

Debra thinks that her boss is hilarious and entertaining too. But she does not do a lot of paperwork, and Debra knows that she has a lot on her desk. Dr. Elise Sheppard is a real enigma; I guess dealing with all the psycho patients over the years your mind starts to look like scrambled eggs after a while.

"Oh, before I forget here's an envelope... I think this should solve the mystery of the gift!"

"Okay, I know that Peter wouldn't send me a gift like this... He's not the romantic type... I'll open it when I get into my office... Thanks Debbie... You're doing a great job!"

"Thanks, Dr. Sheppard!"

Minutes later, Elise enters her very messy office. She puts the basket of goodies on her office chair and pushes her stuff to one side of her desk. The basket is finally on her desk so she can start at it for hours and also work on two towers of case files that are on her chair in front of her desk. It's an eyesore that she doesn't want to attend to right now. Even though she worked on some case files at home it doesn't seem to help. Her workload is just never ending!

Elise sits down and finally opens the envelope.

Dear Dr. Sheppard,

Hello! I hope all is well. I really wanted to take the time to say thank you for your services. I wanted to send a special thank you for putting up with me and my family's behavior as well. I know it wasn't easy, but you've shown that you're a professional who never gave up on me no matter what. I'll never forget your kindness.

I understand that I need a lot of major mental professional help, so I can finally feel like a normal person for once in my life. It's a long journey, and I'm willing to do the work. Thank you for getting the process rolling.

Well, my life has changed a little bit. Colin is going to pre-school now, and he has new friends. Also, he really enjoys his teacher. He told me that she's hot. I almost forgot to tell you that Colin says hi.

The twins are doing an excellent job in school and both are applying to different colleges. It's very nerve-wracking between my wife and me, but I know for sure that all parents go through this stage. Patrick still gets into trouble now and then. I genuinely think he likes to get under my skin. Erin is doing great in school and getting high grades on everything. She's very determined to go to college on the East Coast far away from home. I finally got to meet Erin's boyfriend. Believe me, it hasn't been easy for both parties. He seems okay but I'm keeping my eye on him. I did a background check on him, but nothing comes up. I really hate to say it, but he's clean and he never even received a ticket for jay-walking. As long as my daughter dates this guy, I'm still on it. Mitch is doing great in hockey, and I really hope he gets a full scholarship to any college he wants to attend.

My wife and I are going to see a marriage counselor. I have to say it's not easy but we agreed to go through with it. I thought your therapy sessions were difficult.

Well, I still have my job, and my wife is pleased and she's not going to change the house locks on me anytime soon. I still can't believe I received a higher position after all the drama that I put the company through! I have to laugh; I'm now Peter's supervisor! How funny is that? I have a very strong feeling that he's going to make my new job a living hell from now on. I can't wait for the fun to begin!

About the whole situation at the hospital, can we please forget what happened between us? I'm sorry to say that we can't be friends. It's challenging to explain because you were my doctor. I was your patient and you're now my best friend's girlfriend. It will always be an awkward situation.

I've noticed that Peter seems very happy these days; I guess it's because of you. He's a good man and deserves happiness, and I hope that you can continue to give that to him.

Please enjoy your gift!! Your taste buds will have a full ride of exploring different flavors of coffee from around the world. You really deserve every bit of the bean. Take care and all the best of luck to you in your new job.

Best wishes,
Keith Heiden

Elise is so touched… The gifts that she's gotten from her patients were rude gestures, spit and being cursed at. This gift will take at least a year to finish it. Elise will always remember this very generous present! Life is excellent with a cup of Joe!

Elise leans back in her chair. Suddenly without warning, she falls as her chair rolls out from under her...

"I'm okay!" she calls out as she laughs uncontrollably.

THE END

ABOUT THE AUTHOR

Kimberly and her beloved late husband, Brendan.

It wasn't until years later that Kimberly A. Mercy-Wagner learned how to deal with her disability and worked at being the best person she could be.

However, Kimberly's drive and passion prevailed, and she opens her own paw business with dogs with involves dog training and pet sitting.

Her wonderful husband and an amazing daughter, her family, and friends, especially Ms. Connie Ficco, who is her tutor and editor, as well as her other clients, gave her help and support.

CPSIA information can be obtained
at www.ICGtesting.com
Printed in the USA
LVHW040916030423
743311LV00004B/101